LIES IN LITTLE SUTHERLAND

PIPPA DARLING MYSTERIES
BOOK 8

JENNA BENNETT

WHAT THIS BOOK IS ABOUT

Six months ago, Grimsby the valet dug up dirt on everyone in the family at the behest of his employer, Henry, Duke of Sutherland. During a memorable weekend at Sutherland Hall, Grimsby was killed for it. So was Henry, while the new Duchess, Charlotte, wife of Harold, overdosed on Veronal after confessing to murdering both of them.

That same weekend, at the Dower House in Dorset, Lady Charlotte's former maid, Lydia Morrison—perhaps the mysterious L.M. from Grimsby's notebook of blackmail offenses—received a late-night phone call and disappeared without a trace.

Miss Philippa Darling and her friend, the Honorable Constance Peckham, have spent the last six months looking for Morrison. And during another weekend at Sutherland Hall, this one to celebrate His Grace, Duke Harold's 57th birthday, they get a lead. Shreve, lady's maid to the visiting Countess of Marsden, has seen Morrison on holiday in the Cotswolds.

With the Astley brothers, Christopher and Francis, in tow, the girls set off for Upper Slaughter, only to find, when they get there, that Morrison has been killed before they can speak to her.

Another L.M. bites the dust back in Little Sutherland—local doctor Lionel Meadows, the man who attended Henry, Harold, and Charlotte, as well as their son, future Duke Crispin—and when the constabulary receives an anonymous note accusing Pippa of the crime, the whole thing becomes decidedly personal.

With an imminent arrest hanging over her head, can Pippa prove she didn't do it, and more, figure out who did, before the murderer decides to do away with her, too?

"Murder, like talent, seems occasionally to run in families."

GEORGE HENRY LEWES

CHAPTER ONE

I HAVE OFTEN THOUGHT it fitting that my courtesy-uncle, Harold, Duke of Sutherland, was born in the gloomy late autumn. Not in the sometimes spectacularly colorful yellow and gold of October, nor in the jolly red and green (and white) lead-up to Christmas, but in the gray chill of mid-November, the time of year that gets in your bones and makes you feel cold all the way down to the marrow. It seems suitable for such a rigid, humorless, sour man.

Of course, I was born approximately a week past the midpoint of November myself, so it doesn't necessarily follow. I am, if I do say so myself, a delight. Christopher would agree.

At any rate, it was the middle of November, and we were gathered at Sutherland Hall to celebrate the duke's birthday. (Not mine. We would be commemorating that joyous occasion the following weekend, in the much jollier surroundings of Beckwith Place, and without the presence of His Grace.)

In addition to myself and His Grace, the guests at Sutherland Hall this weekend included the rest of the Astley family: the duke's younger brother, Lord Herbert, Herbert's wife Lady

Roslyn, and their children Francis and Christopher, as well as Francis's fiancée, Miss Constance Peckham.

There was also His Grace's son and heir, Crispin, Viscount St George.

There was Crispin's wife-to-be, Lady Laetitia Marsden, and her parents, the Earl and Countess of Marsden. And then there was Lord Geoffrey, Laetitia's brother, just out of jail and not guilty of murder by decree of the southern circuit of the Assizes.

In a just world, arranging to administer an abortifacient to your pregnant paramour and thus facilitating her death should have resulted in more than a slap on the wrist, if you asked me, especially as the Marsdens could well afford the hefty fine. However, it seemed that the jury had decided to save most of their ire for the woman who had actually, with malice afore-thought, fed Cecily Fletcher the overdose of pennyroyal with the idea of killing her.

Nellie would go to the gallows, of course, unless she pleaded her belly, and given Geoffrey's habits, I wouldn't be surprised if she were enceinte. Meanwhile, Geoffrey was here, back with his family in the lap of luxury, as if nothing had happened and Cecily wasn't dead.

I'm not a fan of Lord Geoffrey's, if you cannot tell. Nor of anyone else in the Marsden family, if I'm honest. Lord Maury isn't so bad, or at any rate better than his wife and children, but Geoffrey is a cad, and Euphemia is a shrew, and Laetitia... well, Laetitia's only crime is that she's marrying Crispin even though she knows that he's in love with someone else, and it's some-what difficult to blame her for that when he proposed to her of his own free will and has made it clear that he won't declare himself to the girl he loves. He's convinced—not without reason —that she'll trample his tender feelings underfoot like a baby grand doing the Charleston, and he also believes—again, not without reason—that his father would disinherit him were he to propose. And he's most likely right: Uncle Harold doesn't like me any better than I like him.

So that's Laetitia. At the moment, she was simpering at Crispin as they did a slow two-step at the far end of the gloomy Georgian drawing room. The fireplace was roaring in an effort to take the chill out of the stone walls, rain was pattering against the windowpanes, and we were tossing back cocktails to keep the cold at bay. And that was when Constance turned to me and said, "Did I tell you, Pippa? Shreve saw Morrison in the Cotswolds."

It took me a moment—you can blame the gin, if you'd like— to make sense of this sentence. At first it was simply a string of words put together in a way that seemed entirely random, and upon a second turnover in my brain, it didn't make a whole lot more sense. Someone had seen someone else in something? In what? A place? A play? And who exactly had seen whom?

But then my brain nudged a name to the forefront, and I reconsidered. "Who is Shreve?"

"Aunt Effie's maid," Constance said.

Aunt Effie is Lady Euphemia, Countess of Marsden. Constance is her niece, so the Marsden and Astley families will be intertwined whether I like it or not. Even if something were to derail Crispin's and Laetitia's ill-fated nuptials, and I'm not holding my breath for that, Constance will marry Francis next summer, and we'll be attached to the Marsdens whether we want to be or not.

But that's next summer, and meanwhile, Crispin and Laetitia will be tying the knot in mid-December. (Indecent haste, if you ask me. They've only been engaged for two months. I think she's afraid that he'll somehow manage to dislodge her if she doesn't get him to the altar fast enough.)

"Your aunt's maid saw Lydia Morrison? Where?"

"The Cotswolds," Constance repeated. "Near Stow-on-the-Wold."

"And what was she doing there?"

By now, a few of the others had started to pay attention to the conversation, as well. Christopher was curled up next to me on the settee, cocktail in hand, while Francis was sitting, a bit more decorously, next to Constance on the loveseat. But Uncle Herbert, Uncle Harold, Lord Maurice, and Geoffrey were playing a manly game of cards at a table nearby, and they had stopped what they were doing to listen, as well. So had Aunt Roz and Lady Euphemia, although the latter seemed more interested in watching her daughter do her best to seduce St George via two-step than to pay the rest of us much mind.

"Shreve was on holiday," Constance said. "The Cotswolds are very pretty, you know. She said that she had always wanted to go."

The Cotswolds are indeed very pretty. And only a few hours away from Wiltshire by motorcar. Now, if only Constance would get to the point.

"Not Shreve," I said patiently. "Morrison. Was she also on holiday?"

Constance shook her head. "She seemed to live there. Or nearby, at any rate. They met at a rummage sale, Shreve said."

Indeed?

"She said—Shreve did—that Morrison looked well, but seemed jumpy. And not as if she was happy to see her. Shreve, I mean. As if Morrison was unhappy to see Shreve. She told her —Shreve told Morrison—that I had been asking about her. That's why Shreve even bothered to mention it to me."

"We should go," I said.

"Go?"

"To the Cotswolds. To see if we can find her."

Over at the card table, play started up again as Uncle

Harold chose a card and put it down. Lady Euphemia took her eyes off her daughter and future son-in-law for just long enough to give me a stare down the length of her nose, and Aunt Roz smiled at me. "Why do you care, Pippa, dear?"

"Because she vanished," I said. "Just up and left one morning in April with no word to anyone."

The same morning we discovered that Aunt Charlotte had killed herself, in fact. I had always suspected that there was a connection. Lydia Morrison had been Aunt Charlotte's maid many years ago, and she had received a telephone call on the evening before her departure. We didn't know whether that call had originated here at Sutherland Hall, of course, but it was possible, and perhaps even likely.

And also, there was the matter of Margaret Hughes. Twenty-three years ago, when Morrison went to work for Lady Peckham, a different maid had come to Sutherland Hall in her place. And Hughes was now dead, clobbered in an alley in Bristol three months ago. There were good reasons why I wanted to assure myself of Morrison's continued health and wellbeing.

"And you're incurably nosy," Christopher said from next to me. He was curled up like a kitten, with his feet on the cushions and his head on my shoulder.

His mother gave him an indulgent look—he's her youngest, and she lost Robbie much too soon—but she did, nonetheless, tell him, "Sit up, Kit. Your uncle won't appreciate you putting your feet on the furniture."

Christopher pouted, but he did swing his feet off the cushions and back onto the floor. He still slumped against me like an empty evening cloak, however. "Is that better?"

"Marginally," his mother allowed. "What's the matter? You can't have overindulged already."

"The floor is cold. The fire's hot. I'm sleepy."

I was, too, now that he mentioned it. The muted light and patter of raindrops and murmur of voices were all soporific. I could barely keep my mind on the conversation.

"I prefer the word curious," I told Christopher. "Or inquisitive, if you will. But not nosy."

"Of course you do, Darling," a voice behind me drawled. After a second, it added a strangled, "Philippa," and I assumed that Lady Laetitia must have elbowed her intended in the ribs as a reminder that he's not allowed to call me Darling anymore.

I grew up as Philippa Marie Schatz in Heidelberg, and then my last name was anglicized to Darling when I landed in Southampton at the beginning of the Great War. 1914 wasn't an opportune time to wander about England with a German-sounding surname.

(I've only recently come to learn that Schatz wasn't actually my father's surname, either, but that's irrelevant to the current issue.)

My arrival in England was more than a decade ago now. Crispin has called me Darling for years, ever since he came down from Eton at eighteen, or certainly since he came down from Cambridge at twenty-one. It has been difficult for both of us to get used to the new rule, not least because I resent it. That was why I tilted my head back and smirked up at him. "I do, Crispin."

Next to me, Christopher made a choking sound, while next to Crispin, Laetitia's face congealed.

The truth is that I would much prefer to call him by his title. In private—by which I mean, when Laetitia isn't present—that's what we do: he calls me Darling and I call him St George. It's the way it has been for years, and we're both comfortable with it. But if she insists on him addressing me by my first name, then she'll have to put up with me returning the favor.

And if I roll the syllables around on my tongue a bit excessively before I spit them out, then so be it.

As for the significance of the, "I do"—

Well, it ought to be obvious. The girl that Crispin fancies himself in love with? The one he's certain would take his declaration of love and trample it underfoot?

She's me. Or I'm she. And I don't blame him for being reluctant. We've spent twelve years being deliberately cruel to one another. It's no wonder if he'd expect more of the same. But I've had some time to come to terms with the idea, since Christopher spilled the beans a month or so ago, and while I would, at one point, have laughed myself sick had my childhood nemesis come to me with pretty words and puppy-dog eyes, the truth is that I like him well enough by now that I would at least endeavor to turn him down without being vicious. It's not his fault that he feels the way he does, poor sap.

Of course it's all moot anyway, seeing as he's engaged to Laetitia and not in a position to declare an attachment to anyone else. And perhaps I haven't quite gotten over my desire to watch him squirm, because I rarely let a chance go by to twist the (metaphorical) knife whenever fate presents me with such an opportunity. The "I do," was supposed to remind him that in a month's time, he'd be facing a woman in front of the altar at St George's, Hanover Square, and she wouldn't be me.

Now I watched his lips part involuntarily, almost as if the blow had been physical. It took a second, and then his lips firmed and his eyes cooled. "Touché, Darling."

"Philippa," I reminded him, and flapped my hand. "Have a seat, St George. We're discussing motoring up to the Cotswolds tomorrow."

"Is that what we're doing?" Constance wanted to know as Crispin and Laetitia made their way over to a chair on the other side of the low table. He helped her down into it before perching elegantly on the arm beside her.

I nodded. "I am, at any rate. You don't have to come. Although I think someone ought, don't you? I'm certain Shreve didn't ask any of the questions I would have asked."

"What questions are they?" Lady Euphemia wanted to know, but just then Christopher said, "I'm in," and I pretended I hadn't heard her in favor of him.

"Thank you, Christopher."

"If you two are going," Francis said, looking from Christopher to me and back, "I'm going, too. I don't trust either of you not to crash the Crossley."

"What about St George?" He'd had more experience behind the wheel than all of us combined.

"You must be joking," Francis said. "He has destroyed more motorcars than the rest of us put together."

"One," Crispin grumbled. "I have destroyed one motorcar. And only because I was drunk at the time."

"You think that's a point in your favor," Francis told him, "but it's not."

"I won't be drunk at nine o'clock tomorrow morning!"

"Knowing you," Francis said critically, "you'll be hung over, and that's just as bad."

"I'm hardly drunk," Crispin snarled, "and I'll stop drinking right now, if it'll make you happy."

"Are you coming with us, then?" I interjected, placidly.

He looked at me. And then at Laetitia. She turned limpid, blue eyes on him. They stayed locked for a moment and then Crispin turned back to me. "No, Darling. We'll stay here."

Laetitia smiled, like a cat with a bowl full of cream. Pleased at keeping him in line with nothing more than a look, perhaps. Or simply pleased that she had kept the two of us from spending several hours in a motorcar together. Even the "Darling," didn't seem to bother her.

"Suit yourself," I told him, since I obviously couldn't care less whether he decided to accompany us or not. "Christopher and me, Francis and Constance, then?"

"I'll drive," Francis said.

"Yes, Francis. We know." Christopher rolled his eyes. "You'll want an early start, I assume?"

"As early as we can make it," I decreed. "If we leave it too late, we may have to stay over."

"I'm sure there are inns," Christopher said with a shrug, as if the four of us, unmarried, rooming together overnight, was nothing out of the ordinary. Which of course it wasn't. I room with Christopher every night. Or if not quite that, we share a flat in London—with separate bedchambers—and can misbehave as much as we want when we're at home. The fact that we don't—because we're best friends, and first cousins, and the next thing to siblings, and most importantly, because Christopher's queer—is beside the point, but Lady Euphemia didn't seem to realize that. Her eyes widened comically.

Aunt Roz's did not. "Don't do anything you'll regret," she said, blandly. To Francis and Constance, I assume. I don't think she knows exactly what Christopher gets up to in London, but she knows very well that he doesn't get up to anything to do with me.

Francis grinned. "Of course not, Mum. If we end up staying somewhere overnight, we'll put Constance and Pippa in a room together, and take turns guarding the door. Won't we, Kit?"

"You can," Christopher said, pulling another little shocked sound from the countess. "But Pippa can take care of herself, and Constance as well. If it were a question of Pippa or me versus a burglar, I'd put my money on Pippa."

"Flattered," I told him, "I'm sure."

"You ought to be." He grinned at me.

"I've said it before," I said. "I'd be happy to share a room with Constance or either one of you boys. But the whole point of leaving early was so that we could make it there and back in one day, with no need to stay over."

Christopher nodded. "Up and out early, then."

"If possible. If we leave directly after breakfast, we can be in the Cotswolds by luncheon, and then back in Wiltshire again for supper, if all goes well."

"Dear me, Darling," Crispin drawled. After an admonishing look from his fiancée, he added, "Philippa. You seem very concerned about not missing any meals. Is there something we should know?"

"Such as?" I blinked at him, and saw the answer materialize in his eyes. I rolled mine. "Good grief, St George. No, I'm not eating for two. Wolfgang and I did not have that kind of relationship. Just because you go around bedding women indiscriminately—"

But that was apparently a step too far. Not for Crispin, nor yet for his fiancée, but the bride-to-be's mother surged to her feet in a flutter of chiffon and lace. "More sherry, Roslyn?"

"Don't mind if I do," Aunt Roz said placidly and held out her glass. As Lady Euphemia walked away with it, Aunt Roz added, with a gimlet stare, "Give it a rest, you two. Flirt on your own time."

It was Laetitia's turn to squeak, offended, and Crispin turned pink to the tips of his ears. "Thanks a lot, Auntie."

"You know better," Aunt Roz told him. She slanted a look at me. "You too, Pippa."

I made a face. "Of course, Aunt Roz."

"If you're leaving early tomorrow, perhaps you should retire soon, to ensure that you get enough rest."

That was as good as an order, and I got to my feet. "That's a good idea. Thank you, Aunt Roz."

"Don't mention it," Aunt Roslyn said as Christopher unwound from beside me. "Sleep well, you two."

Francis and Constance had not been banished, and made no move to stand, so I told the latter, "A moment of your time, Constance?"

"Of course, Pippa." She put her glass of sherry on the table.

"Don't be long," Francis told her, which indicated that he, certainly, had no plans of being sent to his room like a misbehaving child.

I tucked my hand through Constance's elbow and pulled her towards the door to the hallway while Christopher ambled after us. In our wake, Lady Euphemia sank back down on the Chesterfield beside Aunt Roz and handed her the sherry. Crispin met my eyes for a second across the room, but only until his fiancée tugged on his sleeve, and then he turned his attention to her instead. I pulled Constance through the door Christopher caught on the backswing and then allowed to fall shut behind us.

CHAPTER TWO

"WHERE ARE WE GOING?" Constance wanted to know as we reached the hallway, and I tugged her in the direction of the staff quarters.

I flicked her a glance. "I'd like a word with Shreve before we leave Sutherland Hall tomorrow. Just in the event that she knows something she didn't mention to you earlier."

Such as a better idea of exactly where Morrison might be found.

"I can't imagine what that would be," Constance said, but she allowed me to drag her down the hall towards the door to the 'downstairs.' "We won't be interrupting their supper, will we?"

Most likely we would do, but I've never let that stop me before. "Tidwell won't mind. He likes me."

Tidwell is the butler, and he does like me. So does Mrs. Mason, the housekeeper, I believe. And Cook, as well as both footmen. I'm not so sure about the chamber- and parlor-maids.

They were all gathered at table when we walked into the staff kitchen, and there was a moment of absolute silence before

Tidwell surged to his feet. "Miss Darling. Miss Peckham. Mr. Astley." He looked from one to the other of us. "Is there a problem in the parlor?"

Christopher shook his head. "At ease, Tidwell. Miss Darling wanted a word with Shreve."

The visiting maid, a small dumpling of a woman—as different from the tall and elegant Lady Euphemia as it's possible for one woman to be from another—looked startled under heavy brows. Her eyes fastened on Constance. "Miss Connie?"

"Just another question or two about Morrison," Constance explained. "We plan to motor up to the Cotswolds tomorrow to see if we can find her. We wondered whether there was anything else you might know, that would help us in the search."

Shreve looked nonplussed, as if she couldn't quite imagine why finding Morrison was so important. And she might well be right. I wasn't exactly sure why I wanted to take eight or ten hours out of my day to motor to the Cotswolds to look for a woman we now knew was alive and well.

But her departure from the Dower House had been both precipitous and downright suspicious, and I am, as Christopher had pointed out, curious by nature, and as tenacious as a dog with a bone. And not one of those cute, yappy, little breeds, either. Crispin called me a bulldog once, and unflattering though the comparison might be, I won't say that he was wrong.

"I can't imagine what that might be, Miss Connie," Shreve said. "I saw her in Lower Slaughter, but she said it wasn't where she lived."

"Did she seem familiar with Lower Slaughter?" I interjected. "Did she greet anyone while you were there? Did anyone greet her?"

"The rummage sale was at the church," Shreve said with a

wrinkle of her nose. "She was speaking with the vicar's wife when I saw her."

"Did they seem friendly?" Or had it merely been a haggling session over an old chamber pot?

"Friendly enough," Shreve said. "Or as friendly as Morrison ever is. She never was a friendly sort, if you ask me."

There was a stir around the table, so perhaps some of the servants still remembered Morrison from when she had worked for Lady Charlotte. I met Tidwell's eyes across the table, but he didn't say anything. I didn't, either.

"Did you get the impression that Morrison was one of the vicar's parishioners?" I asked Shreve instead. "Did they seem to have that kind of relationship?"

But Shreve shook her head. "Morrison was a Primitive Methodist. She wouldn't attend the Church of England."

Her tone of voice made it sound as if Morrison had turned her nose up at the Anglican church in a way that had offended Shreve, and perhaps others among the staff. Unless Shreve was the strident believer, of course, and had a problem with anyone else having different views from her own.

I couldn't imagine that it mattered either way, honestly, but it was a piece of factual information we might be able to use, especially if there was a Primitive Methodist church anywhere in the Cotswolds.

I flicked a glance at Constance, who said, "Thank you, Shreve," in a polite voice. "We'll let you get on with supper."

"We're sorry to have disturbed you," I added, to the assembly in general. "We three and Francis will be leaving early tomorrow to drive to the Cotswolds. If anyone has a message for Morrison that you would like us to pass on, please get it to one of us by then."

No one said anything to that, and I added, "We won't be

here for luncheon or for tea tomorrow. But would it be possible to get a picnic basket for the trip?"

I turned hopeful eyes on Cook, who informed me that she would be happy to provide us with sustenance for the road, and on that note we withdrew to let the staff get on with it.

"Not much help there," Christopher commented as he and I headed up the central staircase towards the first floor together, while Constance went back to the drawing room and to Francis.

I shook my head. "We'll figure it out. There can't be that many people who live around Lower Slaughter. And what a name, hm?

Christopher didn't answer beyond a commiserating grimace, and I added, "Can you believe that your mother sent us to bed like misbehaving children?"

"I can, actually." He slanted me a look. "You cannot flirt openly with Crispin in front of his fiancée and—more importantly—in front of his future mother-in-law, Pippa."

The unfairness of this quite took my breath away. "That wasn't flirtation, Christopher. He implied that I was enceinte, didn't you hear?"

"He wishes you were enceinte," Christopher muttered darkly, and raised his voice. "Yes, Pippa, I heard. And he oughtn't to have said that. But you can't allow yourself to get riled up that way. Not in front of the Countess of Marsden. Not to mention my mother."

I supposed not. It was just very difficult to resist the bait. "You don't think it was a comment on my figure, do you? Does this frock make me look fat?"

I had bought it recently, to replace a salmon-colored evening frock that I had purchased back in August, in which I had now discovered two separate, foully murdered bodies on two different occasions, not to mention been kidnapped myself.

The salmon frock was gone, wrapped in paper and tossed in the rubbish bin, and I had replaced it with a two-tone dark green velvet frock with gold and bronze embroidery along the hem and decolletage. The heavier fabric was suitable for autumn and winter, and with Christmas coming up, the green was a good seasonal choice. And in addition to that, it matched my eyes.

The velvet was stiffer than the usual silk chiffon or crepe of most of my evening gowns, however, and it didn't drape as easily. Hence my concern that I looked less svelte than usual.

Christopher looked at me with scorn. "No, Pippa. The frock does not make you look fat, nor would Crispin be so foolish as to comment on it if it did. Not only would Laetitia slap him for noticing anyone's figure but hers—"

I snorted. She'd have to blind him in both eyes to avoid that.

"—but you wouldn't let him get away with disparaging yours, either."

"I'm getting better at recognizing the misdirection," I said. "For instance, there was a time when I would have taken—" I cleared my throat and affected Crispin's languid drawl, "—*my, my, Darling, don't you look tart and crisp and good enough to eat?* as an insult—"

Christopher smothered a laugh, not entirely successfully. "That's what he told you at the Dower House in May, wasn't it? About the apple green frock?"

I nodded. "And last month, he told me to wear it because it brings out my eyes. He really is quite adept at saying exactly what he means while making it sound like he means the opposite."

"I think that's just you, Pippa," Christopher said apologetically. "The rest of us knew exactly what he meant."

Perhaps that was true. Everyone else had known about his feelings for me long before I did, at any rate.

"Be that as it may," I said as we reached the top of the staircase and turned left, so Christopher could walk me to my room.

I was back at the far end of the west wing, while he—and Francis and Crispin—were at the far end of the east ditto. Aunt Charlotte had instituted that rule while she was alive. I had always assumed it was meant to keep Christopher and myself apart, as if we weren't cohabiting quite happily together in London, but Christopher had set me straight on that issue, as on so many others, last month, when he'd told me that the real purpose had been to keep me away from Crispin, and vice versa.

It was the room I always occupied when I visited Sutherland Hall, though, and staying elsewhere would have been strange. So I had Constance in the room next to me, and Lady Laetitia across the hall—it must have been Mrs. Mason, or perhaps Crispin himself, who had made the decision to put her as far away from his rooms as she could get—while the Earl and Countess of Marsden had moved into Uncle Harold's and Aunt Charlotte's old chambers. The duke was in the Duke's Chamber, of course, while the Duchess's chamber stood empty, just as it had done when Duke Henry was alive. It seemed to be the fate of the dukes of Sutherland to outlive their wives. Perhaps, if Crispin was lucky, Laetitia would predecease him by decades, too.

"That's a horrible thing to wish for," Christopher said as we turned the corner by Aunt Roz and Uncle Herbert's room and headed down into the west wing.

I peered at him. "Did I say that aloud? I'm sorry."

He shrugged. "It's difficult to blame you, really. It's a pity you don't feel the same way he does, or you could throw yourself at him and convince him to toss her aside so the two of you could run off and live happily ever after."

I shook my head. "He wouldn't do it. Even if I did manage

to convince him that I'd be happy in a garret on the Continent, he wouldn't leave Uncle Harold in the lurch."

"It's hardly in the lurch," Christopher protested. "Father would become Duke of Sutherland after Uncle Harold, if Crispin were disinherited, and Francis would become duke after Father, and in a pinch, if something happened to Francis, I might become duke... but it's not as if there aren't plenty of us to choose from even without Crispin."

"You better not let him hear you say that, or you might give him a complex." I continued, "Besides, I wouldn't put it past His Grace to marry again and make another heir, should he lose his firstborn. Perhaps Laetitia might oblige. She'd lose Crispin, but she'd become Duchess immediately, and the prestige and fortune might be worth it."

Christopher made a face. "That's an unpleasant picture."

Yes, it was. However— "It's not as if it hasn't happened before. Remember Johanna de Vos? She spread her attention fairly evenly between Crispin and his father for the couple of days that the Peckhams were here for Aunt Charlotte's funeral. It wasn't her fault that His Grace had been a widower for less than two weeks and wasn't ready to consider another wife so soon."

"I think Lady Peckham was the one who had hopes in that direction," Christopher said fairly, "although that wasn't a pleasant picture, either."

No, it hadn't been. "Good thing that they're both dead now."

Christopher bit back a snort of laughter. "Yes, a very good thing. Just don't let Constance hear you say that."

No, I wouldn't. Iris Peckham had always loved Constance's brother Gilbert, not to mention her ward, the fair Johanna, more than she cared for Constance, but she had still been Constance's mother.

"As far as Crispin is concerned..." Christopher went on.

I made a face. "He wouldn't throw Laetitia over even if I did declare love and devotion. The fact that I wouldn't be happy living in squalor on the Continent has always been an excuse. I grew up in a flat on the Continent, and he knows it. It would be nothing new to me. He's the one who doesn't want to give up the title and money."

I waited for Christopher to dispute that, and when he didn't, I added, "Besides, he has tied himself to Laetitia now, and he's not the type to go back on his word. They're engaged, and he'll see it through to the bitter end, I imagine. If nothing else, he has that going for him."

"Not sure that's to his credit," Christopher muttered as we came to a stop outside my bedroom door. "Integrity is well and good, but if it ties him down to a lifetime of misery..."

"Then he'll have no one but himself to blame." I reached for the handle. "But I don't think he'll be miserable. They rub along well enough. He might not ever achieve happiness, but between the title and money, and a wife who adores him and will let him get away with murder, and all the many women out there who'll be happy to distract him... I think he'll manage to survive well enough."

"Cynical," Christopher allowed, "but probably true."

I nodded and pushed the door open. "Are you coming in?"

"I don't think I had better. You want to leave early, you said? I should try to get some sleep."

He glanced over his shoulder at the two closed doors across the hall. "Those are Laetitia's and Geoffrey's rooms, correct? Better make sure you lock your door so his lordship can't come in."

"He wouldn't dare," I said. "Besides, haven't you noticed how subdued he is? He didn't try to feel me up even once.

Didn't even try to undress me with his eyes, as the novels put it."

Christopher nodded. "I did notice. But that doesn't mean that he'll continue to behave once the lights are out. Just lock your door, Pippa."

"Of course I'll lock my door," I said. "I'll even keep a handy blunt instrument on my bedside table with which to brain him, should he be careless enough to try to enter. A nice, heavy torch, perhaps. Will that suit?"

Christopher allowed that it would suit admirably, and then we parted ways for the evening. I went into my room, and he ambled the quarter mile or so into the east wing, to where his own room was located. I changed out of my velvet frock and into pyjamas and a robe, and then, of course, I had to visit the lavatory to wash my face and brush my teeth before bed. I was surprised that Christopher hadn't insisted on sticking around so he could protect me on the way there and back.

It turned out to be unnecessary. I saw no one; it was still early, and everyone else was downstairs in the drawing room, enjoying themselves. I could hear their voices, and the music from the gramophone, waft up the stairwell from below. Safely back in my room, I turned the key in the lock before taking the key all the way out of the door and putting it on the bedside table, clear on the other side of the room. I've read enough murder mysteries to know that a sheet of paper under the door and a nail file in the keyhole can be enough to drag the key out into the corridor from whence it can be used to get inside, and I wasn't taking any chances. After that, I hefted the torch on the bedside table to make certain it was heavy enough to crack someone's skull should the need arise, before I crawled into bed and read until my eyes got heavy.

No one disturbed my slumber that night. There were no furtive knocks on the door, nor did anyone surreptitiously try the doorknob. Or if they did, I was asleep and didn't notice. The torch went unused, and when I woke up in the morning, the key was still on the bedside table and the door was locked.

I restored everything to where it should be, and brushed my teeth and fluffed my hair and headed downstairs for breakfast, after a quick knock on Constance's door to let her know that I was up and that I expected to get going as soon as she and Francis—and of course Christopher—were ready.

I was the first one in the breakfast room. Or the first of the family, at any rate. Breakfast was served, so the servants were up already, of course. I filled a plate with buttered toast and grabbed a boiled egg and took a seat.

Christopher dragged himself in five minutes later, decked out in gray flannel bags and a jumper, and dropped down on the seat across from me with his plate of kippers and fried eggs. "Morning, Pippa."

"Good morning," I said, with a searching look across the table. "You're looking a bit peaky, Christopher. I thought you'd be more rested. Did something happen?"

His eyes were heavy and the corners of his mouth drooped.

"Nothing out of the ordinary," Christopher said as he dug his fork into the eggs. "Crispin knocked on my door and wanted to talk."

I opened my mouth to ask what Crispin had felt the need to discuss so late at night, and then closed it again when I realized it was most likely my own "I do."

"And then everyone else came upstairs," Christopher added, aggrieved, "and voices, and doors slamming, and even the sound of a motorcar outside—Crispin going for a drive to fend off his bad mood, I suppose, unless Geoffrey was tired of pretending to be a good boy and decided to go to the village for a drink and a grope..."

Yes, that would be in character. He had done it before. Both here and at Beckwith Place, if memory served.

"He's back and safe, I hope?" I didn't like Geoffrey, but at the same time I didn't want anything to happen to him. Certainly not while he was visiting the Astleys, where we might be held responsible for his wellbeing.

"I have no idea," Christopher said. "I haven't been out to the garage this morning, so I don't know if whoever left has come back. When Francis and Constance are ready to go, we'll see whether all the motorcars are there."

He scooped up a forkful of kipper and conveyed it to his mouth.

Yes, we would do. And hopefully Crispin's Hispano-Suiza wouldn't be the missing one, nose-down in a ditch halfway between here and the village. That had been known to happen, too.

"What was St George upset about?" I inquired. If Christopher was worried about him nose-down in a ditch, it had to be something serious.

He shot me a look. "Do you have to ask?"

I supposed I didn't, not when he looked at me like that. "Never mind." I should have gone with my original instinct and left it alone.

"Much better that way," Christopher agreed and plunged his fork back into the kippers.

"But he's all right?"

"As all right as a man can be, when he's getting married in a month to a woman he doesn't love."

He lifted another forkful to his mouth.

"The fool," I said. "I know I bear some responsibility here —" If I hadn't told him, in a fit of pique, to propose to Laetitia because they deserved one another, he might not have done it,

"—but at the same time, he really did get himself in this pickle all on his own. I'm not responsible for Crispin's actions."

Christopher shook his head. "You're not," he told me when he had swallowed. "You could have been nicer to him—"

I opened my mouth to defend myself, and he added, "—although I know that he wasn't nice to you first."

"No, he wasn't."

"And you're right, you are not responsible for Crispin. You're especially not responsible for him choosing to go through with it now that he knows—or at least suspects—that it was a mistake."

I folded my hands on the table. "Does he think that he made a mistake, though? Every time I've spoken to him, he behaves as if everything is fine and he's right where he wants to be."

"Well, he would do," Christopher said, "wouldn't he?"

I made a face, and he added, "He was distraught last night. Not that he said as much. But the look on his face when you told him, 'I do'..."

I sniggered, and he added, severely, "It wasn't funny, Pippa."

"It was a little bit funny, surely. Laetitia looked as if she'd bitten into a lemon."

"And Crispin looked as if you'd stabbed him to the heart," Christopher said. "Do not make it harder for him, Pippa. I love you, but I love him too, and I don't want you to be cruel. It's one thing for you not to reciprocate his feelings. It's another entirely to twist the knife. Do you want him to be miserable?"

"Don't you think it's possible that if we make him miserable enough, he'll stop pretending he wants this and will throw her over?"

And then he could stop being miserable and start being happy. Or at least reasonably content.

Except... he hadn't been reasonably content even before the engagement, had he? He had been drinking and using dope and bedding women indiscriminately, and that certainly didn't look like happiness, or even contentment. He would only be truly happy if he got what he wanted, I assumed, and when what he wanted was me—

"No," Christopher said. "If throwing her over means a breach of promise suit and Uncle Harold's displeasure, I don't think he would do."

"Not even if I throw myself at him and declare my never-ending devotion?"

"No," Christopher said. "He knows better than to believe that. Besides, you wouldn't do."

"I might, if I thought it would work."

"And then tell him later you were joking?" He shook his head. "No, thank you, Pippa. That would break him entirely, and I won't let you do it. Unless you're suddenly telling me you have feelings you've always said you don't have?"

I wrinkled my nose. "I'm not. I don't. I just feel bad for being the cause of someone's unhappiness, even if it is St George."

"Well, you can't help how you feel," Christopher said and tilted his head alertly. "Someone's coming."

Someone was. I could hear footsteps on the stairs, and then crossing the marble floors of the foyer. A moment later Crispin appeared in the doorway to the breakfast room.

"Speak of the devil..." I said.

He managed a smirk, although the rest of him looked distinctly the worse for wear. "Were you discussing me, Darling? How immensely gratifying."

"You wouldn't say that if you had heard what we were saying," I told him, and leaned back on my chair. "You look terrible, St George. Have you changed your mind, then?"

"About—?" It took a second, and then he shook his head. "Oh, no. I've just come to see you off. Laetitia would kill me if I left her alone here all day."

She probably would do, at that.

"You could bring her," I said, and then made a face as soon as the words were out of my mouth. The last thing I wanted was to spend an entire day in Lady Laetitia's company, especially in the close confines of a motorcar. "What am I saying?"

He sniggered. "Amusing though it might be to watch the two of you hiss at one another like two cats for an entire day, I'll pass. It would be a rather tight squeeze with all of us."

"We could borrow the Bentley," Christopher suggested. "We'd likely all fit in that."

But Crispin shook his head. "If Laetitia and I go, Geoffrey will want to come, too, and even the Bentley isn't large enough for that."

I made a face. "Indeed."

Not that Geoffrey takes up any more space than the rest of us, but he's the type you don't want to get too close to, especially if you're a woman. Add Laetitia and Crispin, and this simple drive to the Cotswolds would be the trip to hell instead.

"We could take two vehicles," I said, "I suppose—"

Crispin and Laetitia could be in one of them, with Geoffrey, and the rest of us in the other, and that way, I wouldn't have to deal with any of the three of them.

He sniggered "It's all right, Darling. I don't want to drive to the Cotswolds and back today anyway. I had a rather rough night."

He did look it. Like Christopher, his eyes were shadowed and heavy. Unlike Christopher, who at least was dressed and ready for the day, Crispin was still in his dressing gown and slippers, with his fair hair as fuzzy as dandelion fluff around his head, instead of slicked back to its usual metallic sheen.

"What happened?" Christopher wanted to know. "When you left my room last night, I thought you were going to bed. You looked ready to drop. But then I heard a motorcar outside. Did you go out for a drive?"

Crispin shook his head. "Must have been one of the others. Geoffrey, or perhaps Francis. I went straight to bed."

"I don't think Francis spends much time at the village pub anymore," I commented, and Christopher shook his head.

"Thank God for Constance."

Yes, indeed. Since the war ended, Francis had developed a rather nasty taste for alcohol and dope. He'd go up to London to smoke opium with his fellow survivors. He'd drink himself into a stupor at the local pub, and he'd dope himself into oblivion with Veronal and sleep for days at a time, all in a determined effort to keep the memories of the trenches at bay. We were all delighted that Constance had come into his life and given him a reason to want to do better.

"Geoffrey, then," Crispin said. "Or perhaps it just sounded like the motorcar was here, when it was passing by down on the lane. When it's quiet, they sound like they're closer than they are."

"I can't imagine that it matters anyway," Christopher said. "I just wanted to make certain that you were all right. You don't look so good."

"I'm fine, old bean." Crispin put a hand on his shoulder for a second and then flicked me a look across the table. "I just came down to wish you both happy travels. You'll be back tonight?"

"That's the plan," Christopher said. "I don't imagine that it can take all that long to find one woman in two very small villages. We'll be back for supper, I'm sure."

Crispin nodded. "I'll see you both then."

He moved towards the door to the hallway. We could hear

him exchange greetings with Francis and Constance in the foyer, and then he headed up the stairs and back to bed while they came inside and took their seats at the table.

CHAPTER THREE

"THERE IT IS," Constance said some three-and-a-half hours later, as we drove into the picturesque village of Lower Slaughter. By then, I had had my fill of beautiful thatched cottages and meandering waterways and most of all, the unending road in front of us. I was feeling cross.

"There what is?"

"The church," Constance said, as if it were obvious.

The trip here had been uneventful, if long. I had started to heartily wish that I had never suggested this outing.

"My derriere has gone to sleep."

"Hop out and move around," Francis said as he stopped the Crossley outside one of the many honey-colored walls surrounding a honey-colored house. They were all built from the same material, probably some sort of local limestone. Even the church, with its square tower and pointy witch's-hat roof, was honey-colored.

"I want to look at it," Christopher said, blue eyes already fastened on the arched windows. He took a first in history at Oxford, and old churches appeal to him.

I made my way out of the backseat—at this point I wouldn't put it past Christopher to crawl across me were I not to get out of the way quickly, and sure enough, he didn't even glance my way as he followed me out onto the grass.

"Go," I told him as I raised my arms over my head and stretched. While the leather seats of the Crossley were among the more comfortable I had experienced—nothing but the best for the late Lady Peckham—it wasn't the same as sitting on the Chesterfield at home. Not after more than three hours of humping along the roads from Salisbury to Swindon to Cirencester and beyond. "We'll take a look at everything else."

"There's not much else to look at," Francis pointed out as Christopher trotted towards the thatched gate in the church wall.

I looked around. No, there wasn't. A few lanes of cottages, and a larger, manor-style house beyond the church. A water wheel spinning slowly in the river. Children's voices from somewhere not too far off. And—

"War memorial cross," Constance said softly, making her way over to it. After a second's hesitation, Francis followed. Constance cleared her throat. "In memory of the men of this parish who laid down their lives in the Great War 1914-1918. Their name liveth for evermore."

"Just one name?"

I made myself move in that direction, too. I don't like war memorials—there are too many of them, and some include the names of people I know, like Cousin Robert's in Beckwith.

Constance shook her head. "Fifteen."

"*Fifteen?*"

There couldn't be more than thirty homes here. Forty on the outside. That was an enormous loss, even for a war that killed fully six percent of the male population.

She nodded. "There are two different Lockeys and two

different Griffins on this list. Two of the four were named Ernest."

"That's awful," I said. At least Aunt Roz and Uncle Herbert had only lost Robbie. I hated to think what would have happened had Francis perished, too.

"I suppose it's a fitting name for the town, really," Constance opined after a moment. "You don't suppose..."

I shook my head. "The name is much older than that. Slohtre—" I spelled it, "is an Old English word that means 'muddy place.' It has nothing to do with the War. Even if I agree that it would be fitting."

There was a moment's pause, and then Francis cleared his throat. "Here's Kit."

We looked up, and yes, there he was, coming towards us from the church gate. "Wrong Slaughter," he announced, while he was still several yards away.

"Pardon me?"

"This is the wrong Slaughter. There's another one, called Upper Slaughter. And that one has a Primitive Methodist chapel."

Francis looked nonplussed, but of course he hadn't been in the servants' dining room for the conversation last night.

"How do you know?"

Christopher had found the vicar's wife, he said. "She told me that the church was built in the 13th century, but that it was renovated less than a hundred years ago. I didn't bother to go in."

No, that wasn't surprising. Not if all the history had been removed from it.

"But you spoke to her?"

He nodded. "She didn't remember Shreve, nor does she know who Morrison is, but she said there's a Primitive

Methodist meeting place in Upper Slaughter, and that Morrison likely settled there rather than here because of it."

"So it's back into the motorcar, then?"

"It's only a mile away," Christopher said. "And there's a footpath. Although the vicar's wife said that it would take twenty-five minutes to walk it. We'd get there much faster by road."

And more dry, if the sky decided to open up. "We can walk about once we get there, I suppose."

"We'll likely have to," Constance said, and headed for the passenger side of the Crossley. "Come along, Pippa."

I came along, and let myself be chivvied back into the backseat. Francis fitted himself behind the wheel, and we were off.

It might have taken twenty-five minutes to walk, but the drive—quite pretty—was much shorter. It was only a few minutes before we rolled into yet another charming little village full of honey-colored houses, with another honey-colored church—this one a Norman style, with a square bell-tower with crenellations, according to Christopher—and the same burbling little river. What looked like a small chapel sat tucked into a row of other buildings on the other side of a stone bridge.

"That must be it," I said.

The others eyed it consideringly. It looked nothing like the church, with its tower reaching for heaven, but there was something about the squat modesty of the barely-curved tops of the windows and doorframe—so different from the defiantly arched stained glass of the church—that nonetheless advertised piety and religious humility.

"Looks like we missed the mass," Francis commented, "or whatever Primitive Methodists call their worship."

I nodded. "It looks empty. I wonder whether there's a

vicarage or whether the vicar—or the priest or minister; do you know what Primitive Methodists call their head bloke?"

"God Almighty, I imagine," Francis said dryly. And added, "No, I can't imagine that anyone who would build that as a church—" He gestured to the humble building, "—would bother with a residence for their vicar."

No, I couldn't either. "He must live elsewhere. I wonder who would know?"

"There's a pub," Francis pointed. "I don't know about anyone else, but I could go for a pint and a Ploughman's."

So could we all, I imagined. Unfortunately— "It's Sunday, and it's just gone noon. Do you think it'll be open?"

Francis made a face. "Likely not, now that you mention it."

He tried the door of the establishment, but it was locked.

"Shall we find somewhere to picnic and bring out Cook's basket, then?" Constance suggested. "Perhaps someone will come by that we can ask about Morrison. Perhaps Morrison will come by. And if not, at least we'll have had food."

"Let's do," Christopher agreed, while I sighed.

"Why didn't one of you remind me that today is Sunday and everything would be shut?"

"Because we came here looking for Morrison," Constance said, opening the boot of the Crossley for the picnic basket, "and besides, I think we all assumed that you were looking for an excuse to get away from Sutherland Hall and Geoffrey, and it didn't matter what day it was."

"More Lady Laetitia than Geoffrey," Christopher added.

"Not to mention His Grace," Francis said. "Give it here, Connie."

He took the basket out of Constance's hand and offered her his other elbow. "Down there by the river looks like a pleasant place."

He headed in that direction. I squinted at it. Sitting on the cold, wet grass in November didn't look particularly pleasant to me, but there was nothing for it, I supposed.

Christopher glanced at me. "We could sit in the Crossley and eat, if you prefer?"

I shook my head. "I think we've all spent enough time in the motorcar for now, don't you? Besides, the food basket has already departed. Better we follow it, and get some air and stretch our legs and then find someone to talk to once we're done. Perhaps there's a vicar's wife in this hamlet, as well."

"No doubt there is," Christopher nodded and offered me his elbow to hang onto across the uneven ground, "although I don't know that the churchyard is an appropriate place for a picnic."

"Certainly not. But we can go there after. It's cold and wet enough that I don't see us lingering long over luncheon."

And indeed we didn't. We ended up crowded together on a bench, which was marginally better than squatting on the wet ground. But the sky was still lowering, and the wind was blustery, and there was rain threatening, and so we scarfed the food as quickly as we could before loading the basket back into the boot of the Crossley.

And it was at that point that footsteps came toward us and, when we looked up, we beheld that village staple, the local bobby.

"Good afternoon, Constable," Francis said politely. The bloke was around his age, with a freckled nose under the regulation helmet.

He nodded back. "Sir. Can I help you find anything?"

I opened my mouth to ask him whether he knew where Lydia Morrison might live, but before I could get the words out, Constance had opened her mouth.

"I don't see a war memorial in this village."

The constable shook his head. "No, Miss. Upper Slaughter

got lucky. Everyone who went to the front from here came back."

"Lucky, indeed," Francis muttered.

The constable nodded. "There were plenty of days I thought I wouldn't make it home."

"Same here," Francis agreed, and with that they were off, reminiscing about where they'd been stationed and whether they had had any friends in common, dead or alive. Which of course they had, and then they started talking about those.

I stood it for about three minutes before I cleared my throat. They both turned to me with identical expressions of mingled annoyance and sheepishness.

"Feel free to talk as long as you want," I said. "But first... we're looking for a woman by the name of Lydia Morrison. The vicar's wife in Lower Slaughter thought she might live here, because of the Methodist chapel. Constance?"

Constance gave a short but concise description of Morrison—late forties, bobbed brown hair turning gray, sallow skin, pointy nose—and the constable nodded. "She's in one of the cottages on the Square. The one with the blue door."

"Wonderful. We'll just have a look. You two keep going for as long as you want."

I headed in the direction the constable had indicated. Christopher followed. Constance dithered for a moment, looking from me and Christopher to Francis and back, before she made the decision that her fiancé might benefit from having another veteran of the War to talk to, and then she scurried after us toward the rows of cottages up ahead.

They were pretty buildings, if I do say so. Very much the type of mental image one gets when someone says 'Cotswold cottage.' Honey-colored, of course, with slate roof tiles, peaked gables, and deep-set, mullioned windows. *Bagshot Square*, the street sign said, *1-8*.

"There's a blue door," Christopher pointed. I looked in the direction he indicated, and nodded.

"Indeed it is. Can you see any others?"

He couldn't, nor could I. We headed for the robin's egg blue, and Constance applied her knuckles to the door. And then we stood back, in a tight row, with Christopher in the middle, and waited.

After half a minute, when no one had answered, Christopher stepped forward and knocked again, more forcefully. Just in the event that Morrison hadn't heard us the first time. I kept an eye on the curtained window next to the door, but there was nothing to indicate that anyone was standing there peeking out at us.

When another few seconds had passed and nothing had happened, Christopher turned to me. "Would you like a go?"

"I don't see the point," I said. "Try the handle?"

He gave me a look. "You try the handle."

I reached for it, and he slapped my hand down. "Not in front of the constable, Pippa!"

No, of course not. I stuffed my hand in my pocket with a guilty look over my shoulder.

"Do you suppose there's a kitchen door?" Constance wanted to know, and I brightened.

"I'll wager there is." Every cottage I had ever seen had had a kitchen door and a kitchen garden of some sort. "Let's go around back and see." I tucked one arm through her elbow and pulled her away from the front door while Christopher followed on our heels.

"Francis..." Constance began, with a glance at him. He and his new friend were still deep enough in conversation that there was no point in interrupting them, if you asked me.

"It's good for him, you know, to have someone to talk to.

Someone who understands more than we do. He's not seeing any of his old friends anymore."

And thank God for that. But still, while I was relieved that he was going without the alcohol and dope, I understood that he'd also lost the people who understood what he'd gone through.

Constance nodded, worrying her lower lip. Christopher waved at Francis and indicated our path around the cottages, and Francis nodded while he made no move to leave the conversation.

On the back side of the row, each little cottage had a small courtyard. Some had gardens, with herbs or flowers growing—dry sticks at this time of the year, of course—while some were bare patches of dirt and brick. We peered up at the cottages as we went, until—

"I believe it's this one," Christopher said. "The garden gate is blue, too."

So it was. We slipped through and into the courtyard.

It was narrow and enclosed, the space largely taken up by a row of pots with twigs sticking up out of the dirt, and by a bench resting against one honey-stoned wall. It might have been a pleasant place in the summer, with the sun shining, the flowers blooming, and the bees buzzing, but under the sullen November sky, it looked gloomy and deserted.

"Private," Christopher commented, looking around at the high stone walls of the courtyard and the higher walls of the surrounding houses.

Yes, it was. No one would be able to see into this courtyard unless they made a real effort. "Let's try the kitchen door."

It was painted the same cheery robin's egg blue as the front door and garden gate, and set into a corner of the courtyard. I draped Christopher's handkerchief over the latch and pushed down on it.

The door resisted—it was a heavy, old thing—but eventually, with a groan, it opened.

We all three froze. However, when several seconds passed with no reaction from inside, we exchanged a look. The sound was loud enough that it should have roused some interest from within, if anyone was there. Yet there was no yell of outrage, nor the pitter-patter of approaching feet.

I gestured to Constance, who leaned forward, into the kitchen, and opened her mouth. "Morrison?" Her voice quavered. "Are you home? It's Constance Peckham."

"We could be wrong," Christopher said softly as we waited for an answer. There was no need for him to spell out what we could be wrong about. We were both thinking the same thing, after all. Constance might not have caught on yet—she's finer-minded than Christopher and I, or at least less distrustful—but we'd both seen enough dead bodies to recognize the signs. "She could have gone to church—"

"The Methodist chapel, do you mean?" I shook my head. "It looked empty, Christopher. There was no singing, nor any sign of life. And surely it's too late in the day for mass—"

He nodded. "But she might have gone home with one of the other parishioners. Or whatever one would call an adherent of the Methodist faith."

"Member?" I suggested. "Fellow worshiper?"

"Perhaps. Might she not have gone home with one of them after the service was over? For luncheon or companionship or something else?"

She might very well have done, of course. "Would she have left her kitchen door open, though? And the chapel was that way." I pointed through the house, towards the front of the square. "Wouldn't she have gone out the front?"

"Who knows? In a place like this—" Christopher gestured to the tiny hamlet with its picturesque cottages and fairytale look, "perhaps people leave their doors open all the time. Mum does too, at home. We only lock up at night."

Yes, of course we did. Or at least we had done, at Beckwith Place. In London, Christopher and I both made certain that the flat was locked up tight whenever we went out, and Evans the commissionaire guarded the entrance to the building.

But that was London, and this was the Cotswolds.

On the other hand—

"Beckwith Place is full of people," I said. "Aunt Roz and Uncle Harold. Francis. Constance now, and you and me back then. If people started wandering in and out—people who didn't belong—one of us would notice. This is a single woman who lives by herself, and not just that, but a single woman who left her last position in a bit of a hurry, as if something was wrong. Not to mention that her counterpart at Sutherland Hall was killed not three months ago. Don't you think she would lock her door when she goes out?"

"She might not know about Hughes..." Christopher demurred.

No, she might not. Hughes had been asking about Morrison that weekend at Beckwith Place, but there was nothing to indicate that she had found her before her death. We hadn't.

"Look," I said, pointing. "There's a keyhole. If someone took the trouble to install a lock, surely it must be for the purpose of locking the door, at least some of the time."

"So what do you suggest we do, Pippa?" Christopher wanted to know. "I'm not walking in. Not with a constable a few yards away."

No, of course not. "Call her again, Constance," I said, and Constance rolled her eyes but did as I said.

There was no answer this time either, and by now Francis

and his companion had caught up, and were standing in the courtyard behind us.

"What's all this, then?" the constable wanted to know, looking from one to the other of us.

"The kitchen door was open," I explained, hiding Christopher's handkerchief behind my back. "But she's not answering."

"Went home with someone after chapel," the constable said, "most likely."

Christopher, who had suggested the same thing, gave me an arch look. I thought about sticking my tongue out, but reconsidered it.

"Do you think perhaps you ought to check?"

The constable stared at me. "This is someone's home. I can't just walk into it."

"You're a constable. Of course you can."

"Not without cause!"

"Isn't this cause enough?" I gestured to the open door with one hand while the other still kept the pocket square behind my back. "The door was unlocked and she's not responding to knocks and calls. What if something's wrong?"

"Everyone's door is unlocked in Upper Slaughter," the constable said.

"Well, I'm concerned for her wellbeing." I turned towards the kitchen, partly visible through the open door. "If you won't check, then I will."

His hand shot out and grabbed me by the arm. "You cannot walk into someone else's house, Miss!"

"We're acquainted," I told him, twitching my sleeve out of his hand.

It was a lie, of course. Morrison had left her post by the time I visited the Dower House in May, so I had never met her. And the constable seemed to know it, because the way he eyed me was dubious in the extreme. I sighed. "Fine. I've never met the woman. But Constance grew up with her."

I indicated Constance. "Morrison was Lady Peckham's lady's maid for twenty-three years," I added. "Until she up and left without notice one day in April. It has taken us six months to track her down."

The constable looked from me to Constance. She did her best to appear trustworthy. It oughtn't to have been a problem, when everything I had just said was the truth, and when she had one of those open, friendly faces, but for some reason she looked extremely guilty.

The constable folded his arms across his chest. "If it has taken you six months to track her down, she clearly doesn't want to be found. Give me one good reason why I should let you go in there."

"Because something might be wrong," I said. "Perhaps you're right, and she went to chapel, and then she went somewhere with someone for fellowship afterwards, and left her kitchen door unlocked through it all. It's not impossible. You might know better than I do whether that's in character. I don't know her, so I can't say with certainty that she wouldn't have done. But isn't it also possible that the reason the door is open is that something has happened to her?"

If I were going to break into this cottage, with the purpose of silencing Morrison, I would do it through this door, in the privacy of this enclosed courtyard with its tall stone walls, where it would be less likely that anyone would see me than if I were fiddling with the front door in full view of everyone in the square.

The constable didn't answer, and I added, persuasively, "What's the harm in taking a look? If she isn't here, she'll never know that you went inside. And if she is, and something is wrong, you might save her life."

I tried to look pleading as my hands worried each other in front of my stomach. Constance did the same, big eyes unblinking as she bit her lip.

Francis, of course, wasn't unaffected by his fiancée's plight. He asked, somewhat apologetically, "Would it hurt, old chap? If you don't touch anything, no one would know that you've been inside."

"We've motored all the way here from Wiltshire to make certain that she's all right," Christopher added, blue eyes limpid.

The constable sighed. "I suppose I might as well. You won't give me any peace until I do, will you?"

It was clearly a rhetorical question, to which the answer was no, we wouldn't. None of us said anything. If he flat out refused to go inside, I wasn't sure what we'd do. It would be difficult to affect entrance without inviting a burglary charge after a flat out refusal. But I was also not prepared to drive back to Wiltshire without seeing with my own eyes that Morrison was either alive and well or dead, so he was right. I would nag him until he did it.

He sighed. "Wait here, please."

"Of course," I said piously, as if going into the cottage had never even entered my mind. Francis snorted. Christopher sniggered. Even Constance smirked. The constable looked from one to the others and shook his head.

"One minute."

He turned to the open door and raised his voice. "Miss Morrison? It's Constable Woodin. Are you at home?"

He got no more of an answer than Constance had done, and after a second, he squared his shoulders and stepped through the doorway.

We gathered in the opening and jostled for space as we peered into the kitchen of the cottage.

It was small and rustic, with a sink below the window to our right, and a small cooker further down the wall. On the other side of the door was a small table and two chairs. An open fireplace on the opposite wall provided heat in the winter months. Beside it were two apertures: a door to the front room, and a staircase that led to the first floor and, I assumed, a bedroom and bath.

"Cozy," Constance commented.

"If you like rustic charm."

She looked around." I don't mind it."

Francis looked like he was taking mental notes. I had rather assumed that the two of them would remain at Beckwith Place after they got married. Francis was the eldest, and would inherit the place from Uncle Herbert eventually, I assumed, although that could be decades, so perhaps he would rather bring his wife to a home of their own while they waited.

Constable Woodin had inspected the front room—why, I had no idea, since, if Morrison was in there, she certainly would have heard us knock and call—and now he came back into the kitchen and made his way toward the staircase.

"Nothing?" I asked.

He shook his head. "Everything looks good. But I'll check the upstairs, too, before we leave."

He put a regulation boot on the bottom step of the staircase and called out, "Miss Morrison? It's Constable Woodin. I'm coming up."

CHAPTER FOUR

I WISH I could say that I was surprised when he came down the stairs again two minutes later, his face pale and his eyes dark under the brim of the helmet.

I wasn't, nor was anyone else.

"Dead?" Francis inquired.

Woodin nodded, looking nauseated. "In bed. Bottle of sleeping draught on the bedside table."

"Suicide note?" I asked, and he gave me a look. I raised my hands. "It's a fair question, Constable. We've had two family members die of Veronal-overdoses in the past few months."

"Three," Constance said.

I flicked her a look. "Three, including Constance's mother."

"The mother who employed Miss Morrison?"

I nodded, although Lady Peckham's murder had had nothing to do with what was going on now. That had been explained at the time. "And only one of them was a suicide."

"Four if we include Kit," Francis said with a glance at him.

"That was intended for me," I answered, with a glance of my own, "and he didn't die—"

Christopher shook his head, and Francis said, "Not that time. Although it was a Veronal overdose. But I'm talking about what happened last month, not what happened at the Dower House in May."

Ah. "Last month wasn't intended to kill either of us. Although if we're considering attempted murders, I rather think Aunt Charlotte tried to get me with a poisoned cup of tea, too, after shooting at me didn't work."

Christopher's brows drew down. "What happened? Why didn't I hear about that?"

"I didn't realize it until the event at the Savoy last month," I said, "with the overturned teacup. The same thing happened at Sutherland Hall in April, only then it was St George who knocked it over. I rather think his mother put something in it, and he saved my life."

"Good for Crispin," Christopher said, and turned back to Constable Woodin, who had been looking from one to the other of us with his mouth open. "Don't worry about it, Constable. It's just that we've had to deal with a few deaths by Veronal this year, and it's just as well to make certain that she did it to herself, and on purpose."

Woodin opened his mouth and closed it again. And opened it again. "As far as that goes..."

"Yes?" We all sounded politely inquiring. Or so I hoped; I would hate to sound indecently nosy.

"Her complexion indicated that she died from suffocation. Which I suppose can happen if the lungs get compromised—"

He glanced at Francis, who nodded grimly. Woodin cleared his throat. "But there was a pillow on the bed, yet not under the victim's head, that may have—"

He didn't finish the sentence, but there was no need for him to go on. We could all picture it perfectly well. Morrison, sleeping the sleep of the just in her upstairs bedroom. (I furnished it with a brass bed and a quilted counterpane and sloped ceilings, but it might, of course, look quite different.) A tall, dark figure made its way into the secluded courtyard under cover of darkness. (Figures are always tall and dark in these circumstances. Aunt Charlotte had been a dainty thing with Crispin's platinum blond hair, and that hadn't stopped her from killing several people, but in my imagination, the figure was tall and dark.) Gloved hands picked the lock on the kitchen door. Careful feet crossed the kitchen slates and went up the steps. I imagined the pillow, lifted in gloved hands and pressed to Morrison's sleeping face. By the time she woke up, it would have been too late, especially if the Veronal had been her own and she had been under its influence.

If she hadn't been, then... well.

In my imagination, the pillow was tossed aside and the bottle of Veronal removed from a pocket and placed on the bedside table next to a waterglass, before the perpetrator slipped back down the stairs and out through the courtyard and away. All while we'd been asleep in our beds in Wiltshire, three-and-a-half hours away.

"I didn't want it to end like this," I said helplessly, and Christopher put his arm around my shoulder and pulled me in.

"There, there. You knew, coming up, that there was a chance—"

"Of course I did," I muttered into the wool covering his shoulder. "She could have died any time between that weekend in April and now, and I wouldn't have thought anything of it. I probably wouldn't even have known. When Hughes died, it was only because the Bristol constabulary contacted Tom that we heard about it at all."

Christopher nodded, patting me. "I know, Pippa. It's frustrating."

"If only Shreve would have told someone a month ago,

when she first saw Morrison. We could have motored up then, and had the chance to speak to her."

Constable Woodin cleared his throat. "If you don't mind, Miss—"

I shook my head. There was nothing to mind so far, at least not beyond the obvious.

"What was it that you wanted to speak to the... to Miss Morrison about?"

"Oh." I sniffed and straightened. "Just about how she received a phone call in late April and left Lady Peckham's employ the next day. She didn't even give notice. Nor did she wait for her wages. Did she, Constance?"

Constance shook her head. "She did say that she would get in touch with Mother when she had a forwarding address, but we never heard from her again."

"But she did leave of her own free will," Constable Woodin clarified.

Constance nodded. So did the rest of us. "Just precipitously," I added.

"And this was more than six months ago."

"The last weekend in April. More like seven months, isn't it?"

The constable didn't answer. "What made you think that something was wrong with Miss Morrison?"

"We didn't," I said, with a glance at the others. "We've just been worried about her, because she left so abruptly and because she never got back in touch."

"And because her counterpart at Sutherland Hall died suddenly and suspiciously in August," Christopher added. "Although that happened in Bristol."

"At any rate," I continued, since I didn't think there was any need to muddy the waters with Hughes's demise, "when Shreve told us that she had seen Morrison—"

"Shreve?"

"The Countess of Marsden's lady's maid. Constance's aunt." I glanced at Constance and clarified, "The countess is Constance's aunt, I mean. Not Shreve. Shreve's the maid. But she was the one who saw Morrison in Lower Slaughter a month ago. But then she didn't mention it until yesterday. We decided to motor up to have a conversation. We certainly didn't expect to find her dead."

"But when you found the door unlocked, you seemed concerned."

"Of course I was. After Hughes, and after Grimsby..."

Constable Woodin arched polite brows, and I continued, "She's the third servant or former servant in my aunt and uncle's household that has died in the past six months."

"Four," Christopher said. When I turned a nonplussed countenance his way, he added, "Wilkins, remember? Although that had nothing to do with this. Whatever this is."

"Of course not. Completely different situation."

Wilkins had also ended up taking his own life, but that had been to avoid being arrested for murder, and it was also totally unrelated to Hughes and Morrison and Aunt Charlotte, and whatever had been going on at Sutherland Hall twenty-three years ago, that had resulted in Morrison being banished to Dorset or Hughes to Wiltshire.

"That's a lot of dead people," Constable Woodin remarked, and I sighed.

"Tell me about it."

Francis's lips twitched. "She seems to have a knack for finding them."

"Do not!" I said, offended. "It was Aunt Charlotte who found your grandfather—" or she pretended to do, anyway, after she had killed him, "—and Crispin found Grimsby, and Uncle Harold found Aunt Charlotte, and... all right, I suppose

Christopher and I found Johanna de Vos, but someone else found Lady Peckham, I wasn't even there for that, and Gladys Long found Freddie Montrose, and Tom found Gladys, and— yes, I suppose I did find Abigail Dole, but it was only because I was the first one to look out the window that morning…"

By this point, Constable Woodin stared at me as if I had grown another head, and I hadn't even got to Flossie Schlomsky or Cecily Fletcher or Dominic Rivers yet. Or the maître d' from the Savoy tearoom, although it wasn't really fair to say that Crispin and I had found him, not when Christopher had spent the past several days with his corpse by the time we got there.

The litany of names had clearly startled Constable Woodin, though, and it was hard to blame him for that. They hadn't all been murdered, of course—or at least Aunt Charlotte hadn't been—but still, it was a long list. No wonder that Woodin's eyes were enormous and his face pale.

"Um…" he said.

"Not to worry. We weren't responsible for any of them. Just like we're not responsible for this one."

Nor would I take responsibility for it in later iterations of this conversation. It was Constable Woodin who had found Lydia Morrison's body, not me. I had simply suspected that it was there.

"And you can prove where you were last night," Woodin said, "I suppose?"

The plethora of dead people in our past seemed to have put us on the suspect list. Or perhaps we had been on it all along. It wouldn't be surprising, I suppose. The person finding the body is always a suspect. I should have been more suspicious of Aunt Charlotte right from the start, instead of focusing most of my attention on Crispin back in April.

"We were at Sutherland Hall in Wiltshire overnight," Francis said. "I don't suppose you'll take our word for it, but you can ring them up—is Upper Slaughter on the exchange?—and inquire of the other guests or staff."

"Wiltshire 1 4," I said helpfully. "The butler is Tidwell and the housekeeper is Mrs. Mason. The hall belongs to the Duke of Sutherland, but he doesn't like me, so perhaps don't inquire of him—"

Christopher hid a smile. "Inquire of anyone you want, Constable Woodin. Cook handed us the picnic basket with her own hands this morning. She can tell you that we were all there then."

"And earlier?"

Earlier?

"Are you suggesting that one or more of us left Wiltshire last night," I wanted to know, "that we motored up here, killed Morrison, and motored back, only to go to breakfast this morning and make the trip all over again?"

"I'm not suggesting anything," Woodin responded. "I merely asked whether anyone can prove that you didn't do."

I scowled at him. "Not in my case. I'm a spinster and I slept alone."

"Same for me," Constance said softly.

"Surely you don't think we did that?" Francis wanted to know. "Would there even be time to drive here and back before breakfast?"

"I think," I said judiciously, even as my heart began to speed up, "that I'm the only one of us who could have done it. Christopher and I both went up to bed early. You and Constance stayed in the drawing room. But St George knocked on Christopher's door later—"

I glanced at him; he nodded, "—so I doubt Christopher could have made it here and back after that. Nor you two, either. You stayed downstairs with the others too late, and we were up too early. I didn't see anyone after I retired, and no one saw me, so I could have made my way down to the garage, taken out one of the motorcars, motored here, murdered Morrison, motored back, and been in the breakfast room when Christopher came down this morning."

"Were you the first one there?" Woodin wanted to know, and I nodded.

"Of the guests, yes. Tidwell and Cook were up, of course. I'm sure the rest of the servants, as well."

Francis grinned. "It's looking bleak for you, Pipsqueak."

"Don't joke about that, Francis," Christopher said. "Constable Woodin doesn't know us. He might not realize that you're not serious."

The constable didn't appear to find the conversation humorous at all, indeed. "Miss Darling—"

"Pippa," I said, "please. And I didn't do it, Constable. I had no reason to want Morrison dead. Why would I drive four hours out of my way—twice!—to kill a woman I had never even met before?"

He couldn't answer that, of course—because I wouldn't do; nor would anyone else. I added, "It was my idea to motor up here. If I had wanted to murder Morrison, I wouldn't have suggested coming here today. I would have kept my mouth shut, and motored up overnight, and slept in this morning, and pleaded a restless night over late breakfast. And you wouldn't have known that Morrison was even dead, let alone that I had had anything to do with it."

Constable Woodin eyed me, but more like someone who was thinking about something else rather than someone who was assessing my potential as a murderer. "I need to report this," he said.

Francis nodded. "What do you want us to do?"

The constable glanced around, distractedly. "Wait, I

suppose. It might take a while. I have to go to the constabulary in Stow-on-the-Wold."

"There's no constabulary in Upper Slaughter?"

He shook his head. "Nor in Lower Slaughter, either. Stow-on-the-Wold is the nearest constabulary to here."

"How far away?"

"Thirty minutes, if I pedal fast."

He grinned. Francis sighed. "Get in the motorcar. I'll take you there."

"What about these three?" Woodin gestured to us.

"We can all squeeze in," I said, "if you're afraid that we're going to contaminate your crime scene if you leave us here. Although, if we stay, we can make sure that no one else walks into the cottage."

He squinted at me. And it was a difficult decision, I could see that. I didn't particularly want to squeeze into the Crossley like a sardine in a can, and I could tell that Woodin didn't, either. He was a strapping, young specimen, with broad shoulders and muscular thighs underneath the regulation trousers. Much more Francis's type than Christopher's. Or if he was Christopher's type, it was in a totally different way. There was a faint resemblance to Tom Gardiner there, and it wasn't just because they were both policemen.

But that's neither here nor there. Leaving the three of us, with our no doubt concerning history with dead bodies, unsupervised outside a fresh crime scene, can't have been a comfortable notion, either.

"We won't touch anything," I assured him. "We swear. Don't we, Christopher? Constance?"

They both nodded, young and innocent and big-eyed.

"The longer we stand here and discuss it, the longer the body will lie up there," Francis said, and that seemed to make the difference. Woodin glanced at him, and something passed between them—perhaps a memory of bodies in the trenches, who knows?—and then Woodin nodded.

"We'll be as quick as we can," Francis told the rest of us. "Do you want to come with us, Connie, or stay here?"

"I'll stay," Constance said.

And that was that. The two men walked out through the garden gate into Upper Slaughter—Constable Woodin shut the kitchen door behind him in a rather pointed manner first—and then Christopher closed the garden gate behind them. It was just as well to make sure no random passers-by could peer into the courtyard and see us standing here, really. And then the three of us looked at one another.

"Sit?" Christopher suggested, nodding to the bench against the wall.

"Don't mind if I do." I took Constance's arm and headed for it. It was long enough to accommodate all three of us, so a moment later she was sitting between us.

Silence descended. Albeit only for a moment, until Christopher broke it again.

"I can't believe we motored all the way here for this."

"By *this*," I said, "I assume you mean another dead body?"

"That, but also the fact that we're sitting here waiting for an influx of constables. Not to mention that we seem to be suspects."

I shook my head. "I'm certain we're not, Christopher. I've never in my life met Morrison. Nor have you. Why would we kill her?"

"I knew her," Constance's voice said, sepulcherally, from behind her hands.

I peered down at her bowed head. "But nobody would suspect *you* of murder."

Constance looks like the very epitome of the well-bred

English gentlewoman, who would never raise a hand against anyone.

Of course, so had Aunt Charlotte, and she had managed to off several people before doing away with herself, but that was neither here nor there. I knew Charlotte. Had done since I was thirteen, and she would never do such a thing.

"Woodin doesn't know that," Constance said.

Perhaps not. But—

"I'm certain Francis will set him straight. They seemed to get on well, didn't they?"

"Let's hope so," Christopher said grimly, "because this is all more coincidental than I like. What are the chances that Morrison has lived here quietly for six months, and then, twelve hours after we hear about her, she's smothered to death? And we have nothing to do with it?"

The chances of that were not very good, when he put it like that. At least not to someone who didn't know us.

But nevertheless— "I didn't motor up here overnight and kill her, Christopher. Why would I do? And none of the rest of you had the time to do it."

Christopher looked dubious. "But will the police believe that?"

"If it's the truth, I don't see that they have a choice. If none of the rest of you had opportunity, and I did, but I didn't do it, then it was someone else. Perhaps she has made enemies since she came here. Was she objectionable, Constance?"

"No more than anyone else," Constance said and took her hands away from her face before sitting up. "Mother seemed to like her well enough."

"This was the maid you told me about, who spent all her time dressing your mother and her ward, and no time helping you, correct?"

She nodded. "But I didn't mind that, Pippa. Certainly not enough to kill her over it."

"No, of course not." If Constance had wanted to kill anyone, it would have been Johanna de Vos, and it would have been six months ago. "But you knew her. None of the rest of us did. Was she the type of person to get herself murdered within six months of moving to a new town?"

"Clearly," Constance said dryly.

I huffed, and she added, "She wasn't the friendliest person I've ever met. Shreve was right about that. She was polite enough to me, I suppose, and she doted on Johanna, but even after twenty years in Dorset, I don't think she had made many friends. She always seemed to think herself too good to fraternize with Cook and the kitchen maid, and she and Shreve clearly didn't get along well."

No, they hadn't seemed to, and that hadn't been because Morrison thought she was better, since Shreve and Morrison had had the same job. Shreve's was even a bit more privileged, I would venture, since Shreve dressed the Countess of Marsden and Morrison merely dressed the Dowager Lady Peckham.

So perhaps Morrison had been envious, and that was why the two maids hadn't gotten along.

"But you think it's possible that she came here, and made herself so objectionable that someone decided to get rid of her?"

"Anything's possible," Constance said.

Yes, of course. I glanced at the door. "I wonder if there are clues in there."

"Constable Woodin would kill you if you went looking for them," Christopher said.

I looked over at him. "Not if he didn't know I had done."

He didn't say anything to that, and I added, "Surely you didn't expect me to sit here and wait politely while there's a crime scene on the other side of the door?"

He shot me a look. "Haven't you seen enough crime scenes, Pippa?"

I had done, to be honest. More than enough. However— "It seems as if I might be a suspect in this one."

"That should make you more eager to keep your distance," Christopher said.

"But what if I notice something that proves I couldn't have done it? Or something that proves that someone else did?"

He didn't answer, and I added, persuasively, "There's plenty of time, and nothing to do but sit here. If it takes thirty minutes to bicycle to Stow-on-the-Wold, it'll take Francis ten or fifteen to motor there. Then they have to make their report, notify the doctor, and arrange for a delegation to come back this way. All I want to do, is go inside and look around before anyone comes to catch me at it."

"Then go," Christopher said. "But don't say I didn't warn you."

I got to my feet, but hesitated. "You don't want to come with me?"

He made a face. "I've had enough of corpses for a while, Pippa. I spent entirely too long locked in with the one at Thornton Heath."

"I'm sorry," I said sincerely. "That must have been awful for you. But this one won't smell, you know. She hasn't been dead long enough for that."

"Nonetheless, I think I shall stay out here, where the air is fresh." He tilted his head back and flared his nostrils. And lowered it again to ask, "Are you afraid to go in by yourself?"

"Not afraid," I demurred. "I would just... like to have company."

I waited, but no one offered to come with me. Both Christopher and I avoided, quite diligently, looking at Constance.

After a long moment fraught with silence, she sighed. "You're shameless, the both of you."

I smiled. "I knew if I waited long enough, you'd agree to go with me."

"And you knew Morrison," Christopher added. "It wouldn't hurt for you to take a look. At the moment, we don't even know that it's Morrison upstairs, and not someone else."

"That's a good point," I agreed. "There's no reason to think it isn't Morrison, of course, but it's just as well to make sure of it. And since I've never set eyes on her..."

"Yes, yes." Constance rolled her eyes. "I said I would go."

"Let's do this, then." I tucked my hand through her arm. "You'll let us know if anyone comes, Christopher?"

"You'll be the first," Christopher said. And added, "Don't touch anything, Pippa. Hands in your pockets the whole time. Remember to cover the handle before you turn it."

"Good of you to remind me. May I have the handkerchief back, then, please?"

He handed it over, and I went through the process of covering the door handle before nudging the kitchen door open.

Constance and I exchanged a look. "After you," she said.

I rolled my eyes, but took a breath before plunging into the kitchen.

CHAPTER FIVE

THE COTTAGE WAS SMALL, so it didn't take long to go through it. We had seen most of the kitchen from the doorway earlier, and actually being inside it didn't uncover anything that looking at it from the door hadn't done. The sitting room didn't offer anything interesting, either. It was a small, cozy room with a fireplace on one wall and the front door and window on the other. I peered through the leaded glass into the square, but the landscape was deserted.

Inside the sitting room, a small sofa with carved arms and legs sat in front of a low table, and a sideboard with two candlesticks and a wireless was off to the side. A basket next to the sofa held skeins of yarn and a pair of knitting needles. Morrison had been in the process of making something soft and rose-colored. I didn't want to remove it from the basket and shake it out—fingerprints, you know—but it appeared too elaborate to be a scarf, so perhaps a jumper or a cardigan. It looked pretty, with an intricate braided pattern, so it was a shame that it would never be finished.

A local newspaper lay in the middle of the coffee table,

dated for two days ago. I wondered whether that meant something—perhaps Morrison's death had taken place a day earlier than we'd thought, and that was why yesterday's paper wasn't here. She hadn't been alive to fetch it.

Although it was just as likely that *The Evesham Journal and Four Shires Advertiser* was a weekly and not a daily. It was perhaps worth looking into, and the police would surely do that if there was a question about Morrison's time of death, but I didn't think we could draw any conclusions from it.

Nothing about the sitting room set up any red flags. Constance and I exchanged a glance and headed back to the kitchen and to the staircase to the first floor.

As I had surmised, there was a single bedroom and a bath up there, with a storage closet under the eaves. The latter was mostly empty. The rooms were comfortably but sparsely furnished, and there were no extras sitting around. Not at all like at Sutherland Hall and Beckwith Place, which are overflowing with detritus from generations of previous occupants.

The bathroom was what you'd expect: small and white and tiled, with a sink, a commode, and a bathtub with feet. Nothing was out of place, and there was no indication that the murderer had used the sink. And why would he, or she, when the murder weapon was a pillow?

The door to the bedroom was standing open, either because Morrison liked to sleep with it that way or because Constable Woodin had opened it and neglected to close it after seeing what was inside.

I hadn't peeked through it into the bedroom yet. Neither of us was particularly eager to do this. It was clear from the dread in Constance's eyes, and I could feel it in the pit of my own stomach.

"It's just for a moment," I told her reassuringly. "As soon as you've looked at her and ascertained that she's really Morrison, you can go back to Christopher. I won't make you stick around."

"But you'll stick around?"

"Just for a quick look at the bedroom. A minute or two, no more."

I didn't think we had been inside the cottage for more than five minutes, and surely it was much too soon for Francis and Constable Woodin to return, but you never knew who else might turn up outside, and thus discover that we were compromising the crime scene.

Constance squared her shoulders, and I did the same, before we stepped through.

The bedroom was as expected: small and tucked under the eaves. A narrow bed sat under a small window, flanked by a night table, while a chair and toiletries table sat against the opposite wall. A sprigged frock was draped across the back of the chair, with a pair of stockings on top. There were no shoes, just a pair of slippers beside the bed, next to a pillow.

The murder weapon, I presumed.

It appeared to be an average bed pillow. Reasonably fluffy, I would say. It was roundish rather than flat. Would that make it more or less difficult to smother someone with it? A denser pillow—less air inside—might make the job easier, but then again, what did I know about the mechanics of murder?

I pictured myself pressing it down over the face of the woman on the bed. Would I be strong enough physically to murder another woman by means of a pillow? She would fight back, I assumed, once she woke up and realized what was going on.

For a man—or for most men—it might be easy. For a woman, perhaps less so.

I slid Constance a sideways glance. She was smaller than me, and less athletic. I might be able to smother her, at least if I caught her asleep and unaware and I had a second or two to get the pillow in place before she awoke. Someone like Laetitia Marsden, on the other hand, I would definitely not be able to murder. Not with a pillow. But Morrison had been twice the age of either of them. She had been asleep and possibly under the influence of a sleeping draught. The vial was there on the night table, in plain view.

With everything else considered, I turned my attention to the bed and its occupant.

Morrison was lying on her back, eyes wide and bloodshot, giving her a strangely startled appearance.

She was a woman of middle age, with bobbed brown hair turning gray. It looked as if it were threaded through with strands of tinsel. The eyes were blue, cloudy under thin brows. Her mouth was open, and there was a trace of blood on the lower lip: perhaps she had bit herself while the pillow was held over her face. The skin was a pasty white, as the blood had already started to respond to gravity and pool in the parts of the body that touched the bedclothes.

Beside me, Constance made a little noise, and I glanced at her. She was biting her lip, and her eyes—brown, not blue—were huge and filled with sadness.

"Is it she?" I asked. "Is it Lydia Morrison?"

Constance nodded.

"Go on, then. Get some fresh air. Sit with Christopher."

"What about you?"

"I'll be right behind you," I said. "Just a minute or two."

"There isn't much here."

No, there wasn't. I still wanted to look at it. "I won't be long. Go on."

I nudged her towards the door. She went, after one final look at Morrison. I waited for her footsteps to start down the stairs before I turned to the toilet table.

Morrison's handbag was sitting there, next to a handker-chief and a door key. The key was for the front door, no doubt. The handkerchief didn't appear to have been used. A pair of small earrings sat next to it. Marcasite, with screw-on backs. Nice-looking, but not fancy and probably not valuable.

I draped Christopher's handkerchief over my hand before I flicked open the clip on the handbag and peered in.

A coin purse sat inside, next to a lipstick and a few other odds and ends. One of them was a small black book, and my heart sped up as I pulled it out. A calendar showing Morrison's movements over the past six months—who she had met and communicated with—would come in handy.

But it was just an address book. I flicked through the pages anyway, but there was nothing of interest inside. She did not have Margaret Hughes's address in Bristol written under H, although that didn't necessarily mean anything. She might have known it and simply not have noted it down.

The Astleys were in there, or at least the ones of them who lived at Sutherland Hall. Iris Peckham's name was under the Ps, with Constance's and her brother Gilbert's names in a parenthesis below, along with Johanna de Vos's. The M page was filled with lots of names: there were the Marsdens: Lady Euphemia and Lord Maurice, Geoffrey and Laetitia. There was Doctor Lionel Meadows, the medical chap in Little Sutherland—which was interesting, considering that there were more than two decades since Morrison had lived in Wiltshire—and there was also a name and an address for an Edith Morrison in Somerset. A mother, or perhaps a sister. Might be a daughter, although that wasn't very likely. Surely someone would have known if Morrison had had a daughter.

Unless that was why Doctor Meadows's name was on the list. If Morrison had been young, and had given birth to a child during the time she had worked for Aunt Charlotte, Doctor

Meadows may have delivered the baby. For all I knew, it might have been his child. Stranger things have happened. Twenty-four years ago, they had all been young, and there was nothing inherently terrible about the local doctor having had a fling with one of the maids at the Hall.

He ought to have married her, though, if that were the case. So perhaps he hadn't been the father of the child. Perhaps someone else had been.

What if it was Uncle Harold? A daughter wouldn't have meant anything to him; he was focused on a male heir, so he wouldn't have cared about an illegitimate daughter. And that would explain why Aunt Charlotte had contacted her good friend Lady Peckham and traded her lady's maid away to Constance's mother in exchange for Hughes.

I gave Morrison a dubious look. Compared to Aunt Charlotte—who had been a beautiful woman—she was nothing to look at. Aunt Charlotte had been attractive up until the day before she died. A little strained at that point, of course—committing several murders and attempted murders can take it out of a woman—but she had still been lovely. Morrison was merely average, and had probably been average in her youth, as well.

Uncle Harold had always struck me as a cold fish, so thinking of him possibly carrying on with Morrison behind his wife's back was difficult, not to mention deeply unpleasant. I did not enjoy the mental images that accompanied the idea. But the idea itself was intriguing. It would explain Morrison's exile to Dorset, if nothing else.

I flipped through the rest of the book, but didn't see anything else of interest, so I stuffed it back into the handbag and snapped the catch closed.

It was probably getting on for the time I ought to go back downstairs, but I took two minutes to open the wardrobe by the wall. A handful of frocks, skirts, and blouses hung in it, all of them perfectly dull and respectable, in drab shades of brown and blue and gray. Morrison's stockings and unmentionables, kept in the drawer below, were likewise plain and boring. No silk stockings or dripping negligees for Morrison. Her nightgown, what I could see of it under the counterpane, was a perfectly serviceable white cotton.

I was about to close the drawer when something that wasn't underwear or stockings caught my eye. Between the fabrics, something dark blue and leathery peeked out. Brows arching, I reached in and nudged the garments aside so I could see what I was looking at.

A deposit book, for the Post Office Savings Bank.

Wasn't that interesting?

Not that Morrison didn't have every right to have a deposit book, of course. She might have been a prodigious saver, for all that she was a maid.

I fished the book out with the use of Christopher's handkerchief, and dropped it on the toiletries table. And made certain to cover my fingertips when I flipped open the cover and prepared to turn the pages.

There turned out to be no need. The first page wasn't even full, and that was despite the original entry having been made more than twenty years ago.

Twenty-three, to be precise. A week into August, 1903, when Crispin was two months old, Morrison had deposited five hundred pounds sterling with the Post Office Savings Bank.

Was it severance pay, to sweeten the move from Wiltshire to Dorset, and from the Viscountess St George to Lady Peckham? Was it hush money? Or, if Edith Morrison was Lydia's daughter (but not Uncle Harold's child), might it have been a gift from Aunt Charlotte to a maid she hated to lose, but who wanted to get away from Little Sutherland before the news of her pregnancy got out?

They were all possible explanations, I decided, as I glanced at the rest of the entries on the page. There weren't many. There had been no corresponding deposit after the flight from the Dower House this summer. Morrison had withdrawn a hundred pounds in May. I assumed it must have been for the cottage and perhaps furnishings, unless it had come furnished. She must have been living off the rest of the cash since. But the updated sum at the bottom of the column showed that even after the withdrawal, what was left was still worth more than the original sum had been when she deposited it.

Galling as it was to realize, Morrison had been worth more than I. Or at least she had been worth more than Miss Philippa Darling. If I were to go to Germany and cozy up to my paternal grandfather, if I were to take up the mantle of Philippa Marie Albrecht, *Gräfin von und zu Natterdorff*, I would be worth a lot more, of course, but I wasn't prepared to forgive my grandfather for disowning my father, even if he had changed his mind about it in the end.

But that was all by the by. There was no part of me that wanted to return to Germany. I was happy being Pippa Darling, cousin to Christopher Astley and confirmed Londoner. Even if that meant that I was worth less money than Lydia Morrison the lady's maid.

And now I really did need to get out of this cottage before Francis and Constable Woodin came back with reinforcements. I shoved the passbook back into the drawer and fluffed the unmentionables over it—the police would find it, and they would also go through the cottage and discover how much was left of the three hundred pounds Morrison had withdrawn in May, unless she had been killed for that cash, in which case they would find none—but there was nothing more I could do. I used my knee to shut the drawer and gave the room—and the corpse—one final look before I headed back onto the landing and down the stairs.

"About time," Christopher told me when I came back through the kitchen door. He and Constance were still seated—or seated again—on the bench by the wall. They were alone, so Francis and Constable Woodin had not beaten me here, nor had anyone else shown up.

"Found something interesting," I told him as I held out his handkerchief.

He gave it a dubious look, but stuffed it back in his pocket. "What's that?"

I wiggled onto the seat between them. "A bankbook."

They both turned to look at me. "Depositbook?"

I nodded. "Opened with a five hundred pound deposit in August twenty-three years ago."

"When we were all infants," Christopher said.

"Right around the time, or so I assume, when Morrison left Sutherland Hall for the Dower House, and when Hughes left the Dower House for Sutherland Hall."

"We didn't live in the Dower House when I was a baby," Constance piped up. "My father was still alive then."

Yes, of course he had been, or Constance wouldn't be here. "I don't expect it matters, but where did you live before the Dower House?"

They had lived in London, Constance explained. "My mother was Uncle Maury's sister, so we lived in Marsden House when I was small. My grandmother lived in the Dower House. After she passed and my father died, that's when Mother moved into the Dower House. I was already at Godolphin then."

"So Morrison moved from Sutherland Hall to London, and Hughes moved from London to Sutherland Hall."

Constance nodded. "I know nothing about the five hundred pounds, though."

I knew nothing about them, either, aside from the suppositions I had made while up in Morrison's bedchamber. That didn't stop me from opening my mouth, preparatory to give my opinion on where the money had come from. But before I could begin, there was the sound of voices from outside the courtyard wall.

"Let's talk more later," I said.

Outside the wall, Francis's voice mentioned something about a blue door, and then the garden gate rattled. Christopher, Constance, and I looked up, innocently, as the gate opened and Francis and Constable Woodin piled in, followed by an older man with a doctor's bag and two other constables in uniform.

CHAPTER SIX

IN THE END, after our official statements had been taken and the crime scene was combed for evidence, the body removed and the doors locked for the last time, the inquest was set for the next day. We were required to give evidence, so we ended up spending the night in an inn in Stow-on-the-Wold anyway, just down the road from the constabulary. After breakfast the following morning, we made our way back to Upper Slaughter, where the inquest was held in the Primitive Methodist chapel, of all places. The funeral would likely be held there, too, unless Edith Morrison, whoever she was, requested the remains be shipped to her in Somerset. She was not present, so I didn't get a look at her, and couldn't determine whether she might be a mother, sister, daughter, or something else entirely.

A few of the locals showed up, to say that Morrison had lived there since June, that she had been polite and pleasant but had kept to herself, and that they couldn't think of anyone who might wish her ill. One villager claimed to have been approached by a young man with golden hair on his way home from the pub late that night, for directions to Morrison's cottage. Or perhaps it hadn't been a young man at all, but the angel of death, come to harvest her soul. This gentleman had arrived in what was either a dark motorcar or a carriage drawn by four black horses. It was difficult to say, apparently. But the old chap, dried out from his night at the pub, had inspected Francis and Christopher, anyway, and had sworn under oath that no, the golden haired young man—or angel—hadn't been either of them, so that was something, anyway.

Constance spoke for all four of us, detailing the conversation with Shreve night before last, and the drive to the Cotswolds yesterday morning, as well as confirmed that the deceased was indeed the same Lydia Morrison who had been Lady Peckham's maid from 1903 until last April.

Constable Woodin collaborated everything Constance had said, and explained that inquiries were ongoing but that the chief constable was not ready to arrest anyone in particular until after a more thorough investigation. And then the coroner returned a verdict of murder by person or persons unknown, and we were free to go.

"That was interesting," I remarked as we were in the Crossley and on our way out of Upper Slaughter and the north Cotswolds as quickly as Francis could reasonably make the motorcar go on the narrow, picturesque roads.

He glanced at me in the mirror. "Not your first inquest, Pipsqueak, was it?"

"Not at all," I said. I had had to attend inquests for quite a few of the dead bodies I had stumbled over in the past half a year. "Nor my first body. At least this one wasn't bloody."

"You weren't close," Francis asked his fiancée, "were you?"

Constance shook her head. "I've known her all my life, of course, so in that sense we were close. But she never liked me, and I never liked her. It was the happiest day of both her and my mother's lives, I think, when Johanna came to live with us. A pretty doll that they could dress."

That was rather sad, not the least for Johanna de Vos. But it was also in the past. All three of them—Morrison, Johanna, and Lady Peckham—were dead.

"I don't suppose you have any idea who Edith Morrison is?" I inquired as the Crossley wound its way down the narrow country lane. "I assumed mother, sister, or daughter, but it could equally well be an aunt or cousin. Not a grandmother, surely. Not unless she's past the century mark."

"Not likely," Constance agreed. "But no, I'm afraid I don't know specifically."

"She never mentioned going to visit family?"

She shook her head. "Not that I can recall. I don't remember her being gone much, at least not in recent years. She had Sundays and Wednesday afternoons off, but she was usually there at the house."

"Letters?"

Constance shrugged helplessly. "It wasn't something I kept up with, was it? People are entitled to their privacy, even if they are staff."

Yes, of course they were. And chances were someone on the staff would fetch the mail, at any rate, and distribute it. If something arrived for one of the servants, the family wasn't likely to even see it.

"Why so curious, Pipsqueak?" Francis wanted to know.

"Edith's name was in Morrison's address book. If it's a mother or sister or cousin or aunt, I don't suppose it matters. But if it's a daughter—"

"Do you have a reason to think Morrison might have had a daughter?"

"I don't have a reason not to," I said.

"How about the fact that she was unmarried and that no one knows about a child?"

"Just because *we* don't know about a child, doesn't mean there wasn't one. Unmarried servants have gotten in the family way before."

Christopher shifted on the seat, and so did Constance. "If that's a dig at Geoffrey, Pippa—"

"It wasn't," I said. "It was actually a dig at Uncle Herbert. Not that it was his fault. Nobody told him. But he did get Maisie Moran up the duff before he married Aunt Roz. Hence why we ended up with that whole mess with Wilkins and Abigail Dole and little Bess."

Francis winced. So did Christopher. Discovering a new half-brother who had ended up dead—by his own hand—before any of us realized he was even family, had done a number on all of us. Not the least on Uncle Herbert, of course, although Christopher had been a little strange since that weekend at Beckwith Place, too.

"Out of curiosity," I said, "has Geoffrey actually impregnated any of the servants? I know Marsden Manor has seen rather a lot of turnover, but has any of it been because he got anyone in the family way?"

"If he has done," Constance answered, "nobody's mentioned it. Although he was only a few years old in 1903, Pippa. He couldn't have had anything to do with Morrison having a child. He was a child himself."

"I know that," I said peevishly. "In fact, I thought perhaps Uncle Harold..."

Two pairs of blue eyes fastened on me with identical expressions of horror.

"Well, there had to be a reason why Aunt Charlotte got rid of her," I said. Reasonably, I thought.

"Yes," Francis said, "but Uncle Harold? I find it hard

enough to believe that Aunt Charlotte let him in her bed, let alone that anyone else would have done. Especially someone who didn't have to."

We pondered that for a moment.

"Maybe she did have to," I said. Geoffrey had been fairly handsy with me, and he was likely worse with the maids. When you're paying someone's salary, it's easier to convince them—and I imagine yourself—that they owe you something.

"His Grace isn't Geoffrey," Francis said, proving that Christopher wasn't the only Astley who could read my mind. "In fact, Uncle Harold has always struck me as the opposite of Geoffrey. A bloke who isn't interested in women at all."

"Men, then?"

I slanted a glance across at Christopher, who shook his head. "We've talked about this, Pippa. Uncle Harold isn't queer. I agree with Francis: he simply doesn't seem very interested in other people. Men or women, in general or romantically."

I made a face. The words 'Uncle Harold' and 'romantically' made for an uncomfortable match. "You don't think he might have been different twenty-odd years ago? I mean, it makes sense. If Aunt Charlotte was enceinte with Crispin and wouldn't let him near her, he might have sought solace elsewhere."

"I can't imagine that he would have settled for Morrison in that case," Francis said. When Constance shot him a look, he added, "No offense, Connie, but she wasn't anything special to look at. Or at least the corpse wasn't. She might have looked a bit fresher when she was young, but she wouldn't have been any great beauty back then, either. And Uncle Harold was the Viscount St George. If he had wanted a woman, surely he could have done better than his wife's lady's maid."

"Someone else, then," I said. "Perhaps someone who was

married already, who couldn't marry Morrison and legitimize the baby—"

"It wasn't Dad," Francis said. I opened my mouth to say that I hadn't for a moment thought that it might have been—history notwithstanding—but Christopher twitched, and Francis added, "No, bear with me, Kit. I know he got Maisie up the duff, but that was before he was married to Mum. He wouldn't have done it after."

In this he was wrong, actually. Uncle Herbert had allowed himself to be blackmailed by Margaret Hughes over a further indiscretion that had happened during his marriage to Aunt Roz. Within a year or so of the time that Morrison had been traded to Lady Peckham, in fact. But now wasn't the time to mention that, nor the time to think about the implications of it. As far as I knew, I was the only one who had overheard that fact. Neither Francis nor Christopher knew about it, although ostensibly Aunt Roz did.

"Uncle Herbert has enough taste not to settle for Morrison," I said. "No offense, Constance."

"None taken," Constance chirped. "I don't know why you're all apologizing to me for casting aspersions on Morrison's looks. It's not as if I have any particular feelings about them."

None of us said anything to that, and Constance continued, "If Morrison was pregnant at all—and we don't know that she was—it wasn't by your father or your uncle. One of the other servants, perhaps? Or someone in the village?"

"She had Doctor Meadows's name and direction in her address book," I said, "although there might have been other reasons for that. He might have delivered the babe. He delivered Crispin. Or he might have helped her get rid of it. Pennyroyal tea wasn't invented in September of this year."

"Or something else might have gone on," Christopher said, "that made Aunt Charlotte decide that getting rid of Morrison was a good idea. The maid might not have been pregnant at all."

I nodded. "You're right. We don't even know that it was Aunt Charlotte who wanted to get rid of Morrison. It might have been the other way around. Morrison wanted a change of pace, and Aunt Charlotte allowed it."

"For that matter," Constance added, "perhaps it didn't originate in your aunt's household at all. Perhaps something was going on with Hughes, and it was my mother who decided to ask her friend for a swap. It might have had nothing to do with either Morrison or the late Duchess of Sutherland."

Perhaps not. "I wonder if anyone is alive who might know the answer?"

"It couldn't hurt to inquire of Doctor Meadows," Francis answered. "I don't know how ethical it would be for him to tell us about Morrison's baby, if she had one, or even tell us that she didn't have one, if she didn't. But it couldn't hurt to ask."

"Cook might remember if Morrison was with child," Christopher said. "She's been at the Hall for a long time. And doesn't she have a child of her own out of wedlock somewhere? Do I remember that correctly from Grimsby's revelations?"

I nodded. Grimsby had indeed dug that tidbit up, and Tom had shared it with Christopher and myself at some point during the investigation.

"Edith Morrison would know," Constance said. "If she's Morrison's mother or sister or cousin or aunt, then there likely is no child."

"We could write and ask, I suppose."

"A note of condolence might be in order anyway," Constance agreed. "If she's on the exchange, I might even be able to ring her up and express how sorry I am for her loss."

I eyed her admiringly. "That's quite cold-blooded of you, Constance."

"Not at all," Constance answered with a little toss of her head. "Just because I have questions, doesn't mean I'm not sincerely sorry. She was my mother's maid for as long as I can remember. I'm very sympathetic to her mother or sister or daughter or aunt."

But not above using that sympathy to get answers. Which was calculating enough to be admirable.

"When we get home, then," I said.

"Back to Sutherland Hall, surely? All our luggage is there."

"Unless Mum and Dad packed it up and took it back to Beckwith Place with them," Francis said.

"Didn't you motor down together? Or did Uncle Herbert have the Bentley?"

The burgundy Crossley—the motorcar we were currently in—belonged to Constance. It had been her mother's car. Geoffrey had motored up to Beckwith Place in it for Francis's and Constance's engagement bash in July, and since then, it has been Francis's domain.

Meanwhile, Aunt Roslyn and Uncle Herbert have a Bentley Touring Car, which Francis had driven before the Crossley fell into his lap along with a fiancée. Uncle Herbert knows how to drive the Bentley himself, of course, but if they were all four going to the same place—Sutherland Hall, in this case—they may all have traveled together in the Crossley.

Francis shook his head. "They had the Bentley. They've probably gone home already."

"But even if Aunt Roz and Uncle Herbert have left, our luggage might still be at Sutherland Hall. We don't live at Beckwith Place any longer."

I glanced at Christopher. He nodded. "We'll get Crispin to motor us up to Salisbury to the railroad station if we have to. Or all the way to London if he wants a break from Laetitia."

"He's marrying Laetitia in a month," I pointed out. "There'll be no break from her then."

"All the more reason why he might want one now."

I supposed that was true. "Sutherland Hall it is, then. We'll regroup once we get there."

And hie ourselves elsewhere as quickly as possible if everyone else had left. There was no way I wanted to spend time at Sutherland Hall without Aunt Roz and Uncle Herbert and the Marsdens to serve as distractions. Uncle Harold had never liked me, and had never made a secret of it. And the closer we came to Crispin's nuptials, the higher the tension ratcheted. Every day was a new chance for something to break —Crispin's sanity, or perhaps my resolve to stay out of it—and every day, in Uncle Harold's view, was another opportunity for the two of us to elope and ruin his plans for his son's future.

As we headed down the road towards Wiltshire, I was fully prepared to have to shove my belongings into my weekender bag and decamping practically as soon as we arrived.

When we did, however, it was to find everything almost exactly as we had left it. We arrived in time for supper, and the same group was gathered around the table as had been there the night before we left.

"Tell us what happened," Aunt Roz demanded as we waited for the soup to be taken away and the fish served. "From the moment you arrived in the Cotswolds until the time you left. Tidwell didn't know much, and we want to hear everything."

"There's nothing much to tell," Francis told her. "We gave Tidwell the important information when we rang up on Sunday night."

Aunt Roz nodded pleasantly. "And now you can tell me the rest."

"We motored up to Lower Slaughter," I said, "and Christopher went to look at the church there. The vicar's wife told us to try Upper Slaughter instead."

"So we motored there," Francis said. "And when we got there, we ate lunch. On a bench by the river, because the public house was closed."

"And the local constable came by and told us where Morrison lived. In a row of cottages on the square in Upper Slaughter. Very picturesque."

"When she didn't answer the knock on her front door," Christopher picked up the narrative, "we went around the back and found the kitchen door unlocked. The constable went inside and discovered her dead in bed. He and Francis motored up to Stow-on-the-Wold for reinforcements while the rest of us waited. And then we had to stay for the inquest this morning."

"And the determination?" Uncle Harold wanted to know.

"Murder by person or persons unknown. We were given leave to go home, and went. And now we're back here."

"And that's all?" My aunt glanced at me.

"That's it," I confirmed. "The drive was uneventful, both going and coming. There were a lot of sheep. The inn in Stow-on-the-Wold was extremely quaint. I shared with Constance and Christopher with Francis."

Aunt Roz didn't say anything, but she looked amused. Uncle Harold looked constipated.

"When we were asked to stay for the inquest," I added, "I think we were all a bit worried that we were suspects."

Across the table, Francis and Constance nodded. Constance looked rather more guilty than Francis. As she should, since she was the one who had broken into Morrison's cottage with me while Francis had been in Stow-on-the-Wold with Constable Woodin.

"I didn't think we were," Christopher said, "although I agree with everything else Pippa said."

"The inquest was held in the Methodist Chapel," I added. "I suppose the funeral might be there, as well, unless Morrison had family somewhere, who requests the body. Would you happen to know anything about her personal situation, Lady Euphemia?"

The countess shook her head. "I'm afraid not, Miss Darling. She was part of my sister-in-law's household, not mine. If we ever had a conversation, I don't remember it."

No, of course not. Why would she possibly remember speaking with a woman who dressed and undressed her sister-in-law for more than two decades, and who lived a quarter mile away from her own home for a large part of that time?

"Perhaps Mrs. Mason would know," I said. "Did she work here at Sutherland Hall when Morrison was Aunt Charlotte's maid?"

This was addressed, by necessity, to Uncle Harold. The look he gave me in return suggested that as far as he was concerned, I was lower on the scale than where Lady Euphemia had placed Morrison, so I shouldn't expect him to deign to respond. Nor did he. It was Aunt Roz who spoke up. "I don't believe that Mrs. Mason has been here long enough for that, Pippa."

"Cook has been here longer," Uncle Herbert added, "and Tidwell. They may know."

"I don't suppose it matters," I said, since it had really only been a ploy to find out whether Lady Euphemia knew who Edith Morrison was. "It's none of our concern what happens to the body. She left Constance's mother's house of her own free will, after all."

"It certainly isn't any of your affair, Darling," Crispin told me. "Incurably nosy, you are."

"You're one to talk," I retorted, since we both knew his penchant for listening at doors and windows, and in secret passages. "You couldn't care less what happens to the body, I'm certain."

He looked surprised. "No, of course I couldn't. I've never set eyes on the woman. Why should I care what becomes of her remains?"

"It's every human's duty to care about the less fortunate," I told him, primly.

"Yes, yes." He rolled his eyes. "Let me know if you'd like a shilling for the wreath, Darling, and I'll be happy to pony up. Until then, keep your do-gooder tendencies to yourself."

"Are you afraid I'm going to rub off on you, St George?"

It wasn't until Lady Euphemia gave an audible gasp, and Laetitia sent a glare my way that could have peeled my skin from my bones, that I realized what I had said. And by then, of course, it was too late. I felt myself turning pink and then pinker until I was the approximate shade of a tomato, all while Crispin watched the progression with a slow smile.

"Not at all, Darling," he said silkily when, I assume, he thought I must have reached peak embarrassment. "You rubbing off on me doesn't worry me at all."

His tone gave the words a suggestiveness that I certainly hadn't intended when I used them. Uncle Harold's brows drew together. "St George."

Crispin snapped back into himself in a rush. For a second, shock—possibly even fear—flashed through his eyes before he straightened. "Yes, Father."

"Apologize to your fiancée."

"Yes, Father." He turned to Laetitia. "I'm sorry. I behaved inappropriately and disrespected you. Can you forgive me?"

It sounded rote, like he had prepared and rehearsed it previously. Or perhaps he had simply been made to say it a lot. Either way, Laetitia smiled graciously. "Of course, Crispin."

She reached out and picked up his hand.

We all waited politely, but when nothing else happened—no attempted murder, no declaration of love—Aunt Roz and Uncle Herbert exchanged a glance, and the latter cleared his throat. "Crispin?"

Crispin removed his gaze from the suction of Laetitia's eyes. It appeared to take a certain amount of effort on his part. "Yes," he said, "Uncle?"

Uncle Herbert gave him a look, and then gave me one.

"Oh," Crispin said. His cheekbones darkened. "Sorry, Darling. I spoke inappropriately and disrespected you. Can you forgive me?"

I arched a brow. "I don't know, St George. Did you rehearse that sentence?"

The smirk came back, and so did the sparkle. "As a matter of fact I did, Darling."

"Philippa," I reminded him. "And of course I forgive you. Although it was my own fault, really. I should have known better than to give you an opening like that. I know how hard it is for you to resist temptation."

Lady Euphemia gave another gasp, and Laetitia flinched. So, for that matter, did Crispin.

"Pippa," Aunt Roz said tiredly.

I nodded. "Yes, Aunt Roslyn. I apologize."

"Apologize to Crispin," Aunt Roz said. "Not to me."

"Of course." I turned to him. "My apologies, St George. I spoke inappropriately and disrespected you. Can you forgive me?"

Francis converted a snort into a cough, while Constance hid a smile. Christopher smirked without bothering to hide it. So did Crispin. "Of course, Darling. I know how hard it is for you to resist temptation."

"Touché," I said. "But it's Philippa, remember? You don't want to upset your fiancée."

"Of course not." He turned to her. "I'm sorry, Laetitia."

This time he actually sounded sincere, which was more than I would have expected. Laetitia, however, did not sound remotely as loving as last time, when she told him, "Of course, Crispin." There was no adoring smile to go with the words this time. Instead, she gave me a narrow look before she reached out, and the fingers she wrapped around his hand were possessive.

"Thank you, Pippa," Aunt Roz said blandly, as if nothing at all had happened.

"No problem, Aunt Roz. I'm sorry I overstepped. Thank you for correcting me."

That seemed to be more than Francis could handle, because he snatched up his napkin and began to cough into it, loudly, while Constance patted him on the back.

"Never mind, Pippa," Aunt Roz said. I nodded and went back to my supper.

CHAPTER SEVEN

WE HAD to give Shreve the news, of course, which we did after supper, while the others were gathered in the drawing room again.

"You have no idea who would have wanted to do away with her, do you?" I asked after Constance had imparted the news. "Did she mention anything about being afraid of anyone when you spoke to her?"

Shreve shook her head. "No, Miss Darling. She seemed more upset about me being there than about anyone else."

That tracked with Morrison having left the Dower House because she was afraid, anyway.

"Did she ask you any questions about what had happened at the Dower House after she'd left?"

"She had heard about what happened to Lady Peckham and the young miss," Shreve said, "and she asked if it was true that Master Gilbert was the one who had done for them both."

She gave Constance an apologetic look. My friend's jaw was tight, but she didn't say anything.

"Anything else?" I inquired. "Did you tell her about Lady

Laetitia's betrothal to the Viscount St George, perhaps? Or about Cecily Fletcher and Lord Geoffrey's stint in jail while waiting for the Assizes?"

Someone at the table made a noise that might almost have been a smothered laugh. I didn't look up to see who it was. It wasn't Shreve. In fact, the maid seemed appalled that I had brought it up.

Although she answered straight-forwardly enough when I pinned her with a look. "Yes, Miss Darling. I told her about Lady Laetitia and Lord St George. Not about Lord Geoffrey."

"That was perhaps just as well. I suppose she conveyed her felicitations to Lady Laetitia on the catch. Err... match?"

"No," Shreve said succinctly. Behind me, someone made that same noise again. I ignored it again. If someone was misbehaving, it would be up to Tidwell or Mrs. Mason to deal with, not me.

"Truly? That's a shame." I turned to Mrs. Mason. "You didn't know Morrison when she worked for Lady Charlotte, did you, Mrs. Mason?"

The housekeeper shook her head. "I'm afraid not, Miss Darling. That was before my time here."

"Yes, that's what Aunt Roz thought. You've been here longer, haven't you, Tidwell? Do you remember Morrison from back then?"

"Not well," Tidwell said, with a glance at Mrs. Mason. "It's been a long time, and we had Hughes for many years after that."

Yes, of course they had had. "I assume someone told you what happened to Hughes?"

"The young lord," Tidwell said; meaning Crispin, I assumed. "He had learned of it from Master Christopher, he said."

I nodded. "Well, now Morrison's dead, too. You can't think of anyone who would want them both gone, can you?"

"No, Miss Darling." Tidwell's tone was dry. "I'm not in the habit of killing unsatisfactory staff. Especially not after they've left the family's employ."

No, of course not. "I wasn't insinuating that you would do such a thing, Tidwell. Although... you said 'unsatisfactory'?"

"Lady Charlotte seemed happy enough with Hughes's help," Tidwell said blandly, and let the rest of the sentence hang temptingly.

"You mean you liked Morrison better?"

"Not to say liked," Tidwell demurred, "but I thought her a better maid than Hughes."

I exchanged a glance with Constance. If Aunt Charlotte had given up the superior maid to Lady Peckham, the need to get Morrison out of Sutherland Hall must have been great. And that did make it sound as if the swap had been Aunt Charlotte's wish, not Constance's mother's. If Aunt Charlotte had been doing Lady P the favor, surely she wouldn't have allowed herself to end up with the worse maid in the doing of it?

"You wouldn't happen to know whether Morrison was enceinte when she left," I asked, "would you, Tidwell?"

He looked at me blankly. "Enceinte, Miss Darling?"

"Pregnant," I said. "Up the duff. In the family way. Expecting."

Tidwell nodded. "I know what it means, Miss Darling. I would not be in a position to have had such information."

"No, of course not," I said. "Never mind, Tidwell. Forget I asked."

He took pity on me. "I was head footman when Lydia Morrison worked here. I don't recall a relationship with anyone. She must have kept it quiet, if so."

"Did she have any particular friends amongst the staff, do you recall? Someone who might remember the details?"

"I don't believe so," Tidwell said. "She came from Somerset with Lady Charlotte, and was only here for a couple of years before she left again. The only person I remember her being close to, was milady."

Until milady shipped her off to London and Lady Peckham.

"Thank you, Tidwell," I said. "We won't keep you from your supper any longer."

He nodded. "Thank you, Miss Darling. Miss Peckham."

The other servants murmured their goodbyes, and we took our leave.

"Anything?" Constance wanted to know when we were out of the staff quarters and on our way down the hallway toward the drawing room and the others.

I glanced at her. "Not aside from the obvious. You?"

She shook her head. "No one seemed particularly murderous."

My lips twitched. "Did you think someone might be? The staff would have had even less time than the rest of us to motor from Wiltshire to Upper Slaughter and back before breakfast. We just come downstairs and eat. They have to cook the food first."

"Not all of them," Constance said. "Tidwell doesn't make breakfast."

"Of course not. But he's the last in the household to go to bed. When everyone else has retired, he goes around and turns out all the lights and makes certain all the doors are locked."

"That means nobody may have noticed him leaving," Constance said.

She had a point, of course. Or would have had, had I been able to wrap my head around Tidwell as the main suspect.

As it was, I tried, but it was impossible. I shook my head. "I don't think it's Tidwell, Constance. He had no reason to want Morrison dead. He hasn't seen her in twenty-odd years, I imagine. She hasn't been back here in that time, as far as I know."

By the time Lady Peckham got here for Aunt Charlotte's funeral, Morrison had already left her employ a week or so earlier.

"But he did know her twenty-odd years ago," Constance pointed out, "and no one else did."

"Cook might have done. But you're right about that."

Constance looked mollified, and I continued, "Although if something was going on with them back when they were both employed here, something that made him want her dead—"

"Such as a baby on the way," Constance interjected.

I nodded. "Such as. But if so, don't you think he would have followed her to London and killed her then? He's had plenty of time and opportunity since she left. It's not as if she's been in hiding."

Not until the past six months, at any rate.

Constance didn't say anything to that, and I added, "I'd believe it of Cook or Mrs. Mason before I'd believe it of Tidwell. He really is the best part of Sutherland Hall. Surely you've heard me say so?"

"I'm fairly certain you think the best part of Sutherland Hall is Lord St George," Constance said dryly and tucked a hand through my arm. "Whatever were you thinking earlier, Pippa? Aunt Effie looked as though she was about to have a coronary. And I wouldn't be surprised if Laetitia tried to poison you later. Don't drink anything you haven't poured out yourself for the rest of the time we're here."

"Don't worry," I assured her, "I won't." I learned that lesson after what happened at the Dower House in May, and had it reinforced last month at the Savoy. "I won't touch anything from anyone other than you and Francis and Christopher."

"And your aunt and uncle, I suppose."

"Roz and Herbert," I said, "yes. Harold, no."

She shook her head. "No, of course not. He looked like he was about to expire, too."

No doubt. "As for what happened," I said, "I got carried away, I suppose. It's easy to do. I get into the back-and-forth, the way one does, and I forget that people are listening."

She nodded. "That's understandable. Although it would be easier if you would simply admit..."

"Never mind," I told her. "He's marrying your cousin in a month. And whether anyone believes it or not, I don't feel that way about him."

"Of course you don't."

"I don't!"

"That's what I said," Constance said.

I grumbled. It had clearly been sarcasm—or at least I would have staked my life on it being sarcasm—but there was no point in arguing about it, and at any rate, we had reached the drawing room, and I didn't want to have this conversation with an audience.

The parties had arranged themselves much as they had done three nights ago, with a few exceptions. Lady Euphemia was playing cards with her husband and son, and His Grace, Duke Harold, tonight. Aunt Roz was sharing the sofa with her husband instead. They were sitting across from their sons in the conversation area. Christopher and Francis were going over more of the details from our trip to the Cotswolds, it seemed. I caught Constable Woodin's name on Francis's lips as I slithered up to the chair where Christopher sat, and perched on the arm.

He smiled up at me. "There you are. What news?"

I shook my head, as Constance made her way around the

table to the other chair, where Francis was sitting. He snaked an arm around her waist and pulled her down on his lap. She squeaked and flushed, but didn't protest.

"None, I'm afraid," I answered Christopher's question. "No one claimed to know anything about why Morrison may have left Sutherland Hall twenty-three years ago, or for that matter any reason why Aunt Charlotte may have wanted to get rid of her."

Christopher's body stiffened for a second. If he hadn't been leaning against me, I don't think I would have noticed. As it was, I felt it clearly, and looked down at him.

He wasn't looking at me, just staring straight ahead. Uncle Herbert, on the other side of the table, must have noticed something wrong, too, because he was looking at his youngest son with an expression of concern.

It didn't last long. Christopher's stiffness melted away after a second or two, and so did Uncle Herbert's look of worry. I thought about bringing it up, to face the issue head on, but then I decided that any interrogation would be better kept for a more private moment, when everyone in the family—and beyond— wasn't present to hear our conversation.

"I think I may inquire of Doctor Meadows tomorrow," I added, and Uncle Herbert's face took on another look of concern.

"Why would Doctor Meadows have anything to do with Miss Morrison's death, Pippa?"

"Oh," I said, "I don't think he had anything to do with her death."

Although now that he had brought it up, perhaps I ought to consider that possibility. If she had been with child twenty-three years ago, and he had been the father—or he knew that someone else had been, like Uncle Harold—might he have motored up to the Cotswolds to kill her?

It was difficult to imagine a reason why, or even how, he might have done it. Take the issue of transportation, first of all. Did Doctor Meadows own a motorcar? I rather thought not. Francis had motored to the village and brought him back to Sutherland Hall in April, when Duke Henry first expired, before we had any inkling that the late duke's death had been a murder.

Without a motorcar, the doctor couldn't have made it from Wiltshire to the Cotswolds and back overnight, and the owner of any car he hired might have thought the whole thing a bit strange and worthy of notice, which isn't what you want when you set out to commit a murder. I certainly would have done, had someone hired my car for a seven-hour drive, only to stay inside the destination for just a few minutes.

Then again, Doctor Meadows was a physician, and of everyone, it would make the most sense for a physician to make house calls in the night. So in that sense, someone might actually believe it. Even if Little Sutherland to Upper Slaughter was rather a long distance to go for a house call.

And then there was the question of how Lionel Meadows would have discovered that Lydia Morrison had relocated to Upper Slaughter, because as far as I knew, the maid Shreve wouldn't have had any reason to search him out to tell him, and without Shreve, none of us would have known.

And besides, as I had already pointed out to Constance just a few minutes ago, anyone who had wanted to get rid of Morrison had had the past twenty-three years to do it. This— what happened two nights ago—couldn't have been because of something that had happened back then, or at least not because of something that was known back then. If it was cause for murder now, surely it would have been cause for murder then, too? So why wait almost a quarter century, when Morrison had been readily available at the Dower House all this time?

Anyone with the ability to motor to the Cotswolds three nights ago, would have had the ability to motor to Dorset any time these past twenty-three years.

Indeed, Marsden-on-Crane was only about half the distance from Sutherland Hall to Upper Slaughter, so for convenience's sake, it would have been much easier to go to Dorset to do the deed.

"Then what do you think Doctor Meadows can tell you, Pippa?" Aunt Roz wanted to know, and yanked me back to reality.

I blinked, and reordered my thoughts quickly. "I simply thought, since she had his name in her address book—"

That was as far as I got before Francis turned to me. "You ought to be ashamed of yourself, Pipsqueak. You were supposed to wait outside the cottage while Woodin and I motored to Stow-on-the-Wold for reinforcements. Not sneak inside and dig through the crime scene."

Aunt Roz's eyes widened, and so did Uncle Herbert's. Pippa!" Aunt Roz exclaimed, while Uncle Harold at least managed a slightly more questioning, "Pippa?"

"We didn't dig," I said, guiltily.

"We?" Aunt Roz looked from Christopher to me and back. I guess no one thought Constance would have had anything to do with it.

She flushed. "It was me, Roslyn. We wanted to make certain that the dead person was, indeed, Morrison, and I'm the only one who has seen her."

"All I did was sit outside and keep watch," Christopher added, self-righteously.

His mother rolled her eyes. "So you let your cousin and future sister-in-law go inside by themselves?"

Christopher threw his hands up. "Damned if I do and damned if I don't, is that it?"

"Clearly," I told him. "Don't worry about it, Christopher. It was a nice, clean crime scene. Nothing much to see at all. We were careful not to touch much. Her address book was in her handbag and her passbook in her unmentionables drawer, under a lot of boring cotton and wool."

"Dear me, Darling," drawled Crispin's voice from behind me. I had no idea where he had come from, all of a sudden. He hadn't been here—nor Laetitia—when Constance and I entered the room. Outside for a cigarette or a romantic stroll through the gardens, perhaps. He had a whiff of the outdoors about him, a chill, crisp, autumnal sort of scent, mixed with the clean odor of rain. "How terribly ill-mannered of you, pawing through other people's unmentionables."

"You would know all about pawing, St George," I retorted with a look up at him. "Where have you been, pray tell? The center of the garden maze?"

Constance, who had once walked in on Crispin and another young lady sharing the wrought iron bench in the middle of the maze, made a choking sound and buried her face in her hands. Her cheeks were bright red.

Crispin looked at her, and must have been reminded of the occasion, too, because he flushed. He returned his attention to me. "One of these days, Darling—"

"Don't make promises you can't keep, St George. As I was saying—"

I turned back to Aunt Roz and Uncle Herbert, who had been watching the exchange with something halfway between horror and amusement, "I did paw through her unmentionables. Not while she was wearing them, obviously. I'm not some people. They were decently stored in a drawer in her wardrobe. But that's not what we were discussing. She had Doctor Meadows's name in her address book, and I thought I might pay him a visit tomorrow, before we leave Sutherland Hall."

"Didn't you speak to Doctor Meadows in April?" Aunt Roz wanted to know. "Wasn't that where you were headed when…"

"When Aunt Charlotte decided to practice her target shooting from Christopher's bedroom window, yes." I nodded, as I tried to ignore the reaction from behind me. Or the lack of reaction, perhaps. And not from Crispin; the sense of stillness, of interrupted breathing, came from the card table. Uncle Harold, most likely. It was no surprise that he didn't like to be reminded of his late wife's attempted murder of me, especially in front of the Marsdens.

"That was not a question about Morrison," I added. "That was about Grimsby and whatever secret he had dug up that got him and Duke Henry killed."

The silence from the card table became more charged.

"But that's neither here nor there at the moment," I concluded. "This would just be a question about Morrison. And it's not as if any of us has to worry about being accused of her murder. We were all here in Wiltshire when she died. Hours away from the Cotswolds."

There was a breath during which no one said anything, and then—

"Of course we were, Darling," Crispin said. "Speaking for myself, I was in Kit's room until after midnight. I wouldn't have had the time to motor to the Cotswolds and back before breakfast the next morning."

"I'm not so sure about that," I told him, "considering the speed with which you usually move. Although for the record, I wasn't accusing you."

He rolled his eyes. "There's a first time for everything, I suppose. Thanks ever so, Darling."

Laetitia cleared her throat, and he added, with a grimace, "Philippa."

Uncle Harold cleared his throat. "Of course you didn't do,

St George. Nor did anyone else here. It's as Miss Darling said: none of us had the opportunity to motor up to the Cotswolds and murder that poor woman. Not without being missed. Ergo, none of us did it."

"Precisely," I said. I don't like to agree with Uncle Harold—I don't like Uncle Harold, period—but needs must. "I'm simply curious as to who did do, so I think I'll take a walk to the village after breakfast tomorrow, and have a conversation with Doctor Meadows. Just because he didn't have any answers about what went on last time, doesn't mean he might not know something about what's happened now."

"I'll come with you," Christopher said.

"Thank you, Christopher." I included the rest of the family in the next statement. "And nobody better shoot at us from the house when we come out from behind the trees this time."

Laetitia sniffed. "As if anyone here would do such a thing."

"It's happened to me twice," I pointed out. "The second time was at Marsden Manor in September."

"My stars!" Countess Euphemia slapped a hand to her bosom, while her husband looked startled.

"It was the morning of the shoot," Francis said. He had been in just as much danger of being hit by the wayward bullet as I had been. It had passed within a foot of us both. "We were outside on the lawn, the three of us." He indicated me and Christopher. "The bullet came from the woods, passed between us, and embedded itself in the wall."

"Constable Collins dug it out," I added, "later that afternoon."

"And you think someone shot at you deliberately?" Lord Maury sported a concerned wrinkle between his brows.

"At the time," I said, "we assumed that someone mistook me for Cecily Fletcher from a distance, and was aiming for her."

Everyone's face darkened at that, since no one wanted to be reminded of Geoffrey's crimes. Geoffrey himself looked particularly wooden, but he assured me, "I would never, Miss Darling."

"At this point," Christopher added, "we suspect it was the *Graf von und zu* Natterdorff who fired the shot, and he was aiming for Pippa deliberately."

"The German gentleman? Why would he do that?"

"Didn't he propose at the end of the weekend?"

"As it turns out," I said blithely, since Crispin apparently hadn't shared this information with his future parents-in-law, nor perhaps even his future wife, "I'm the *Gräfin von und zu* Natterdorff, and Wolfgang didn't want to share his inheritance with me."

There was utter silence following this announcement. My family—Aunt Roz and Uncle Herbert, Francis, Christopher, and Constance—had already heard all about it, of course. Christopher and I hadn't wasted any time in letting everyone else know. But Crispin, who had also been there for the denouement, apparently hadn't seen fit to let his father in on the secret, because Uncle Harold gaped at me in a way that indicated strong surprise.

I pretended that I couldn't see it, because gloating would be impolite. "He tried to marry me to get his hands on my share of the money, but he also tried to kidnap me as well as murder me several times—along with Christopher, once or twice—so we think it quite likely that he saw an opportunity at Marsden Manor that weekend and took it. I didn't have the chance to ask, so of course we may be wrong, but it makes sense."

There was another pause, then—

"You—" Uncle Harold cleared his throat. "You're a German countess, Miss Darling?"

The way that he, very carefully, avoided looking at his son

and heir indicated that this information might have made a difference earlier. Before Crispin proposed to Laetitia and got himself tied to wedding her, at the threat of a breach of promise suit. At a point when he could have made a different choice and pursued someone else.

And while I knew that there were other reasons for why he hadn't pursued me—we hated each other, and I would have laughed myself sick had he gone down on one knee and pledged devotion, and he knew it—I also understood what his father's reaction would do to Crispin, and presumably to Laetitia, who would undoubtedly give him grief about it.

So I went against my own first instinct, which was to rub the duke's nose in it, after all the years he had believed me to be beneath him and his family. Instead, I said calmly, "Only on paper. The Weimar Republic did away with the German nobility in 1919. And that's fine. I'm happy to be Pippa Darling."

"But the estates," the Countess of Marsden said, with a glance at her daughter. "The money and land..."

"The German government is welcome to it. I'm certainly not going back to Germany to claim my inheritance."

What if they wouldn't let me leave again? No, better to simply let them absorb it all. Germany could use all the help it could get, what with the post-War reparations and the poverty and the madness of Herr Hitler and all the rest of it.

"Yes," Christopher said and put an arm around my waist. "Stay with us, Pippa."

"Thank you, Christopher," I told him, as I put my own arm around his shoulders and held on.

CHAPTER EIGHT

NOTHING of any note happened on our way down to the village the next morning. Part of me was braced for it, especially when we came out from behind the small copse of trees that had shaded us from the Hall, and we could see where the shot had come from back in April, but nothing actually happened. We made it down the hill and into the village without ending up in the ditch with dirt on our knees and blood on the palms of our hands this time.

Little Sutherland is a nice little hamlet, made up of a few narrow, cobblestoned streets lined by brick and stone cottages. It's not quite as picturesque as Upper or Lower Slaughter, but not far removed, either. The stone is grayish rather than honey-colored, and the layout is a bit flatter and less rambling. But it's a lovely place for all that.

The infirmary is located just off the town square, and we made our way there.

Déjà vu hit again as we pushed the door open and walked in. And not only because we had done the same thing seven months ago, with blood running down my arm from where the bullet had nicked me on its way past, but also because part of me was afraid that we would walk in on another dead body.

We had discussed driving to the Cotswolds to see Morrison, and Morrison had been dead when we arrived.

We had discussed walking to the village to talk to Doctor Meadows. What were the chances that Doctor Meadows would be alive when we got here?

The chances were good, as it happened. We walked in, and a few seconds later, the door to the surgery opened and Doctor Meadows stepped through. "Oh," he said when he saw us. "It's you two. Is everything all right?"

His sleeves were rolled up to his elbows, and he had a towel between his hands that he was using to dry them. Perhaps he truly had been in surgery, and we had interrupted him with his hands in someone's intestines.

My stomach did a slow roll and I tore my eyes away from the towel and focused on the doctor's face instead.

"Everything is fine," Christopher assured him. "Everyone is alive and well."

The doctor gave me an up-and-down look. "No bullet wounds this time?"

"None at all," I said. "No bullet wounds, no scraped knees, nothing like that. No one tried to take us out on our way to the village this time around."

He nodded. "What can I do for you?"

"We just had a question," Christopher said, with a glance at me. I indicated that he should continue, so he did. "You've been the doctor here for a long time, haven't you?"

"Since before you and your cousin were born," Doctor Meadows nodded. "My father was the doctor before me."

"When Aunt Charlotte was young, she had a maid by the name of Lydia Morrison. Would you happen to remember her?"

"Of course," Doctor Meadows said readily. "She came here from Somerset with your aunt, and went back there, or perhaps it was somewhere else, a few years later."

He didn't look as if the question had opened up any kind of wound, old or new. Nor did his voice sound like it.

"It was London," I confirmed. "And then from there to Dorset with Lady Peckham. Constance's mother, you know."

"Young Francis's girl." He nodded. "I've seen her come and go a few times, but we haven't met."

"Constance is lovely," I said. "You'll like her. Although we were talking about Morrison. Who was Constance's mother's maid almost as long as Constance has been alive. Until April, when she left the household suddenly."

"After Lady Peckham died?"

I blinked, and then I realized that of course, Doctor Meadows would have attended Lady P upon her death. She had been here at Sutherland Hall when it happened, for Lady Charlotte's funeral, and when the younger set—all the Astleys, Constance and Gilbert Peckham, Johanna de Vos and myself—decamped for the Dower House, Lady Peckham had stayed behind to provide Uncle Harold with moral support.

She had ended up dead a day later, but I hadn't given it much thought at the time, since it had happened in Wiltshire while we'd been in Dorset, and since Johanna de Vos's murder had taken precedence at that point. But now I realized that yes, of course, the staff at the Hall would have called in Doctor Meadows when Lady P died, and for him, that death would loom larger than Johanna's.

"Before," I said. "Otherwise she would have been here with Lady P that week, I assume. She left Lady Peckham's employ right around the time Lady Charlotte died. And Duke Henry and Grimsby."

"Her departure was rather abrupt," Christopher added.

"She didn't even wait for her pay, and she didn't leave a forwarding address. Constance has been worried."

"Naturally," Doctor Meadows agreed. He dropped the used towel on top of a nearby table and began to fasten his cuffs. If he had someone in surgery in the other room, he wasn't in any hurry to get back to them. Perhaps he had simply been washing up after breakfast.

"We didn't know what to do about it," Christopher continued, "but this weekend, the Marsdens are visiting. You know that Crispin is engaged to marry Lady Laetitia Marsden?"

Doctor Meadows nodded and glanced at me. I rolled my eyes. It really must be true what Christopher had said, that absolutely everyone knew how Crispin felt about me.

"Well," Christopher continued, "Lady Marsden's maid mentioned that she had seen Morrison on holiday last month, so we motored up to the Cotswolds a few days ago."

"Word has spread," Doctor Meadows nodded.

"Has it, really? Well—" I folded my arms across my chest, "your name was in her address book, so we thought perhaps you could shed some light on what happened."

He stared at me. "Shed some light upon her death, do you mean? Dear me, no. I haven't seen the woman in more than twenty years. I wouldn't know anything about it."

"Why would she have your contact information in her book after all these years?"

"Perhaps the book is twenty years old," Doctor Meadows said, and of course there was a possibility of that.

"But you did know her when she worked for Lady Charlotte?"

"I know all the locals," Doctor Meadows said. "Gentry and otherwise. Everyone gets ill, Miss Darling."

Yes, of course. "Can you remember Morrison needing your

services for anything in particular? Illness or injury? Anything else?"

Pregnancy, just as a for-instance.

"She wasn't here very long," Doctor Meadows said, "and nothing in particular comes to mind."

He did appear to be thinking about it, to do him justice. Unless he only appeared to be thinking about it, to throw off suspicion.

"You must have seen her for something," I insisted. "You knew who she was."

Doctor Meadows nodded. "But not necessarily because she sought out my services for her own self. She was there with Lady Charlotte for most of her ladyship's appointments while she was expecting young Crispin."

Of course. Uncle Harold wouldn't have been bothered about supporting his wife for those, nor is it something fathers in general do, I suppose.

"But Morrison was never, for instance, pregnant herself?"

He stared at me as if I had lost my mind. "No, of course not. Or not during the time she was here in Little Sutherland. I have no idea what may have happened later."

"And you haven't thought of anything else of interest having to do with Crispin's birth?"

That's what we had come down here to inquire about in April: the initials L.M. that Grimsby the valet had scribbled on Crispin's blackmail dossier. I still didn't know whether they referred to Lionel Meadows, Lady Laetitia Marsden, Lydia Morrison, or someone else.

Next to me, Christopher moved uncomfortably, and I reached out and took his hand without looking at him. "Just another minute, Christopher."

"No," Doctor Meadows said. "I already told you that there

was nothing out of the ordinary about young Crispin's birth. He was a few weeks early—"

I nodded. That's normally a cause for stigma—your standard 'premature baby' (note the quotes) is born seven or eight months after his parents' marriage—but of course that wasn't the case here. Uncle Harold and Aunt Charlotte had already been married several years by the time Crispin came along.

"—but he was healthy and well-formed, simply a bit on the small side, and he outgrew that by the time you were three or four."

Christopher nodded. "We're much of a height now. And have been for a while. We went off to Eton looking like twins."

"Sounded like them, too," I agreed.

What would any reasonable person think, after all, but that Christopher and Crispin Astley, in the same year at Eton, were brothers? The only difference between them is coloring. Crispin inherited his mother's platinum hair and gray eyes, while Christopher has the sunny blond hair and blue eyes of the rest of the Sutherlands. But that difference isn't enough to take away from the fact that in every other respect, they're practically identical. Christopher's nose is perhaps a shade longer, and they've both picked up some scrapes and scars along the way that are different, but for all intents and purposes, they look enough alike to be twins.

All of which was neither here nor there. I turned back to Doctor Meadows.

"So there's nothing you can think of to tell us? You don't know why Morrison would have left Aunt Charlotte's employ as soon as Crispin was born? You can't think of anyone who might have wanted her dead?"

Doctor Meadows looked startled. "My dear girl, of course not. It's been almost a quarter of a century since I last saw her. And surely, if something had happened back then that someone would have wanted to kill her for, they would have done it by now?"

You'd think so, wouldn't you? Except—

"I don't suppose you know anything about what happened to Hughes?" I wanted to know.

"Margaret Hughes? Lady Charlotte's maid, do you mean?"

"The one that replaced Morrison, yes."

"I'm afraid I don't," Doctor Meadows said. "What happened to her?"

"Well, she's dead, too."

I kept a close eye on him when I said it, but all I could see was genuine shock.

"It happened a few months ago," Christopher added, "in Bristol. She went there in July. Aunt Charlotte was dead, you know, and my mother has no need for a lady's maid, so my father gave her a bit of money and a friend of ours gave her a lift to Bristol. And a month or so later, we heard that she had been killed in a robbery."

"You don't say?" Doctor Meadows seemed politely interested, but nothing more. "That's terrible. But no, I hadn't heard anything about that."

"Isn't it just awful? Both of them dead—all three of them, if you count Aunt Charlotte, or all four, if you count Lady Peckham—and all within six months of each other. It's hard to imagine that there isn't a connection."

Doctor Meadows looked at me for a moment. "Your aunt left a note, I thought?"

He very delicately didn't call it a suicide note, although that was what it had been. "And Lady Peckham's son took responsibility for her death, didn't he?"

Yes, of course he had done. Gilbert couldn't have killed either Hughes or Morrison, any more than Aunt Charlotte could have done. So no matter how circumstantial and coincidental the whole thing seemed to be—perhaps I ought simply to call it suspicious—Aunt Charlotte's and Lady Peckham's deaths were explained. Someone else had killed Hughes and Morrison. And it wasn't likely to be Doctor Meadows. There wasn't a single whiff of guilt about him.

"Thank you for your time," I told him, with a squeeze of Christopher's hand. "We won't keep you any longer."

He beetled at me under lowered brows. "There's nothing wrong?"

"Nothing beyond what we've already mentioned," I said brightly as I turned towards the door. "If that changes, you'll be the first to know."

Doctor Meadows nodded. He kept his eye on us as we crossed the infirmary floor, but he didn't say anything, just watched as we let ourselves out and shut the door behind ourselves.

"So that's that," Christopher said when we were standing on the cobblestones under the gray skies of the November morning.

I nodded. "I had hoped that he might have had something to contribute, but I'm not really surprised that he didn't."

Morrison hadn't lived in Little Sutherland for a long time, and the address book might simply have been twenty years old.

"If she were his paramour back then," Christopher opined, "he gave no sign of it."

I shook my head. "That doesn't mean she wasn't. But there's also no reason to think she might have been. We don't even know if she was enceinte when she left. She might have been—and probably was—a perfectly buttoned-up spinster with a mother named Edith in Somerset."

Somewhere nearby there was a slam, as of a door shutting, and Christopher looked around. There was nothing to see, and after a moment he turned back to me. "Shall we head back?"

I tucked my hand through his arm. "We may as well. If Doctor Meadows doesn't know anything, I doubt anyone else here would. Perhaps we can talk Constance into trying to ring up Edith Morrison on the telephone, and see what she has to say."

"I don't see why we shouldn't give it a try," Christopher agreed, and pointed us in the direction of the road out of the village and back up to Sutherland Hall.

AS IT TURNED OUT, Constance was more than happy to ring up the exchange and ask for Edith Morrison. However, the lady was not on the exchange, and there was nothing we or the operator could do about it.

"Let me try," Francis said, and took the earpiece out of Constance's hand. "Operator? Can you connect me with the constabulary in Stow-on-the-Wold?"

That, the exchange operator could do, and a few moments later, Francis was speaking to Officer Woodin. Three minutes after that, we had the answers we had been looking for.

"Edith Morrison is Lydia's mother. According to Woodin, who had it from the constabulary where the mother lives, they've barely seen one another in the past twenty-five years. Our Morrison will be buried in Upper Slaughter, Woodin said. Her mother might travel there, but then again, she might not. She's elderly and hasn't seen her daughter in a quarter of a century, so I got the impression—and so did Woodin—that she doesn't much care that her daughter's dead."

"I'm not sure that I do, either," I said. "I was mainly interested in what their relationship was, or more specifically, whether Edith might be Lydia's daughter. If she isn't, and if they haven't had much contact, it's unlikely that Edith would know anything that pertains to Lydia's murder."

Francis nodded. "Shall we head back to Beckwith, then? You've spoken to Doctor Meadows. Mum and Dad already left. There's nothing more to do here, is there?"

There wasn't.

"I'll go upstairs and pack," I said, and turned towards the staircase with Christopher right behind.

When we came downstairs again, each of us clutching our weekender bag, it was Uncle Harold, of all people, who talked us into staying for luncheon. He was in the foyer, and caught sight of us coming down the stairs. And instead of letting us leave quietly, he insisted that as luncheon was only a few minutes away, we ought to stay and partake before making the drive back to Beckwith Place and from there, to Salisbury and the train station.

There's only an hour's drive between Little Sutherland and Beckwith, and less than that between Beckwith and Salisbury, so there was no chance that we'd starve before we got there. But he appeared sincerely concerned about it—or at least he seemed sincerely concerned for Christopher; I'm sure he couldn't care less about me—and there was no reason to upset him by saying no, so we acquiesced with good grace. Francis and Constance came back inside from the Crossley, the Marsdens and Geoffrey appeared from whence they had occupied themselves, and Crispin and Laetitia drifted in from wherever they had been. For once, he didn't appear to have been recently kissed, so perhaps they hadn't been together.

"I hear you're headed home," the latter said to Christopher.

Christopher nodded. "We would have left already, but Uncle Harold invited us to stay for luncheon."

Crispin flicked a glance at his father. "Without saying goodbye?"

"We didn't want to interrupt," I said. "Just in case you were doing something important."

He glanced at me, but didn't say anything. "All the way back to London?" he asked Christopher instead.

The latter nodded. "Tomorrow, I imagine. By the time we get to Beckwith Place, it'll be time for tea. By the time we could make it to Salisbury and the train, it would almost be time for supper. By the time we got to London—"

Crispin nodded. "Might as well wait until the morning."

Yes, indeed. Francis could take us to Salisbury after breakfast, and we'd be in London by afternoon.

"It's been lovely," I told Duke Harold politely. "Thank you for inviting us."

Christopher nodded. "Yes, thank you, Uncle Harold."

His Grace inclined his head. "It's always a pleasure, Christopher."

The statement rather pointedly excluded me, and I'm sure we could all hear it. I was under no illusions, and I'm sure no one else was, either. But there was no point in commenting on it. Aside from the fact that I was in Uncle Harold's home, and that I shouldn't be rude to our host, any complaint would simply serve to make me look like a brat.

So I kept my mouth closed, and ignored Lady Laetitia's smirk, and the Countess of Marsden's ditto, not to mention the color in Crispin's cheeks. Instead, I devoted myself to my plate.

"This is delicious. Cook has outdone herself."

"Marvellous tripe," Francis agreed blandly.

Uncle Harold cleared his throat, and Francis told him, "Sorry, Uncle Harold," but without bothering to sound like he meant it.

"Never mind, Francis," Uncle Harold said.

Francis nodded, and looked down at his plate. The corners of his lips were twitching. I could see Constance slanting a look at him along the table.

And it was around that point that the sound of a motorcar entered the courtyard and came to a stop.

"Are we expecting someone else?" Crispin wanted to know, looking around the table. We were all present, except for Aunt Roz and Uncle Herbert, of course. Perhaps something had happened to the Bentley, and they had had to return to Sutherland Hall instead of going on to Beckwith Place?

His Grace didn't answer. From the foyer, we could hear Tidwell's measured steps as he crossed the marble in the direction of the door.

The hinges squeaked, and then Tidwell's voice said, "Good afternoon, Constable."

I arched my brows, and Christopher arched his right back.

There was the murmur of voices in the foyer, too faint to make out, and the sounds of... not quite a scuffle, but the shuffling of feet.

"One moment—" Tidwell's voice protested, breathlessly, but whoever he was talking to quite obviously did not heed the warning, since, a moment later, his figure appeared in the door to the dining room.

One of the village bobbies, in full uniform. I recognized his face, in the vague sort of way that one recognizes someone one has seen about but doesn't really know. I had no idea what his name was, but I knew that I had seen him before.

He stopped in the doorway to look around the table. Lady Laetitia, the Countess of Marsden, Constance. Me.

"Your Grace," Tidwell intoned, elbowing the constable out of his way as he stepped across the threshold, "may I present Constable Daniels—"

Daniels didn't wait for the response. "Miss Darling," he said instead. "I'm afraid you'll have to come with me."

CHAPTER NINE

FOR A MOMENT, no one spoke. I waited for Uncle Harold to take the reins—he was the Duke of Sutherland, and we were in the dining room at Sutherland Hall—but His Grace must have been just as taken aback as the rest of us, because he uttered not a word. Nor did Crispin, for that matter. It was Tidwell who spoke up. "You can't simply walk in on His Grace's luncheon guests, Constable Daniels."

Daniels flicked Uncle Harold a glance. "My apologies, Your Grace."

Uncle Harold inclined his head. I would have expected a bit more outrage, to be honest, but perhaps he was simply too surprised, or too curious to see what would happen next, to interfere.

"Why?"

I wasn't the one who asked. It was Francis who bristled on my behalf. "Why do you want to take Pippa away?" he added.

Constable Daniels turned his attention to him. And contemplated him for a moment in silence before he said, politely enough, "We have a few questions about a murder."

"I already told the police in Stow-on-the-Wold everything I know," I protested.

He turned back to me. And although he looked as if there was something he wanted to say, he couldn't quite bring himself to do it. "If you would come with me, Miss Darling?" he said instead.

For all that it was a question, and perfectly bland, there was no mistaking that it was an order. I got to my feet. "Will you at least give me leave to retrieve my jacket? It's cold outside."

The constable hesitated. For long enough that Christopher rolled his eyes and got to his feet. "Here, Pippa." He shrugged out of his own jacket and put it over my shoulders. "I'll fetch yours and bring it to the constabulary."

It took effort to get my voice to cooperate. "Thank you, Christopher."

I didn't know what was going on, but based on Daniels's demeanor, it was serious. Perhaps Constable Woodin had discovered my foray into Morrison's cottage, and had decided to arrest me for interfering with an investigation. And then he had rung up the Little Sutherland constabulary to do the honors, so he didn't have to make the trip here himself. The situation gave off that sort of whiff. There were no handcuffs, and Constable Daniels hadn't said, "You're under arrest for the murder of—" but I really did get the impression that something like that was coming. Perhaps as soon as we were outside in the courtyard.

"We'll be right behind you," Christopher said, with a glance at his brother.

Francis pushed to his feet. "I'll bring the Crossley around."

Constance made to get up, as well, but he put a hand on her shoulder. "Stay here, Connie. There's nothing you can do to help. We'll figure out what's going on and come back for you."

Constance looked mulish, but I supposed she realized that

there was no point in all three of them sitting outside the constabulary waiting to hear what was happening inside. In the absence of Uncle Herbert, Francis was the head of the family—the small branch of it that I belonged to—and since Uncle Harold, the *de facto* head of the Sutherlands, didn't seem inclined to take a hand in whatever was going on, the responsibility fell to Francis.

And to Christopher, of course, who would never let me go off on my own, whether he had any authority or not.

"We'll be five minutes behind you," he told me, as he headed out of the room.

I nodded, a bit shakily. Francis gave me a comforting sort of look. "Chin up, Pipsqueak. We'll figure it out."

On the other side of the table, Crispin made to get to his feet. His fiancée put a delicate hand on his arm to keep him in place, although it was the glare that his father directed his way that made him subside back into his chair.

"It's all right, St George," I told him. "You tried. Francis will handle it."

Crispin sent a look at the doorway where Francis had vanished, but he didn't say anything. Constable Daniels took the opportunity to put the next phase of operations into place.

"If you'll come with me, Miss Darling."

The request was polite enough, but the tone—not to mention the meaty paw he wrapped around my upper arm—made it clear that I had no option but to obey.

"You don't have to manhandle me," I told him, a bit breathlessly, as he steered me through the door and down the hallway towards the foyer. Tidwell scurried in front to get to the door first. "I'm coming willingly."

Daniels didn't say anything to that, nor did he slow down appreciably. I could hear the sound of voices and movement from upstairs. Hopefully Christopher and Francis wouldn't be back in time to see Constable Daniels forcibly dragging me across the marble floor of the foyer, because I didn't think either of them would take kindly to that spectacle, and what happened after that would likely end in one or both of them being arrested for interference with an apprehension.

Tidwell flung the front door open, and stood aside.

"Thank you, Tidwell," I managed. Constable Daniels grunted and yanked me across the threshold.

"Good luck, Miss Darling." Tidwell watched as Constable Daniels pulled me across the gravel to the police issue Crossley Tender parked outside. I crawled into the backseat without demur—I certainly wasn't stupid enough to attempt to make a break for it—and Daniels slammed the seat back, practically crushing my kneecaps as he did it, and fitted himself behind the wheel.

"I don't suppose you intend to tell me what this is about?" I tried when he had engaged the motor and we were on our way out of the courtyard with the roofs of Little Sutherland spread out before us, at the end of the narrow lane that led down the hill into the village.

He shot me a look in the rearview mirror.

"That's what I thought." I sat back and folded my arms, and tried to take comfort in the scent of Christopher that emanated from the tweed jacket I was wrapped in.

The drive wasn't long enough to allow me to move beyond being scared and getting more so. Just a couple of minutes later, the Tender pulled up outside the Little Sutherland constabulary, and I was hauled from the backseat and inside. I ended up in a chair in front of a desk with Constable Daniels staring at me across the surface.

I pulled Christopher's jacket a bit tighter around myself and dredged up whatever courage I had left. "Do you plan to tell me what this is about now? Because I told Constable

Woodin in Stow-on-the-Wold everything I know about Morrison several days ago."

He didn't say anything, just looked at me, so I continued, "I would have testified at the inquest, but they only wanted to hear from Constance. I can't imagine what more I can do at this point. She's dead, and I don't know who did it."

Constable Daniels opened his mouth. "Who's dead?"

I blinked. "Lydia Morrison. Isn't that what this is about?"

Obviously not, because he asked, "Who is Lydia Morrison?"

Who is—?

"Lydia Morrison," I said, "was Lady Iris Peckham's maid. Before that, she was Aunt Charlotte's maid. The late Viscountess St George. Uncle Harold's wife."

Daniels looked confused.

"Morrison worked for Aunt Charlotte," I tried again. "Then she went to work for Lady Peckham. This was all a long time ago, when Crispin—the current Viscount St George—was a baby. Now she's dead."

"In Stow-on-the-Wold?"

"In Upper Slaughter, actually. But yes, the constabulary in Stow-on-the-Wold handled the case."

Daniels nodded. "And what did you have to do with it?"

"Nothing at all!"

My voice had turned shrill, and I took a breath and moderated it. "We motored up there—Francis, Constance, Christopher and I—because Constance wanted to see Morrison. When we got there, she was dead. We were asked to stay for the inquest so Constance could identify Morrison as the maid who had worked for her mother for twenty-three years. Morrison had only lived in Upper Slaughter for six months or so, so no one there knew her well."

"Interesting," Daniels said.

I eyed him. "They didn't tell you much, did they?"

"They told me nothing."

Well, that wasn't fair, was it? If the chaps in Stow-on-the-Wold had asked him to detain me for questioning, they ought at least to have told him why.

"What happens now?" I wanted to know. "Do we wait for someone from the Cotswolds to make it here?"

The look he gave me was strange. "Why would someone from the Cotswolds be coming?"

"Isn't that what this is about?"

Clearly it wasn't. He looked as confused as I felt.

"Perhaps we should start over," I suggested. I was breathing a bit more easily now, that it appeared I was not about to be arrested for Morrison's murder, or even for (possibly) contaminating her crime scene. "Would you care to tell me what this is about, Constable Daniels?"

Daniels hesitated, before he nudged a piece of paper across the desk towards me. "Don't touch it."

I wouldn't have done anyway, or at least I don't think so. Since he had specifically instructed me not to, I kept my hands firmly in my lap as I leaned forward.

It was a bog-standard piece of stationery, thick but not ostentatious. Bare of any kind of logo, of course. A couple of lines were scratched on it in what looked like fountain pen, by someone who was either not well-educated enough to have received lessons in penmanship, or who had tried hard to disguise their handwriting.

DOCTOR MEADOWS IS DEAD, the note said, in spiky, uneven capitals that listed to the right. PHILIPPA DARLING DID IT.

The spidery words hit me like a fist to the chest, and I sat back on the chair. It was a mostly involuntary reaction, an unconscious attempt to put space between myself and the accusation. "That's ridiculous."

My voice was breathless, like I had had the wind knocked out of me, which of course was exactly what had happened. There was a rushing sound in my ears.

Daniels arched his brows. "Which?"

I flapped my hands indignantly. "Both! Doctor Meadows isn't dead. I saw him myself, just a few hours ago. And he was alive and well."

His eyes sharpened. "So you did visit the infirmary this morning."

It wasn't a question, more of a confirmation of something already suspected—or alleged—but I nodded. "I did."

"And he was alive when you left him."

"Of course he was!"

"Can anyone verify that?"

"Christopher," I said. And then—I wasn't at my best, and I suppose that might explain it—my mind finally caught up with the implications. "Wait. You mean that it's true?"

"What's true?"

"About Doctor Meadows," I said. "That he's dead."

He nodded. "I'm afraid so."

"But he was alive just a few hours ago!"

"That's usually how it happens," Daniels said dryly.

"Well, I had nothing to do with it!"

"And you say that Mr. Astley can verify that?"

I nodded. "We were together the whole time. On the way there, while we were speaking to Doctor Meadows, and on the walk home."

"You were never apart?"

"Not until we reached Sutherland Hall. Then, we were in our separate rooms for the time that it took to pack our bags. We were supposed to go home this afternoon. But that wasn't long enough for either of us to run back to the village and attack the doctor."

"And Mr. Astley will confirm this?"

"Of course he will," I said. Not only was it true, but it was Christopher; he would confirm it whether it was true or not.

Constable Daniels hummed something under his breath. If it was supposed to sound like words, I couldn't make out what they were. "What did you and Doctor Meadows talk about?"

"Lydia Morrison," I said.

"Why would you inquire of Doctor Meadows about a woman who died in the Cotswolds?"

"His contact information was in her address book," I said. "I thought they may have been in contact since she left here."

Daniels eyed me. "How do you know who was in Miss Morrison's address book?"

"Oh. Um... I happened to get a look at it?"

It sounded less certain and more like a question than I wanted it to. Constable Daniels lifted his lip. It wasn't of the same quality as one of Crispin's sneers, which are a thing of beauty, but he got his point across. "Try again, Miss Darling."

"Fine." I threw my hands up. "I snooped, all right? She had been murdered, and I was curious, and the address book was right there... You can't blame me for taking a look."

He looked like he could very much blame me for taking a look. But Morrison's murder wasn't his concern, nor was my involvement in it. After a moment, he abandoned the topic in favor of his own case. "When did you leave the infirmary this morning?"

"I have no idea," I said. "We left Sutherland Hall after breakfast. I don't know how long it took us to walk down to the village. We spoke to Doctor Meadows for a few minutes. I didn't check the time when we left again. We arrived back at

Sutherland Hall about thirty minutes before luncheon. We packed our bags, and prepared to leave."

"Why didn't you?"

"Uncle Harold talked us into staying for luncheon," I said.

Constable Daniels nodded. "And Doctor Meadows was alive when you left the infirmary."

"Of course he was," I said. "He said goodbye to us. Christopher and I let ourselves out the front door into the High Street."

"Was anyone else about?"

I hadn't seen anyone. Little Sutherland isn't anything like a metropolis, and on a chilly, gloomy November day it's even quieter than usual.

"Someone must have seen me, though," I added.

"What makes you say that?"

I indicated the note, still sitting there on the surface of the desk. "If I hadn't stirred from Sutherland Hall all day, I could have simply said so and this wouldn't be an issue. Someone saw me in the village and decided to implicate me."

Daniels eyed the note in silence for a second. "Any idea who that might be?"

"None. I don't really know many people here. Aside from Doctor Meadows, most of the ones I know were up at the Hall."

He didn't respond to that, and I added, "Where did it come from? It couldn't have been posted. Not between the time I last saw Doctor Meadows and when you came and fetched me from the Hall."

That had been a matter of a hour and a half, at most. Probably less. Certainly not enough time to write a note, post it, and have it delivered. His Majesty's Royal Mail doesn't move that quickly.

"We don't know of anyone else who has seen Doctor Meadows this morning," Constable Daniels said. "You were alone at the infirmary?"

"Other than Christopher and Doctor Meadows, as far as I know. Although someone might have been in the back room, as long as they were quiet about it."

He tilted his head. "Do you have any reason to think someone was there?"

"That's where Doctor Meadows came from when we arrived," I said. "He was in the middle of drying his hands and rolling down his sleeves." I hesitated. "Although for all I know he might have been doing the washing up. He lives above the infirmary, doesn't he?"

The constable nodded.

"Well, then I suppose he might have been upstairs when we arrived. I don't think I heard anyone come down the stairs, though."

"And what did you talk about?"

He waited with a pen poised over a piece of paper while I repeated the conversation that had taken place, as verbatim as I could recall it.

"And Mr. Astley will confirm this?" he asked at the end of it.

"Of course he will. He's probably outside right now."

I glanced at the front door. Daniels did the same, but he didn't get up from behind the desk. "And that was when you left?

"That was when we left," I confirmed. "We stood for a moment outside the front door while we pulled on our gloves and fastened our scarves, and then we walked back up the hill."

"And when you got there?"

"We packed," I said. "When we came down the stairs to leave, Uncle Harold talked us into staying for luncheon. And then you arrived."

"But Doctor was definitely alive when you left the infirmary."

I nodded. "Ask Christopher if you don't believe me."

I had thought that that might be enough for him to let me go, but no. He changed the subject again. "Tell me about the people up at the Hall. Who knew that you were going to the village this morning?"

"Everyone," I said. "All the guests, and at least some of the staff. Francis and Constance took breakfast with us. So did Aunt Roz and Uncle Herbert. And whoever wasn't at breakfast would have heard us discuss it after dinner last night. I can't imagine that anyone didn't know."

"Tell me again who's at the Hall this weekend." He pulled a clean piece of paper over to take notes.

"There's Uncle Harold and Crispin, of course, and the staff. You probably know them better than I do, but there's Tidwell, and Mrs. Mason, and Cook, and Sadie—she's the parlor maid—and Hugh and Alfie, the two footmen, and a kitchen maid, and a couple of chambermaids, and the grooms and gardeners...."

Sutherland Hall is a large estate, with a large staff. It made me long for my little flat in London, where all I had to worry about was Christopher and Evans the doorman.

Constable Daniels nodded for me to go on, and I did. "The Earl and Countess of Marsden are visiting, with their son and daughter and a maid. The daughter is engaged to marry Crispin. They've all been here before, and I'm sure you must have seen them. They aren't the sort of people one would overlook."

Daniels nodded.

"Then there's His Grace's brother, Lord Herbert Astley, and his wife, Lady Roslyn. But they left during the time Christopher and I were in the village. I'm sure they're back at Beckwith Place by now. It's only about an hour's drive from here."

"Did you see them?" Daniels interrupted the smooth flow of my delivery.

I blinked at him for a moment while I recalibrated. "Before they left, do you mean? Yes, they were at breakfast. We said goodbye."

And it had only been meant to be for a few hours anyway. We had been headed to Beckwith from here after luncheon.

"In the village," Constable Daniels clarified. "Or in the lane coming or going?"

Oh. I shook my head. "I'm afraid we didn't. They must have passed through Little Sutherland while we were inside the infirmary."

Daniels nodded. "Go on, please."

"There's not a lot more to say," I said. "Christopher and Francis are outside in the motorcar waiting for me. I'm sure you've met them both before. They've been visiting Sutherland Hall for decades."

Daniels nodded.

"The only other guest is the Honorable Constance Peckham. She's the niece of the Marsdens, and Laetitia and Geoffrey's cousin, as well as Francis's fiancée and an old friend of mine from school."

"And then there's you."

I nodded. "Yes, of course." I go where Christopher goes. Unless Christopher goes to a drag ball. Then I'm not allowed to come. But otherwise, we go together.

Daniels glanced down at the list of names he had scribbled. "You mentioned a maid?"

I had, in fact, mentioned a lot of maids. However— "Lady Marsden brought her maid along. Her name is Shreve. She's the one who told us about Morrison."

"What about Morrison?"

"That she had seen Morrison in Lower Slaughter," I said. "That's why we motored up there."

"And found Morrison dead."

"That's correct."

"And the reason you wanted to speak to Doctor Meadows this morning, was to ask him about Morrison."

I nodded.

"Was he able to give you any of the answers you wanted?"

"I'm afraid not," I said. "He said he hadn't seen Morrison in more than twenty years, and he had no idea who might have wanted to kill her."

Silence reigned for a moment, and then I added, "Would you mind telling me what happened to Doctor Meadows?"

He looked at me, with that expression that said, as clearly as words, that I must be stupid for missing the fact that the doctor was dead. I added, while doing my best to control my impatience, "Specifically. Did someone shoot him? Strangle him? Hit him over the head with the proverbial blunt object?"

"That," Constable Daniels said.

"In the infirmary, or...?"

"In the surgery," Constable Daniels said.

Then someone might truly have been in there while Doctor had conversed with Christopher and me in the front room. "Did you find the murder weapon?"

Constable Daniels allowed as how they hadn't. The murderer must have taken it with him when he left.

"What about the note? Was it left behind at the scene?"

But no, likely not. Not with the wording the way it was. There was no need to mention Doctor Meadows's death to anyone who was already looking at his corpse.

"It came through the mail slot," Daniels said. His eyes flicked to the front door and the slit in it. "I picked it up and read it. I went to the infirmary. I found Doctor Meadows dead.

I set a couple of constables to work on the crime scene. Then I motored up to Sutherland Hall to fetch you."

"Well, I didn't do it," I said. "If I had killed him, I wouldn't give the police a note implicating myself. Nor would Christopher. That would be stupid."

Daniels didn't respond to that, and I went on. "Where did it come from? Did someone write it in the infirmary? Did you check the doctor's stationery or desk blotter?"

"We're doing that," Constable Daniels confirmed.

"Good." I nodded decisively. "Because if it didn't come from there, if the killer brought it with him, that makes it premeditated, you realize. That—" I indicated the note, "isn't something someone writes and carries around with them unless they plan to use it."

"Do you recognize the handwriting?"

I flicked another glance at it. "Who would recognize that? It's all capital letters. It could have been written by anyone."

It could have been written by *me*, with the pen in my left hand. Not that I mentioned that.

"Can you think of anyone who might want to accuse you of murder?"

There were plenty of people who might not quibble about having me out of the way for a while, with Laetitia and her mother at the top of the list. But to accuse me of murder, they would have had to have known that Doctor Meadows was dead, and how would anyone who hadn't left the Hall all morning know that?

Constable Daniels hummed. "You may go, Miss Darling. But only back to Sutherland Hall."

I opened my mouth to protest—I was meant to go to Salisbury and London today, or at least tomorrow—and he added, "Surely you understand that, after an accusation like this, we can't have you leave. I don't want to arrest you—"

"You'd better not," I said, "because you have no proof other than this note, and it's pure speculation."

"—but the Chief Constable would also have something to say about it if I let you motor away before the inquest. You'll be required to give evidence, if nothing else."

Yes, of course I would be.

"Fine," I said. "I'll stay for the inquest. As long as Uncle Harold is willing to continue to put us up at Sutherland Hall."

He looked a bit surprised at that—perhaps he didn't realize that Crispin's father heartily despises me; I ought to have put him on the list of people who would be happy to have me out of the way—but he nodded. "You're free to go, Miss Darling. If your cousin is waiting outside, let him know I'd like a word."

I told him I would do, and headed for the door.

CHAPTER TEN

MY COUSIN WAS INDEED WAITING OUTSIDE—
BOTH of them, in fact—and I told the one I assumed
Constable Daniels wanted to speak to that his presence was
requested inside the constabulary.

"And don't try to be cute, Christopher. You're literally the
only thing standing between me and a cell."

"That's ridiculous," Christopher said as he unwound
himself from the passenger seat. "May I have my jacket back?
Yours is there."

He indicated the backseat, where my coat was neatly
folded on the cushion. I shrugged out of his tweed and handed
it to him.

"Not that ridiculous. Have him show you the note."

"Which note?" He twitched his sleeves down.

"The one accusing me of murder." I snapped my own
jacket open preparatory to putting it on. He moved to help me
and I shooed him away. "Go, Christopher. If you waste any
more time, he'll think we're conspiring."

Christopher muttered something—it sounded like, "I'll

show him conspiring,"—but he went. I finished wrapping my jacket around myself before I crawled into the backseat and met Francis's eyes in the mirror.

"There's a note?"

"Capital letters in black ink. Shoved through the mail slot in the door after the murder."

"That's interesting," my cousin commented after I had repeated the accusation.

"Isn't it? Someone either saw me—saw us—coming or going, although if they did, they would have seen Christopher too, because we didn't separate at all. Or someone knew I was going to be there—with or without Christopher—and decided to frame me."

"The only people who knew that you were going to be there are the people at Sutherland Hall," Francis said.

I nodded. "Precisely so."

He eyed me in the mirror. "I spent the morning with Constance."

I huffed. "I know it wasn't you, Francis. Or Constance, for that matter. Not only had neither of you any reason to kill Doctor Meadows, but you certainly wouldn't frame me for it if you had done."

"I'm simply mentioning the fact that I have an alibi, Pipsqueak."

"And the police may care about that," I said, "but I don't. Although I suppose it's a good thing you do, really. Someone did it, and when they can't prove that it was me, they'll have to look for someone else."

There was a moment's pause while I scowled and while Francis thought, and while the door to the constabulary stayed stubbornly closed. It was too soon to expect Christopher back out—of course it was—but I was still watching the door, waiting.

"He was alive when you saw him?" Francis asked.

I glanced up and caught his eyes on me in the mirror. "Doctor Meadows, do you mean? Yes, he was. We spoke. It was definitely him, alive and well. Whoever killed him, killed him after Christopher and I had gone."

"Did he have any information about Morrison?"

I shook my head. "He remembered her, but he said he hadn't had any interaction with her since she left Aunt Charlotte's employ. And that's another thing."

"What's another thing?"

"If the same person killed Doctor Meadows as killed Morrison, and perhaps Hughes, too—"

"A traveling serial murderer?" Francis said with interest. "Do go on, Pippa."

I flicked him a look. "It sounds farfetched, I know. But bear with me. If the same person killed all of them, and for the same reason, why would that person not kill Doctor Meadows *before* we had the chance to speak with him? Why wait?"

"It sounds as if he had nothing of interest to say," Francis pointed out, "so why not let you speak to him?"

"Yes, of course." I nodded. "But if he didn't know anything of interest, why kill him at all?"

He opened his mouth and closed it again. And opened it again. "Perhaps, as they say in the novels, he knew something he didn't know that he knew?"

"Then why take the chance that he'd figure it out? Or tell me? Or us?"

"Because you wouldn't know it for being significant even if he did tell you?"

"But if no one but the murderer would recognize its significance, and yet it was significant enough to commit murder over... why wait twenty-three years? Why not murder him back then, when no one was curious?"

Francis shrugged somewhat helplessly. "I don't know, Pippa. Perhaps it had nothing at all to do with Morrison. Perhaps Doctor Meadows was having an affair with the butcher's wife, and the butcher saw you and Kit come out of the infirmary, and thought he'd take the opportunity to get rid of his wife's lover while framing you."

I tilted my head contemplatively. "All right. I'll take your word for it that the butcher's wife would be worth all this excitement. But if so, why not frame Christopher?"

"Kit's the Duke of Sutherland's nephew," Francis said, "and Crispin's best friend. Best not to frame him."

Yes, that was true. While I was merely the girl Crispin was hung up on, but not the one he was marrying. The poor relation, the half-German orphan, only there on sufferance. It would be safe to frame me.

"Is the butcher's wife worth committing murder for?"

"How am I supposed to know?" Francis shook his head. "I have no idea, Pippa. I don't imagine so. But it could be the baker's wife, or the greengrocer's wife, or anyone else's wife, for that matter. Or perhaps Doctor Meadows did something at some point—medically, don't you know—that upset someone. Someone's child caught the measles and died, and the parents still aren't over it."

"But that happens," I said. "Not usually, I know; I had the measles, and I was fine—"

Francis nodded. "We all had the measles and were fine. But sometimes someone isn't fine. And if someone's child died from the measles—or scarlet fever, or an allergy to bees—and the parents blamed Doctor Meadows..."

Yes, of course. And it might not have been a child at all, it might have been a woman in childbirth or a man with an injury of some sort. When a person is unhinged enough to commit murder, what made them decide to in the first place might not make sense to the rest of us.

Francis nodded when I said as much. "I'm sure Constable Daniels will look into Doctor Meadows's patients."

"You don't think he'll simply arrest me for murder?"

Especially if Uncle Harold pushed for it? Which he might do, if he thought it was important enough to get me out of the way before Crispin's wedding to Laetitia. He did have the Chief Constable's ear.

"If he tries, I'll remind him that there are other avenues of investigation," Francis said. "Besides, I wouldn't be surprised if we see Scotland Yard soon. Kit rang up Tommy before we motored down here."

"Rang up— Tom Gardiner, do you mean? Is he coming?"

"When does he not," Francis wanted to know, "when Kit phones?"

Fair point. "Scotland Yard isn't taking over the case, though. Are they?"

"I have no idea," Francis said cheerfully. "I can't imagine that they would do. It isn't particularly exciting, is it? Village doctor brained with doorstop? The only thing that makes it interesting, is that it might be connected to Morrison's murder, and perhaps Hughes's murder. But those are in two different jurisdictions, and Hughes's murder was months ago..."

I nodded. "For all I know, they've already arrested someone for that. I don't know that they haven't. It might simply have been a robbery, the way that they thought."

"And Morrison might have gotten on the wrong side of a Primitive Methodist," Francis agreed, "while the butcher or baker did for Doctor Meadows."

"Precisely. Although I imagine that Tom might know about Hughes, at least. She had his card in her handbag—that's why the Bristol detectives rang him up in the first place—and he probably asked to be kept *à jour*. If they arrested someone, they might have let him know."

"We can ask him when he gets here," Francis said, "which he'll likely do in the next few hours."

"That reminds me. Constable Daniels said that I can't leave. I have to stay for the inquest. Christopher too, I assume."

"We thought as much," Francis nodded. "Our second inquest in a week. Exciting times."

After a moment, he added, "Crispin will be delighted."

"His father won't be." Nor would Laetitia. Or her mother.

"That's all right," Francis said. "He won't kick you out. He can't really kick us out, and that means you're staying, too."

I supposed it did. "What a muddle this is."

"You ought to be used to it by now," Francis said. "It's hardly your first murder case, is it?"

No, of course it wasn't. But the question was clearly rhetorical, so I didn't answer it, just let him go on.

"It'll be all right, Pipsqueak. Nothing we haven't dealt with before. And nothing to do with us, except peripherally."

He turned the key in the ignition of the Crossley. "Here's Kit now. Let's get you back to the Hall and tell Uncle Harold the good news."

"Sounds lovely," I said.

Meanwhile, Christopher had approached the vehicle. "Not so fast, Francis. Constable Daniels wants a word with you, too."

"With me? Why?" But he disengaged the motor and dropped the key in his pocket.

"No idea," Christopher said as he opened the passenger door. "He asked whether I was alone. When I said no, that you were here too, he asked me to send you in."

"But I wasn't even in the village this morning." Nonetheless, he stepped out of the motorcar and adjusted his coat.

"I assume he just wants confirmation of something or

other," Christopher said, fitting himself into the front seat. "Off you go, there's a good chap. Don't say anything you'll regret."

Francis eyed him. "Not sure what that would be."

"Anything we would regret, then." Christopher's quick side-eye included me in the 'we'. "Anything to suggest that either of us was complicit in Doctor Meadows's murder. Or Morrison's ditto."

"I wouldn't," Francis said. "Besides, you weren't."

"Just make sure the constable knows that, if you please."

Francis nodded. "I'll be back shortly."

He made his way to the front door, and Christopher twisted in his seat to address me. "Are you all right, Pippa?"

"Fine," I said. "Why wouldn't I be? He didn't indicate any plans to arrest me, did he? Or suggest that he thought I was guilty?"

Christopher shook his head. "Although I don't know that he believes you to be innocent, either, necessarily. There's the note, and I suppose he has to take it seriously."

"An anonymous note!"

"I know. But it's an accusation, and he has to look into it. I didn't get the idea that he thought it particularly credible."

"I should hope not," I said, disgruntled. "Why on earth would anyone think I'd murder Doctor Meadows? I can probably count the times I've met him on one hand. The only time he treated me, was six months ago when the bullet just missed me."

I had never lived at Sutherland Hall, and never spent much time here, either. Unlike Christopher, who had eleven years of visits with Crispin before I showed up from Germany.

"I've met him more often than that," Christopher said. "I broke my arm once, when I was seven or so, and Doctor Meadows had to set it. And that wasn't the only time something happened when Crispin and I played together, either.

But all the childhood illnesses and such I had, I went through at Beckwith Place, with Doctor White. Including the influenza."

I had gone through the influenza with Doctor White, too. Before coming to England, I'd had a few of the standard child-hood illnesses in Germany, and then there were the years I had spent at the Godolphin School in Salisbury, while Christopher was away at Eton. None of which translated into much time spent in Little Sutherland with Doctor Meadows.

"He suggested that you might be in the family way," Christopher added, "and that Doctor Meadows refused to give you something for it."

I snorted. "I hope he didn't suggest that you were the father of my non-existent child?"

"He did," Christopher said calmly. "I set him straight, of course. Then he suggested that it was Crispin's."

I rolled my eyes. "For the record, if I had been stupid enough to get myself up the duff by St George—and what an idea, Christopher!—I wouldn't visit the Sutherland village doctor to have it taken care of. I'd go to someone in London, where I live."

And where they would be less inclined to speculate about the identity of the baby's father.

"I made certain to point that out," Christopher nodded. "I also reminded him that Crispin is engaged to Laetitia, and that nothing good will come of asking that question of anyone else."

I shuddered. No, indeed. I could just picture Laetitia's face now, if Constable Daniels were to bring up the possibility. Not to mention Uncle Harold's ditto.

"I did my best to impress on him the absolute ridiculous-ness of the notion," Christopher assured me. "I got the feeling that he believed me. Or at least he believed that I believed it. Although, since we were together every minute of our visit earlier, there was no way you could have murdered Doctor Meadows even if you were expecting.”

“Good,” I told him decisively. “Did he ask you about anything else that I should know? Or let anything interesting slip?”

“Nothing he didn’t already tell you, I’m certain,” Christopher said. “I told him that we’d heard a door slam a minute or so after we left the infirmary, while we were still standing outside in the lane.”

“Did we hear a door slam?”

“I did,” Christopher said. “I don’t know about you. We didn’t discuss it. But I certainly heard something of the sort.”

So had I done, now that I thought about it. “I wonder whether that was when the murder took place?”

“I hope so,” Christopher said, “since we were indubitably together, and in full view of everyone in the village.”

“If anyone saw us.”

“Someone saw us,” Christopher said. “Whoever wrote the note.”

“Did Daniels tell you about it?”

He nodded. “Showed it to me, told me it had come through the mail slot shortly after the murder. Asked me if I recognized the writing.”

“And did you?”

He shook his head. “Something like that could belong to anyone. We all write abominably with our left hands. All except for Crispin.”

“Why except for Crispin?”

“He’s naturally left-handed. I remember all the crying when we were small. Uncle Harold tied his left hand behind his back so he couldn’t use it, and made him learn to write with his right instead.”

I scowled. “Bastard.”

He shrugged. "It's common practice. Although I can't imagine why anyone would bother. As long as he knows how to write, who cares which hand he uses to do it?"

Certainly not I. "Didn't people used to believe that being left-handed meant you were evil?"

"Hundreds of years ago," Christopher confirmed. "But all sorts of things were thought to be evil back then. We know better now."

"Are you certain about that?" It was St George, after all. Evil seemed to fit.

Christopher rolled his eyes at me, and I smirked. "So he can write with both hands, is what you're saying?"

"Equally well, too. He kept the left-handed writing from Uncle Harold and practiced on his own time. At Eton, he'd use both. Sometimes at the same time."

How interesting.

"It sounds like anyone except perhaps Crispin could have produced the note, then. Did Constable Daniels think it might have originated at Sutherland Hall?"

"He didn't suggest it," Christopher said judiciously. "Although the insinuation that I might recognize it did rather lend itself to that interpretation. It's not as if I know any of the villagers' hands."

No, it wasn't. "I don't suppose the writing paper looked familiar?"

"It looked like writing paper." After a second he added, "At least it didn't have the Savoy Hotel logo in the corner."

I made a face. "Don't remind me."

Wolfgang Ulrich Albrecht, the late—or perhaps still-breathing—*Graf von und zu* Natterdorff, had corresponded with me via Savoy Hotel stationery for several months after he moved out of the upscale Savoy Hotel and into humbler accommodations. I didn't appreciate the reminder, of the subterfuge or of Wolfgang himself.

"We could check Uncle Harold's study," Christopher said, "once we get back to Sutherland Hall."

"Do you suppose he'll allow you to skulk in his study, peering at his stationery? Besides, he was in there when we came back up from the village earlier. I noticed the lights were on when we crossed the courtyard."

"That doesn't mean anything," Christopher protested. "He could have gone out and left the lights on."

"Are you accusing your uncle of killing Doctor Meadows and framing me for murder, Christopher?"

He didn't answer, and I added, "I'm fairly certain I saw his head, too. Someone was in there, sitting at the desk. And it couldn't have been Uncle Herbert. He had already left by then."

"Dad wouldn't have gone in Uncle Harold's study anyway," Christopher said.

"He might have done, if there was something your uncle asked him to look at."

Christopher snorted. "And what do you suppose that might be? Uncle Harold has always been extremely territorial about the Hall. He hardly even took Dad's input when it came to burying Grandfather."

"In justice to your uncle," I said, and it pained me to have to be fair about it, "he had a few other things on his mind at that point."

Like his wife's funeral, and the fact that she had been responsible for killing his father.

Christopher shrugged sulkily.

"At any rate," I added, "it's not just the study that has stationery. The library does, too, not to mention all the guest rooms. You never know when one of the guests—Lady Laetitia, for instance—might get the urge to pen an explicit love note to St George."

Christopher made a face. "Did you have to put that image into my head? Although I suppose you have a point. Even if there's similar stationery in Uncle Harold's study, or for that matter all over the house, we wouldn't know whether any of it had gone missing this morning."

"Mrs. Mason might know," I said. "Not about the writing paper in the study or library, but in the guest rooms. I'm sure the maids do the replenishing when they do the rooms every morning. Someone might remember having had to replace a piece of note paper this morning."

"I don't suppose it would do any harm to ask," Christopher said. "Whoever wrote the note had to have known that Doctor Meadows was dead—"

"Or that he would die, if the note was written beforehand." In which case it was premeditated murder.

"—but how could they know, if they were all at the Hall this morning?"

"Perhaps they weren't all at the Hall this morning. We can ask Francis when he comes back out, whether he knows where everyone went after breakfast. And if he doesn't know, we can ask Constance, or Crispin, or even ring up Aunt Roz and Uncle Herbert and ask them."

"We ought to do that anyway," Christopher said. "And let them know we won't be coming home today, and why."

I suppose we ought. "At least they were long gone when this happened."

"Long gone when it was discovered, at any rate. Hopefully Daniels won't get any ideas about asking them to come back. They must have been driving through Little Sutherland at around the same time as the murder."

So it seemed, if that had taken place shortly after Christopher and I had seen him.

"Here's Francis now," I said, as the door to the constabulary opened and the latter came out. He shut the door behind himself and strode towards the Crossley.

"Well?" I asked as he fitted himself behind the wheel. "What news?"

He flicked me a glance in the mirror. "Nothing you don't already know."

"Did he tell you not to leave?"

"Sutherland Hall, do you mean?" He cranked over the motor. "Yes. We're all expected to stay. You two are expected to attend the inquest whenever it's set. The rest of us are to make ourselves available for questions later."

The Crossley rolled off down the road.

"Questions about what," I wanted to know, "precisely?"

Francis's eyes flicked to mine in the mirror again. "Whether either of you two had a reason to want Doctor Meadows dead. You're not in the family way, are you, Pippa?"

"Certainly not," I said with a sniff, while Christopher snorted.

"Is he still on about that? I thought I talked him out of that idea."

"Seemingly not. He asked me about it."

"What did you tell him?" I wanted to know. "You didn't suggest that there's anything like that going on with me and St George, did you, Francis?"

I love my cousin, but he does occasionally display a strange sense of humor. It was the time in the trenches, I assume, that taught him to find amusement in things that the rest of us wouldn't find funny. I wouldn't put it past him to perpetuate this story for the simple sport of it.

"St George, is it?" He glanced at his brother. "All he

suggested to me, was that the two of you were trying to hide a pregnancy. There was no mention of Little Lord Fauntleroy."

I made a face. "I don't know which is less likely, honestly."

"Me," Christopher said. "Clearly. While you're not interested in me, I'm also not interested in you. Crispin, on the other hand, likes women—"

"And how."

"—and he also likes you specifically."

"None of which has anything to do with whether I would have anything to do with him. But I take your point, Christopher. So Constable Daniels was still on about that, then, Francis?"

"Seemed to be," Francis said, maneuvering the Crossley up the lane towards the Hall. "I can't wait until Uncle Harold has to field questions about it."

He sniggered.

I rolled my eyes. "Oh, joy. Nor can I."

CHAPTER ELEVEN

WE DIDN'T HAVE to wait long. Francis and his sense of humor wasn't about to let this chance go by. We were barely inside the foyer—Tidwell was still in the process of shutting the front door behind us—when Crispin skidded onto the marble floor. He was followed a few seconds later by his fiancée and his father, in a much more leisurely fashion.

By the time they arrived, Crispin had assured himself that I was there, and in one piece. Christopher was the first person he looked at, but only for as long as it took to ask, "Is everything all right?" before he turned his attention to me. And while I usually can't tell from his face that he has romantic feelings for me, in this case his expression was unguarded for at least half a second before the blinds slammed down.

"Fine," I told him. "Nothing to worry about. Just a few questions."

"Why you?"

I hesitated. Did I tell him about the note, or wait until we had more privacy? If that was even possible, with Laetitia dogging his heels like a faithful Retriever.

"It wasn't just Pippa," Christopher said. "The constable spoke to me and Francis, as well."

Crispin shifted his attention to Francis. "Why you? And why not Connie?"

"It wasn't about Morrison," I said. "As it turns out, there was a murder in the village this morning, while Christopher and I were there."

Behind Crispin, Laetitia gasped and clutched her hands to her breast. If she had killed Doctor Meadows—and I had no reason to think she had done; I simply like to imagine her guilty of various offenses—it was a convincing presentation of innocence.

"Who's dead?" His Grace wanted to know.

"Doctor Meadows," Christopher told him. "Sometime between the time Pippa and I left the infirmary, and when luncheon was served."

There was a moment of silence. Then—

"Dreadful," Uncle Harold said. "And the constable wanted to speak to you because...?"

"He wanted to make certain that Doctor was alive and well when we left him," Christopher said, "which he was, of course. We would have said something about it had he not been. And then he wanted to know whether we had noticed anything out of the ordinary. Anyone skulking around or behaving suspiciously or whatnot."

"And had you done?"

Uncle Harold looked from him to me and back with penetrating blue eyes. The chandelier gilded his grayish hair almost back to its youthful buttery blond.

"Not in the least," I said cheerfully. "The street outside was as empty when we left as it had been when we arrived. We were only inside the infirmary for a few minutes, and all of Little Sutherland seemed content to stay inside this morning.

It's the weather, I suppose."

"And that was all?" Crispin asked, a trace of worry still in his tone. "It seemed rather more pointed than that when Daniels manhandled you out of the dining room."

"That was all, truly. I'm afraid we'll have to impose on your hospitality for a few days longer. Constable Daniels wants us to keep ourselves available for the inquest."

"We were the last people to see him alive, it seems," Christopher added. "Aside from the murderer, of course."

Crispin nodded. "Of course. I'll let Mrs. Mason know that you'll be staying."

"That's all right," I said. "I'd be happy to do so." It would give me an opportunity to ask the housekeeper about the stationery in the bedrooms.

Tidwell cleared his throat. "With your permission, Your Grace—"

He turned to me, "Miss Darling—"

And again to Uncle Harold, "I'll have the bags taken back upstairs."

He snapped his fingers at Hugh, the first footman, who was hovering in the background. The latter snagged Christopher's and my weekender bags from the corner of the foyer, where we had dropped them earlier, and headed for the staircase.

"And now I'll speak to Mrs. Mason," Tidwell said and stalked towards the kitchen wing with measured steps.

"That's you told, Darling," Crispin said as soon as the butler was out of range. None of us dared speak until then, I assumed. I certainly didn't.

I nodded. "Serves me right for trying to fraternize with the staff."

"Is that what you were doing? I didn't realize you held Mrs. Mason in such high regard."

"I don't," I said. "Nothing against Mrs. Mason, of course.

But you know as well as I do that I adore Tidwell. If I were going to fraternize with anyone, it would be him."

"Naturally." Crispin smirked. I smirked back, and only then remembered that we were standing in the middle of the foyer, surrounded by some of our nearest and dearest, who certainly wouldn't get, or appreciate, the joke. The look Uncle Harold directed my way was fishy in the extreme, while Laetitia looked scandalized. I'm not sure whether it was my stated passion for the butler or the rapport between Crispin and myself that bothered her, although it might have been both.

I cleared my throat. "If you'll excuse me, I think I'll follow Tidwell."

I didn't wait for anyone to respond, although the silence that spread behind me, as I walked towards the green baize door to the servants' quarters, was loud. I had no doubt whatsoever that everyone exploded into speech just as soon as the door shut behind me.

TIDWELL HAD ALREADY MADE it to the servants' sitting room before I caught up. Shreve was nowhere to be seen today —she must be upstairs in Lady Euphemia's chambers—but Tidwell stood in conversation with Mrs. Mason while one of the maids looked on. As I came through the door, Mrs. Mason and Tidwell moved apart, and they all turned to look at me.

"Miss Darling," Mrs. Mason said politely after a moment. "I understand that you will be staying with us for a few more days."

"Not by choice," I answered. And added, "I mean... yes, Constable Daniels wants Christopher and myself to attend the inquest, whenever it takes place. And that means that Francis and Constance will be staying too, I assume."

I glanced at Tidwell, whose face was impassive, before

focusing on Mrs. Mason again. "Doctor Meadows has been murdered, in case no one told you."

Mrs. Mason pressed her lips together, but nodded. "Tidwell just now informed me."

"I wanted to ask about the writing paper," I said.

Mrs. Mason looked nonplussed. "The writing paper, Miss Darling?"

"In the bedrooms. And, I suppose, in the library and study."

"What about the writing paper?" Tidwell wanted to know. Behind him, the maid stared at me, bug-eyed.

"The constabulary received a handwritten note accusing me of killing Doctor Meadows," I said. Coolly, I thought, although the maid gasped and slapped a hand to her chest.

An expression of irritation crossed Mrs. Mason's face. "Don't you have something to do, Sadie?"

Sadie looked chagrined, like she didn't want to have to leave before she could hear the rest of the story. Nonetheless, she got to her feet. "Yes, Mrs. Mason."

She shot me a look on her way to the door. I ignored her, and so did Mrs. Mason and Tidwell.

"What's this about writing paper?" Mrs. Mason asked again when the door had shut behind the maid.

"As I said, the constabulary—"

"Yes, yes." She brushed it aside. "Do they know that it came from here?"

"I don't think they have any idea where it came from. But I thought I'd ask, since writing paper is so easy to come by at Sutherland Hall. There's some in every nightstand, as well as some of the common rooms."

"In the servants' quarters, as well," Tidwell said, "although I assure you, Miss Darling, none of the staff would accuse you of murder."

"Of course not." That possibility hadn't even crossed my

mind. Perhaps it ought to have done, but I had not upset any of the servants enough that they'd do something like that, as far as I knew.

"The staff was working this morning," Mrs. Mason said stiffly. "No one on my staff had the opportunity to go to the village and commit murder."

No, I hadn't thought so. "I only wanted to ask about the writing paper in the guest rooms, and whether you had had to replace any of it today."

The note would have been written in the early part of the day, I assumed, before the maids had had the opportunity to turn over the rooms.

"Or perhaps tomorrow," I added. "You might make note of it, if any of the rooms need more writing paper tomorrow morning."

Mrs. Mason nodded. "To answer your question, Miss Darling, Master Francis used a piece of writing paper for a note to Miss Constance. It was in her room this morning."

"I'm not worried about Constance or Francis," I said. Neither of them would accuse me of murder. Nor would they kill Doctor Meadows in the first place.

"His Grace uses the stationery in the study," Tidwell contributed, "when he has correspondence. His Lordship has a desk with writing paper in his sitting room. He uses that, or occasionally the stationery in the library."

"No private love notes from the stash in his bedside drawer?"

"Not recently," Tidwell said blandly. "The last time His Lordship kept his correspondence private was in August."

I made a face. August was when Crispin and I had had that acrimonious exchange of letters that had culminated with me telling him (in writing) to propose to Laetitia because they deserved one another. I should be grateful that he had kept that whole thing under wraps, I suppose. The servants, not to mention Uncle Harold, would have had a field day with it.

"Lady Laetitia's writing paper always needs replenishing," Mrs. Mason added, gossipy. "I believe she uses it to write little love notes to Master Crispin. The maids see them in his room."

And giggled over them, no doubt. "Crumpled and in the rubbish bin, I hope?"

Tidwell looked preternaturally bland. Mrs. Mason's lips twitched. "I'm afraid not, Miss Darling. They go in his night table drawer."

Ugh. "Of course they do." My nose wrinkled. "I suppose he takes them out every so often, and reads them to himself when he can't sleep at night?"

"You would have to ask him," Tidwell said blandly. "Although I'm certain you understand, Miss Darling, that the bin wouldn't be the proper place for love notes from the future Viscountess."

Yes, of course I understood. I wasn't stupid. Or at least I don't like to think that I am, all evidence to the (sometimes) contrary. If Laetitia wrote her betrothed love notes, and he consigned them to the rubbish, it wouldn't bode well for future marital bliss. So of course he couldn't do that.

The notes I had sent in the past, including the one that had exhorted him to propose to Laetitia, were another matter, of course. They weren't the sort of thing a man would keep, no matter how besotted he might be. But hopefully he had disposed of them in the fire, and not anywhere where the servants had access to them, because that would be beyond embarrassing.

I eyed Tidwell and Mrs. Mason, to see whether either of them betrayed any sort of knowledge of the kind of correspondence that might have put Crispin in his place and made him propose to the bane of my existence. They both looked perfectly bland, like they would have had no idea what I would be thinking about.

I cleared my throat. "Anyone else?"

"Lord Geoffrey needed a refill this morning," Mrs. Mason said. "So did his mother, but she sent a letter to Marsden Manor. It went out in the mail bag."

"But Geoffrey had an unaccounted-for letter?"

"That doesn't mean anything, Miss Darling," Tidwell advised me. "He might have been taking notes from a book or doodling or working out the clues for a cryptic crossword. Or he might have put a letter in the mailbag when no one was looking."

Yes, of course he might have done. And Geoffrey, of everyone here, would have had the least motive to murder the local doctor, it seemed. He had visited Sutherland Hall only once or twice before, and it wasn't likely that he would have run across Doctor Meadows on any of those occasions. No one had died, nor, to my knowledge, been ill or grievously injured.

On the other hand, Geoffrey wasn't an enormous fan of my humble self, so if I had to pick someone in the household as the most likely to frame me for murder... well, it mightn't be Geoffrey, actually. I would put his sister above him on the list, along with, possibly, her mother, and certainly her future father-in-law. But Geoffrey did have motive of a sort, not just because I had rejected his advances before, but also because he might possibly hold me at least partially responsible for the month or so he had just spent in jail.

And accusing me of murder when he had just been acquitted of it himself, did have a certain poetic justice.

Tidwell cleared his throat, and I came back to myself with a rush. "I'm sorry. I should go join the others. Thank you for the help."

I avoided looking at them both as I backed out of the

servants' sitting room and then turned tail and scurried back to the front part of the house.

I did not go back to the foyer, however. I couldn't hear anyone's voices that I knew—not from there—so instead, I made my way down to the end of the west wing, past the study, the boot room, and the gunroom—where Aunt Charlotte had found the rifle that she had used to take that potshot at me back in April—all the way to the servants' staircase. From there, I climbed to the first floor and came out practically in front of my own bedchamber. The corridor was empty, and I ducked inside my room and dropped on the bed with a heartfelt groan. It had been a terribly long day, and it wasn't even teatime yet.

I knew very well that I wouldn't be allowed very much time to myself, of course. If Christopher didn't come and find me soon, Constance would do. We were probably all in our rooms getting settled back in. Unless the others had stayed downstairs, and I was the only one up here.

I was still wearing the skirt, jacket, and brogues I had put on for the walk down to the village this morning—the same skirt, jacket, and brogues I had decided would be fine for the trip back to Beckwith Place in the Crossley. They were decidedly not fine for tea at Sutherland Hall, so after allowing myself two minutes to moan into the counterpane, I got back to my feet and began to systematically divest myself of my current garments. My weekender bag had been unpacked again (by one of the maids, I assumed) and the clothes hung back up in the armoire. I slipped my favorite blue-and-white afternoon frock off a hanger and pulled it over my head, smoothing the fabric over my hips. After slipping my feet into a pair of appropriate T-strap shoes and checking my face in the mirror—I needed more lipstick—I called it good and turned towards the door.

The hallway outside was still as desolate as when I had arrived. I put my ear to the door of the room next to mine—

Constance's, or it had been before we tried to move out before luncheon. There was no murmur of voices from within, so I moved on, alone.

Sutherland Hall is built in a U-shape, with an east wing, a west wing, and a central wing. This last was where the Duke's and Duchess's Chambers were located, across from the main staircase down to the foyer. The Duchess's Chamber has been sitting empty for years. The late Duke Henry's wife died before him, and of course the same was true for the current duke and Aunt Charlotte.

After his father's death in April, Uncle Harold moved out of his room in the corner of the east wing and into the vacated Duke's Chamber. I would have personally waited a bit longer before I occupied the bedroom, and bed, where my father was murdered, but to each their own.

That left the old heir's chambers empty, and Crispin should have moved in, after his father left, but for one reason or another he must have decided to stay in his existing suite. I'm sure he was comfortable there. And I could well imagine why he wouldn't want to occupy the chamber next to his father's. Sutherland Hall is solidly built, but there are secret passages honeycombing the place, and Crispin likes his privacy.

Not that I was headed towards Crispin's chambers, of course. No, I was aiming for the room across from his, namely Christopher's. The others may all be downstairs, but Christopher might be up here.

There were no sounds emanating from the Earl's and Countess's suite, nor were there any voices from behind Francis's door. I wasn't surprised. My cousin wasn't the type to drag his fiancée off for a tumble between luncheon and tea. That was more Geoffrey's speed, I thought. And perhaps Crispin's, or more likely, Laetitia's.

Not that Francis was the type to engage in a slap and tickle in public either, of course. That wasn't what I meant. No, Francis and Constance were undoubtedly downstairs, behaving like the properly courting adults that they were.

Besides, if Francis wanted to engage in impropriety with his fiancée, he could do that in the privacy of Beckwith Place.

I didn't bother to put my ear to Christopher's door. If he were there at all, he'd be alone, and probably not talking to himself. Nor did I bother with a knock. Instead, I wrapped my hand around the handle and turned it. The door opened, into an empty room.

"Christopher?"

I looked around. Christopher's weekender bag had also been emptied and the clothes hung in the wardrobe. And like me, Christopher must have taken the time to change out of his plus-fours and into proper trousers, because the outfit from this morning was thrown haphazardly across the bed. He would either tidy it away when he came up to change for supper, I assumed, or perhaps one of the maids would do it.

"Christopher?"

There was no answer the second time either, not that I had expected one. I pulled the door closed behind me and turned towards the servants' staircase. (There is one at the end of each wing; this one came out beside the conservatory on the ground floor.)

And then I hesitated.

The upstairs was deserted. There was no indication that anyone was up here. No voices, no sounds. No sign of any of the guests or for that matter the maids. The footman who had carried the bags back upstairs was gone now. The rest of the guests were probably gathered downstairs in the sitting room or parlor—or library or garden maze—waiting for tea to be served. I would never get a better chance to search Crispin's quarters.

Did I think it was likely that he had penned the note accusing me of murder?

Not at all. There was a time—April—where I would have been delighted to believe so. I had been convinced back then that he had not only murdered Grimsby the valet, but his own grandfather as well. I had believed that he was capable of practically anything, including shooting at me.

I no longer believed that. I certainly didn't think that he wanted to hurt me in any way. What I wanted, not to be too precious about it—was an excuse to look at the notes in his bedside table. I'd check the blotter in his sitting room too, of course—there was bound to be a writing desk there—but I doubted very much that I would find an inky mirror imprint of the spiky accusation from the note. It would serve as an excuse if anyone saw me, however.

I glanced down the hallway one final time—still empty—before I squared my shoulders and reached for the door handle.

I HAVE NEVER BEEN PRIVILEGED to visit Crispin's chambers. Whenever I came to Sutherland Hall as a child, we played outside—he had an early habit of abandoning me in the hedge maze—or we crawled around the attics, or we behaved properly in one of the rooms downstairs. The game room or library, as likely as not. (When I say 'we,' I mean myself, along with Crispin and Christopher. Francis and Robbie were both too old to spend time with us.) Then Crispin and Christopher went off to Eton (and I to the Godolphin School for Girls, where I met Constance) while Robbie and Francis went to the Front.

All of which is to say that there has never been any reason, nor any opportunity, for me to go beyond this particular door.

I knew that it would lead to a sitting room. Crispin also has a bedchamber as well as a dressing room in his suite, but I took care not to walk straight into either of those. I would have to invade the bedchamber sooner or later, at least if I wanted a look at Laetitia's love notes—or to see whether my own correspondence was hidden anywhere—but for now, I stepped into the sitting room and closed the door quietly behind me.

The suite seemed unoccupied. The sitting room was empty, and the door connecting it to the bedchamber stood open. I could see the corner of an opulent four-poster through the opening, neatly made. There were no sounds emanating from the other rooms.

"Crispin?" I ventured, so softly that only someone on this side of the door to the hallway would have heard me. "St George?"

There was no answer, and so I breathed a little easier as I proceeded to look around.

The sitting room looked just like every other room at Sutherland Hall: old, luxurious, and staid. A comfortable Chesterfield sat in front of the fireplace, with a well-stocked bar cart against the wall. The Viscount St George could stay up here and get blotto in the comfort and privacy of his own chambers, it seemed—and he probably did do, when it was just him and Uncle Harold in residence.

A roll-top desk sat against the opposite wall, and I made my way to it.

It had been left open, and I could see a stack of notepaper inside, along with envelopes, stamps, and the like. It looked very much like the paper Constable Daniels had shown me earlier.

That meant nothing, of course. Everyone in the house had access to the same sort of paper, and there was no reason to think that Crispin, in particular, had been behind the note.

The blotter was stained with ink, and I peered at it for signs that it had been used to blot the anonymous note. There were none—signs, I mean; and again, there was no reason to think it would have been—and I moved on.

You may ask why I was tiptoeing through Crispin's rooms when I didn't suspect him of trying to frame me.

Six months ago, he would have been at the top of my suspect list. Back then, I not only thought him capable of murder, but also believed he would have happily framed me for any number of crimes he himself had committed.

That was before I got to know him better, and also before Christopher had, somewhat reluctantly, convinced me that I was the apple of Crispin's eye, and that he would never, under any circumstances, do anything to harm me.

But that's neither here nor there. Tidwell and Mrs. Mason had mentioned love notes, and I wanted a look at them. While Crispin would never accuse me of a murder I hadn't committed, I wouldn't put the same past Laetitia.

I couldn't explain why she would have bothered to murder Doctor Meadows—surely not simply to frame yours truly for his death—but it couldn't hurt to take a look at what she had written, and how her handwriting compared to that in the note.

I left the desk and made my way towards the door to the bedroom.

It, too, looked very much like every other room in Sutherland Hall. A big, old bed with a goose feather mattress and a fancy counterpane, opposite a gently popping fireplace. There was no one up here—or weren't supposed to be—so there was no need to keep the fire going during the day, but the maids had kept it banked and ready to be manipulated into full flame again as soon as dinner started. It was almost winter, and too cold to do without the extra heat.

The bed was big enough for two, and I contemplated it for a moment with my head tilted. Did Crispin sleep on one side or the other—and if so, which?—or was he the type to sprawl in the middle, taking up most of the space?

The latter, I decided, the spoiled, little, rich boy. He wasn't used to sharing, and would probably spread out over as much of the bed as possible, leaving his fiancée—did she ever share it—to perch on one of the sides.

I had a reason for wondering, I assure you. I was trying to determine which bedside table the letters were most likely to be in. But if Crispin didn't have a side, then it didn't matter. I headed for the closest night table, ran my eye over the water glass, carafe, ashtray, etcetera, that littered its surface, and pulled the drawer below open.

Here was more of the same writing paper, along with the usual items one finds in someone's bedside table. A torch, in the event of a power cut. Matches, in event of the same, or perhaps simply to light a cigarette if a lighter wasn't available. A handkerchief. An envelope, slightly different from the others, a bit smudged.

From me, perhaps?

I reached in and fished it out with two fingers and turned it over. There was no name on the front of it, but it was open. From the looks of it, it had never been gummed down. An empty envelope Crispin had used to store something important in, then, perhaps.

I reached in, and found a single sheet of writing paper, folded, and a piece of slightly crumbled newsprint: carefully cut out but a bit the worse from wear after being jostled in the drawer for some amount of time.

One side showed a headline about the general strike, dating the newspaper to May of this year, some six months ago. There was no reason I could think of why Crispin would be interested in that. It hadn't affected him in the least. The strike had been going on while we'd been at the Dower House for Constance's and Gilbert's weekend party, but Crispin had motored there from Sutherland Hall, unlike Christopher and I, who had had to take the train from Waterloo Station to Salisbury first.

I turned the clipping over and saw, immediately, why it had been excised from the paper: it was Aunt Charlotte's obituary from the week of her funeral. *Dearly beloved*, the obituary said, *wife and mother, died suddenly but peacefully in her bed.*

Which, yes, was the truth. I had seen her that morning, and she had looked like she were asleep. She had also looked as if she were already laid out for the funeral, with her nightgown buttoned to her throat and her hands folded across her chest. Whatever else it did, an overdose of Veronal made the recipient slip off into eternal sleep with no outward signs of either foul play or discomfort in the proceedings.

Not that there was any question about foul play in this case, of course. Aunt Charlotte had left a note, in which she had confessed to killing both Duke Henry and Grimsby. The newspaper clipping didn't mention that, either.

I slipped it carefully back into the envelope and pulled the notepaper out instead.

My darling boy, it began, in loopy, girlish cursive. *If I am still alive when you find this, do not try to revive me.*

I winced. I had read those words before. This was the note that Aunt Charlotte had left on her escritoire before she downed a triple measure of Francis's Veronal and lay down to die. The police must have given it back after the investigation, and Crispin had held on to it.

I was breaking all sorts of rules of law and decency by being here, and it was even worse that I was reading something so personal. I folded the note up without finishing it, cheeks hot, and stuffed it back into the envelope. I dropped the latter back into the drawer and then I nudged a few other things on top of it so it wouldn't be so obvious that someone had been here and pulled it out. That done, I pushed the drawer shut and made my way around the bed to the other night table. I might feel guilty, but not enough to stop me from further snooping while I had the chance.

The other side of the bed looked similar to the one I had already been on. There were no water glass and no carafe, so whether Crispin sprawled in the middle or not, he presumably entered the bed from the side closest to the door. On this side lay a book—Dorothy L. Sayers's recent release, *Clouds of Witness*—with a bookmark. He had made it a couple of chapters in, I noticed. I had finished the book a month or so ago—although in justice to him, he had been somewhat busy this autumn, with a new fiancée and all. He may have had other things on his mind when he went to bed.

In any case, his laziness was my gain. I knew the ending, and knowing that he was reading the book meant that I could spoil it for him the next time the opportunity came up.

Which I would ensure that it did sooner rather than later, of course. I don't let the opportunity go by to ruin Crispin's fun. First I would have to come up with a way to introduce the subject without letting him know that I had been in his room and seen the book, but that probably wouldn't turn out to be a problem. He's laughably easy to wind up for someone who knows him well.

It was in such a pleasant state of anticipation that I pulled open the night table drawer and came face to face with the stack of love letters from Laetitia.

One might have expected a neat collection with, perhaps, the addition of a pink ribbon. If so, one would have been disappointed. (I, needless to say, had no such expectations. As I had blurted out in front of Tidwell and Mrs. Mason, I hadn't expected him to keep Laetitia's letters at all. Upon further deliberation, of course he would have done—she would have had his hide had he not kept them—but I knew better than to believe that he'd done so out of sentimentality. No, it would have been purely out of self-preservation, and as such, no such romantic adornment as pink ribbon was necessary.

I reached in and lifted the wad of stationery. It was a thick bundle, not all of it on the same paper. He must have kept notes from other places and other times, as well. A quick rifling through the stack showed me that the notes were all written in the same hand: sleek and elegant, less girlish than Aunt Charlotte's, but aggressively feminine. I was frankly surprised that every lower-case I wasn't dotted with a little heart.

My nose wrinkled. It might have been the scent of roses that wafted from the paper—had she dunked it in cologne before sending it off?—or perhaps it was simply that words like 'my dearest darling' were littered across the pages. I didn't read the letters—of course not; I would never read someone else's private correspondence, or only in the most dire of circumstances, which this wasn't—but the endearments were so pervasive that a simple skim of my eyes over the paper noted them.

It was all just too much. My mouth puckered, and I dropped the bundle back into the drawer and shoved it shut before rubbing my hands against my skirt. My palms itched, as if I had touched something sticky. Something saccharine and sweet, that threatened to turn my stomach.

But that was all by the by, I told myself. I hadn't wanted to know how explicit Laetitia's love notes to Crispin were. I had wanted a gander at her handwriting, to see whether it matched, in any respect, that of the anonymous letter writer.

And the answer was that I couldn't tell. They had nothing in common, certainly. Laetitia's hand was feminine and elegant, while the anonymous note had been spiky and accusatory. But had Laetitia taken the pen in her left hand and scrawled the few words I had seen... well, who knew whether she might not have approximated the same effect as the note?

This had been a waste of time and effort. I left Crispin's

bedroom as I found it, and made my way across the floor to the door to the hallway.

I was approximately six feet away from safety when it happened. I had looked right and left before stepping through the door into the hallway. (The last thing I wanted was to be spotted sneaking out of Crispin's chambers.) The fact that the east wing had been empty was what had given me the impetus to leave the suite. I crossed the threshold and pulled the door shut behind me. I turned towards the servants' staircase and was just about to make my way in that direction when a scream at the other end of the hall pierced my eardrums.

I winced and turned, in time to see Laetitia come down the hall towards me like a fury, skirts flapping around her calves and bob bouncing, face twisted in anger. Behind her, her mother smirked.

"You!" Laetitia shrieked, the pitch of her voice close to that range where only bats would be able to hear it, and getting louder as she approached. "What are you doing in my fiancé's room?"

I thought about taking the cowardly way out, by throwing myself through the door into the servants' staircase and escaping that way. I had enough time to do it, or would have done, had I moved immediately. I didn't, because when it comes right down to it, I don't avoid confrontation, even when someone comes at me with claws extended and murder in her eyes.

I would honestly not have been surprised had she wrapped both hands around my throat and squeezed. I wouldn't have been surprised had she attacked me in other ways, either, perhaps by backing me into the wall and knocking my head against it a few times. It looked very much as if something like that was coming. But some semblance of sanity must have reared its head before she reached me, or perhaps it was the fact that I stood my ground and that the sneer on my face was worthy of Crispin at his most abhorrent.

"What do you think I'm doing in your fiancé's room?"

A flicker of uncertainty crossed her face, and I added, "I was looking for a sample of his handwriting to see whether he was the one who shopped me to the constabulary, of course."

Laetitia blinked.

"Someone told the local constabulary that I killed Doctor Meadows," I reminded her. "I thought it might have been Crispin."

She recovered. "He would never!"

I snorted. "Of course he would have done. He despises me."

Or so I would have believed, a few months ago. Now, of course, I knew better. But Laetitia didn't know that Christopher had come clean about Crispin's feelings for me, to me, and what Laetitia didn't know wouldn't hurt her.

"The note doesn't match his handwriting in any case," I told her. "Nor does it match yours, in case you wondered."

There was a beat of silence. "Mine?"

"I happened to find your stack of love letters in the bedside table." I smirked. "I hope you don't mind that I took a look. It was just to make sure that you hadn't tried to frame me for murder. Honestly."

I had no idea whether she believed me or not. Probably not, as I made no effort to sound sincere about it.

But my statement seemed to have rendered her speechless, at any rate. She stared at me, goldfish-like, with her mouth open and her cheeks flushed. It's difficult to make a woman as lovely as Laetitia Marsden appear anything but beautiful, but in this case she did look rather simple.

I gave her a patronizing little nod. "If you'll excuse me."

She didn't say anything, or lift a hand to stop me, so I took the couple of steps towards the servants' staircase and pulled the door open. "I shall see you both downstairs," I told them, before I ducked inside and headed down.

TOM MADE it to Little Sutherland in time for tea. We were just gathering in the sitting room for the genial beverage when there was the sound of a motorcar on the gravel in the court-yard, and I twitched on my chair like the proverbial scalded cat. I'll readily admit that by that point I was jumpy, as well as moderately concerned for my future wellbeing. I thought I had made it clear to Constable Daniels that I had had nothing to do with the murder, but who was to say that some sort of new evidence hadn't come up, something that implicated me more definitively than a hastily scrawled anonymous note? Anyone who wanted to frame me, and who had access to Sutherland Hall and my bedchamber, might have taken the opportunity to procure some item of mine with which to salt the crime scene.

Thus, when I heard the sound of a motor arriving outside, my first thought was that the local authorities were back, this time to drag me off to a jail cell in Little Sutherland.

And it must have shown, because Christopher's eyes flew to mine across the table. "All right, Pippa?"

I nodded vacantly while I peeled my ears for further sounds from the front of the house. After a moment, I heard Tidwell's measured footsteps cross the marble of the foyer, and then the sound of the front door opening. A slight pause followed, and then—

"Good afternoon, Detective Sergeant," Tidwell said politely.

I whimpered. Not even a constable, it seemed, but a detective sergeant. They were coming to arrest me for certain.

"Shhh!" Christopher hissed. His ears were pricked. Wave

the title Detective Sergeant in front of him, and only one thing —or one person—comes to mind.

"Good afternoon, Tidwell," Tom Gardiner's voice said, and I slumped like a marionette with the strings cut. Christopher, on the other hand, stiffened as if someone had given him a jolt, and fastened his eyes on the entrance to the room. He was quivering like a Pointer.

Tom's steps came closer, and Christopher forgot to breathe. I kicked him in the shin under the table. "For goodness's sake, Christopher, show some decorum."

"Says you," my cousin told me rudely, but he did relax against the chair back, just in time for Tom to appear in the doorway and for Christopher to look at least a bit less like it was Christmas morning and like all his desires had been fulfilled at once.

Francis raised a hand. "Tommy! Over here!"

Everyone in the family—with the likely exception of Uncle Harold—knows and loves Tom. He and Francis attended Eton together for a few years. He was Cousin Robert's contemporary and best friend, until Robbie died at the front, and in the time since Christopher and I came up to London, Tom has endeavored to keep Kit out of trouble.

He's a good bloke. Christopher is head over heels in love with him, of course. Tom has some fondness for Christopher, too, although I've never been entirely certain whether it's romantic in nature, or simply the result of Christopher being Robbie's little brother. But Tom comes running whenever Christopher calls, or whenever he believes that Christopher needs help, and perhaps that says enough.

While Tom made his way into the room, Francis glanced at the clock ticking away on the mantel. "He must have broken the Meadowlands record on the way here."

He must have done, indeed. Or at least it hadn't taken him

long at all to get from Whitehall to Wiltshire. He must have jumped into the first available motorcar the very moment his phone call with Christopher had concluded.

Now he gave Francis a nod in response to the latter's greeting, but he didn't join us. Instead, he approached Uncle Harold, who was holding court with the Earl and Countess of Marsden at a separate table.

"Your Grace." He bowed politely, before turning to Maury and Effie. "My Lord. My Lady."

"Detective Sergeant Gardiner." Lady Euphemia inclined her head a bare inch. She remembered Tom, of course. They had both been at Beckwith Place for Francis's and Constance's engagement celebration in July, and Tom had also shown up at Laetitia's engagement do at Marsden Manor in September. "To what do we owe the honor?"

The words were polite enough, although the tone relegated Tom's presence from honored guest to unexpected gate crasher. Specifically, she addressed him the way she would one of the servants, or perhaps a constable from the village. Someone distinctly below her in importance.

He didn't rise to the bait. I would have been tempted to do, so more power to him.

"Kit rang me up and informed me that someone had tried to frame Pippa for murder," Tom said instead, calmly. "I thought I ought to take a look."

Something about the response made Lady Euphemia's spine lose its iron rigidity. I can't imagine what she was thinking—perhaps that Tom was sweet on me, and that was why he had come all this way to make sure I was all right. And if so, I was no threat to her daughter's designs on Crispin, which must have been relieving. Although what she thought I could do about Crispin's and Laetitia's nuptials at this point I don't know. They were properly engaged, with a wedding date only a month hence, and the banns in the process of being read.

But at any rate, her reaction was too obvious to miss. Tom waited a moment for her to respond, and when she didn't, he added, "I hope you don't mind."

The sentiment was undoubtedly addressed to Uncle Harold, as the head of the household, but it was Crispin who answered. "Don't be daft, Gardiner. Nobody wants Philippa to be arrested for a crime she didn't commit."

The pregnant pause that greeted this pronouncement indicated clearly that although he might not feel that way, there were several people present who would be more than happy for me to be arrested for any reason whatsoever. The silence virtually reverberated with the (unspoken) sentiment. Crispin cleared his throat. "I'll just go and have a word with Tidwell about a room for you. Excuse me."

He inclined his head politely to his father and his future mother-in-law. To Laetitia he added, "I'll be right back."

She pouted, of course, prettily, but didn't say anything that might stop him. Crispin put his hand on Tom's shoulder. "Go and join Kit and Francis, there's a good chap."

He nudged Tom in our direction. The latter gave Uncle Harold another inclination of his head and another, "Your Grace," before he followed the advice. By then, Crispin was halfway to the door. His expression was that of a man happy to make his escape.

I sniggered as he passed by our table, and then I reached for the teapot and an empty cup and saucer. "Cup of tea, Tom?"

"Don't mind if I do, Philippa." He sank down on the empty chair between Christopher and Francis. "Good afternoon, Astley. Miss Peckham. Kit."

Their eyes snagged and held for a moment. Until Francis

cleared his throat and broke the spell. "Good to see you, Tommy."

"You, as well," Tom told him. He seemed less perturbed by the interruption than Christopher, whose cheeks were flushed all the way up to the tips of his ears. "Thank you."

He nodded politely at the cup of tea I placed in front of him.

"Don't mention it." I sat back. "Christopher said he rang you up, and you decided to drive to Wiltshire to make certain he—or we—were all right?"

"I wasn't worried about Kit," Tom said and lifted the cup and saucer for a sip. "Nobody accused *him* of murder."

"We were in the infirmary together," I told him, "so they may as well have done. If Doctor Meadows was murdered while we were there, it could have been either of us."

He placed the cup and saucer back on the table and eyed me. "And was he murdered while you were there?"

"Of course not," Christopher said. "Aside from the fact that you should know us both better than that, we were together the entire time. Neither of us could have killed him without the other one seeing, and I assure you that we didn't do it together. As far as we knew, he was still alive and well when we sat down to luncheon."

"The first we heard that he wasn't," I added, "was when Constable Daniels arrived."

"And that's when you found out about the note accusing you."

It wasn't a question, but I nodded. "When we reached the constabulary, yes. He didn't mention it on the drive. But he showed it to me once we were in the village."

"What did it look like?" Tom wanted to know.

"Like a note. Like any note. Plain writing paper. Plain

black ink. Spiky, uneven letters, as if someone had written them with his non-dominant hand."

"No point in checking the grates for mutilated newsprint, then."

"The classic cut-and-glued letters, do you mean?" I shook my head. "No, none. The note was hand-written, but not in a fist anyone would be likely to recognize."

"We'd all produce something very like it," Christopher added, "if we tried.'"

"Have you tried?"

Christopher and I glanced at one another, and then at Francis and Constance. Then we all shook our heads.

"I suppose it couldn't hurt to make a parlor game of it," Christopher said, looking around. "Tidwell?"

The butler materialized next to the table. "Master Christopher?"

"Note paper," Christopher said. "Enough for everyone. And pen and ink."

Tidwell nodded. "Of course, Master Christopher."

He vanished as quickly and silently as he had appeared. A minute later he was back, to place a stack of notepaper and a pen and inkwell on the table. "Anything else, Master Christopher?"

"No," Christopher said, "thank you, Tidwell."

Tidwell faded away. Christopher took a breath and uncapped the inkwell.

CHAPTER THIRTEEN

"YOU CAN'T BE SERIOUS," I said, as he dipped the pen in.

He flicked a glance my way. "Whyever not? Tell me what to write, Pippa."

"Doctor Meadows is dead," I quoted, "Philippa Darling did it."

Christopher ran the nib of the pen across the paper. I watched the chicken scratch he produced with his left hand for a moment before I added, "That looks close enough to what I remember to pass for it. But it certainly wasn't you who wrote the note, Christopher. We were together when it was delivered. There's no need for you to prove that you didn't."

"In the interest of fairness," Christopher said, with the tip of his tongue sticking out of his mouth as he did his best to get his non-dominant hand to cooperate, "we should all have to prove ourselves."

After a moment, when he had finished the scrawl and laid the pen down, he added, "If we want everyone else to submit a sample, it won't do for me to refuse, will it?"

Of course it did, when it couldn't have been him. But I didn't quibble, just watched as Tom picked up the pen and marked the sheet of paper with Christopher's name and the date, before handing the pen and a blank sheet across the table to Francis. "Go ahead, Astley."

Francis took the pen with a grimace and went to work. "For the record," he said, eyes on his effort, "it wasn't me, either. I haven't left the Hall today. Or hadn't, until Kit and I hared off into the village after Pippa and the constable. Connie can confirm."

Constance nodded. "We were together from breakfast until luncheon. Neither of us left the grounds."

"Do you happen to know if anyone else did?" Tom wanted to know, and Constance bit her lip as she thought about it.

"Christopher and Pippa, of course. Laetitia dragged Lord St George into the hedge maze after breakfast..."

I snorted. Tom arched a brow at me, and I said, "It's the middle of November. Surely they could find a better place to canoodle."

"I'll have you know, Darling—" a familiar voice drawled behind me, and I raised a hand.

"Spare me, St George." Whether he was about to tell me that any place is a good place for canoodling, or it was the fact that Laetitia could make any place a good place for canoodling, I didn't want to hear it.

Part of me expected him to make his point anyway, but he didn't. "As you wish." Instead, he leaned over my shoulder and let his eyes rove over the table. "What's all this, then?"

"An experiment," Tom said, gathering up Francis's scribbled note while watching as Constance took the pen in her left hand and began writing. Her letters were more precise and less spiky than Francis's.

And as such, also less like the note I had been shown at the constabulary.

Not that I had believed, for even a moment, that Constance had written it.

"I'll go next," Crispin said, as Constance started on her second sentence. "You're planning to test everyone, I assume?"

"Unless you have a better idea."

But Crispin didn't. "Good luck explaining this to my father," he merely said instead.

He left his post behind me—I breathed out, surreptitiously—and made his way to the empty chair on the other side of Constance. There, he pulled a sheet of writing paper towards himself and waited for Constance to pass him the pen before he started his own exercise.

"Is that your dominant hand?" Tom asked after a moment, as the letters took shape across the paper, beautifully controlled and in straight lines, not spiky at all.

Crispin flicked a look at him. "I'm naturally left-handed. I had it beaten into me to use my right hand—"

I winced, and he added, "Not literally, Darling. Don't worry."

"I wouldn't put it past your father," I said. "Christopher said he tied your left hand behind your back so you wouldn't use it."

"Among other things." He switched the pen to his other hand and kept going. "I won't say it was fun. But I learned to write like a proper gentleman, and there was no permanent damage done."

No, indeed. The letters he produced with his left hand weren't any different from the ones he produced with his right. Neither line looked anything like the chicken scratches Francis and Christopher had come up with.

"Definitely not you," I commented, and he put the pen down with a look at me.

"No. But then you knew that, didn't you?"

Of course I had done. Six months ago I might have suspected him of trying to get me in trouble with the police for the fun of it. Now I knew that he'd never make that choice.

"Yes," I said. "I did do."

Tom grabbed the pen and used it to write Crispin's name on the sheet of paper, and then handed the pen to me, along with a blank sheet. "Might as well do this properly."

I arched my brows, although I accepted the pen. "You think I would accuse myself of a murder I didn't commit?" Not to mention a murder I hadn't had the opportunity to commit, since I had been with Christopher and had an alibi.

"No," Tom said. "But if we're going to do this, we'll do it right. This way, no one can say I didn't turn over every stone."

Indeed not. I took the pen and began to scratch letters across the paper. The result looked quite a lot like what Constable Daniels had shown me, albeit no more so than what Francis and Christopher had produced.

"I can't wait to see how my father responds to this," Crispin said, watching my letters take shape with his chin on his hand.

"Do you think he'll refuse?"

His eyes flicked up to my face for a second before dropping down to my hand again. "I don't see how he could. Not without looking exceedingly suspicious."

"You don't think he's guilty, do you?"

I pushed the pen across the table to Tom, who used it to write my name on the sheet of paper bearing my artistic contribution.

"My father?" Crispin said. "It's you, so on the one hand, I wouldn't put it past him."

No, I wouldn't either.

"On the other, why would he want Doctor Meadows dead? And why now? We haven't seen Doctor since my mother died."

"He was here when Lady Peckham passed," I pointed out. "Sorry, Constance."

Constance waved her mother's death away as if it didn't matter. "Never mind, Pippa."

"*We* weren't here when that happened," Francis pointed out, and Crispin nodded.

"The last time I saw Doctor, was the morning Mum died."

"Perhaps so," I agreed, "but he must have attended Lady Peckham. Even if we were elsewhere when it happened."

"He did do," Tom agreed. After a moment he added, with a comprehensive glance around the table at us all, "What? *You* may have been at the Dower House, but *I* was here. At least until I motored down to Dorset after you. Doctor Meadows was here. I spoke to him."

"Did anything happen on that occasion that might have caused—" I lowered my voice, "His Grace to want to get rid of the doctor?"

Crispin shifted on his chair, and Tom eyed me as if he suspected me of having lost the plot. "If I thought so," he asked me, "don't you think I would have said something about it?"

I didn't answer, since the answer was self-evident, and he added, "No, Pippa, nothing at all happened. Everyone was upset, but other than that, they behaved perfectly well."

"Why would you suspect my father, anyway, Darling?" Crispin wanted to know. He kept his voice low enough that the Duke wouldn't hear. I chanced a glance in the direction of Uncle Harold, and saw that he was talking to Lady Euphemia.

"I don't," I said, "necessarily. You were the one who brought him up, if you'll recall."

He looked chagrined at the reminder, and I added, "Although surely he makes for a better suspect than almost everyone else here. He and Doctor Meadows have lived less than a kilometer from one another for decades. The rest of us barely knew the man."

"Kit and Francis knew him," Crispin protested. "You did. Aunt Roz and Uncle Herbert certainly did—"

"You did, too."

He rolled his eyes. "If I had wanted Doctor Meadows dead, I wouldn't have done it today, nor would I have tried to pin it on you."

No, I knew that.

"If my father wanted Doctor dead," Crispin continued, "he wouldn't have done it when Laetitia and her family were visiting, either. As you said, they've known each other for decades. Practically any other day would have been better than today. It's much easier to come and go unobserved when you don't have a house full of guests."

Yes, of course it was. "Nonetheless," I said, "if your father killed Constance's mother, and Doctor Meadows knew about it—"

They both stared at me, open-mouthed.

"What?" I wanted to know. "Lady Peckham came here with the clear purpose of snagging the title of Duchess, either for herself or her ward. And if he didn't want to get remarried, because it was only a week since Aunt Charlotte died, after all—"

I stopped talking when Constance pushed her chair back.

"Connie?" Francis asked.

Constance looked at him, and then at me, and then she turned on her heel and headed for the door, but not before I—before all of us—had seen the tears gathering in her eyes.

"We're going to talk about this, Pipsqueak," Francis told

me, before he bolted after her. Guilt curled through my stomach, but I stayed in my seat and watched as they disappeared through the door into the hallway, one after the other. At the speed Francis was going, he was likely to catch up just a meter or so down the hall, and even at this moment—perhaps especially at this moment—I knew that it would be better to let him deal with the situation. I would have to grovel later—and I would do—but not until Constance had calmed down.

"Bloody hell, Darling," Crispin said. "Not your finest moment, was it?"

"Clearly not." I shook my head. "I get going, and then I don't think about what I'm saying. The same thing happens when I get angry."

"You don't say?"

He didn't wait for me to respond, just added, "Whether or not Lady Peckham had her eye on my father when she turned up for the funeral—and I sincerely doubt that she did, Darling, as my mother had only been gone a week and a half at that point—but even so, you do know that my father wouldn't have killed her, don't you? Why would he do? All he had to do was say no."

"Of course I know that."

I shot a guilty look at Uncle Harold, whose attention must have been caught by the precipitate departure of Constance and Francis. He was watching the door with a wrinkle between his brows.

"Perhaps not the nicest reminder for Constance either, Pippa," Christopher murmured, "that her brother killed her mother."

I winced. "Perhaps not. I'll apologize when I see her next. She knows I'm prone to speaking before I think, so hopefully she'll forgive me."

"At any rate," Crispin said, "my father did not kill Lady Peckham—correct, Gardiner?"

Tom nodded.

"—and thus His Grace would have had no reason to kill Doctor Meadows, either. Besides, if he had done—killed Lady P, I mean—and the doctor knew about it, why wait six months to get rid of him?"

"He could pin it on me if he waited until now?" I suggested. "Two birds with one stone and all that."

"Safer to arrange it as an accident when no one else was around," Crispin opined. "Surely you're not actually accusing your host of murder, Darling?"

"Of course not. As I said, I get going, and..."

He nodded. "Well, my job here is done."

He pushed his chair back. "Let me walk you to my father's table, Gardiner, so I can get an up-close look at his face, and that of my future mother-in-law, when you tell them that they're suspects in a murder."

Tom opened his mouth, most likely to say that they were not, neither of them, suspects in Doctor Meadows's murder, but Crispin waved him down. "Don't ruin it, Detective Sergeant. Just let me enjoy the moment."

"Of course, Lord St George." Tom got to his feet too. Crispin waited gallantly while Tom gathered up the writing paper and pen, and then they headed across the floor towards the head table. "I'll come and find you later, Kit," Tom told him over his shoulder, which sounded quite a lot like a dismissal to me.

Christopher nodded, and then he and I watched them walk away, at least until I noticed Laetitia glaring at me like she would quite like to make me the next murder victim, and at that point I came back to myself and turned to Christopher.

"Would you like to see the expression on His Grace's face, too, or shall we get out of here?"

"I wouldn't turn it down," Christopher said, and nudged his chair backwards, "but I think we ought rather to find Francis and Constance so you can apologize. She's your best friend—"

"You're my best friend."

Although admittedly Constance and I had become closer in the past few months than we'd ever been in our Godolphin days. I suppose she was my best friend of the female persuasion, unless that was Aunt Roz. Then again, Roz was my aunt, and perhaps that doesn't count. And Christopher would certainly never provide me with a fiancée or wife who would take that place, so perhaps he was right, and Constance truly was my best girlfriend.

Either way, I owed her an apology. "Lay on, McDuff."

He glanced down at me. "Shouldn't you be telling her that?"

"I doubt she'll want to duel me, Christopher."

"I wouldn't be too sure," Christopher said as he held the door open for me with a polite bow, and let me precede him into the hallway. "She's nowhere near as meek and mealy-mouthed as you led me to believe she was back in May."

No, she wasn't. "I think she's gained some confidence as she has grown up," I confessed. "She was very quiet as a girl."

"She's still quiet. Just not the pushover you said she was." He looked around the foyer and raised his voice. "Tidwell?"

"Master Christopher?"

"Did you happen to notice which way Francis and Constance went? Upstairs? Outside? Somewhere else?"

"I did not," Tidwell said. And added, "No one has come through the foyer in the last few minutes."

"Thank you, Tidwell." Christopher turned me around and

nudged me back down the hallway. "The conservatory, do you suppose? Or the library? They wouldn't invade Uncle Harold's study or the below-stairs, I assume, and if they didn't go through the foyer..."

"They may have taken the servants' stairs up to the first floor," I suggested, as I double-timed it down the hallway through the east wing, "and now they're holed up in Francis's room, or in Constance's, making whoopie."

"Constance did not look to be in the mood for whoopie. We'll check the library and conservatory first, and if they're not there, we'll go upstairs."

He bypassed the door we had come out of, from behind which a low murmur of voices could be heard—at least no one was volubly objecting to Tom's instructions—and pushed open the door to the library. "Francis? Constance? Are you here?"

There was no answer, nor was there one from the game room next door when we tried there next.

"And small wonder," I said, avoiding the glassy stare of a zebra whose head and neck was decorating the wall. "It's not precisely comforting, is it?"

Christopher shook his head. "This room always gave me the pip when I was little."

"It gives me the pip now. And I don't think Francis is very fond of it anymore, either. After everything, I rather think he'd like to avoid anything dead, even if it's just a zebra."

"You may be right." He shut the door behind us and continued towards the end of the hall. "The conservatory, then? And if not there, the upstairs."

I nodded. "The conservatory might be a bit chilly. It's sunny, but it is, after all, November."

"I imagine they have ways of keeping warm," Christopher said, and pushed the conservatory door open.

I had been wrong, I realized. The conservatory wasn't cold

at all. Rather the opposite, in fact. A wave of humid, warm air hit us in the face as soon as the door opened. If I stayed in it, it would probably make my makeup run.

Constance wears less of that than I do, so that didn't mean anything. She and Francis might still be inside. I followed Christopher across the threshold into the jungle.

It was six months since I had been in the Sutherland Hall conservatory. I had spent a memorable few hours there the night Grimsby the valet was murdered, while I waited for Christopher to come back inside from their assignation—or blackmail handoff—in the rose garden. It had been a spooky experience, even before we knew that the valet was dead. It had rained that night, thunder had rumbled and lightning flashed outside, and inside the conservatory, leaves and branches had rustled as if brushed by invisible—or invisible-to-me—bodies. And then, at the end of it, after Christopher came back inside, we realized we were shut in, that Tidwell had locked the door between the conservatory and the rest of the ground floor for the night.

"Francis?" Christopher raised his voice. "Constance? Are you in here?"

There was no answer, and I backed out into the hallway with a heartfelt, "Thank God. I would have melted had we stayed in there any longer."

Christopher nodded and shut the door. "Upstairs, then, I suppose."

He reached for the unobtrusive door to the servants' stairs. I followed him into the narrow space and up.

This was the same staircase I had come down earlier, after digging through Crispin's belongings. It comes out at the end of the east wing, just down from Crispin's suite and the door to Christopher's room. Francis's room, the same one he always stays in when he's visiting Sutherland Hall, is beside it. The door was shut, but we could hear the murmur of voices from within. They stopped when Christopher applied his knuckles to the wood.

"Are you decent?" he directed through the door. "It's us. Kit and Pippa."

There was another murmur—perhaps Francis was inquiring whether Constance wanted to be bothered with me so soon—and then my cousin's voice. "It's open."

Christopher twisted the knob, and in we went.

"I'm sorry," I said, just as soon as I had cleared the threshold. "I didn't mean to upset anyone. I just get going, and I get caught up in the mystery of it all..."

Francis and Constance were sitting side by side on the edge of the bed. Fully dressed, thankfully, and not doing anything beyond holding hands. Constance's eyes were a bit puffy, and her hair perhaps a bit more ruffled than it ought to be, but otherwise, it didn't seem as if my unpleasant reminder had done anything too awful.

"You should write a novel," Francis said disagreeably. "Maybe you'd get some of this infernal plotting out."

Christopher snorted as he shut the door behind us. "Don't think she isn't doing just that. The flat is all over pieces of paper where she's started and then discarded *Secrets at Sutherland Hall.*"

Francis sniggered. "What's to write about that? The old man tasked his valet with digging up dirt on all his family members, and then they both ended up dead."

"It was interesting," I said. "Not so much what happened, but the possibilities of what might have done. So many possible motives. So many ways it might have turned out."

After a moment's contemplation, I added, "If I were to write it, I would have taken some poetic license in how I worked the plot. The reality didn't end up being very interesting in the end. There was no denouement, and no big show-down in which Aunt Charlotte was arrested. She just killed herself and took all the fun out of it…"

"This is what I'm talking about," Francis said, after exchanging a glance with Christopher. "You could stand to be a little more empathetic, Pipsqueak."

"I wouldn't say it where Crispin could hear," I protested. "Besides, you have to admit it would be much more interesting if there was more to it. Just like it would be more interesting if—"

I bit my tongue before I could blurt out that it would have been much more interesting if Uncle Harold had wanted to get rid of Constance's mother, and now he had killed Doctor Meadows because the doctor knew what he had done. Francis must have realized what I had only barely managed to bite back, because he scowled.

"You would so, Pippa. You've said much worse things than that to Crispin in the past."

"Not recently," I said.

He tilted his head. "Since when did you start becoming concerned with his feelings?"

"Since Christopher told me—" I frowned and switched tactics. "Actually, that's not quite true. The debacle in April was when I first started to notice how his father treats him, and I've been feeling a bit sorry for him ever since. Although I'll admit that it wasn't until last month, when Christopher told me—"

"Christ Almighty." Francis rolled his eyes. "Did it really take Kit to lay it out for you before you realized that our prat of a cousin has been making cow-eyes at you for years?"

It didn't seem like a question that required a response, so I didn't dignify it with one. Besides, it made Constance giggle, and I appreciated that more than I wanted the chance to snipe back at Francis. "Really, Pippa," she said, her voice uneven, "if I could see it that first weekend at the Dower House..."

"He was mean to me!" I protested, even as my insides collapsed with relief that she didn't seem to be angry with me anymore. "And if he wasn't mean, then he was mocking me, always embarrassing me with innuendo and insinuation..."

Constance's lips twitched. "And it didn't cross your mind that a man who called you Darling in every other sentence might be harboring romantic feelings?"

I made a face. It hadn't crossed my mind, no. I had heard the mockery—still heard the mockery sometimes—but nothing else. I suppose I could hear the truth behind the mockery now, too, but only since Christopher had come clean about Crispin's feelings. And even a month later, there were still times when I doubted that Christopher had told me the truth. It was honestly just so difficult to wrap my head around the possibility that the Viscount St George had been nurturing tender feelings for me for the best part of five and a half years. It was difficult to credit him with tender feelings at all, for anyone. It was all the more difficult to credit him with feelings of any sort, other than disdain, for *me*.

"At any rate," I said, "it's more comfortable to turn everything into a mystery novel in my head than deal with the fact that real people died because of other, real people's motives. I don't want to think about the fact that someone is trying to frame me for murder. It's easier to speculate about what might have happened, in a different world, if Laetitia killed Johanna because she wanted Crispin for herself, or if Uncle Harold killed your mother because—"

I stopped when I heard a noise outside in the hallway. Something small and soft, like the scuff of a shoe on the carpet runner. For a moment, time hung suspended as we all stood there, barely breathing, waiting to hear what would happen next. From the expectant silence from outside, I got the feeling that whoever was out there did the same thing.

Christopher looked at me. "Should we see if anyone's there?" he inquired, not quite *sotto voce.*

I opened my mouth, but before I could speak, there was the shuffle of rapid footsteps outside, and then the sound of a door opening.

"Bloody hell," I muttered, and lunged for the door.

CHAPTER FOURTEEN

NO ONE TRIED to stop me. And when I turned the knob and wrenched the door open, the hallway outside was empty. There was no way to know who among the residents, guests, or staff had been there, nor where he or she had gone. I considered knocking on Crispin's door to see whether he'd respond, although if he didn't, it wouldn't prove anything one way or another. He could be inside his rooms and simply choose not to open the door for me. So could anyone else, for that matter. And while Crispin's—and Christopher's—rooms were the closest, there was also the servants' staircase at the end of the hall, which was perhaps the likeliest place for the eavesdropper to have gone.

"You were saying?" Francis inquired dryly from behind me, and I shut the door again and turned to him with a grimace.

"Not something that I wanted anyone else to overhear. Just that it's easier to make something fantastical out of the mad things that have happened in the past six months, than dwelling upon the reality that Aunt Charlotte killed two people before killing herself, and Gilbert killed two people before going on the lam, and Uncle Herbert had an illegitimate son none of us knew about—"

Christopher made a face.

"—and he killed the mother of his child and then himself." Wilkins, I meant, of course; not Uncle Herbert. But there was no point in saying that, since the others all knew it, too. "And my long-lost cousin from Germany tried to murder me several times—and you too, Christopher!—before kidnapping me and putting me on a freighter in the middle of the North Sea. All of that's very real, and none of it is pleasant. It's much more enjoyable to speculate about the ways things didn't happen."

"I suppose that's true," Francis admitted. "I'd be much happier if Aunt Charlotte hadn't turned out to be a murderess and I hadn't had an older brother no one ever told me about."

That last was a moot point now, of course, and it was on the tip of my tongue to say so, but that was probably one of those unempathetic statements I should try to avoid making.

"And I'd be much happier if my mother wasn't dead," Constance piped up, "and I suppose I would rather have it have been His Grace who killed her, rather than my brother."

My lips twitched, and so did Christopher's. "I appreciate that," I said, "and I'm sorry to have upset you, Constance. It was not my intent to make light of what happened to your mother. I just get carried away thinking about things, you know."

She smiled. "I'm well aware of that, Pippa. We spent five years together at Godolphin. I'm well aware of how you get carried away with things. There's nothing to apologize for."

There was quite a bit to apologize for, and it was nice of her to forgive my transgression so easily. I said so.

"You're quite welcome," Constance said. "Besides, I'm not surprised that you're a bit out of sorts. It must be difficult to be accused of murder. Especially when there's nothing to prove that you didn't do it."

I turned towards Christopher—he could prove that I didn't do it—and Constance added, "Except Christopher, of course. But everyone knows that he'd lie for you."

Well, yes. He would. But—

"Surely you don't think that I killed anyone, Constance?"

"Of course not," Constance said. "But it still can't be comfortable to have everyone's suspicions cling to you like this. It's no wonder if you're tetchy."

"I'm not—" I bit back the rest of the denial, since I was only proving her point. "Well played, Constance."

She smirked at me, and I added, "And yes, I suppose I'm a bit upset. Not so much because I'm afraid that I'll be arrested. I had no motive, and moreover, Christopher and I really were together when Doctor Meadows was killed. He was alive and well when we left the village."

"Or at least when we left the infirmary," Christopher supplied. "Who knows what happened once we walked out?"

"I know what happened," I said. "Someone else walked in and killed him."

Nobody said anything, and I added, "But as I was saying, yes, it is a bit upsetting that someone has gone out of their way to accuse me of murder. Someone obviously dislikes me quite a bit to be willing to do that."

"Unless you were just handy," Christopher said.

"If so, you were just as handy."

He nodded. "But I'm the Duke of Sutherland's nephew. You're the poor relation. It's a lot less risky to accuse you."

I gave him a look. "Thanks ever so, Christopher."

"In that case," Constance said, "all we have to do is figure out who dislikes you enough to want to frame you for murder."

Her fiancé snorted. "In this household? It could be practically anyone."

I rolled my eyes. "And thanks ever so to you too, Francis."

He sniggered. "Present company excepted, of course. But there's the fair Laetitia, her parents—or at least her mother; I suppose her father isn't so bad—"

"Uncle Maury is quite nice, really," Constance agreed. "Certainly too nice to frame anyone for murder."

"I wouldn't put it past Geoffrey, either," Christopher added. "You did have a hand in his spending two months in jail, Pippa."

I nodded. I had already considered this, and yes, small wonder if Geoffrey wanted a bit of his own back. "Does either of you have any idea what Geoffrey was doing between breakfast and lunch? Would he have been able to get to the village and back?"

"We saw Francis's parents off," Constance said, "and then we went upstairs to pack our own belongings so we could leave once the two of you came back. I didn't see anyone else during that time."

"Francis?"

He shook his head. "Uncle Harold went to his study after breakfast. I have no idea how much time he spent there. It might have been the entire morning. Laetitia and Crispin started out in the hedge maze, although I can't imagine that that would have been comfortable for too long. I didn't see the earl and countess until luncheon, nor Lord Geoffrey."

"Perhaps we should inquire of the maids," I suggested, and Christopher made a sound that was half snort, half giggle.

"Surely he must have learned something from what happened in September, don't you imagine?"

"I wouldn't be too sure," I said. "He got away with it. There's no reason why he wouldn't do it again." Especially as I suspected that Geoffrey's womanizing ways were more of a compulsion than something he actively chose to do, not something he could simply stop. "Although I expect he might be a bit more careful in future about who he gets in the family way. If it's a maid, that's one thing. He can pay them off. If it's a highly born young lady who expects marriage, that's something else entirely."

"At any rate," Christopher said, "it sounds like no one knows where Geoffrey was between breakfast and luncheon. He might have been in the village framing Pippa for murder."

"Would he kill Doctor Meadows simply so that I'd be arrested for it, though? That seems excessive." I glanced at Constance, who might reasonably be expected to know Geoffrey better than the rest of us.

"It would be excessive," she agreed, "although I'm not certain Geoffrey always thinks things through, you know?"

"Or he might have had his own reasons for wanting Doctor Meadows dead," Francis supplied. "Say, for instance, that Geoffrey misbehaved with one of the local girls. He has visited Little Sutherland before. He might have gone home with someone after a pint at the pub."

He might very well have done. It sounded quite like something he would do.

"And she might have found herself in the family way," Francis continued. "And he might have petitioned Doctor Meadows to do something about it. He wouldn't have wanted to risk it again himself, I imagine."

"And when Doctor Meadows refused, he killed him?"

Francis shrugged, and I admitted, grudgingly, "I suppose it isn't any worse than any other scenario we've come up with."

"Rather better than some," Francis said, "if I do say so myself."

"It would help if we knew what he was doing between breakfast and luncheon. If he has an alibi, it can't be him."

"It would help if we knew what everyone was doing," Christopher said. He turned towards the door. "I think I'll go inquire."

"Of whom?"

He glanced at me over his shoulder. "Anyone who'll talk to me. Will you come?"

"I suppose I might as well." I trotted after him towards the door. Francis and Constance didn't move from the bed, and I added, "Not coming along?"

"We'll stay here for a bit," Constance said demurely.

I nodded. "Don't do anything I wouldn't do."

"Doesn't leave us with much," Francis informed me. "Best of luck finding someone to take your place before you're arrested, Pipsqueak."

"Tom's here," I said. "I'm not worried."

And then I was outside in the hallway, and could close the door behind me. Christopher stood on the other side of the corridor, in front of Crispin's sitting room door, and once I had shut Constance's door behind me, he applied his knuckles to it.

There was no answer from within, and he did it again. "Crispin? It's me, Kit."

But Crispin was either not inside, or not answering the call, and after a moment, Christopher turned to me. "Must have been someone else."

"Or he simply doesn't want to speak to us." I looked around. "Whoever was out here must have gone into his room, or yours, or through the stairwell door. There aren't any other doors near enough."

"You don't suppose Laetitia or Geoffrey might have made it to their mother's door if they ran?"

I eyed it. "I suppose it's possible. Although I'm not knocking on that."

Christopher shook his head. "Nor I. We can check my room, I suppose, although I don't know how likely it is that anyone would duck in there."

Not at all likely, I would say. Aside from the Viscount St George, the rest of us—those of us who might have felt comfortable with taking refuge in Christopher's room—had all been together. And Crispin would have had no reason to duck into Christopher's bedchamber when the door to his own sitting room was no farther away.

"Any sign that the maid has come and gone?" I wanted to know. Perhaps the person we had heard in the hallway had been one of the maids, who had been worried about being caught eavesdropping.

He shook his head. "Not since this morning. They won't be turning the beds down until later."

"The chambermaids might know where everyone was between breakfast and luncheon," I said. "Or at least they would know whether anyone spent that time in their room."

"We should inquire." He glanced at the door to the stairwell and seemed to change his mind. "Let's go this way."

'This way' was up the east wing to the central section and around the corner to the central staircase. We clattered down, and headed for the kitchen wing, where we stumbled into the servants' dining room in time to interrupt the servants' tea.

"Oops." I stopped just inside the door. "Apologies."

"Oof," Christopher added as he ran into me and knocked me forward a step. "Sorry."

"No matter, Master Christopher. Miss Darling." Mrs. Mason looked from one to the other of us. "If this is about Detective Sergeant Gardiner's accommodations, Master Crispin has already—"

"No," Christopher said, and flushed, while I added, "I'm sure he has done. This is about something else."

Mrs. Mason waited, eyebrows elevated, and so did everyone else. They were all excruciatingly polite, and made me feel more out of place for it.

Christopher cleared his throat, clearly as uncomfortable as I was. "We just wanted to ask the chambermaids whether any of the guests or family were in their rooms during the time between breakfast and luncheon." He glanced around the table.

One of the younger women giggled and blushed when their eyes met, and Christopher looked horrified. Mrs. Mason fixed the poor girl—she couldn't have been much over eighteen—with a basilisk-cold stare. "Do you have something to say, Mabel?"

Mabel did her best equivalent of a seated curtsey. "Just that Lord Geoffrey Marsden spent the time between breakfast and lunch in his room, Mrs. Mason."

"Alone?"

Mabel flushed again. "Yes, Miss Darling. He..." She shot Mrs. Mason a look. "Well, he..."

"Flirted," I said bluntly.

She nodded. "Yes, Miss Darling. He tried to tell me that I didn't have to tidy the room, but that I could stay and keep him company."

Mrs. Mason became, if possible, even more wooden. "You said no, Mabel. Did you not?"

Mabel looked terrified. "Yes, Mrs. Mason. His lordship told us about Lord Geoffrey's trouble in Dorset, and he warned all of us to stay away from Lord Geoffrey."

A couple of the other young women nodded.

Christopher cleared his throat. "So Geoffrey was in his room between breakfast and lunch. Anyone else?"

Mabel nodded. "Miss Constance. She was packing her bag because they—you—were supposed to leave for Beckwith Place. And your mother and father."

"And Francis, I suppose," I said. "Anyone else?"

But Mabel shook her head. "I don't know about Master Francis, Miss Darling. I'm responsible for the rooms in the west wing."

She glanced at one of the other maids, who cleared her throat. "I saw Master Francis. He was also packing to leave. I didn't see anyone else on the upper floor."

That left the older Marsdens as well as His Grace and Crispin unaccounted for, then, as well as Laetitia.

"What about the lower floor? Did anyone see anyone there between breakfast and luncheon?"

Sadie, the parlor maid, spoke up. "His Grace worked in the study this morning. Master Crispin took his fiancée to the hedge maze after breakfast." She hesitated. "Or perhaps she took him."

More likely that, I thought, although that might have been my biases. "How long did they stay there?"

"Long enough," Sadie said with a saucy smirk that disappeared as soon as Mrs. Mason glanced her way. She added sullenly, "I don't know, do I? I had work."

"What about the Marsdens?"

"The Earl and Countess of Marsden," Hugh the footman said, "stayed in the breakfast room when His Grace went to the study. After that, they were in the library for part of the morning. Or perhaps she was in the library while he was in the game room. She had a letter to write, she said."

I exchanged a glance with Christopher. That was everyone accounted for, then, and for the most part, they didn't have an alibi among them. Uncle Harold had been alone in the study, and could have left without anyone noticing. The earl and countess had been separated, and one of them could have left without the other noticing. Geoffrey had been alone in his room, and no one would have noticed if he had made himself scarce for a while. And as for Laetitia and Crispin, even they may not have been together the entire time. They certainly hadn't spent all of it outside in the hedge maze. Not in this weather.

"Thank you," I said politely. "We're sorry for keeping you from your tea."

"Yes," Christopher nodded. "You've been very helpful. As you were."

He stepped backwards to the door and fumbled for the knob. We ducked through the door and out of sight.

Outside in the hallway we faced one another and breathed out.

"Awkward," Christopher opined.

I nodded. "Couldn't have picked a worse time for it, either. Just standing there watching as their tea got cold."

"Oh, I'm certain we could have done." He turned me around and nudged me down the hallway. "What did we learn?"

I started moving while I endeavored to parse the answer. "Not much. You and I have an alibi, and we may be the only two people at Sutherland Hall who do. Mabel can't have been in Geoffrey's room for all that long. The Marsdens were in separate rooms, according to Hugh. Uncle Harold was in the study, and your parents and Francis and Constance came and went, it seemed."

He slanted a look my way. "Surely you don't suspect my parents or my brother of killing Doctor Meadows?"

"Of course not," I said irritably. "I'm just pointing out that it's a good few hours between breakfast and luncheon. You and I had time to walk to the village, talk to Doctor Meadows, walk back, and then pack our bags before going downstairs. Any one of the others could have made it to the village and back, too, with no one seeing them."

"Geoffrey, his parents, and Uncle Harold, do you mean?"

"Or Laetitia, in the event that she and Crispin didn't spend hours in the hedge maze, which I'm sure they didn't. The weather is neither warm nor particularly pleasant, and staring at the spot where Grimsby breathed his last would lose its appeal rather quickly, I would think."

"And if Uncle Harold was doing business in his study," Christopher offered, "he might have called Crispin in to talk business."

"Thus leaving Laetitia at loose ends." I nodded. "She's someone I could very well imagine framing me for murder."

Christopher agreed. "We might just go out to the carriage house and the stables, and see whether anyone took one of the motorcars or horses out this morning."

"As long as we go by the boot room. I don't fancy getting my shoes dirty."

He glanced down. "Of course, Pippa. Although I can go by myself, you know."

"I don't mind," I said, as we headed for the boot room. "Just give me a chance to change my footwear and it'll be fine. It won't take but a moment."

There were several pairs of Wellies lined up by the boot room door, and I unbuckled my strap shoes and looked around for a likely pair.

"These must be Uncle Harold's," Christopher said, nudging an oversized pair with the toe of his shoe. "Too big for you."

I nodded. I'm not particularly dainty—a couple of inches taller than Constance, albeit shorter than Laetitia and her mother—but this particular pair would drag after me if I tried to walk in them.

"Aunt Charlotte's," Christopher added, and nodded to the pair on the other side. "Or perhaps one of the maids'. Certainly not Laetitia's, and I doubt Constance brought Wellies to the party."

"If she had done, they'd be in the Crossley by now." But yes, this pair was dainty—as Crispin's mother had been—and would likely pinch my toes. They were also neat and clean, quite unlike the other two pairs.

"I suppose you'll have to wear Crispin's boots," Christopher said and kicked the pair in the middle. "They'll be big on you, but not so big that you won't manage."

"Yes, thank you, Christopher. I'm sure I can do."

He and Crispin were both of a size, and their clothes and shoes were, too. I knew exactly how big Christopher's feet were, as it wouldn't be the first time I had stuffed my own into a pair of his slippers for warmth.

The Wellies were all over dried mud, as they would be, had Crispin worn them to walk in the garden maze with Laetitia. They fit well enough, however. Not so well that I didn't have to concentrate on lifting my feet as we made our way across the courtyard, but also not so poorly that my feet slipped out of them. They rubbed up and down on my heels with every step, but they stayed on.

"Are you certain you don't want to stay in the house?" Christopher asked again as we made our way around the corner of the conservatory towards the stable and the old carriage house. He gave me a concerned look.

I shook my head. "It'll take a minute longer to get there, but we have time. Supper won't be for hours yet."

"I just don't want you to be uncomfortable. You're not wearing much."

I was wearing considerably less than he was, for certain. Men get undershirts, then regular shirts, then waistcoats, and jackets. All I had was my chemise and my rayon frock. And while I could have asked him to take his jacket off and give it to me, I could also have picked up a macintosh from the boot room. That was if I had thought about it, of course. I hadn't done, so now I was shivering, and stalking stiff-legged towards the stable.

"I'm fine, Christopher. It's only a few more yards."

We reached the carriage house first, and ducked inside.

It wasn't warm, of course, although it was a bit warmer than outside. The wind was less chilling for one thing, and there was no stinging moisture in the air.

"All the motorcars are here," Christopher commented, looking from Crispin's blue Hispano-Suiza to Constance's burgundy Crossley, to her aunt and uncle's green Daimler and Uncle Harold's newly acquired Rolls Royce Phantom. The only thing missing was Aunt Roz and Uncle Herbert's Bentley, and that would be back at Beckwith Place by now.

Christopher raised his voice. "Alfred?"

Alfie was the second footman, who had also, since Wilkins's demise, obliged as chauffeur for Uncle Harold when the latter desired to go somewhere. His Grace apparently didn't think it appropriate for a peer of the realm to be behind the wheel of his own motorcar.

"He must be up at the house," I said when no response came. "There's no need for him to be here, is there? I'm sure Uncle Harold isn't planning to go anywhere before supper. And Alfie has duties inside, as well."

"He wasn't at tea in the servants' hall," Christopher said as he followed me out.

"Nor was Tidwell." I closed the door behind him. "The two

of them were probably cleaning up after the family before sitting down for their own meal."

Christopher gave a shrug. "Let's take a look at the horses, then."

We headed for the stables, where the air was much warmer, and full of snorting and movement. Manes tossed and tails flicked as horses nickered.

"All present," I said.

Christopher nodded. "But if anyone had ridden to the village this morning, the horse would be back now."

I looked around. "Where are the grooms?"

"Having their tea, too, I wager." Christopher looked around as well. "Or a sit-down when they're not needed. Back there."

He pointed to a door in the back of the stable, through which we did indeed find the two grooms sharing... not tea, but a pint and a game of cards across a rickety table.

When Christopher pushed the door open, they both jumped to their feet, one of them so quickly that his chair turned over. Guilt was marked clearly across both of their faces. One of them gulped. "My—"

Christopher waved a hand. "Not Crispin. Christopher Astley."

Neither of them said anything, but they did look a bit more relaxed once they knew that it wasn't Uncle Harold or his son who had caught them soldiering in the middle of the workday. Knowing Crispin, I would have thought that he'd be more likely to join them than tell his father what he'd seen, although I suppose I might be wrong. Uncle Harold might have beaten those sorts of egalitarian inclinations out of him.

"We wanted to know whether anyone had taken any of the horses out today," Christopher said. "Sometime this morning, perhaps."

The two grooms exchanged a glance. "We did," one of them

said. I didn't know his name, I was chagrined to realize. I ride, but only when I can't get out of it, and they were both new since the last time I had visited the Sutherland Hall stable. Perhaps I wasn't as egalitarian as I'd like to think.

The other groom added, "The weather's not good enough for any of the guests to want to ride today."

There was a trace of something in his voice that might have been humor, but that might equally well have been the condescension of a man—or boy, he wasn't much more—to the upper class who was too delicate to do what was necessary.

Christopher, to his credit, ignored it.

"When was this?" I wanted to know. "That you rode out?"

They both turned to me. A second passed before the first chap told me that it had been this morning after breakfast.

"Did you happen to see anyone on your ride? Where did you go?"

They had gone across the fields, it seemed, and they both agreed that they hadn't seen a soul.

"Not even Christopher and myself walking down to the village?"

They exchanged a glance, but were adamant that no, they hadn't seen anyone. "Sorry, Miss Darling," one of them said.

"That's all right." I smiled pleasantly. "Carry on. We'll see ourselves out."

I stepped back and Christopher shut the door. We didn't speak until we had left the stable and were outside in the wet again.

"They could have done it," I said. "They were out here by themselves. No one kept tabs on them. They could have ridden to the village, killed Doctor Meadows, and tried to frame me."

Christopher nodded, although he seemed to disagree, or at least he delighted in playing devil's advocate. "Why would they do, though, Pippa? You don't even know their names. I'm surprised that they know yours."

I was too, frankly. "Be that as it may, they do know it. One of them could have written the note."

"Would they have access to the note paper?"

Perhaps not, now that he mentioned it. The grooms didn't tend to come into the house much. They certainly wouldn't be welcome in the library or drawing room. And it wasn't likely that they'd have their own supply of writing paper and ink in the back of the stable, was it?

"Let's go," Christopher said, and took my elbow.

"Where?"

"I want to see whether there's writing paper in Wilkins's rooms above the garage. And I want to talk to Alfie."

"Do you think he might have gone to the village this morning? Or might have seen who did?"

Alfred was a local, so he might have had his own reasons for doing away with Doctor Meadows. He certainly knew my name, and unlike the grooms, he would have had easy access to the Hall and to the writing paper. He probably also knew that of everyone here, I was the person he could most safely accuse without repercussions.

Christopher didn't answer, just pushed open the door to the garage and started past the motorcars, over to the staircase by the back wall. I followed more slowly, peering into and around the vehicles as I passed them. One of them might have made a trip to the village this morning, but how would one know which?

The nearest vehicle was Crispin's Hispano-Suiza, and I put my hand against the metal covering the motor. The surface was cold against my palm, and I dropped my hand again. The motor would have been hot directly after the trip, I assumed, but that was hours ago. The fact that it was cold now proved nothing one way or the other.

Christopher headed up the stairs. By the time he reached the door at the top, I had just got to the bottom, and I stopped there and waited instead of dragging the too-big Wellies from step to step.

"Try the latch," I suggested after a few seconds, when there had been no answer.

He squinted down at me. "I don't want to walk into the man's private quarters without warning, Pippa. He's a servant, but he still has the right to privacy in his own quarters."

"You knocked," I said, beginning to climb. "Isn't that warning enough?

Besides, he probably wasn't even here. He was most likely up at the house, doing footmanly things under Tidwell's beady eye.

"He might be asleep," Christopher said, although he reached for the handle anyway.

I snorted as I stopped two steps below him. "In the middle of the workday? Not bloody likely, is it?"

He didn't answer, and I added, persuasively, "Just open the door, Christopher. I'm sure the place is empty, and all we want to do is look at the desk blotter."

"Fine." But he took a breath before he twisted the knob and pushed the door in. And hovered on the threshold, swaying. "Oh, God."

CHAPTER FIFTEEN

"GO AND GET TOM," I told Christopher, staring at the body laid out on the floor just inside the door. It was clearly Alfie—I could tell by the uniform, and also because I had seen the footman before—and he was equally clearly as dead as a door nail. The side of his head was caved in, sandy hair sticky with blood. For a moment, my vision tunneled as I remembered Frederick Montrose, and Abigail Dole, and Dominic Rivers, and their broken skulls—and then I pulled myself back together and gave Christopher a poke. "Kit!"

He blinked and turned to me, face blank. "I don't want to leave you alone with—"

He gestured at what was left of Alfie, but without looking at him.

"He won't hurt me," I said, and tried to keep my voice steady. I didn't want to be left alone with the corpse either. However, needs must. "Go, Christopher. The sooner you can find Tom, the sooner we can both leave this to him."

Christopher hesitated. "I know he won't hurt you. But maybe there's someone else..."

He glanced around the small room.

"Whoever did this is long gone," I said steadily. "The blood is dry in patches. This happened hours ago. Go on, now. You'll be faster than me, especially in these Wellies."

He gave me one more look, searching my face to be certain that I meant it. I must have looked as if I did, because he gave a nod. "I'll be back as quickly as I can." He turned on his heel. A moment later, I heard his shoes clatter down the stairs, and then, shortly after that, the carriage house door opened and closed.

It was silent. I took a breath and turned my attention to Alfie.

I didn't want to move any closer to him. The bottoms of our shoes—or in my case, boots—were wet. I could see the imprints of Christopher's shoes coming and going. By moving nearer, I might destroy some sort of evidence. Or if nothing else, Tom would be able to see just how far my curiosity had taken me.

Instead, I peered around the room from the vantage point inside the door, keeping my feet planted inside the Wellies.

The body lay a few feet away. It was located stomach down halfway into the small room. His head was turned sideways, so I could see half of his face, including one open, staring eye, slightly filmed.

I shuddered, but forced myself to keep looking.

The wound was on his left temple and the side of his head, and it wasn't difficult to put together what had happened. He had opened the door, perhaps because someone had knocked. That someone had whacked him on the left temple with something—most likely a right-handed attacker—and Alfie, taken aback by the attack as well as the force of it—had swung to his right and staggered, as he had fallen away from the door and into the room. From the position of his arms, and the fact that his face was mostly intact, he had likely been alive at least long enough to catch himself before face-planting into the hardwood floor. His nose looked straight and there wasn't any evidence of a nose bleed, so it didn't seem to be broken.

But once he was on the floor, someone had taken another whack at him, unless I was mistaken. I'm no kind of expert (even if I have seen more than my fair share of deaths from broken skulls), but it did appear as if there might be two different areas of impact. One on the temple, likely the first blow, enough to break the skin and cause a knot, and then another a bit further back, deeper and more fatal. That was where the skull had caved in and where most of the blood was coming from. From all I knew, there might have been more wounds, too, but I wasn't about to go any closer to make certain of it.

I looked all over the floor, but there was no sign of the murder weapon. Whoever the killer was, he (or she) hadn't left it behind when he fled. If, indeed, fleeing was what he had done. More likely, he had simply shut the door behind himself —or herself—and had walked calmly downstairs and out of the carriage house and... where? To the stables? Back to the Hall? Elsewhere?

It was difficult to imagine that anyone other than one of the residents could have done this, although it wasn't impossible. Alfie likely had friends as well as enemies in the village. Coming here to kill him would have been a risk, but someone might have done it and gotten away without being observed. Someone had managed to kill Doctor Meadows without anyone seeing, and this was no different.

But at least Alfie hadn't killed Doctor Meadows. Or if he had done, someone else had returned the favor.

Could Alfie have been paid to kill Doctor Meadows? And when the person who hired him had showed up to pay for the murder, he had killed Alfie instead of handing over the money?

It didn't seem likely, frankly. Alfie wasn't the type of person one would hire for a murder, nor did he seem like the type of person who would take the job. Not only did he have a job already, and one that likely paid all right, but he was young—younger than me by a year or so, I'd wager—and fresh-faced. Too young to have partaken in the war. Someone with no experience with killing.

I eyed the blood again. How long did it take for blood to dry on a wet and cold November day? Long enough that Alfie had been lying here when Christopher and I made our way down to the village this morning, or had he been hit later, when we'd been upstairs packing our bags?

Had anyone seen Alfie at all today, other than his murderer?

None of the servants had seemed worried about him not being there for tea, so perhaps it wasn't an unusual occurrence.

It was at this point that I heard the door downstairs open and close again. There was the rustling of fabric and the thumping of feet on the dirt floor of the carriage house.

"It's us," Tom's voice called up, just as I began to worry that the murderer was back and that I would need to prepare to protect myself. I breathed out and relaxed again.

He bounded up the stairs two steps at a time and nodded to me. "Pippa."

"Tom," I said, and stepped back as best I could in the narrow space. "I didn't touch him to make certain, but he looks dead to me."

Tom's eyes flickered over the body. "I would agree. *Livor Mortis* has set in. He's been lying here for several hours."

"That's what we thought." I flattened myself against the wall as he squeezed past. "I haven't gone any closer to him than this. I can't see a murder weapon anywhere, but I think he was hit at least twice."

Tom nodded, as he squatted down beside the body. Christopher drifted into the doorway behind me, eyes fixed on what was happening.

"I had Tidwell ring up the Little Sutherland constabulary," Tom added, presumably directed at me, since Christopher would have been there when he did it. "Why don't you go downstairs and wait for them, and instruct them where to go? It shouldn't be long before they get here."

Neither of us moved. "Me," I asked, "or Christopher?"

He flicked me a look. "Both of you, if you don't want to watch me examine the body."

There was no part of me that wanted to watch him examine the body. "I can do without that, thank you."

"Shouldn't someone stay with you?" Christopher wanted to know. "Just in case."

He didn't say in case of what, but then we both—we all three—knew that he wasn't worried about anyone attacking Tom, or Tom doing anything he oughtn't do. Christopher simply didn't want to leave Tom before he had to.

"I'll go," I said. "You can stay here. Although... may I borrow your jacket?"

"Of course." My cousin shrugged out of it and draped it over my shoulders.

"Thank you." I stuffed my arms through the sleeves. "Who else knows about this? Should I prepare for the entire population of Sutherland Hall to be gathered outside the carriage house?"

"His Grace, Duke Harold, and the Earl and Countess of Marsden were still in the drawing room when Kit found me," Tom said. "Everyone else had left."

There wasn't likely to be anything to worry about, then. Uncle Harold wouldn't care enough about Alfie to come out to see what was wrong, and Laetitia's parents didn't know the footman.

"Be sure to intercept any of them that do show up, Pippa. I don't want anyone else up here that doesn't need to be. Or in the carriage house, either."

"Of course not." I took the reminder as it was intended: a prod to get me going. "Come find me when the constables arrive, Christopher."

My cousin promised that he would do, and then I sloshed my slow way down the stairs and across the carriage house floor in my too-big Wellington boots and shut the door behind me.

I had been prepared to spend the time by myself, slowly soaking up mizzle until I was wet all the way through. It would take the constables at least fifteen minutes, I imagined, to gather themselves and their paraphernalia and make it here from the village. Even so, I won't claim that I was surprised when, a few minutes later, I saw Crispin come around the corner of the conservatory towards me.

"Darling." He was breathless when he stopped in front of me. He even went so far as to grab me by both arms as he peered into my face, something he rarely does. "What happened? I heard that Kit came running into the drawing room to fetch Gardiner. Are you all right?"

"Fine," I said. "I'm not the problem."

He glanced over my shoulder to the carriage house door behind me. "What is the problem?"

"Someone killed Alfie," I said.

Crispin reared back, dropping both hands from my arms as if I had pushed him. "Pardon me?"

"Alfred the footman. The one who chauffeured your father around now that Wilkins is gone."

"I know who Alfred is, Darling." He shot another look at the carriage house. "He's dead? What happened?"

"Blunt instrument to the head," I said, and watched him wince. "I don't know what kind. It wasn't left at the scene."

"The scene?"

"He's on the floor just inside the door upstairs. It looked like he opened the door to someone, and that someone hit him in the temple with something. And then hit him again for good measure once he was down."

"Ouch."

"You can say that again."

He opened his mouth, and I added, "Don't. This isn't the time for humor, St George."

"Of course not." He gave my face another look. "Are you certain you're all right?"

"As right as I'm likely to be," I said, "after finding the footman dead."

He looked concerned, and I added, "I'm fine. It just brings back memories."

"Of course it does. Do you need to sit?" He looked around. "Why don't we go inside, and—"

I shook my head. "Can't. Tom sent me out here so I could tell the constables where to go when they arrive from the village."

"I'll do that. You go back inside and get warm. You're shivering. Here."

He pulled a flask from somewhere and handed it to me, after twisting off the top. "Only a sip or two. It's strong stuff. But it'll help."

It did. I handed the flask back with a delicate cough as the heat from the alcohol curled through my stomach. "Thank you."

"Don't mention it." He capped the flask and tucked it away whence it had appeared. "Go on, Darling. I'll stay here until the constables arrive, and then I'll fetch Kit and bring him to you."

I hesitated. It was tempting, I'll admit. I was cold and wet, and I couldn't stop seeing Alfie's head in my mind. "Are you certain you don't mind?"

"I don't mind at all. Off you go." He waved me off, and then watched me slosh away. "Are those my Wellies you've got on?"

"I imagine they must be," I said over my shoulder. "I found them in the boot room. I left my own shoes there, so I'll put them back when I get inside."

"No worries, Darling. You're welcome to anything of mine that you want or need."

It wasn't the first time he had said something like that, although it was the first time he had sounded sincere about it. And of course I had to ruin it. "Don't let Laetitia hear you say that."

His face closed. "I won't. Go on, now. Don't dawdle."

He flapped a hand in my direction, clearly desirous of having me take myself off as quickly as possible. I wondered if I ought to apologize—the reminder had been like a cold bucket of water, probably for both of us—but in the end there was no point. He was engaged, and reminding him of that fact wasn't telling him anything he didn't know. It was, in fact, telling him something he ought to have remembered before he started saying romantic things to me.

So I simply nodded, and walked away. When I flicked a glance over my shoulder, just before I turned the corner of the conservatory into the courtyard, he was still standing there, but facing the carriage house. He hadn't cared enough to watch me walk away, it seemed.

• • •

INSIDE THE BOOT ROOM, I stepped out of Crispin's Wellingtons and into my own shoes, and then thought about what I wanted to do next.

Christopher, Crispin, and Tom already knew what had happened. So did Uncle Harold and the Earl and Countess of Marsden, according to Tom. And Tidwell had been instructed to phone the constabulary, so Tidwell knew. That surely meant that the rest of the staff was in the process of being told, as well. Crispin had found out somehow, so Laetitia must already know, or if she didn't, surely her mother would inform her. That left Geoffrey—who would probably be told, as well, but I had no plans to inform him—and Francis and Constance.

They had been upstairs in Francis's room when we left them earlier. Assuming that such was still the case, I headed in that direction: along the rest of the west wing to the servants' stairs, and up to the first floor. And because I was still a bit chilled from standing outside—and I suppose from the murder —I stopped in my room to wrap a shawl around my shoulders before going back into the hallway to find my cousin and his fiancée.

And that was when the door to Laetitia's room opened, and the future bride stepped out.

I stopped. So did she, and her eyes narrowed. "What are you doing here?"

"I live here," I said. "Or rather, I'm visiting. My room is just there."

I pointed to it.

Her eyes narrowed further, to where they were just two pale blue slits. "Why aren't you with your little cousin?"

My 'little' cousin?

"You mean Christopher?" That was rich, given that he was precisely as big as Crispin, and several months older. Laetitia had practically robbed the cradle when she got herself engaged to St George. She's at least two years older than he is, if not more. "He's outside, with Tom and Crispin."

Her lips tightened.

"Crispin didn't want me standing outside in the cold," I added, sweetly, "so he volunteered to wait for the constables in my stead. He was standing outside the carriage house the last time I saw him."

Unless the constables had arrived by now, and then Tom wouldn't need Christopher or Crispin to stick around any longer. Tom might not be allowed to stay, either. Scotland Yard cannot simply invite itself into the middle of a local investigation. They have to be invited in by the Chief Constable, and so far that hadn't happened. I doubted the Chief Constable knew that Tom was even here.

"I heard that the two of you spent some time in the garden maze this morning," I added.

Laetitia squinted at me. "And what if we did do?"

"It must have been cold. How long did you stay outside?"

"Not long enough for it to be a problem," Laetitia said with a smirk. "We kept one another warm."

I smirked back. "He's good at that, I hear."

Her face turned stony, and I added, "Did you happen to see anyone else while you were out there?"

"In the garden maze? Of course not."

"Somewhere else?"

"You and your cousin were on your way into the village," Laetitia said with a toss of her head. The glossy black wing of her Dutch Boy haircut swung against her jaw. "Two of the grooms were saddling the horses. One of the footmen was talking to them."

That sounded as if Alfie had been alive when Christopher

and I walked to the village. Unless she was referring to Hugh, of course, although as far as I knew, he had had no reason to be outside by the stables.

I asked for a description, but Laetitia gave me an elegant shrug of a single shoulder. "How should I know? All I saw was the uniform."

Of course. "What happened after you came inside?"

She blinked. "What do you mean? Nothing happened."

"What did you do? Did you and Crispin go somewhere else together?"

"Oh." She stuck her bottom lip out in a pout. Had I been Crispin—or another bloke, any bloke—I might have thought it charming. As it was, I mostly wished I could slap the expression off her face. "No. His Grace had some business with Crispin, so I went upstairs to my room to freshen up."

"Did you see or speak to anyone? Your brother? Your parents?"

But Laetitia said she hadn't done, and furthermore, she objected to me interrogating her. "You're not with the constabulary. You have no business asking me these questions."

"That's fine," I said. "I just wanted to know whether you had an alibi or not."

"I don't need an alibi! I didn't go to the village. There was no time for that."

"I'm not worried about the village," I said. "I meant an alibi for the footman's murder."

"The—" She staggered a bit, so on the face of it, at least, this was news. But of course you can't always tell when someone's pretending, and her reaction didn't make me take her off the suspect list. Not that I had any reason to put her on the suspect list in the first place—she had no motive that I knew of; certainly not if she couldn't tell Hugh and Alfie apart—but as far as I was concerned, everyone in the house was on the suspect list until I knew that they couldn't have done it.

"Someone killed the footman?"

I nodded. "Bashed him over the head with the proverbial blunt instrument."

"The same footman that I saw?"

"I assume it was the same footman." How would I know, when she couldn't describe him beyond the gray uniform? "Were they arguing when you saw them? Did either of the grooms look like he wanted to commit murder?"

"Of course not," Laetitia said with another toss of her head. "It was a perfectly civil conversation."

"Good for them. And when you came inside, Crispin went somewhere with his father, did you say?"

"To the study, I assumed."

"And you went upstairs. By yourself."

She nodded.

"That's a shame," I said.

She blinked. "Why?"

"It's obvious, isn't it? If Alfie was alive when you saw him, then he was killed after you went inside. And if you were alone in your room from then until luncheon, you have no alibi."

She stared at me. I smiled sweetly. I had no reason to think she was involved, of course. I simply wanted to rattle her. But it seemed as good a place as any to end the conversation, so I gave her a nod and left her standing there in the hallway.

FRANCIS'S ROOM was empty when I reached it, so he and Constance must have gone back downstairs. I knocked, and then opened the door.

The east wing of Sutherland Hall faces the formal gardens,

as well as the stable and carriage house. I made my way over to the window and peered out.

I only wanted to see whether the constables had arrived yet, or whether Crispin was still standing in front of the carriage house, shivering and flapping his arms like a chicken.

Instead, what I saw was him and Christopher on their way back to the Hall, just a glimpse of two fair heads, platinum and gilt, before they ducked around the corner of the conservatory. They had their heads together and their mouths were flapping. Christopher's hands were flying, as well. He likes to express himself physically.

There was nothing else to see, the carriage house sat silent, so I pushed off from the window and hurried into the hallway and up to the central wing and the main staircase.

I was halfway down the stairs to the foyer when the two of them stepped through the front door.

"Thank you, Tidwell," Crispin said, and looked up. "Darling."

"St George. Christopher." I finished my descent and handed Christopher the jacket he had lent me earlier.

He shrugged it on. "Thank you, Pippa."

"Your Wellies are back in the boot room," I informed Crispin. "Your fiancée is upstairs, or was, the last time I saw her."

He glanced at the stairs, but made no move to ascend.

"I assume the constables arrived," I added, "and that's why you're here?"

Christopher nodded, smoothing down his lapels and situating the jacket across his shoulders. "Tom came down to say that they had requested his help, since he's here. So he stayed."

I nodded. "What now?"

"Upstairs," Christopher said, "if you don't mind."

He tucked his hand through my arm and pulled me towards the staircase. "We shall see you for supper, Crispin."

Crispin blinked. "Certainly, Kit."

I glanced at him over my shoulder as Christopher pulled me towards the stairs, and the look he gave me was as confused as the feeling that permeated my own being.

CHAPTER SIXTEEN

"DID YOU AND TOM HAVE A SPAT?" I inquired as we reached the top of the staircase and Christopher dithered for a moment before turning left.

He flicked me a look. "Whatever do you mean?"

"Something is wrong," I said bluntly. "You don't usually carry me off by myself the moment you come inside unless something is wrong. You have to forgive me if I suppose you've had a disagreement."

He shook his head. "No disagreement."

"If not that, then what? Didn't want to see the corpse again?"

It was hard to blame him for that. I had been happy to get out of the carriage house and away from the dead man, too.

"I don't mind the corpse," Christopher said, and then made a face. "What am I saying? Of course I mind the corpse. But no, that's not why."

He steered me around the corner and down the west wing towards my room. The hallway was empty now. Laetitia was long gone, as of course she would be. It occurred to me to wonder whether she was inside her room, and if so, whether she could hear us. It didn't occur to me until after the words, "What, then?" had fallen out of my mouth, however.

I followed it up immediately with, "Never mind."

Christopher nodded. "Best wait until we're inside."

He opened the door to my bedchamber and scanned the room before pushing me through the doorway. I arched my brows again, but went. He followed, and shut the door behind us.

"I don't know how we can make it any more secure," I told him over my shoulder. "If you have a secret to tell me, we may have been better off outside."

"We may have been, at that. But we're here now." He gestured to the bed. "I suppose we'll simply have to whisper."

"You're worrying me," I said, as he folded down next to me.

"I'm worried myself."

But that was all he said. After some seconds had ticked by in silence, I prodded. "What are you worried about, Christopher? Are you certain nothing's going on with Tom?"

"Nothing's going on with Tom," Christopher said. "Nothing like what you're thinking, at any rate. He's fine, as far as I know. And he came running when I rang him up, so I'd say everything is hunky-dory. Other than the ostentation of dead bodies, of course."

Yes, other than that. "I believe what you're talking about is an ostentation of peacocks, but never mind that. If not Tom, then what is it?"

"It's Crispin," Christopher said.

I furrowed my brows. "What about him?"

He glanced at me. "I'm worried that he's mixed up in this."

I recoiled a few inches, to where I could see him more clearly. "What do you mean? Mixed up in what? Alfred's murder? The anonymous note? Morrison's death?"

"All of it," Christopher said.

I shook my head. "That's silly, Christopher. He has no reason to be mixed up in any of it. Why would he be?"

He didn't answer, and I added, "Besides, he was with Laetitia this morning." Constance had said so, and so had Laetitia herself.

"Only for part of the morning," Christopher said wretchedly. "They went inside at some point."

"And Uncle Harold invited Crispin into the study for a business matter," I said. "That's what Laetitia told me."

"But he could have left there, and gone to the village, and then when he came back, killed Alfie so Alfie couldn't tell anyone that he had taken the H6 out."

I thought about it. "I suppose it's possible. But why would he bother?"

He didn't answer immediately, and I added, "Do you really believe that, of everyone here, Crispin would try to frame me for murder? What happened to 'he's been in love with you for five years, Pippa?' Isn't he the last person at Sutherland Hall who would do that?"

"He has motive," Christopher said, half truculent and half glum.

"For framing me?"

"For wanting Alfie dead. If he killed Doctor Meadows."

"That's a big if," I said. "Besides, you saw his writing sample in the drawing room earlier. There's no chance that he wrote the anonymous note."

"He could have made it look bad on purpose," Christopher said stubbornly. "Or perhaps he had Alfie write it for him. Perhaps that's why Alfie's dead."

I stared at him, torn between rolling my eyes and smacking him over the head in order to beat some sort of sense into him.

"What has gotten into you, Christopher? You've never believed Crispin capable of murder before."

"I didn't think that he killed Grandfather," Christopher corrected. "Or Johanna de Vos. Or Gladys. Or Abigail Dole. Or—"

I raised a hand. "I get it. You didn't think he was capable of killing anyone else. But you do think he might have killed Doctor Meadows? Why on earth would he have done?"

"Not only that," Christopher said miserably, "but I think he might have killed Morrison. And Hughes."

I stared at him. For once he had rendered me speechless.

Not for long, of course. Nothing renders me speechless for long. "Bloody hell, Christopher! What madness is this? Why on earth would he do any of those things?"

"It's a long story," Christopher said. He was squirming uncomfortably on the counterpane.

I eyed him for a moment. "Well, it's a good thing we have plenty of time, isn't it? Supper isn't for hours yet."

Christopher took a breath. "You were there in July."

"At Beckwith Place?" I nodded. That had been the visit when the celebration of Francis's 30th birthday and his engagement to Constance had been interrupted by the murder of Abigail Dole on the croquet lawn. "But that's all resolved now. We know who Elizabeth's father was, and how he was related to the Astley family. Crispin had nothing to do with it. You said so yourself, just now."

"Do you remember that afternoon, when Tom spoke to Dad in the study? Crispin rang up the pub and asked Wilkins to bring him a bottle of scotch as an excuse for getting him up to Beckwith Place, and the two of you left the study and went outside and around the house to the study window..."

"And you were there." I nodded. "Sitting on the ground

under the window, listening to the conversation. Of course I remember."

We had had to be exceptionally quiet when we joined him on the ground, so the group inside the study wouldn't notice us. There had been Tom, and Uncle Herbert, and Sammy, the constable from the village—Beckwith, not Little Sutherland—and eventually there had been Wilkins the chauffeur, as Tom confronted him with being Uncle Herbert's illegitimate son, Elizabeth's father, and Abigail's murderer.

"And you remember Hughes blackmailing Dad, before Tom took her and little Bess to Bristol."

I nodded. It had been quite an unpleasant experience, as a matter of fact. And worse than eavesdropping on the original conversation had been having to discuss it with Uncle Herbert afterwards.

"I wasn't there for that," Christopher said, "but you told me about it. About what she said."

I thought back. It had been four months ago, so hardly a long time, everything considered, but it felt like a lifetime. "She knew about Wilkins. That he was Uncle Herbert's son with the maid from before Uncle Herbert married Aunt Roz."

Christopher didn't answer, and I added, "Until then, Uncle Herbert hadn't known that Wilkins existed."

"But she also reminded him that it had happened again," Christopher said, his face disconsolate.

I nodded. "Yes, she did. And when I asked him, Uncle Herbert said that Aunt Roz knew all about that. Otherwise, I would have been tempted to tell her."

I loved my uncle, and I owed him for taking me in and taking care of me since age eleven. But my aunt was my mother's sister, so I owed her more.

"Wait—" I squinted at him. "Are you telling me that your mum doesn't know? He lied to me?"

"I'm sure Mum knows," Christopher said hollowly. His hands were clasped between his knees, and he was staring at them, fixedly. "I know, too. I've known since July."

"When you were sitting on the ground outside the study window," I said, putting two and two together. "They talked about it."

He nodded.

"Why didn't we hear it? Crispin and I?"

"They'd finished by the time you arrived outside the window," Christopher said.

I waited, but he didn't say anything else. I opened my mouth to ask him to clarify, but then I closed it again, and really thought about it. Christopher was concerned about Crispin, that Crispin might have killed Hughes, Morrison, and Doctor Meadows.

And Alfie, I suppose, although Alfie was probably only dead now because he knew something about Doctor Meadows's killer. Not like the other three, who had been murdered—or so I suspected—because of something that had happened twenty-three years ago, when Crispin was a baby, and when Hughes and Morrison had switched places.

And then I thought about that afternoon four months ago, of coming around the corner of Beckwith Place beside Crispin, with the sun shining down on us and the bees buzzing, and seeing Christopher on the grass underneath the study window, with tears streaking his cheeks and a look of horror on his face when he had seen us—no, when he had seen *Crispin*—approach.

"No," I said, shaking my head.

Christopher didn't answer, just looked miserable, and I added, "His brother's wife? Why would your father do that?"

Bedding the maid and begetting Wilkins as a callow youth was one thing. Bedding his sister-in-law while his own wife was enceinte—Christopher was born barely two months before Crispin—was another matter entirely.

"I expect she asked him to," Christopher muttered.

I stared at him, appalled. "Who? Aunt Roz?"

She would have been in her first trimester when Crispin was conceived—perhaps feeling poorly, perhaps nauseated and disinclined to intimacy—but that was no reason to send her husband to someone else.

You wouldn't find me doing something like that. If I were suffering with my husband's spawn, and he wanted to get frisky, he had better just hold that thought until I felt better, or he'd find himself without both wife and child.

The fact that Crispin's face popped into my head at this juncture doesn't even deserve a mention. It was only because it was something he would do, I told myself, and there was certainly no other reason for it.

"Not Mum," Christopher said with a snort. "Mum would never. I meant Aunt Charlotte."

"Aunt Charlotte asked your father to bed?"

"I assume she would have done. Or perhaps she did ask Mum. It might have been a mutual decision."

I stared at him, the way I would have stared at someone who was leaping around the courtyard with bells on his shoes and a crown of flowers on his head. Someone who had taken leave of his senses. "Whatever are you blathering about, Christopher?"

"Isn't it obvious?" Christopher asked. "Aunt Charlotte and Uncle Harold had been married for several years by then. Mum had Francis and Robbie, and was having me. Aunt Charlotte had no one. Uncle Harold wanted an heir—"

"And you think Aunt Charlotte asked your father to give her one? And your mum agreed?"

Christopher shrugged as if it didn't matter, when I knew full well that it did. "Keep it in the family, no?"

I sat back and thought about it. "I suppose there might be something to that. I can understand Aunt Charlotte's side of it, at any rate. Uncle Harold must have been impatient. And it's never the husband's fault, is it? If she couldn't provide him with an heir, he'd simply get rid of her, and find himself a different wife."

"Precisely," Christopher said. "One way or the other."

The other way being divorce, I assumed, if the one way was murder. Or vice versa.

"She'd be out on her bum, no longer the Viscountess St George, with no chance of ever becoming the Duchess of Sutherland. Not to mention that no one else would want her, if she was barren."

"Except she wasn't," Christopher said. "She had no problem getting with child when Dad got involved."

Ugh. I made a face. "Let's not discuss that part of it, Christopher. But yes, I could see Aunt Charlotte throwing herself on your mum and dad's mercy. *Help me give him an heir.* I could even see Aunt Roz taking pity on her, with her two children and another on the way."

Christopher nodded, even as his face twisted. "That's one way to assure that there's no question about legitimacy, anyway. Crispin is a Sutherland through and through."

Indeed. "I don't see what was in it for your dad, though. It wasn't because he wanted to bed his brother's wife. Uncle Herbert has always been goofy about Aunt Roz. And if Uncle Harold had no heir, Uncle Herbert would become Duke of Sutherland if he outlived his brother. With Crispin in place, Uncle Herbert is one step farther away from the dukedom."

"But his son would become duke either way," Christopher

said. "Francis in the event Uncle Harold had no heir, and Crispin otherwise."

He hesitated a moment and added, "I never got the impression that Dad particularly wanted to be duke. He's happy at Beckwith Place with Mum and his hobbies."

"He could have your mum and his hobbies at Sutherland Hall."

"At Sutherland Hall, he would be too busy for hobbies," Christopher said. "The estate doesn't run itself, after all."

After a moment, he added, "Besides, none of this matters, does it? It happened."

"You believe it happened," I corrected.

He slanted a look my way. "I'm fairly certain it did do. I heard the conversation. You didn't. Dad admitted it."

"There's no way to know for certain," I said firmly. "Crispin might still be Uncle Harold's son. I'm sure he was still bedding his wife, too."

"But it's more likely that he's Dad's, isn't it? If Uncle Harold couldn't get Aunt Charlotte up the duff in several years of marriage, what are the chances that it happened at the same time that Dad was trying?"

Not good, I would have to say.

"All right," I conceded. "I accept your premise. But it doesn't explain why you think Crispin would kill anyone."

"Doesn't it?"

He didn't wait for me to answer, just went on. "What if he found out about this during that weekend in April? This was probably the secret that Grimsby was holding over Aunt Charlotte's head, you know. The secret that she killed Grimsby and Grandfather over. She may have told Crispin that Morrison knew, as well. But he couldn't go anywhere to deal with it right after Aunt Charlotte's death. Uncle Harold kept him at Sutherland Hall until the funeral, remember?"

I did remember that. Christopher and I had gone back to London, and the tabloids had been quiet about Crispin's exploits for an entire fortnight because he was buried in Wiltshire.

"By the time he got to the Dower House for the weekend party it was two weeks later," Christopher continued, "and Morrison was long gone. Then in July, there was the engagement party for Francis and Constance, and he learned that Hughes knew, as well. So he waited a month to throw off suspicion, long enough for Hughes to get settled in Bristol, and then he drove there and got her alone in an alley and hit her over the head and made it look like a robbery. Tom went to Beckwith Place after Bristol, to make certain that Dad—and I suppose Mum—had an alibi, but I don't think he went to Sutherland Hall to check theirs."

"No," I agreed, "why would he? Hughes hadn't black-mailed either of them."

"So far as we know," Christopher said darkly. "At any rate, it's only a few hours from Little Sutherland to Bristol. He could have easily motored there and back in a day."

Yes, of course he could have done. Especially in the Hispano-Suiza.

"And Morrison?" I asked.

"Until this weekend," Christopher said, "none of us knew where to find Morrison. And he did want to come with us, remember?"

"You think he motored up there by himself? And back, overnight? That's farther than Bristol."

"If anyone could do it," Christopher said, "Crispin could. He makes the trip from Wiltshire to London all the time. He's used to traveling on his own. He's also used to staying up all night. The Bright Young Set often cap off their parties with breakfast."

Yes, of course they did. However— "I don't think he runs much with that crowd anymore, Christopher. Between Gladys getting killed, and Cecily Fletcher and Dominic Rivers ditto, and Ronnie Blanton being stuck in the country to kick the dope habit, and Hutchison and Ogilvie... well, we all know what happened there. I get the feeling that Laetitia keeps him on a pretty short leash these days. The last time I saw him in London, it was for supper at the Criterion and a play. Almost staid."

"He could have done it," Christopher insisted. "He would have arrived in Upper Slaughter sometime between three and four in the morning, most likely. It wouldn't have taken long to kill Morrison. She was asleep. All he had to do was hold the pillow over her face for a few minutes. He'd have been back here by the time breakfast was served."

Which he had been. Groggy and in his dressing gown and slippers, but present. "And you think he would be doing all of this because he didn't want to lose his spot in the succession?"

"If he's Uncle Harold's son, he's next in line to be the Duke of Sutherland when Uncle Harold goes," Christopher said. "If he's Dad's, he's the youngest of four. Or three now. But still behind Dad, Francis, and me for the dukedom."

"And you think he cares about that?"

He looked at me. "Don't you?"

Did I?

He cared about it enough not to pursue a relationship with me even though he supposedly wanted one. He had told me himself that the reason he didn't declare himself to the girl of his dreams—before I knew that the girl of his dreams was me— was that his father would disown him.

I had reflected at the time that yes, a Crispin deprived of all his creature comforts would be a miserable companion. He was used to a certain level of ease, and denuded of it, I imagined he would suffer, and no doubt make everyone around him suffer, as well. But I had encouraged him to declare himself anyway, because love was worth the loss of luxury, and I had assured him that if the girl loved him, she'd be happy to live with him anywhere, even if that was the proverbial Parisian garret. And instead of listening, he had made the choice to propose to Laetitia Marsden.

"You may have a point," I said reluctantly.

Christopher nodded. "I don't like it any better than you do, Pippa. I love Crispin. But it hangs together."

It did. Or at least it did if one suspended disbelief here and there and didn't look too hard at a few of the details.

"What about the anonymous note?" I queried. "Why would he try to frame me? If you're to be believed, he loves me. And even if you're wrong and he doesn't, I thought we had worked things out after the engagement, and we were friends again. Or if not friends, at least friendly. Not enemies."

When he had been among the group that had taken me off the German freighter last month, he had certainly seemed happy and relieved to find me alive and mostly well.

"I thought so, too," Christopher said. "I can't explain that. But otherwise, it makes sense."

"But you can't just disregard the things that don't fit!"

I could hear my voice becoming shrill, and I took a couple of breaths and counted to ten before I tried again. "If he killed all those people—and I'm not saying that I believe you, Christopher. It may make sense on paper, but that doesn't mean that I believe it—but if he did, chances are that he wrote the note, as well. Who else but the killer would know that Doctor Meadows was dead?"

"Someone else might have gone by and seen the body," Christopher suggested.

"And that person happened to have in their pocket a piece

of writing paper and a fountain pen? A piece of paper that matches what we use here at the Hall? Not to mention that instead of just letting the constables know what had happened, they decided it would be a good opportunity to frame me instead of trying to get help, the way any innocent person would do?"

Christopher made a face, as if to say he couldn't argue with that, and I went on. "There's simply no reason for Crispin to try to frame me. That seems like a vindictive little jab of the sort that Laetitia would take pleasure in. The only reason to do it, is to be petty and mean, because it's not as if anyone would actually believe it. I had no motive, and I was with you when Doctor died."

"I don't know what to tell you," Christopher said helplessly. "It's not as if I want to believe it myself, Pippa."

"Then don't," I told him. "I can't believe that you think your cousin capable of murder, Christopher. And not just murder, but serial murder. Three of them, over as many days, plus Hughes. I'm surprised you're not trying to hang Duke Henry's and Grimsby's murders on him, too."

"You already tried that," Christopher retorted, "back in April."

"And you didn't believe me then. What makes you think he wouldn't have committed those crimes, if you think he committed these?"

"Aunt Charlotte confessed," Christopher said.

"She might have been protecting him. God knows she doted on him."

There was a moment's pause while Christopher eyed me. "You're not serious, are you, Pippa?"

"I don't know," I said. I had brought up the previous deaths in an effort to persuade Christopher to realize how mad his position was, but now I wasn't certain what I thought. "I believed Aunt Charlotte's note at the time. But if you want me to consider that he might be a murderer now, we ought to consider whether he was a murderer then, too. The reason Duke Henry and Grimsby were killed, is probably the same reason that Morrison and Hughes were."

"The fact that Crispin isn't Uncle Harold's son," Christopher nodded. "And it's true that Aunt Charlotte couldn't have killed them. But that doesn't mean that she didn't kill Grandfather and Grimsby back then."

"But Crispin might have been part of it. They may have done it together."

"Fine." Christopher folded his arms across his chest. For some reason, this idea seemed to bother him a lot more than the possibility that Crispin was guilty of killing Hughes, Morrison, and Doctor Meadows. It must be the family connection. "Convince me."

I didn't want to convince him—not of this—but he was eyeing me expectantly, so I cleared my throat and got on with it. "I suspected St George at the time. You know that. We talked about it."

He nodded.

"I don't think that he had an alibi for either murder. He was out and about the night Grimsby was shot. He was the one who unlocked the conservatory door for us, remember? And anyone in the house could have gone into Francis's room and taken some of his Veronal."

"It was Aunt Charlotte who served Grandfather his tea, though," Christopher pointed out. "If Crispin had received the tray from one of the servants, I think they would have mentioned it, don't you?"

"Perhaps. Perhaps not. Although it might have been both of them together."

Christopher allowed as how that might have been possible.

"I suppose you think he was the one who shot at you, then? That day we walked to the village?"

"If we're talking means and opportunity," I agreed, "he might have done. A gun is considered more of a man's weapon than a woman's, I think."

The gun room had been open to anyone in the house, so Crispin could as easily have fetched the rifle and pointed it out Christopher's window as his mother. And he might have been the one who shot Grimsby while Aunt Charlotte poisoned Duke Henry. Poison is considered more of a woman's weapon than a man's, at least if you listen to the novelists. The great equalizer, and all that.

"And Aunt Charlotte knew what he had done," Christopher continued, "so she rang up the Dower House, to give Morrison time to get away, and then Aunt Charlotte wrote the note taking the blame, and took the rest of Francis's Veronal, and went to sleep."

"And Crispin let her?"

Christopher hesitated. The suggestion seemed to have given him pause, as it ought to have done. While Crispin and Uncle Harold had always had a contentious relationship, he and Aunt Charlotte had always been close. There was no way that the Crispin I knew would have allowed his mother to die for crimes he had committed. Or allowed her to die at all, if there was something he could have done to prevent it.

"I think we ought to talk to him," I said.

Christopher widened his eyes. "To Crispin?"

"He deserves a chance to tell us why we're wrong, don't you think?" And in the event that we were not wrong, a chance to explain his side of the story.

He shook his head, most violently. "Absolutely not. I'm not telling my cousin that I suspect him of murder."

"Then what do you suppose we do? Tell Tom and let him

deal with it? That doesn't seem quite fair, Christopher. St George is your cousin. I think you owe him better than that."

"There's no need to tell Tom," Christopher said, without touching on the other part of my statement. "He knows already."

Something cold settled into my chest. "What do you mean, Tom knows already? What does he know?"

"He said that it was all too much of a coincidence," Christopher said. "For Morrison to die the same night that Shreve told us where to find her. For Doctor Meadows to die the same morning we went to speak to him. And for Alfie to die the same morning as Doctor Meadows, when he might have seen someone take a motorcar or bicycle out of the carriage house."

I nodded. "I agree with Tom. It's all very suspicious. I just don't see why any of it implicates Crispin particularly. No more than anyone else."

"I've just explained it to you," Christopher said. "If he isn't Uncle Harold's son, then he would want to silence anyone who knows that. Who else has that sort of motive?"

"Laetitia," I said triumphantly. "If Crispin doesn't become Duke of Sutherland, she won't become Duchess. And you know she's marrying him at least partially for that. Besides, out of everyone here, she's the most likely to try to frame me. You can't convince me that Crispin would do that."

"I suppose that might be true," Christopher said grudgingly.

"You don't have to sound so displeased. It's not as if we want Crispin to be guilty."

He didn't answer, and I changed the subject. By a degree or so. "Did Tom find a murder weapon?"

"Not during the time I was there," Christopher said. "But the constables started turning over the carriage house when I left, so unless the murderer took it with him, I'm sure they'll find it."

So was I. The carriage house was full of handy weapons, like tire irons and wrenches. There was no need to bring your own into that kind of environment. Just use whatever was handy. As the person who killed Doctor Meadows had done. And the person who killed Morrison, too.

"What do we do now?" I wanted to know. "You're not willing to confront Crispin. Tom's busy. I certainly don't want to talk to Laetitia about any of this. Is there anything else we can do?"

"Search Crispin's room for clues?" Christopher suggested.

I waved the proposal away. "I was in there earlier. There's nothing there."

His brows arched. "You were in Crispin's rooms? Whatever for?"

"Not that," I said, since I could see what he was thinking. "It was earlier, before tea. I was looking for a sample of Laetitia's handwriting. I didn't know that you—or Tom—would make everyone write the anonymous note for comparison."

"But in Crispin's room? Wouldn't it have been better to look in her own?"

"Mrs. Mason told me that she writes Crispin little love notes," I explained, and couldn't keep my face from puckering as I said it, "and that he's honor-bound—or duty-bound—to hold onto them. I thought I would take a look."

"And did you find them?"

I nodded. "They're all there, in his night table drawer. A great, big stack. Her fist looks nothing like the anonymous note."

"Of course not." He snorted. "Admit it, Pippa, you only looked because you were curious. Not because you thought it would prove anything."

No, of course not. Whoever wrote the anonymous note wouldn't have used their own usual handwriting. That would have been too easy.

"How risqué were they?" Christopher wanted to know. He was trying to hold back laughter but not succeeding very well. "Did they make you blush, Pippa?"

"I didn't read them," I said, appalled. "I don't read other people's private correspondence, Christopher."

Christopher looked disappointed. "I would have done."

"You would not have enjoyed them, I assure you. They were full of outlandish endearments. Dearest darling pussycat, and the like."

"Ewww." He wrinkled his nose.

I nodded. "Precisely. I also saw Aunt Charlotte's note. The one from April."

Christopher sat up straighter. "The suicide note? What did it say? Anything pertaining to what we've been talking about?"

"I didn't read that either," I said. "Just the first line or two, enough to recognize it. That's all I read last time, as well."

Christopher didn't say anything, just sat silently. The silence was somehow very loud.

"It makes sense that he would keep it," I pointed out. "It was the last note his mother wrote to him. I have all the letters my mother wrote to me from Germany during the War."

They were somewhere. I couldn't tell you exactly where—it was seven years since she had died, and I had moved to London since then—but I knew I hadn't thrown them away.

"We should take a look," Christopher said.

"At the note? I don't know, Christopher. I've already been in Crispin's room once today. I don't fancy going back."

"But no one saw you," Christopher protested.

"I'm sorry to burst your bubble, but Laetitia saw me, in fact.

I had to tell her that I suspected Crispin of writing the note, and I was looking for a sample of his handwriting."

He stared at me. "She can't possibly have believed that. Surely she must know that you and Crispin have corresponded before. You ought to be familiar with his fist."

"She seemed to believe it," I said doubtfully, "although I suppose I might simply have dazzled her with my brilliance. But she saw me. And she might even have mentioned it to Crispin."

Who, if he was guilty of multiple murders, certainly wouldn't be happy to find me snooping around in his quarters for a second time today.

"Then you can stay here," Christopher said and rolled to his feet. "I want to read that letter."

He headed for the door. I trailed after. "There's not going to be anything interesting in it, Christopher. Even if you're right and they did commit the murders together, she wouldn't risk putting anything incriminating into a letter that the police would read."

"She was my aunt," Christopher said over his shoulder, "and he's my cousin. I might catch something that the police didn't." He reached for the doorknob.

"It's his," I said, a bit desperately. "It's personal. You have no right to it."

"There might be something there that proves that he didn't do it," Christopher said.

I watched him head into the hallway as the words ricocheted around in my head. I hesitated for barely a second before I followed.

"Wait for me."

CHAPTER SEVENTEEN

"YOU DON'T HAVE to come inside with me," Christopher said as we navigated the hallways from the west wing to the east. "If your conscience is bothering you, that is."

"That's below you, Christopher," I informed him as we trotted past the top of the stairs and the doors to the Duchess's Chamber and, five seconds later, the Duke's Chamber. "It sounds like something nasty and sarcastic that Crispin would say."

He flicked me a look. "And yet you won't invade his privacy to read his personal correspondence."

"It's personal! And I already did invade his privacy, don't forget. I have no objection to doing it again. I simply think the letter is a dead end, and we should leave it alone."

It was the final thing Crispin had left of his mother. We had no right to it.

Christopher didn't attempt to counter this very reasonable objection. "I just want a look at it," he said stubbornly.

I threw my hands up. "The whole thing is mad. You cannot possibly believe that Crispin is behind this. Why would he be?"

"If not Crispin," Christopher inquired as we turned the corner to the east wing, "then who?"

"I told you that. Lady Laetitia. She has every reason to want Crispin to become Duke of Sutherland so she can become duchess. And unlike him, she has coldblooded murderess written all over her."

Christopher snorted. "Why don't you tell me how you really feel, Pippa?"

"I just did. I feel as if Crispin is incapable of doing this, and that she is very much capable of it. He wouldn't frame me for Doctor Meadows's murder, Christopher. She would do."

Christopher didn't answer, just stopped in front of the door to Crispin's sitting room and glanced at me. "Last chance. Do you want to come inside with me, or stay in the hallway?"

"I'll stay," I said. "I've invaded St George's privacy enough for today."

He nodded. "Give the alert if anyone turns up."

"What sort of alert would you like?" I wanted to know as he turned towards the door.

He glanced at me over his shoulder. "Anything you can think of, Pippa. Two raps followed by three on the door?"

Certainly. Because rapping on the door in the rhythm of 'Duke of Sutherland' wouldn't appear suspicious at all.

"I'll do my best," I said, flapping a hand at him. "Go on. The quicker you do, the less likely I'll have to do anything at all. The letter is in the night table drawer on the side of the bed nearest the door. The obituary is there, as well."

He flashed me a grin before ducking through the door and shutting it behind himself. I leaned against the wall opposite the door to Christopher's bedchamber and fastened my eyes on it, the better to look as if I had some purpose in being here.

I don't know if you've ever been in the position of lookout, while you wait for someone to finish something they shouldn't be doing, that could get the both of you in trouble if you were caught. I have done—it wasn't the first time Christopher had put me in this position, nor was the opposite a lie, actually—and it's nerve-racking. The seconds tick by agonizingly slowly. It feels like every minute is ten, and like the ordeal will never end. It also feels as if you're liable to be caught at any second. If you're lucky, the person inside the room is quick and no one sees you standing there, but occasionally you're not lucky, and the door to the servants' stairs opens, and the Duke of Sutherland steps through.

I must admit that I was surprised to see him. Perhaps even shocked. Of all the people in the Hall, Uncle Harold was the last I would have expected to use the servants' stairs to get around.

Or perhaps not the last. That might have been Lady Euphemia, who always looked as if she were smelling something rank—probably me. But His Grace was certainly near the top of that list.

He looked equally surprised to see me. He stepped through the door, saw me standing there, and for a second, appeared as if he wished to duck back inside the stairwell. Then he looked from me to the door of his son's room, and his eyes narrowed.

"Miss Darling."

He does occasionally call me Philippa. Or did, when I was a child. The older I get, the less frequent it seems to be.

I dipped at the knees. He *was* the Duke of Sutherland, and I have been taught manners. I'll be polite to the man, especially in his own house, even if I do not particularly like him. "Your Grace."

I think of him as Uncle Harold, but I rarely call him that. Certainly not when he's addressing me formally.

"What are you doing here?"

"Waiting for Christopher," I said brightly, indicating the door across the hallway. "He's changing."

The duke looked mollified. Most likely he was happy that I wasn't lying in wait for his son and heir, or perhaps he appreciated the fact that I left Christopher to change in peace. In truth, if this had been a real situation, I would have been inside Christopher's room with him. I have seen him change plenty over the dozen years or so that we've lived together. As it was, I merely smiled politely and waited for His Grace to take his leave. It wouldn't do to have Christopher step out of Crispin's room while Crispin's father stood here.

"I don't suppose you can tell me what's going on in my carriage house?" the duke inquired.

I blinked. "Didn't Christopher explain when he fetched Tom earlier?"

Uncle Harold shook his head. "Kit fetched Detective Inspector Gardiner, but without telling the rest of us what had happened. I assumed it had something to do with that sad affair in the village—"

"Doctor Meadows, do you mean?"

He nodded. "—but then I saw several additional constables arrive and proceed into my carriage house. I thought perhaps you could enlighten me. You seem to know everything that goes on around here."

That sounded like a dig, and I wanted to take offense to it. But he was my host for the week, and nothing good would come from sniping back at him. I stuffed the inclination and took a breath before I told him, pleasantly, "I'm sorry to be the one to impart bad news. Something has happened to Alfie."

"Alfie?"

"Alfred," I said. "The footman?"

The duke nodded. "Of course. The one who occasionally serves as chauffeur now that Wilkins is gone."

"That's the one."

I don't know why I expected any sort of emotional response to the announcement, whether for the mention of Alfred or Wilkins, who had been Uncle Harold's nephew, even if no one had known that. Needless to say, there was no emotional response whatsoever.

"What was he doing in the carriage house?" Uncle Harold inquired. "I haven't required the use of the motorcar today."

"I'm afraid I don't know." Although it was a valid point. On a day when Uncle Harold wasn't going anywhere, Alfie had no business around the garage. He had duties in the house instead.

"And what happened to him?" Uncle Harold wanted to know.

"It looked as if someone hit him over the head with a blunt instrument."

Uncle Harold blinked. "Indeed?"

"That's what it seemed like to me. I don't know who or with what, although it's possible that the constables have found the murder weapon by now."

A noise to my right brought my head around in that direction. It took only a second for my mind to translate it into the sound a doorknob makes when it's turned, and I blanched. What a time for Christopher to come out of Crispin's room!

But then it turned out to be the door to the servants' staircase again. I had a single second to breathe out in relief before the door opened and I saw who stepped through.

"Father." Crispin looked from Uncle Harold to me. His brows drew together. "Darling?"

I managed a smile. "I'm sorry for loitering outside your door, St George. I'm waiting for Christopher to finish changing. I suspect he wants to get out of the clothes he wore when we found the body."

Crispin nodded and turned towards his own door. "If you'll excuse me."

I watched helplessly as he reached for the handle. There was nothing I could do. I couldn't rap on the door to alert Christopher; not with both of them standing here. And while I could have tried to keep Crispin here in the hallway, the jig would have been up when Christopher came out of his rooms anyway. Best, perhaps, to let Crispin go inside and catch his cousin *in flagrante*. Christopher might be able to talk his way out of the situation, and at least Uncle Harold wouldn't be privy to the confrontation.

I forced another smile and a pleasant nod. "Of course."

Crispin—who could no doubt see that it was forced—hesitated for a moment, eyes flicking between me and his father. But eventually he gave Uncle Harold a polite nod—"Father,"—and me another one, "Darling,"—before he pushed his door open and disappeared inside.

Uncle Harold eyed me.

"I think I'll see how Christopher's getting on," I said, and cut across the hallway to the opposite door. It felt somewhat like I was running away, but it was also moderately obvious that Uncle Harold wasn't going to leave me standing here, in the hallway outside his son's room, while his son was inside. "I'll see you at supper, Your Grace."

"Miss Darling," His Grace nodded, and watched as I ducked into Christopher's room.

I shut the door behind me and put my back against it before directing a bright, "How are you not finished yet, Christopher? You're taking forever!" to the empty room.

I couldn't replicate Christopher's voice, of course, so I had to keep talking to myself instead. Which I did by walking away from the door towards the window while I uttered the sort of inanities one might utter when talking to an invisible man in the middle of changing his clothes.

I kept it up for what felt like another eternity—offering to tie his tie for him, brushing imaginary lint off imaginary lapels; the whole thing took probably less than a minute, but felt longer—and then I turned back towards the door. "I'll just see you later," I told the empty air as I wrapped my hand around the handle and turned it. "I simply don't have the patience for this."

I pulled the door open and stepped into the hallway. Uncle Harold must have believed the subterfuge, because he was gone. I scurried across the hall and pushed Crispin's door open without knocking. They must still be in there, I figured, because surely I would have heard them yelling at one another had they emerged into the hallway while I'd been inside Christopher's room.

But perhaps I was wrong. I had expected to find them face to face, brandishing index fingers at one another. Instead, the suite of rooms was quiet. I stopped halfway into the sitting room and listened.

Could they have left without making any noise so I hadn't heard them?

But if so, why hadn't Christopher come into his own room? Surely he would have guessed that I would be there, if I wasn't in the hallway?

Or had they, perhaps, gone down to the parlor for a drink? But no, Crispin kept a drink cart in his sitting room—I was looking straight at it—so if bonding over alcohol was what they'd wanted, they wouldn't have had to leave for that.

Or—the back of my neck prickled—was Christopher right and I was wrong, and Crispin had caught him snooping and had killed him?

That would explain the silence.

My head lifted as I heard a muffled sound from the bedroom. Was someone crying? Had Crispin attacked Christopher and now he was mourning? Or had Christopher defended himself, and hurt Crispin, and now he was upset over it?

I strode in that direction and reached for the door.

It didn't occur to me to knock first, or to announce that I was there. As a result, when I walked in on Crispin, bare-chested and halfway out of his trousers, all I could do was stare.

For a second or two, until I swung on my heel and faced the sitting room, my cheeks burning. "Gah!"

"If you insist on arriving without notice," Crispin told me, not bothered in the least from the sound of his voice, "I'm afraid you'll get what you get."

After a moment he added, "It's not as if you haven't seen it all before."

I addressed the empty sitting room, even as I listened to the rustling of cloth behind me. "You know very well that I haven't. Just because you look like Christopher, doesn't mean you *are* Christopher."

And just because I had seen Christopher in the altogether —or as near as made no difference—didn't mean that this was at all the same thing.

I looked around the sitting room and saw no one. And while I had only gotten a glimpse of the bedroom before Crispin's semi-nudity had sent me running, I hadn't seen Christopher there, either. He wasn't in the logical place, on the edge of the bed. So where was he? Was he hiding, or had Crispin truly whacked him over the head and stowed him under the bed, preparatory to getting rid of him? Was that why he was changing his clothes, because he had gotten Christopher's blood on them?

Or, I realized as I looked at the little ormolu clock ticking away on the mantel, perhaps he was simply changing because it was getting close to cocktail time. Although that didn't explain where Christopher was.

"You can turn around now," Crispin informed me. "I'm decent."

I snorted. "I doubt that."

"I can't imagine what you might mean." He was tightening the belt of a rather nice dressing gown around his waist. The trousers were back on, or perhaps this was another pair, but the V of skin where he hadn't drawn the lapels of the gown close enough, was bare.

I averted my eyes and looked around the bedroom, as surreptitiously as I could manage. There was no sign of Christopher, dead or alive. For a moment I thought about asking about him, but then I decided against it. If Crispin didn't know that he had been here, if Christopher had heard him coming and had tucked himself away somewhere, I didn't want to give him away.

"Looking for something?" Crispin inquired solicitously, and I pulled my attention away from the rest of the room and back to him. He was still fiddling with the green brocade belt that belonged to his dressing gown.

"Of course not. Who would I be looking for?"

He smirked. "I thought perhaps you were wondering whether Laetitia was present."

It hadn't even crossed my mind, and I said so. "I suppose you got cold and wet standing outside."

"A bit of it, yes. Nothing a change of clothes and a nip of brandy won't cure. Can I interest you in a glass?"

He came towards me. I stepped out of the way and got a sardonic eyebrow for my trouble. He didn't say anything, just brushed past me, through the doorway and into the sitting room. Before I followed, I gave the bedroom one more comprehensive look. There was still no sign of Christopher, and no indication that he had been here.

"Don't mind if I do," I said and followed him into the sitting room.

"What's that?" He shot me a look over his shoulder from where he was standing in front of the bar cart. "Oh... brandy? Or something else?"

"Whatever's convenient," I said as I made my way over to one of the armchairs and took a seat. "Thank you."

"Don't mention it." He filled two glasses, crossed the floor to give me mine, and then took his own over to the other armchair and seated himself on it. After a sip of the honey-colored liquid and a pleased hum, he fixed me with a stare. "Do you plan to tell me what you're doing here, or just pretend that my finding you outside was a coincidence?"

"I don't know what you're talking about," I told him staunchly, and took a sip of my brandy.

He nodded, albeit not as if he believed me. "I'm sure. Where's Kit?"

"In his room," I said. "As I told you."

"And you left him there to follow me in here?" He arched a brow. "What will he say when he comes out and finds you gone, do you suppose?"

"I don't imagine he'll say much," I said. "He'll assume I've gotten tired of waiting and gone back to my own room, I daresay. Or perhaps downstairs."

Crispin nodded pleasantly. "Not likely to look for you here, then?"

"I imagine that this would be the last place he'd think to look for me," I agreed breezily, even as I wondered where this line of questioning was headed and whether I just imagined that it had a slight threatening quality to it.

But no. Surely Christopher wasn't right, and Crispin wasn't

thinking about strangling me and hiding me in his dressing room until he could get rid of my body?

My fingers tightened around the glass until I worried that I would accidentally break it. And then I forced myself to relax while telling myself that I was being silly. If Crispin attempted to do anything to me, I would brain him with the brandy glass. That would give Christopher time to intervene. I wasn't alone, I reminded myself. Christopher was still here somewhere. There was only one way into and out of Crispin's quarters, and it was the door in the sitting room. Christopher couldn't have left without me seeing him. He had to be hiding, biding his time.

"You know, Darling," Crispin said, watching me spiral, "if you were to tell me what's going on, I might be able to help."

"Nothing's going on," I said, a bit too fast. And then, to hide it, I took another swallow of brandy. It burned going down, and I coughed. I don't think I could have looked more guilty had I tried.

Crispin rolled his eyes. "Of course not. Where's Kit, really?"

I was still catching my breath. But my eyes flicked—entirely involuntarily, I swear—to the door to the bedroom.

"Truly?" He eyed the door speculatively for a moment before turning back to me. "Are you certain? We were both in there just a few minutes ago, and I didn't see him. Unless he was hiding under the bed...?"

I didn't answer. For all I knew, Christopher might have been hiding under the bed. All the old seventeenth-century beds are high off the ground; the better to keep the mice out, you know. And Christopher is slender, so there'd be plenty of room for him underneath the frame. Although it was far more likely that he would have taken refuge in the dressing room, I thought.

Crispin surged to his feet. I watched as he stalked towards the door to the bedroom, contemplating whether it would be better or worse for me to call out.

While I was still contemplating, Crispin raised his voice. "Come out, Kit. I know you're there."

There was a moment during which nothing happened, and during which I wondered whether I was wrong and Christopher had, somehow, made it out of Crispin's rooms without me seeing him. It was also a moment during which I kicked myself for having come in here for no reason, when Christopher wasn't even here.

And then there was the sound of footsteps from the other room, and the sulky appearance of my cousin—and Crispin's cousin—in the door to the bedroom.

"You just couldn't keep your mouth shut, could you?" he asked me.

I sniffed. "He's not stupid, you know. When I showed up here for no reason, he could tell that something was going on."

"Much obliged," Crispin said dryly as he returned to his chair. "Have a seat, Kit. Tell me what's going on. Feel free to get yourself a drink if it'll make the confession come out easier."

"Don't mind if I do." We sat in silence while Christopher splashed a finger of brandy into a glass before coming over to perch on the arm of my chair. I surmised I might have been forgiven, at least a little bit.

Crispin looked from him to me and back. "Am I right in thinking that the two of you have concocted another fantasy in which I'm guilty of murder?"

I raised my hands. "Don't look at me. I didn't believe it."

That single eyebrow rose. "Not even for the past few minutes, when you've been sitting here wondering whether I strangled Kit with a belt before you came in?"

"Perhaps then," I admitted. "You have to admit you were acting sinister on purpose."

He sniggered. "Perhaps just a bit."

He turned to his cousin. "What's going on in your head, Kit? Who am I supposed to have murdered this time?"

When Christopher didn't answer—because he was sipping on his brandy, probably for the express purpose of avoiding having to answer—I said, "Everyone from your grandfather and your mother to Doctor Meadows and Alfie."

His eyes widened. "My mother wasn't murdered!"

"But all the others were."

"Not by me!" Crispin said. "Why would I murder Alfie, for God's sake? Or Doctor Meadows? The man's never been anything but nice to me."

"He was there when you were born," I pointed out, and he looked at me in silence for a moment. I could almost see the thoughts clicking through his head, adding up, one on top of the other, and as usual—he's always been smart—it didn't take long for him to arrive at a conclusion.

"I see what this is about. How long have you known?"

"I only found out about an hour ago," I said, while Christopher confessed, "I listened outside Father's study window that weekend in July when the story about Wilkins came out."

Crispin nodded. "I thought you looked at me rather queerly when Philippa and I turned up."

"You mean—" I looked from one to the other of them. "The two of you haven't discussed this?"

Neither of them said anything, and I turned to Christopher. "You discovered that your cousin was your brother four months ago, and the two of you didn't talk about it? Then, or since then?"

"There was nothing to discuss," Christopher defended

himself. Which was rich, if you asked me, and also entirely false. There was quite a lot to discuss, in my opinion.

Crispin must have agreed, because he snorted. "If I had known what you overheard, I would have brought it up, Kit. Don't you think it's something we ought to talk about?"

"No," Christopher said. "The walls have ears, and you never know who might be listening. Besides, you left a few hours later, and it's not as if there weren't plenty of other things to figure out at that point."

That was true. Wilkins had been dead, and there had been the question of what to do with little Bess, not to mention Crispin's obsession with talking his father into buying the Rolls Royce Phantom. But—

"It was four months ago," I pointed out again. "It's not as if you haven't spoken since."

"But that was about other things. And there was always something else that took precedence. First you met Wolfgang, and then Crispin proposed to Laetitia, and I wasn't about to bring it up during the engagement party at Marsden Manor—"

No, certainly not.

"And then you got yourself engaged to the bastard—" Crispin supplied, and I turned to him.

"It wasn't a real engagement. And he wasn't a bastard then."

"He was always a bastard," Crispin said. "You just hadn't realized it yet."

Christopher gave him an approving nod. "Quite right. And he tried to kill you—" This was me again, "—and kidnapped me, and then he kidnapped you, too. When was I supposed to have a heart to heart with Crispin about anything else?"

"Between those happenings?" I suggested, and Christopher threw his hands up. Literally. Brandy splashed everywhere.

"Bloody hell." He eyed the spots on his trousers ruefully.

"Fine, Pippa. It wasn't something I wanted to discuss, all right. That sort of thing is much better kept under wraps. Once you say it out loud—"

"It becomes real," Crispin finished. "And I don't think anyone wants that."

Christopher shook his head. "I certainly don't. I have no designs on the title. I'd have to get married and produce an heir if I were Duke of Sutherland. And I know what you said, Pippa, but you'll have to excuse me. I have no desire to wed you and bed you just to keep up the succession."

Crispin eyed me over his glass. "Is that a possibility?"

"No," Christopher said, at the same time as I qualified, "Not a very likely one, I suppose. If we're both unmarried at thirty, we said we'd consider it. But—"

"Pippa isn't likely to last to thirty," Christopher said. "Or at least I thought not, until a few months ago."

A few months ago, that statement might have confused me. As it was, I knew that he was referring to Crispin's engagement to Laetitia. And so did Crispin. His cheeks colored.

"You wouldn't be first in line anyway," I told Christopher. "Francis is first after your father. And you know that he and Constance will have children."

"You never know who can or cannot have children," Christopher said, and I watched Crispin wince at the reminder. Christopher winced, too, once he realized what he had said. A beat of silence followed. Then we all took a collective breath.

"With that out of the way," Crispin said, "what were you trying to prove, skulking around in my dressing room, Kit?"

Christopher muttered something.

"He was being daft," I said, so Christopher wouldn't have to. "Here's the thing, St George. On paper, what we just discussed serves as motive for every one of these murders.

Grimsby figured it out and told your grandfather, who called your mother on the carpet. Lydia Morrison left your mother's employ when you were a few months old, presumably because she knew the truth. Margaret Hughes was her replacement, and she figured it out, most likely from Grimsby but perhaps from Morrison or your mother. Doctor Meadows delivered you, so he might have known. He did know that you were born 'prematurely—'" I used my fingers to make quotes around the word, "—which would indicate that the delivery date didn't line up with your father's... with Uncle Harold's expectations."

"And you thought I killed them all?"

"No," I said, with a glance at Christopher. "I know you wouldn't do that."

"You thought I'd killed Grandfather and Grimsby in April."

"That was before I got to know you better," I said.

He muttered something non-committal, and I added, "Come now, St George. You rescued me from a fate worse than death a month ago. You can't tell me we aren't friends."

"She's got you there, old man," Christopher opined, and Crispin scowled for a moment before acquiescing.

"Very well. We're friendly, and you didn't believe me guilty of murder."

"Not this time," I said. "But you have to admit it's all a bit suspicious. First your mother kills her father-in-law and his valet, and then herself. Then her former lady's maid goes missing. Her current lady's maid is murdered. Then her former lady's maid is murdered. Then her doctor is murdered. Then the footman, or perhaps I should say chauffeur, is murdered—"

"Someone left that night," Christopher interrupted. "The night before we motored to Upper Slaughter. I heard a motorcar."

Crispin shook his head. "It wasn't me. I went to bed after

we spoke, and I didn't wake up until morning. I only woke then because I had set an alarm."

"You did seem rather sleepy at the end of our talk," Christopher confirmed. "Unusually so, I'd say. I don't suppose you ate or drank anything that might have put you to sleep?"

Crispin sneered. "I assure you that I can hold my liquor, Kit."

I rolled my eyes. "Not like that, you nitwit. He's wondering whether someone doped you."

"Not that I can noticed. But I suppose it's possible. You and I didn't have anything to drink while we were talking. Before that, it's anyone's guess."

"I assure you I didn't go out of my way to dope you," I said dryly. "I wouldn't have minded if you'd come along with us. Nor would Francis or Constance."

"The obvious suspect," Christopher said, "is your fiancée. You wouldn't hesitate to accept a drink from her, and she had incentive to..." He floundered for a moment before settling on, "...to keep you home."

"Aside from that," I added, "Laetitia also has the most to lose if the truth comes out. Apart from you, of course, Crispin. But you said you didn't motor up to the Cotswolds and kill Morrison, and someone did."

"And you think it was Laetitia?"

I opened my mouth, but Christopher got there first. "That would depend on what she knows—"

Crispin turned to him. "I certainly haven't told her!"

"I didn't think you had done," I told him calmly. "It isn't news we want to get out, is it? But she may have found out the same way Christopher did."

Perhaps even by listening to the very same conversation. The Marsdens had been there at Beckwith Place that weekend, and Crispin had been with me, so there was no telling where

Laetitia had been. She might well have been outside the door to the study with her ears peeled.

"That's a bit disingenuous of you, Darling," Crispin commented. "It's not as if you are above dropping at eaves yourself."

No, I wasn't. "Nor are you."

He smirked. "We're both as bad as the other, then. But that doesn't mean that Laetitia is in the habit of pressing her dainty ears to keyholes."

I sniffed. "I'm afraid I hadn't noticed her ears. Although I don't suppose they'll remain dainty for long, considering the weight of the diamonds you gave her."

"Dear me," Crispin said, "is that jealousy I hear, Darling?"

"You wish. Not only would I not have the Sutherland diamonds as a gift, I'm sure she'll end up with holes the size of grapes in her earlobes. Overly ostentatious, heavy things, they are."

"Be that as it may," Christopher said, "other than Crispin himself, she has the most to lose if word gets out that he's not the heir to the Sutherland title. How are her skills behind the wheel, Crispin? Could she have made it to the Cotswolds and back while we were sleeping, if she made certain to dope you to make sure you wouldn't go looking for her?"

"I wouldn't go looking for her anyway. I'm not going to misbehave in my ancestral home with her brother next door and Philippa across the hall."

He flicked a glance at me, and seemed to realize what he'd said, because he flushed. "How long of a drive did you say that it is?"

Christopher told him how long it had taken Francis to motor from Sutherland Hall to Upper Slaughter the next day, and Crispin nodded. "Anyone could make that drive overnight. And any of the motorcars in the garage—or at least the

Phantom or the H6, or the Marsdens' Daimler—could have made the trip easily."

"She said you were called into the study by your father, St George, after the interlude in the maze this morning. Is that correct?"

He nodded. "The interlude, as you call it, was a cigarette. The weather wasn't conducive for necking in the outdoors. But yes, Father had some paperwork for me to look over regarding the situation."

"Which situation?"

"The engagement," Crispin said. "The marriage. The dowry." He flapped a hand.

"Your bride-to-be wasn't invited to look at it?"

"That would defeat the purpose," Crispin said. "No, she pushed off, and so did Father after handing me the stack and telling me to go through it."

"And how long would you say you were in the study? Long enough for your fiancée to make it to the village, kill Doctor Meadows, and come back?"

"It's not a far distance," Crispin said. "I wouldn't be surprised."

There was a moment of silence. "Do you believe she might have done?" I asked.

He looked at me for a moment. "It seems that someone did do, doesn't it? And there are only so many of us who have motive. Or opportunity."

"It wasn't us," I said, with a glance at Christopher. "Not that Christopher wouldn't kill for you, and not that I wouldn't help him get rid of the body if he did kill someone—"

They exchanged a glance and smirked.

"But we wouldn't kill someone over this." Preserving Crispin's place in the succession wasn't important enough to me to kill someone over, especially if the news getting out would get Laetitia off his back.

"I was stuck in the study with the paperwork," he said. "Not that I can prove that."

"I'm sure Uncle Harold would swear that he left you there with a task and a stack of paper," Christopher told him, "if it came to that."

Crispin nodded. "No doubt. We should have a talk, Kit. Long overdue though it is."

Christopher agreed. "Will you excuse us, Pippa?"

"Of course." I pushed to my feet. "I'll go get ready for supper. I'll see you both downstairs later."

They both nodded. Neither made a move to get up. I walked to the door and let myself out.

CHAPTER EIGHTEEN

"ACCORDING TO THE CORONER," Tom said, "Alfred died during the same time period as Lionel Meadows, and from the same sort of wound."

It was hours later. The cocktail hour had come and gone, and so had supper, before the constables finished their inquiries in the carriage house and left. The van from the mortuary had taken Alfie's body away, and the coroner—a chap from Salisbury, since Doctor Meadows wasn't around to do the honors—must have had time to compare the bodies, if what Tom said was true.

"A wound caused by what?" I wanted to know. I was perched on the arm of Christopher's chair in a corner of the game room, with a glass of gin and tonic in my hand.

Laetitia made a moue of distaste. "Really, Miss Darling—"

"I want to know," I said. "These were people we knew. I realize they were strangers to you, but—"

"Enough, Darling," Crispin said. He was perched on the arm of Laetitia's chair in the same fashion I was, and she looked up at him adoringly when he came to her rescue. "Just because you're as cold-blooded as a snake, doesn't mean that everyone is."

I sniffed, offended. "I'm not cold-blooded, St George. Quite the opposite, in fact. I knew Alfie. I'm upset that someone killed him. I'm sorry that it's unpleasant to think about, but I want to know who did it. And how."

"With a wrench," Tom said calmly. "We found it on the floor of the carriage house, under one of the motorcars."

"Which motorcar?"

"The Daimler," Tom said, as Laetitia blanched and Geoffrey's head came up, "but I don't think that matters. Whoever used it, simply tossed it out of sight on their way through the carriage house after committing the crime. The fact that it ended up under the Daimler and not one of the other motorcars was simply the luck of the draw."

"Fingerprints?" I wanted to know.

Tom shook his head. "Whoever did it wore gloves. Everyone does these days."

"Especially this time of year," Christopher agreed. "And whoever did it would have come from the outside. Not strange if he—or she—kept their gloves on. Even in the infirmary."

Tom nodded. "Not strange at all."

We were all gathered in a corner of the game room, with the exception of Geoffrey, who had joined the older generation for a game of cards. With Aunt Roz and Uncle Herbert gone, it was just Uncle Harold and the earl and countess left, and they needed someone for a fourth. A game Geoffrey was now ignoring in favor of listening to our conversation.

He had been strangely subdued this weekend. Which had been pleasant, don't get me wrong. Fending off Lord Geoffrey's advances was always a chore. But it did cross my mind to wonder whether the personality change—and his current rapt attention—signified anything murderous.

He had been alone in his bedchamber for part of the morning, so he could have gone to the carriage house, and from there into Little Sutherland, without anyone noticing. He might have murdered both Alfie and Doctor Meadows. Although surely, after such a close call just weeks ago, he wouldn't want to risk the gallows again so soon?

Besides, what would his motive be? He hardly knew either of them.

Unless his mind had been destroyed by what had happened to him, of course, and he had lost the plot. He didn't like me much, so trying to frame me for the crime might have been motive enough. And his sister despised me, which was additional incentive for getting me in trouble, I assumed.

"...don't you think, Miss Darling?"

"I certainly do," I said, still in my own little world. And then I blinked awake. "Wait... what?"

Laetitia was looking at me. So was everyone else. "Don't you think it likely," she repeated, or at least I assumed it was a repetition of the previous question, "that this is all connected? From the maid to Doctor Meadows to the footman?"

Her eyes were challenging, while Crispin's were flat, opaque. Christopher's were worried; I could feel his concerned gaze on the side of my head. Tom's expression was cautious, and when he met my eyes, he gave an almost imperceptible shake of his head.

"I'd hardly think so," I said, in spite of knowing full well that it was almost certainly all connected. "Most of us never even met Morrison, and the rest of you haven't seen her for months. It's much more likely that she ran afoul of someone in Upper Slaughter. Shreve said that she wasn't very friendly. She probably rubbed someone the wrong way."

"And the other maid?" Laetitia wanted to know. "Did she rub someone the wrong way, too?"

"She must have done." I turned to Tom. "You were there—afterwards, I mean. There was no indication that it wasn't simply a random crime, was there?"

Tom shook his head. "The Bristol constabulary had their eyes on a few of the usual suspects, they said. The ones with a penchant for money and the lack of self-control not to grab for it, you know. She was a relative newcomer with enough of the ready to catch someone's notice."

Thanks to Uncle Herbert's blackmail payment. And also, Hughes had been Aunt Charlotte's lady's maid for a number of years, so it wouldn't be surprising if the latter had provided a little something for Hughes in her will, as well. Or if Uncle Harold had done, as severance when he let her go.

"The same was true for Lydia Morrison," Tom added. "A single woman of a certain age with the means to purchase a nice home. She might have been a bit too flash around the village or chapel, perhaps. Someone might have decided it was worth the trouble to go inside her cottage that night, and when she woke up, he or she had to silence Morrison with the means available."

"Have you heard anything new since the inquest?" I wanted to know.

Tom shook his head. "They have no reason to communicate with me. None of this concerns Scotland Yard."

"But surely the constables do at least believe that the doctor's death, and that of the footman, are related," Laetitia insisted.

Tom pretended not to have noticed the not-quite-furtive-enough glance she directed my way. "Of course. Two men killed within a half mile of each other, the same morning, and with the same weapon. It's likely that the same hand wielded it both times."

"And are they any closer to figuring out whose hand that might have been?"

I rolled my eyes. "They don't think it was mine, so there's no need to look at me like that."

"The note said it was you," Laetitia said.

"I'm well aware of that." I turned to Tom. "Were you able to get everyone's writing sample earlier?"

"I'm afraid I had to abandon the experiment," Tom said apologetically, "when Kit came and fetched me. I would finish now, but everyone is a bit too much under the influence, I'm afraid. Such things are better done sober."

"Every sample I saw looked the same anyway," Christopher said, and Tom nodded.

"I don't suppose the constables had anything interesting to say earlier?"

"Not to me," Tom said. "They accepted my help because I was here, and I have dealt with more crime scenes than they have, but I'm not involved in the case otherwise. There was no need to update me on what they'd discovered."

"But you must have heard them talk to each other." Francis fiddled lazily with the fringe on Constance's evening frock as he spoke. "They've interviewed the villagers, haven't they? Hadn't anyone seen anything this morning?"

"One woman saw Pippa arrive and then leave again," Tom said with a glance at me. "She said Pippa was accompanied by a young man who looked like Lord St George."

Laetitia made a face. I shook my head, and so did both Christopher and Crispin.

"I was in the study looking at paperwork," Crispin said, while Christopher added, "We left Sutherland Hall while Crispin and Lady Laetitia were in the garden maze."

Tom nodded. "The witness said that the people she saw only stayed inside the infirmary for a couple of minutes, and that they looked no different when they left than when they arrived."

No, of course not. We had had no reason to scurry away like guilty people.

"I assume she didn't see it necessary to check on Doctor Meadows," I said, and Tom shook his head.

"She's also not the person who wrote the note. The constables tested her, and she spelled Philippa wrong."

Yes, that's easy to do, between the double and single Ls and Ps.

"Someone else mentioned having seen a black motorcar at the approximate time of the murder," Tom continued, "and we're assuming that was Lord Herbert and Lady Roslyn motoring through Little Sutherland on their way to Beckwith—"

"Before," I said, and Tom broke off to look at me. I clarified, "It must have been before the murder. Doctor Meadows was still alive when we left the infirmary, and we didn't see the Bentley on our way home, did we, Christopher?"

Christopher shook his head. "They must have been past the infirmary before we came out. And as Pippa said, he was still alive then."

Tom didn't respond. Instead, he informed us blandly, "There's enough room to park behind the infirmary, and there's a spot of oil on the ground there that indicates that a motorcar might have stood there for a bit earlier today."

"Why just today?" I wanted to know. "Why not yesterday, or the day before?"

Francis shook his head, and Tom said, "The heavy rain last night would have washed away anything from before this morning."

"But it's been raining off and on most of the day. Surely

anything from this morning would have been washed away too?"

He shook his head. "I'm afraid not, Pippa. The mizzle hasn't been heavy enough to wash away an oil slick. The storm last night would have done."

"Do you suspect Aunt Roz and Uncle Herbert, then?"

Tom hesitated, and Christopher turned to stone next to me. Across the table, Francis's brows lowered.

"I'm not in charge of the case," Tom said eventually, "so it doesn't matter what I think. But I can tell you that Constable Daniels hasn't sent anyone to Beckwith to bring them back here. Or hadn't, as of this afternoon."

"Has he spoken to them?" Christopher wanted to know. The tension in his body was evident in his voice too, now.

"He said he had done," Tom confirmed. "Your parents said they hadn't seen either of you after you left Sutherland Hall, and they didn't notice anything out of the ordinary while they motored through the village."

He didn't add, "but of course that's what they would say." I heard it, nonetheless. And so must Christopher have done, because he asked again, "Do you suspect my parents of murder, Tom?"

"No, Kit," Tom said. "Of course not."

"You suspected my father enough that you stopped by Beckwith Place after Hughes was killed."

"That was for their protection," Tom said steadily. "Not because I thought either of them was guilty."

"And he did have an alibi," I said. "Didn't he? You said that he did do."

Tom nodded. "He had been with Lady Roslyn all day. And with Francis and Constance that night."

"My parents aren't murderers," Francis said stiffly.

"I agree," Christopher said, and I nodded.

"Aunt Roz and Uncle Herbert had no reason to want Doctor Meadows dead. They certainly had no reason to kill Alfie. Doctor Meadows was still alive when Aunt Roz and Uncle Herbert left Sutherland Hall."

That might not have been the reason Alfie was killed, of course. The footman-cum-chauffeur might be dead now because he knew something about the night Morrison died. Such as who had been behind the wheel of that motorcar Christopher said he had heard leave, for instance.

But we had tried to make it sound like there was no connection between Morrison's murder and what had happened here, and now we were stuck with it.

I got to my feet. "I think it's time I turned in. It's been a long day, and this might be the last night in a while I get to sleep in my own bed, if Constable Daniels decides to arrest me tomorrow."

Laetitia's eyes glinted in delight. Everyone else—save for Tom and Crispin—assured me that he wouldn't do. I was fairly certain that Crispin didn't join in because his fiancée wouldn't like it, but the fact that Tom didn't protest did, I must admit, fill me with a measure of worry. If Tom thought I might be arrested, there seemed a real chance that it might happen.

And Christopher seemed to have come to the same conclusion, because he pushed to his feet, too, protectively. "I'll walk you up, Pippa."

"He's not going to haul me off between here and my room, Christopher," I told him.

He directed a narrow look at Tom across the table. "Perhaps not. But I'd rather not give him the opportunity."

Tom rolled his eyes. "I have no authority to arrest anyone, Kit. I'm here as a guest."

"And if he wanted to arrest me," I added, "neither your

presence, nor the fact that I was in my room, would make any difference."

Tom shook his head. "But I solemnly swear that I won't break your door down overnight to take you off to prison."

"I appreciate that. You'll forgive me if I lock myself in in spite of your assurances."

Unless I missed my guess, and it truly had been one of the villagers who had murdered Alfie and Doctor Meadows—and Morrison and Hughes, and perhaps Duke Henry and Grimsby —there was a murderer on the loose in Sutherland Hall, and I'd feel better with a locked door between myself and whoever it was.

"You do that," Tom said. "In fact—" He glanced around the circle of faces, "—you should all do that. Lock your doors, don't wander the halls overnight, and if it seems like a good idea, spend the night with someone else."

Laetitia turned doe eyes on Crispin. He flushed.

I scoffed. "I'm certain a locked door will be sufficient. Along with, perhaps, a cricket bat."

"I'm afraid I would have to visit the carriage house for that," Crispin said, "and I assume that's off limits, Gardiner?"

Tom nodded. "Just for the time being, you know. If you need a motorcar tomorrow, I'm sure that can be arranged. As long as you'd be allowed to leave, of course."

Crispin's eyebrow rose. "Is there a particular reason I might not be allowed to leave?"

"None that I know of," Tom said, which didn't really answer the question. And Crispin must have realized it, although he didn't pursue the subject any further. He did catch my eye for just a second, though.

"On that note," I told Christopher, "let's go, if you're seeing me up."

"We'll all go," Francis said, and got to his feet. "Up you come, Connie."

He extended a hand to his fiancée, who allowed herself to be assisted to her feet. Crispin offered his elbow to Laetitia, who latched on with a clear look of ownership, and we headed for the door, with Tom bringing up the rear.

The Marsdens and Uncle Harold called it a night at the same time—it was hard to say whether it was because of our discussion, or whether they had simply finished their game at the same time we were leaving—but the three older adults headed up the main staircase while Geoffrey attached himself to our party as we made our way down through the west wing. Behind me, I could hear Geoffrey making inquiries of Tom as to what was going on, and Tom repeating the advice about keeping the bedchamber door locked overnight due to the recent murder on the premises.

Geoffrey blanched, I saw, when I glanced over my shoulder as we entered the staircase.

The servants' stairs are narrow, so we had to proceed up two by two. Christopher and I went first, followed by Francis and Constance, then Crispin and Laetitia, and finally the two unattached gentlemen.

Had there been any justice in the world, of course Tom would have been escorting Christopher—I'm certain Christopher would have liked that—but that would have left me prey to Geoffrey, so it was just as well that he didn't. Besides, I was equally sure that once we got upstairs, Christopher would deposit me in my room, wait for the door to close, and then Tom would find an excuse for walking my two cousins and Crispin to the other wing.

And right on schedule—

"I'll see the three of you to the other side of the Hall," Tom told Christopher—and by extension, Francis and Crispin—as the three of them saw their various charges to their various bedroom doors. Geoffrey hesitated in his for a moment, but ended up going inside without a word to anyone. He hadn't even looked at me. We heard the key turn in the lock and then the scrape as it was removed to, I presumed, a safer spot on the bedside table.

Tom nodded approvingly. "Make certain you all do that."

I fully intended to. I also planned to wedge a chair under the handle, to ensure that no one could break the door down and come in. Or not without making a lot of noise, at any rate.

But first— "We'll have to visit the facilities before bed, you know."

"We can wait," Christopher offered dutifully.

I shook my head. "Don't be silly, Christopher. If anyone accosts me in the next five minutes, I'll scream loudly enough that you'll hear me, even on the other side of the Hall."

He looked doubtful, and I added, "Besides, whoever is doing this seems to have set me up as scapegoat, haven't they? They aren't likely to kill me."

Unless my death was set up as a suicide, of course, wherein I ostensibly killed myself and left a convenient note taking the blame for it all, the way Aunt Charlotte had done.

Or not done, as the case may be.

"I have no plans of committing suicide," I announced, preemptively. "If I'm discovered dead in the morning, with a note taking responsibility for all the murders, know that I didn't do it."

Christopher snorted. "As if I would ever believe something like that."

"Nor would I," Francis added, and Constance nodded.

"We'll avenge you, Pippa."

"Hopefully that won't be necessary," I said, "but thank you."

"Would you like me to fetch you something from the gunroom?" Crispin wanted to know, solicitously, and I rolled my eyes.

"No, St George. I'm not worried."

Christopher nodded. "Very well, then. Good night, Pippa. See that you survive until morning."

I promised I would do, and then I watched the four men wander down the hall toward the central wing.

"If you'd like to use the loo first," I told Constance, "I'll stand guard."

She nodded. "I'll just fetch my sponge bag."

She disappeared into her room. I did the same.

CHAPTER NINETEEN

I GAVE my room a quick once-over as I gathered my supplies. Nothing seemed out of place or out of order, but with just a few seconds to look around, it was difficult to be certain. I promised myself I would do a more thorough search before I went to bed, before grabbing up my things and heading back into the hallway.

To my surprise, Laetitia was waiting, as well. "I might as well come along," she said airily, as if someone had invited her. "We all need to use the lavatory, and this way no one is alone."

"The more, the merrier," I agreed. I didn't particularly want her here, of course, but it did make sense for us all to go as a group, and this way I wouldn't have to worry about Geoffrey getting over his strange restraint and sidling up to me while I was waiting for Constance.

The latter ducked inside the loo with her sponge bag while Laetitia and I stationed ourselves outside. On either side of the door, with at least three feet separating us.

"You don't really believe that we're in danger, do you?" were the first words out of her mouth.

"I can't imagine that *you* are," I answered. "You don't know anything about what's going on, do you?"

She shook her head. "Do you?"

"I know who had motive and opportunity," I said.

She straightened. "Who?"

"I'm not telling you. Then you'd be in danger, too."

That wasn't the reason, of course. But as expected, it stopped her from asking any further questions. Instead, she sank her teeth into her lower lip and stared at me.

"Just out of curiosity," I asked, "did you happen to hear a motorcar leaving Sutherland Hall the night Morrison died?"

"I was in my room," Laetitia said. "In the west wing." After a moment she added, sounding annoyed, "Crispin was tired."

The implication being that had he not been, they would have spent the night together.

"So he mentioned," I said, and I don't think I sounded particularly one way or the other about it, although she gave me a narrow look. I added, "I don't suppose you'd have any idea why anyone would want to make sure that he slept through the night that night, would you?"

There was a beat. "Did someone do that?"

"It seems as if someone might have done," I said. "He slept unusually soundly, he said. Almost as if someone wanted to make certain of it."

There was another moment of silence before Laetitia said, "Perhaps you should inquire of your cousin."

My back stiffened. "What is that supposed to mean? Which cousin?"

"Crispin and your cousin Kit went up together," Laetitia inquired, "didn't they?"

It was less a question than a slightly malicious reminder, and I'm happy to say that I kept my temper when I told her, "So they did. But Christopher had no reason to dope Crispin.

And if you intended it as a dig at Francis, he doesn't take Veronal anymore."

Laetitia looked politely skeptical, and I scowled. "Neither of them would have had any reason to put Crispin to sleep, because neither of them had a motive for killing Morrison. Why would either of them—either of *us*—want her dead? We've never even seen her!"

Unlike Laetitia, who had grown up a quarter mile down the lane from Morrison. Not that that was likely to have had anything to do with the maid's murder, but it was still a fact.

"Why would anyone?" Laetitia asked. It sounded rhetorical, but the expression in her eyes said otherwise.

I opened my mouth to answer, but before I could get the first word out, the lavatory door opened, and Constance stepped out, smelling of cold cream and mint. "Next," she said brightly.

I shut my mouth again, chagrined. Laetitia eyed me for a moment, perhaps hoping that I would go on, but when I didn't, she ducked inside the lavatory before I could even inquire as to whether she wanted to go first. Constance arched her brows. "Something wrong?"

"Nothing more than the usual," I said. "I almost told her who I suspect of killing Morrison, and why."

If Constance hadn't opened the door, I would have blurted out the whole thing, and without knowing whether Laetitia knew about it or not.

"Well, don't tell me," Constance said, as the water turned on inside the lavatory. "I don't want to know."

"Safer for you that way, no doubt."

Not that I thought Constance was in any danger whatsoever. I doubted that what was going on had anything to do with her.

She shook her head when I said so. "I don't see how.

Although if you're looking for people with motive, I'm on the list, you know."

I blinked. "What on earth are you talking about, Constance?"

"Well, you never even met Morrison, did you, Pippa? Nor did Francis or Christopher. Of course neither of you would kill her. But I knew her. And I didn't like her very much. She was always nice to Mother and to Johanna, but she wasn't nice to me."

"Well…" I cast about for something to say. "I suppose, if you want to look at it that way."

It seemed a poor motive for murder, though. Especially when Lady Peckham and her ward were both dead now, and neither of them by Constance's hand.

For a second—just a second, I swear—I wondered whether it was possible that Gilbert Peckham had taken the blame for his sister, and it was in fact Constance who had murdered their mother as well as Johanna, and now she had murdered Morrison, too.

Then reason reared its head, and I shook off the delusion. "Don't be silly, Constance. Nobody would take that seriously as a motive for murder."

"Anything can be a motive for murder," Constance said serenely. "It depends on the person doing the murdering."

Yes, of course it did. "But you'd have to be mad to kill your mother's maid over something like that. Especially when she was already miles and miles away and you didn't have to deal with her ever again."

Constance shrugged. "I'm merely mentioning it. You just never know."

You didn't. Although I was fairly certain that I didn't have to lose sleep over this particular possibility. "Tom's right, anyway. It's none of our concern. The Bristol police are dealing with Hughes, and the Stow-on-the-Wold constabulary is dealing with Morrison, and Constable Daniels is dealing with Doctor Meadows and Alfie. None of them need our help to figure this out."

"No," Constance agreed. "You should stay out of it, Pippa. You'll be much safer that way."

Yes, indeed. And while that statement might have sounded like a threat to anyone who didn't know Constance, I didn't think she had threats in her, let alone murder. "I'll do that. Do you want to go to your room while I wait for Laetitia, or would you prefer to stay here with me?"

"I'll wait with you," Constance said placidly, and leaned against the wall next to me with every appearance of someone settling in for the duration.

Laetitia emerged from the lavatory a minute or two later, trailing the scent of roses and her diaphanous negligee. As I ducked into the loo myself, I reflected that she really is unfairly attractive, even without a single speck of makeup on her face. I'm certainly not ugly—I was looking at myself in the mirror, so I could see the truth for myself—but the best thing that can be said about me is that I'm cute. Meanwhile, Laetitia is the sort of gorgeous that can launch ships and start wars, and that makes grown men trip over their own feet in the streets and lose track of their conversations.

For a moment, while I scooped cold cream out of the jar and slapped it on my face, I wondered whether Christopher might be right and Crispin really could have killed multiple people to preserve his future with her.

I didn't think that Christopher was wrong about Crispin's feelings for me. Not now that I had had some time to come to terms with the idea of them. But there was also the fact that he had never acted on those feelings, and had proposed to Laetitia instead of me. I liked to pity him for being trapped in an engagement with a woman he didn't love, but the truth was that he had never once displayed any regrets for having made that decision.

So yes, he might imagine that he loved me. It might even be true. But when it came right down to it, he had chosen Laetitia over me. And having once made that choice, how far would he go to keep her?

She was gone by the time I came back out of the lavatory, and I don't know why that should have come as a surprise. "Where's Laetitia? Surely she didn't leave you here alone?"

"I sent her back to her room," Constance said. "She was being herself—"

I translated 'herself' as 'annoying and condescending.'

"—and she wasn't supposed to be here in the first place, so I got rid of her. We didn't need her. You and I do very well on our own."

Constance tucked her hand through my arm as we headed down the hallway towards our respective doors.

"Of course we do." I peeled my ears as we passed Laetitia's door, but I couldn't hear anything from within. "Are you worried, Constance? We can share tonight if you'd rather."

We'd done it before, both at Godolphin as children, and more recently, at the Dower House in May.

But Constance shook her head. "I'm not worried. Even if there is a murderer on the loose, he has no reason to want to murder *me*. I don't know anything. Although... would *you* feel better if we shared, Pippa?"

I shook my head. "I'm fine. Not at all worried."

That was a lie, of course. But if anyone came to kill me, I'd rather not put Constance in the line of fire. Whoever was doing this wasn't concerned about collateral damage, or Alfie would still be with us, and there was no reason to risk Constance by putting her in bed next to me.

And at any rate, I was more concerned about who the murderer was, and what would happen to him, than I was about being murdered.

She squeezed my arm. "Are you certain?"

"Positive," I said steadily, and stopped outside her door. "Here we are. Do you want me to come in while you check the room?"

She shook her head. "No one was there when I fetched my sponge bag earlier. And someone has been in the corridor every second since. I'm sure it's empty."

"Wait here, then," I said, "until I get to my door, and then we'll go in and lock our doors at the same time."

She nodded, and I wandered down the hallway to the next door. "Be sure to put something under the door handle before you go to sleep," I told her.

"You, too," Constance said, holding her door open. "On three?"

We counted to three and then we both stepped across our respective thresholds and turned the keys in the locks. I took mine over to the nightstand and put it next to the water carafe. That done, I grabbed the chair from the escritoire and wedged it under the handle.

After that I did go over the rest of the room for anything that shouldn't be there, but saw nothing out of the ordinary. My clothes were where they should be, and my toiletries ditto, and nothing had been added that I could see, other than the replenished water in the carafe. After all that, I changed into my favorite pair of blue satin pyjamas and crawled onto the bed with a pen and a notepad. Perhaps if I wrote things down, it would be easier for me to figure them out.

Chronologically, then:

Uncle Herbert had bedded his brother's wife twenty-four years ago. From what my uncle had told me in July, Aunt Roz was aware of what had happened. That either meant that she'd known all along, and it had been agreed upon between them that Uncle Herbert would do this to help Aunt Charlotte, or everyone had become aware of the situation in April of this year.

But no, Uncle Herbert and Aunt Charlotte, at least, must have known all along. They could both count, and must have known when Crispin arrived—early, according to Doctor Meadows, may he rest in peace—whose child he was likely to be. The same went for Morrison, I assumed.

Aunt Roz might have found out in April, although it was just as likely that she had already known. It depended on whether her husband and/or her sister-in-law had talked to her about it, before or after the fact, twenty-four years ago. For Uncle Herbert's sake, I hoped it had been him, and that he'd breached the subject before he did anything, although at this point the issue seemed to have been resolved either way.

Crispin had certainly learned the news in April, probably while eavesdropping. I remembered an instance during dinner that weekend, when he had given Uncle Herbert a wholly unexpected and surprisingly nasty glare across the supper table. I had wondered at the time what it had been about, but if Crispin had just learned that Uncle Herbert was his biological father, and that he himself was not the legitimate heir to the dukedom, that would explain the animosity.

By that point, Duke Henry had been dead, although we didn't yet know that he had been murdered, and Grimsby would be shot later that night. Crispin had had motive and opportunity to kill them both. In fact, back then I had been convinced that he had done just that. Until two days later, anyway, when Aunt Charlotte had committed suicide and left a note confessing to the crimes.

Crispin had seemed sincerely distraught about his mother's

death, both then and earlier this evening, so he probably hadn't killed her. He likely hadn't even known that she had been planning to kill herself. He would have stopped her had he known, I assumed. It must have been her own decision, one she had taken without consulting anyone else, and without letting her son know that she knew—or thought she knew—that he was a murderer.

No wonder he had been distraught that morning. Not only had he lost his mother, but she had killed herself to protect him.

That was if any of this had happened, of course, and I didn't know that it had. I knew that Duke Henry, Grimsby, and Aunt Charlotte were all dead, but up until this weekend, I hadn't considered (again) that Crispin might have had anything to do with it. Aunt Charlotte had confessed, and I had believed that she'd been responsible.

But if she hadn't been, if Crispin had killed Duke Henry and Grimsby, then he could be responsible for every murder since then, too. Hughes in July—he had been there at Beckwith Place the weekend Tom had motored her and little Bess to Bristol—Morrison three nights ago, and Alfie and Doctor Meadows today.

But he wasn't the only person who had been at Sutherland Hall in April, and at Beckwith Place in July, and back here in Little Sutherland this weekend.

I could take Christopher and myself out of contention, I thought. Christopher hadn't known that Crispin was his brother until July, and I had only found out today. Neither of us had killed anyone.

Francis had been present for all three occasions, but I wasn't sure, even now, if he knew about Crispin. He hadn't been listening under the study window in July, nor had he been eavesdropping in April, as far as I knew. And even if he did know, he had no reason to want to protect that knowledge. If

Crispin was found to be Uncle Herbert's youngest son instead of Uncle Harold's legitimate heir, that would only benefit Francis.

He was out, then, along with myself and Christopher, and of course Constance, who hadn't been here in April and who had no motive to kill anyone, except perhaps Morrison.

Aunt Roz and Uncle Herbert had motored through the village earlier. They had left Sutherland Hall before either murder had been discovered, but they would have had time, I thought, to commit them. Alfie before they left the Hall, and Doctor Meadows on their way through Little Sutherland. There was that oil slick out back of the infirmary that Tom had harped on earlier. It needn't be from the Bentley, of course, but it had come from some motorcar or other, and we had several of those available.

Tom or Constable Daniels would have thought to inspect the motorcars for oil leaks, surely. I wished I had done that when we'd been out in the garage earlier, but of course I hadn't known about the oil slick at that point. Tom had only brought it up this evening. And it was too late to go out there now.

Or was it? I peered at the window. It didn't seem to be raining anymore, although it was dark and uninviting outside, while I was comfortably curled up here, warm and dry and safe.

A hummed snatch of song from next door made me consider that I could get dressed and fetch Constance, and the two of us could go to the carriage house together. It would still be dark and wet and perhaps scary, but we'd have each other's company. But that might put Constance in danger, and if anything happened to her, Francis would surely have my head.

That wasn't worth the risk. And I couldn't even leave myself while someone was awake and could hear me.

I had better get back to the list of suspects, then.

Aunt Roz or Uncle Herbert could have taken the Bentley to Upper Slaughter the night Morrison was killed. Uncle Herbert usually does the motoring, and he would definitely be able to make it to the Cotswolds and back overnight while Aunt Roz stayed here to provide an alibi. Add to that that he hadn't even been awake to see us off the following morning, and he might very well have been gone all night with none of us the wiser.

But while they could perhaps have done it, I didn't know why they would have bothered. Like Francis, Uncle Herbert would only benefit from having Crispin declared ineligible for the title, and then there was the anonymous note. Both my aunt and uncle had had access to the paper and a pen with which to write it, and of everyone here, they were the two people we knew for certain had been in the village this morning (aside from Christopher and myself). But it was hard to imagine that either of them would have tried to implicate me.

The only purpose of the note, it seemed to me, was to stir up trouble. I hadn't killed Doctor Meadows, and I had Christopher to alibi me. There was always the chance that Constable Daniels wouldn't believe Christopher, of course, but that seemed like a long shot.

And it was possible that Aunt Roz and Uncle Herbert (or whoever else might have penned the note) had surmised as much. That it would be safe to accuse me, because I wouldn't be a real suspect, not with Christopher to vouch for me.

But if so, why bother to write the note in the first place?

So no, while I had to keep Aunt Roz and Uncle Herbert on the list of suspects, I wouldn't put either of them anywhere near the top of the list. No motive for the murders, and no motive for framing me.

Onwards, then. To Uncle Harold.

He had been at Beckwith Place in July, and knew that Tom

had chauffeured Hughes to Bristol along with little Bess. And of course Uncle Harold had heard us make plans to motor up to the Cotswolds to talk to Morrison. He had the same access to the same motorcars as anyone else, and more of a reason to write the anonymous note. Uncle Harold abhors me, as well as deplores his son's feelings for me.

But Uncle Harold might not even know that Crispin wasn't his son. Crispin had found that out by eavesdropping, which Uncle Harold was surely above doing. And if Aunt Charlotte had killed Duke Henry and Grimsby to keep the knowledge of Crispin's paternity from him, surely it was safe to assume that he didn't know?

And if he didn't know, he had no motive. For any of it.

Laetitia and the other Marsdens hadn't been here in April, although they had been present both at Beckwith Place in July and here this weekend. Laetitia might have doped Crispin to give herself time to motor to Upper Slaughter and back. Of everyone here, he was surely the one most likely to try to invade her bedchamber in the middle of the night, so ensuring that he couldn't do might make sense. And she had tried to shift the blame for that onto my cousin, whether she had intended the dig to be at Christopher or Francis.

She would kill me without batting an eye, I thought, if I tried to come between her and Crispin. It was difficult to say how much of that was trying to hang onto the title and fortune, and how much was trying to hang onto Crispin himself, but she was at least capable of murder in the right—or wrong—circumstances.

Then again, so are most people if the conditions require it.

And here we were, again. I made a face as I scribbled the next name on the pad.

Crispin, Viscount St George. Future Duke of Sutherland.

Or as the case may be, simply Crispin Astley, youngest son

of Lord Herbert Astley, without even an Honorable in front of his name.

He had every reason to want to keep his paternity quiet. If word got out, he'd lose everything. His reputation, his inheritance, his pretty fiancée, his father's regard, such as it was—or at least the regard of the man he had thought was his father for almost all of his twenty-three years.

On the other hand, there were the rest of us. He'd gain two brothers, a father, and a stepmother, all of whom already loved him and would fold him into their family with cries of joy. There was me, although as a pseudo-sister I surely left something to be desired. And with all that, we might still be a poor exchange for the Sutherland title and fortune.

So yes, Crispin had a lot to lose. He had known about his parentage since April. Duke Henry had been giving him a difficult time as it was that weekend, ranting about his grandson's recklessness and profligacy and loose morals, not to mention the unsuitability of getting himself emotionally attached to someone like myself. All of it must have grated, even before the final, big discovery. And on top of that, the old man had been approaching ninety. Giving him a nudge toward eternal sleep might not have appeared as such a sin under the circumstances.

Crispin had known where to find Hughes, and no one had checked his alibi for that day. He had known where to find Morrison, too, and had even wanted to go with us to see her. He would have had no problem making it to Upper Slaughter and back overnight. The excuse about the sleeping draught—if it was an excuse—might have been to explain away both why he was groggy the next morning, and why no one would have been able to rouse him overnight. Just in the event someone had tried to knock on his door while he wasn't there.

He said that he had spent half the morning today in Uncle Harold's study, but he had been alone, and there had been no reason why he couldn't have left and gone to the village. I had seen someone through the study window when Christopher and I arrived back at Sutherland Hall from our walk, but I hadn't looked closely enough to determine whether it had been Crispin or Uncle Harold. There had been no reason to look closely, not at the time. I had assumed it was Uncle Harold, but there isn't much difference between platinum and gray-blond hair in lamplight.

If Crispin had left the study, Alfie might have seen him, which would explain why Alfie had to die. And as for why he had decided to implicate me... well, as I had told Christopher, Crispin was the last person here who would accuse me of murder. The man who—supposedly—loved me.

And what a perfect cover that was. He would have known, of course, that I was in no danger of being arrested for the murder. He knew, better than anyone, that Christopher and I stick together. He'd have had every reason to think that we'd step into the infirmary together, talk to Doctor Meadows together, and step out again together.

He had even told Christopher to be careful, and had reminded him of what had happened the last time Christopher and I had walked to the village.

What better way to ensure that Christopher didn't leave my side for so much as a second?

I popped the top of the pen between my lips and gnawed on it.

This all hung together far better than I wanted it to. I didn't want Crispin to be guilty. My inner eye supplied me with an image of him, hands tied behind his back, shirt-collar turned down, and a rope around his neck—and when the rope jerked, I jerked, too, and made a face when I realized it.

It was a fact I couldn't avoid, however. If he were found guilty of—I counted in my head—anywhere from four to six murders, there was no chance that the House of Lords would afford him the kind of leniency that they had shown Geoffrey. It would be the hemp fandango, for certain.

His motive—killing numerous people to keep his illegitimacy quiet—wasn't likely to gain him any favors, either, with the peerage or the population at large.

I grimaced. This was doing absolutely nothing to help me relax for sleep. Seeing things in black and white, written starkly on paper, only made them look worse. I shoved the paper and pen onto the bedside table and swung my legs over the side of the bed. I wasn't going to get to sleep anytime soon, so I might as well take the opportunity to go to the carriage house to look for oil leaks.

CHAPTER TWENTY

THERE ARE multiple ways out of Sutherland Hall. None from the second floor, of course, not unless I wanted to open the window and slide down the wall—which I didn't. There's the front door, that Tidwell guards during the day. There are the double doors from the drawing room onto the terrasse. There's the conservatory door at the end of the east wing. There's the boot room door next to Uncle Harold's study in the west wing, that also opens into the courtyard. There's the kitchen door into the kitchen garden, accessible through the servants' wing, which I wasn't about to invade.

I peered out into the hallway before I left my room, to make certain everything was quiet and that no one was lying in wait. The hallway was empty and still, save for the muffled sound of snoring from down the hall. Geoffrey, or perhaps Tom. I didn't move closer to ascertain the source one way or the other. Constance also made little snuffling noises in her sleep, but from Laetitia's direction there was no noise at all. Perhaps she had made her way over to Crispin's wing after we were all in bed, and her room was empty.

I placed my brogues carefully on the floor beside me as I pulled my door shut and locked it. I was as careful as I could, wincing at every scrape the giant old key made in the lock. When I could pull it out and drop it into my dressing-gown pocket, I let my breath out as quietly as I could. Then I bent to pick up the shoes, and the key fell out of my pocket and clattered against the wood floor with a racket that cut through the still of the night like a gunshot.

The snoring cut off with a surprised snort. Constance's snuffles stopped, as well. For a moment, nothing happened. I held my breath, dirty brogues clutched to my nice, clean gown, while I waited for one of the doors to open. The key lay accusatorily in the hardwood gap between the wall and the carpet runner.

There was the soft noise of blankets shifting, and a body moving on a mattress. Someone was getting comfortable. The snoring started up again, more softly. I bent, as silently as I could, and grasped the key. It went back into my pocket, and then I tiptoed to the door to the servants' staircase and eased it open. I slipped across the threshold onto the landing and shut the door behind me again, as quietly as I could. When the green baize had settled into the frame, I flitted down the stairs in my bare feet and out into the ground floor hallway. I slipped my brogues on in the boot room, the last thing I did before I opened the door and stepped out into the night.

The rain had let up, but it was still overcast and misty, and the dark bulk of the Hall towered over me as I made my way across the courtyard, around the fountain, and along the wall of the conservatory. Every light in the Hall was out, at least as far as I could tell, and with no moon and stars, it took a few minutes before my eyes fully adjusted to the dark. By then, I had left the wall of the conservatory behind and had struck out down the drive towards the carriage house.

It was only now that it occurred to me to wonder whether Constable Daniels had set a guard.

But no, surely not. What was there to guard, after all? The constables had spent all afternoon and most of the evening here, picking over the crime scene. Whatever there had been to find, surely they must have discovered by now.

As I flitted down the grass and gravel, I imagined myself stumbling through the carriage house doors, directly into the arms of Constable Daniels or one of his cohort. There'd be no way to convince him I had nothing to hide then. If sneaking around the crime scene in the middle of the night didn't cement my guilt, I didn't know what would do.

For a moment, I thought about going back. Of simply turning around and returning to my room without breaching the carriage house doors.

But I was already here, so close to where I wanted to be. And all I wanted was a quick look underneath the motorcars; surely there wasn't anything wrong with that? It wasn't as if I planned to touch anything. And I certainly didn't plan to venture up into the rooms above the garage, where Alfie had been killed.

Just in case, I made certain to wrap my hand with a corner of my dressing gown before undoing the latch and pulling the carriage house door open. It screeched like a needle on a gramophone, and for the second time tonight, I froze in place, certain that someone must have heard me.

I could even imagine that I felt, from within the darkness, the same breathless anticipation that I felt myself, as if someone was in there, just waiting for me to make the next move.

In the event that I wasn't simply imagining things, but that Constable Daniels truly had left a colleague to stand guard, I raised my voice. "Is anyone there? This is Pippa Darling."

Better to make myself known now, I figured, than be caught

in the act of looking suspicious. I wasn't actually going to do anything suspicious, after all, so it was a risk that seemed worth taking.

There was no answer, not even the scuff of a shoe, so I must have imagined someone's presence. I stepped across the threshold into the darkness and pulled the door shut behind me. At that point, I thought it would be safe to take the torch out of my pocket and turn it on—no one was awake to see it from up at the Hall—and it was when I flicked the switch and the beam of light shot out, that there was the very distinct shuffle of someone, or something, from farther into the garage.

My heart jumped onto my tongue and continued beating there. I had to swallow hard to be able to speak, and when I did, my voice shook. "Hullo? Who's there?"

It's a cat, I told myself. A cat, or perhaps a hedgehog, or some other small woodland creature that I—or the light—had startled into flight. Something cute and furry that would never hurt me, and that was more afraid of me than I was of it. Certainly not something, or someone, who knew that I was standing here, quaking in my brogues, expecting the worst.

There was another noise, from the left this time, and I swung the torch that way. "Stop!"

Whoever it was did, which argued against a cat or hedgehog, or anything with four legs. They don't tend to listen that well, or respond as accurately.

"Who are you?" I tried. "Show yourself!"

I don't know what I expected. I suppose I was still clinging to the hope that there might be a constable from the village here, or perhaps Tom himself, trying to teach me a lesson about wandering about in the middle of the night and putting myself in danger.

What I did not expect was for something to come flying out of the darkness toward me. I raised both arms to protect my head—it's automatic, in case you wondered—and the projectile hit my arm.

The blow knocked the torch from my hand, and I squealed and fell back. The torch hit the ground with a tinkle of broken glass. So did I, with a grunt.

The light didn't go out, but it might as well have done. The torch spun away from me, coming to rest underneath the Marsdens' Daimler, and lay there, illuminating nothing but dirt and the undercarriage of the motorcar.

My arm felt as if someone had hit it with a bicycle pump—most likely because someone had done—and I clutched it to my chest, blinking away the tears that filled my eyes. And that was when something big and dark bore down on me from out of the darker darkness, and something black descended on top of me.

I screamed, but it was buried under a… was that a car blanket?

It was, I decided, as I clawed at the muffling folds with my only functioning hand. In the background, I could hear the sounds of someone scrambling away, stumbling over and around things and barging into the motorcars with dull thumps of metal, and then the garage door opened with a squeal. There were rapid footsteps running away, and then the reverberating bang as the door slammed back into the frame and hung there, shivering. By then I had gotten the blanket off my head into my lap, and was carefully brushing the folds away from my injured arm. There was no need to hurry, after all. Whoever had been here was gone, and I wasn't reckless enough to charge after him, or her, into the night.

I'll admit it: all I wanted to do at that point was to retreat to my room. But I had dragged myself here, specifically to check which—if any—of the remaining motorcars were leaking. If none of them were, that would point to the Bentley having been parked behind the infirmary this morning—or yesterday morning by now. But if one of the others had developed a leak, at least it would go some way towards exonerating my aunt and uncle.

I wiggled under the Daimler, careful to lean only on my good elbow, and reached for the torch. There was no oil leak here, anyway. Then, once I had it in my hand, I got to my feet, carefully, with the help of my functioning arm while I kept the other tightly clutched to my chest.

With the mystery intruder out of the way, it was an easy job to navigate around to each of the motorcars to peer underneath them for any signs of an oil slick. The Marsdens' Daimler was clean, as mentioned, and so was Constance's Crossley. I hadn't really suspected otherwise. Francis would have checked the Crossley for problems both before and after the trip to Upper Slaughter, and if any of the Marsdens were guilty, it was probably Laetitia, who was as likely—perhaps more likely—to borrow Crispin's H6 as her parents' Daimler.

The Hispano-Suiza or the Rolls Royce, then. I bent to peer under the Phantom. The ground was pristine, of course. The Phantom was practically brand new, only in the possession of His Grace since August, and hardly used since then. There was no reason to think it would have developed a leak so soon.

It was with a feeling of inevitability that I directed the light from the broken torch under the rear of the Hispano-Suiza. I wasn't even surprised when I saw the light reflected in the sticky black puddle that was slowly sinking into the dirt floor.

THE SECOND SHOCK of the night—or perhaps it was the third or even fourth by now—was when I opened the garage door to the outside and found myself face to face with another tall, dark silhouette.

Or it might have been the same one, for all I knew.

I stumbled back, and then squealed when the figure shot out a hand and grabbed my arm to keep me upright.

It was the bad arm, of course. I let out a very unladylike expletive, and Crispin sighed. "I knew that was you."

"Whatever do you mean?" I wanted to know, offended, as I cradled the arm against my chest again.

"Who else would be sneaking about the crime scene in the middle of the night?" He glanced beyond me into the darkness of the carriage house before turning his attention back to me. "What's wrong with your arm?"

"Someone threw something at it," I said.

His eyebrow twitched. "What, pray tell? Or should that be whom?"

"It should be who, but the answer is that it was a bicycle pump. I suppose the wrench wasn't available anymore."

He sighed. "You're not making any sense, Darling. What are you doing here?"

"I could ask you the same thing," I said.

"I heard the door slam," Crispin said, with a glance at it. "If you're sneaking around, Darling, you should be more circumspect. I'm surprised the entire house didn't hear you."

"It wasn't me slamming the door, you git. It was whoever hit me with the bicycle pump."

"Whomever," Crispin corrected, not without a smirk.

I rolled my eyes. "You want me to believe that you heard the door—from the other side of the house, no less—and you decided to come out and see what was going on?"

"Fine," Crispin said. "I was in my sitting room earlier, having a night cap and thinking about things, and I saw you come out of the boot room and tiptoe across the courtyard. I didn't get down here until now because, unlike you, I decided to get dressed before I ventured out."

He gave my pyjamas and dressing gown a halfhearted sneer.

I returned the favor. He had taken the time to dress head to toe in tweed, with plus-fours, socks and shoes, shirt and waistcoat, and even a tie. The only thing missing was the hat, and he probably regretted leaving it off, as the mizzle beaded on his hair. Mine was turning curlier by the second.

"Are you certain you weren't on your way somewhere?" I inquired suspiciously. "That's a lot of clothes to put on just to follow me to the garage."

"I'm positive, Darling. I could have put the evening kit back on, I suppose—it was handy—but it didn't seem like quite the thing for the occasion."

No, for him to traipse down here in full black tie would have been even stranger than this.

"I suppose Laetitia would have had something to say about it, had you come to my rescue in your jim-jams," I said maliciously.

His voice didn't change. "Let's keep Laetitia out of this, if you don't mind. You still haven't told me what possessed you to leave your room and venture out to the carriage house in the middle of the night. Secret assignation?"

I snorted. "Hardly. There's no one here for me to assign with. And it's not the place I would choose, is it?"

"So why—?"

"I wanted to see whether any of the motorcars leaked," I said. "You were there when Tom talked about the oil slick behind the infirmary. I thought, if one of the cars here was leaking, at least it would exonerate Aunt Roz and Uncle Herbert."

He nodded. "And what did you discover?"

"Someone else doing the same thing. Or doing something else. I have no idea. I stepped inside and turned on my torch, and he—or she—threw the bicycle pump at me. And then he threw a blanket on top of me before he ran away."

Crispin's lips twitched.

"It's not funny," I said defensively. "I think my arm is broken."

It wasn't, of course. I would likely have a nasty bruise tomorrow, but I felt none of the greasy nausea that I associated with broken bones, so I was likely good in that respect.

But of course Crispin didn't know that, so he gave it a concerned look. "Would you like me to help you splint it? There's no doctor in the village anymore, that I can take you to see."

"I'll be fine," I said. "I'll let Francis take a look tomorrow. Or Tom. Someone with some experience. Perhaps it's only bruised."

"And who was it who threw the pump at you?"

"No idea," I said cheerfully. "He knocked the torch out of my hand first, so I couldn't see much, and then he threw the blanket on top of me so I could see even less. Clearly he knew I would recognize him, if I got a good look."

Crispin hummed, and I added, "It could have been you, for all I know. Your story is highly suspicious, you know. It's very late, and I was quiet leaving the house. You oughtn't to have noticed me come outside."

He rolled his eyes. "I'm not sure what to tell you, Darling."

"The truth would be nice."

"That is the truth."

Fine. "Did you see anyone when you came in this direction, then? Whoever it was ran out of here just a minute or two before you showed up? You must have seen him."

To be honest, I didn't know whether that was true or not. If Crispin had gone out through the front door, or the boot room door, the person who had been here, might have had time to cross the lawn and the terrasse before Crispin came around the corner.

"I'm afraid I didn't," Crispin said, and I couldn't tell whether he was telling the truth or not. He might have seen someone, or he might not. He might have been here himself, maiming me, or he might not. "Just out of curiosity, does one of the motorcars leak?"

"Funny you should ask. Yours does."

He got a strange look on his face. "Mine?"

"The Hispano-Suiza. Feel free to take a look."

I handed him the broken torch. He hesitated a second before he took it. "Wait here."

I had no intention of going anywhere, and told him so. He ducked inside the carriage house and left me standing outside the door. I put my back against the wall and peered up at the Hall while I waited. It was still silent and dark. Whoever had been out here, clearly hadn't been stupid enough to turn on any lights when he or she got back inside.

Or had it been Crispin?

I didn't like to think so, obviously. But the fact that he had shown up here, fully dressed, a few minutes after my attacker had absconded, was suggestive, to say the least. He might have wanted to check out the oil slick situation for himself, and I had caught him at it. And now he was inside the garage, looking at something he had already looked at, so I wouldn't think he'd already been inside.

Although there had been no need for all that. When I introduced myself earlier, he could have simply stood up and told me what he was doing—the same thing I was—and I wouldn't have thought anything of it. Why maim me and run away to avoid being recognized, only to come back as himself five minutes later?

Or perhaps he really had been drinking alone in his room

when I came out through the boot room door, and he had decided to follow me. We all had a lot on our minds lately, and Crispin had more than most.

If he had done, and had decided to follow me, he ought to have seen my attacker, however.

And if he had done, but wouldn't admit it, perhaps it was someone he wanted to protect, like Laetitia. Her room had been silent earlier, so it was at least possible that she was the one out of bed.

There were all the other Astleys, too, but I wasn't any more likely than Crispin was to want to get Christopher or Francis in trouble, and as for the Marsdens, it was nigh on impossible to imagine either Lady Euphemia or Lord Maury creeping out of bed and down the drive under cover of darkness. Why would they?

Beside me, the door squealed again, and broke my train of thought. Crispin came through, his face grim.

"Well?" I said when he didn't speak.

He nodded. "You're right. My motorcar has a leak."

Yes, indeed. "I assume you didn't motor to the village this morning and kill Doctor Meadows?"

He looked at me, seemingly searching my face for something. Whatever it was, it mustn't have been there, because he shook his head. "I was with Laetitia in the maze, and then I was in my father's study."

"But someone else could have taken the H6 out."

"Anyone who wanted to. The keys are in the car."

Yes, of course they were. When I didn't answer, he glanced up at the Hall. "Are you ready to go back inside? There's nothing more to be discovered here, I think."

No, likely not. I started up the driveway with him beside me.

Part of me wondered, distantly, whether I ought to be

worried. I had made a good case for why Crispin was the murderer. And here we were, alone together, after I had made it obvious that I was investigating. If he had already killed multiple people, it would be nothing to kill me too, or so I assumed.

Although if it had been him in the garage earlier, it would have made more sense to do it then, in the dark, before I knew who he was. When he wouldn't have had to look me in the eye as he wrapped his hands around my throat and squeezed.

I shivered, and he cast me a look. "Cold?"

"A bit, but that particular reaction was something else."

He didn't ask what—perhaps he guessed—but he offered, "Would you like my jacket?"

"I'm all right, thank you. We'll be inside in a minute."

After a few steps, I added, "Out of curiosity, which way did you leave the house earlier? Surely not the boot room door."

He shook his head. "Down the servants' stairs and out through the conservatory."

"Was the conservatory door locked when you got there?"

"As tight as a tick," Crispin said, which made sense. If my attacker—assuming he was someone other than Crispin—had come and gone through the conservatory, Crispin would have seen him for certain.

I slanted him a look. "I'm fairly certain that I've figured out what this is about, you know."

He slanted one back. "I imagine you have done, Darling. You and Kit both. We talked about it earlier, in fact."

We had done, and if he didn't want me to bring it up again, he gave no sign of it.

"There are only so many of us here this week who could have made that trip to the Cotswolds and back overnight," I said apologetically. "Francis and Christopher have no motive, nor does Uncle Herbert, and I can assure you that I don't care one way or the other who the next Duke of Sutherland is."

"I'm sure you don't, Darling."

"But even if *I* don't, there are people who do. Or would do, if they knew the truth."

He nodded. "Go on, then."

"Well, there's the Earl and Countess of Marsden, for one. They would quite like their daughter to become Duchess of Sutherland, I imagine."

"I imagine so," Crispin agreed. "Although I don't see Maury or Euphemia motoring around smothering people or bashing them with wrenches, somehow."

I didn't, either. "Geoffrey missed the gallows by a hair, so he isn't likely to risk his freedom again so soon. His sister, on the other hand..."

A corner of his mouth turned up. "Yes, Darling. Tell me about Laetitia."

"She's a horrible cow and you oughtn't to have proposed to her," I said bluntly. "I take full responsibility for telling you to do so."

"Thank you, Darling."

"Unfortunately, that's water under the bridge, or at least it is unless we want to commit a murder of our own."

I waited, but he didn't tell me to go ahead and plot Laetitia's demise. In the absence of that, I continued. "Now that the title is within reach, I wouldn't put it past your fiancée to kill untold masses of people to hang on to you. She likes you well enough on your own, but the title and fortune would tip the scales, I imagine. She would also frame me for murder without any compunctions whatsoever. Nothing would make her happier than to get me out of the way."

In fact, I was probably next on her list, if getting me arrested didn't work.

Crispin made a noise, but it was hard to say whether it was laughter or something else. I glanced at him, but he merely cleared his throat and gestured for me to go on.

"She could have made the drive to Upper Slaughter," I said. "She was there when Hughes left for Bristol in July, so she knew where to find her, and she had time to go to the village while you were dealing with Uncle Harold's paperwork this morning. And I don't think she would have hesitated to borrow your motorcar."

"No," Crispin confirmed. "She has used it before. But you don't know her the way I do, Darling."

I made a face. "Certainly not."

"You know what I mean. She really isn't so bad when you get to know her."

"I'll take your word for it. Are you telling me that you don't think her capable of murder?"

He hesitated. "I think we're all capable of murder in the right circumstances. Or the wrong ones. When the stakes are high enough that murder seems the easiest way out."

"Well, that's the case for Laetitia. And then, of course, there's you."

He nodded. "Yes, I'm well aware of what you think of me."

"I'm not sure you do," I said, "but you can't deny that you had motive."

He shook his head. "Not at all, Darling. I also had means and opportunity. It's my motorcar that's leaking. I could have motored to the Cotswolds and back overnight, more easily than most of the rest of you. It wouldn't be the first time I've gone without sleep. I could have told you and Kit that I was doped to throw suspicion off myself. I could have shut myself in the study yesterday, and then sneaked out through the boot room door. When Alfie saw me come back from the village with the bloody wrench, I could have killed him, too. I had the opportunity to do all of it, and a better motive than most."

Yes, indeed. "I'm not going to say anything to anyone," I said, as we reached the door to the conservatory and he opened it for me and bowed me through. "Thank you."

"Don't mention it." He shut the door behind us, and locked it, and we headed in.

"I don't care about most of these people," I continued. "Grimsby was a blackmailer, and so was Hughes. Morrison was unkind to Constance, and anyone who's unkind to Constance can't possibly be a nice person."

His lips twitched, and I added, "Doctor Meadows seemed like a decent chap, and it's awful about Alfie. But it's in Constable Daniels's hands, and not mine. I'm going to leave well enough alone and not get involved."

Crispin nodded. "I'm sure that's the safest thing you can do."

We reached the door at the other end of the conservatory, and he opened it and waited for me to step through. Outside in the hallway, I lingered. "I should make certain that the boot room door is locked. We don't want anyone who doesn't belong to be able to get in."

"I'll walk you," Crispin said.

"That's not necessary. I made it down here on my own earlier." And I had assumed that he'd want to take the quickest route up to his own rooms.

"It seems the least I can do," Crispin said, "with your arm out of commission. What would you do if anyone attacked you between here and there?"

"Scream loudly," I told him, since there wasn't much else I could do.

"Better just to let me accompany you." He eyed the arm

dubiously as we set off. "Are you certain you don't want anything for that? Laudanum? Or perhaps a sling?"

"It's already better," I told him, even as I still held it cradled against my body. "If it's not well again by tomorrow, I'll wrap a scarf around it and ask Francis to take a look."

We headed down the east wing, past the game room, library, and drawing room, and into the central and west wing, where Crispin locked the door between the boot room and the outside while I watched.

"Are you certain about not wanting a gun?" he inquired when we were walking again, past the gun room this time.

I shook my head. "I'll lock myself in when we get upstairs. I'm not worried."

"As you wish."

He put a hand against my back and nudged me forward. I stepped into the servants' staircase and started climbing.

Throughout the whole experience, from when he had first turned up outside the carriage house until now, I had been aware of the fact that he might have murdered several people. He knew that I suspected him, and I knew that he might choose to murder me too.

It didn't feel as if that was his plan, honestly—why would he offer to fetch me a gun if he planned to try to kill me?—but I knew it theoretically, at least.

What I hadn't thought about at all was the fact that he was supposed to be in love with me. That lasted until we came out in the west wing hallway, just down from the door to Laetitia's bedchamber (as well as my own), and he stopped to look at me.

"Here we are."

Here we were, standing outside my door, quite like a girl and the suitor who had escorted her home at the end of a normal evening out.

I swallowed. "Thank you for seeing me to my door, St George."

He smirked. "Any time, Darling. Do I get the usual reward for my trouble?"

The usual reward being... a kiss?

"I don't think your fiancée would approve of that," I said, even as I felt my cheeks heat.

The smirk widened. "I'm quite certain that she wouldn't. But what Laetitia doesn't know won't hurt her."

I supposed not. But even so— "Do you plan to proposition other girls after you're married, as well, St George?"

He grinned. "No, Darling. This is my last hurrah before donning the old ball and chain. I figure I'd better make the most of it."

"Well, you'll have to make the most of it without me," I told him. "Although I do appreciate the effort, St George."

"Any time, Darling. Sweet dreams."

I gave him my thanks, and then I unlocked my door before hesitating on the threshold. He was still standing there, waiting for me to duck inside, and he was right: what Laetitia didn't know wouldn't hurt her.

So I turned back, and slung an arm around his neck, and went up on my tiptoes, and brushed my lips across his cheek before I whispered in his ear. "Good night, St George. Sleep well."

I didn't wait to see his reaction, just turned my back to him and disappeared into my room. I did notice, however, as I stood inside waiting, that several seconds passed—several very long seconds—before I heard him walk away.

CHAPTER TWENTY-ONE

I WALKED to breakfast the next morning like a person to the gallows, just waiting for the other shoe to drop. The rest of the night, after listening to Crispin walk away, had been spent going over the evidence in my head, over and over again: all the threads, all the intricate, small plot-lines, until I fell into a restless slumber, haunted by hangmen and dead bodies and black things covering my head. I overslept, of course, and woke up as frazzled and divided in spirit as I had been when I turned in.

It had also occurred to me, a bit belatedly, I'll admit, that Crispin's sly comment about the ball and chain might not have been in reference to Laetitia. He might have been talking about being arrested this morning. There was a whole month left until he got married. Plenty of time for kisses. But they were likely to be scarce in prison.

There was no part of me that wanted to see anyone, but I knew that if I didn't show my face downstairs, Christopher would come looking for me. So I donned a warm skirt and jumper, in deference to the gray November morning as well as the chill that permeated from my center out to the other parts of me.

There was no one about when I opened my door, nor when I reached the bottom of the servants' staircase. The smell of cooked bacon hung in the air, and I could hear the murmur of voices from the breakfast room.

I set off down the hallway, only to slow a few seconds later, as I noticed that the study door was open. I drifted over and lingered on the threshold for a moment to peer inside.

This was where Crispin had spent part of the morning yesterday, several hours going over paperwork, or perhaps only the few minutes necessary before scurrying through the boot room and across the courtyard to the carriage house. Twenty or thirty minutes would have been enough to motor to the village and back, and if the study door was kept shut, no one might realize that he had left at all. And there was plenty of blank paper around on which to write the anonymous note.

I peered around again, carefully, before ducking through the open door and into the room. Hopefully no one would catch me in the minute or so it would take for me to check the desk blotter for any sign that the anonymous note had been written in this room.

I stopped beside the desk and pushed the tangled papers on top aside. And there—yes, a sheet of blotting paper, with ink spots still on it. I bent over and peered at it, doing my best to translate the random squiggles and constellations into what might have been words.

Surely that was an inverted P and half an H for PHILIPPA? And a bit above that, the line and half the backward curve of a D? For DOCTOR or perhaps DEAD? Or even DARLING?

My heart sank slowly into what felt like my stomach. This didn't look good for Crispin, whether he was guilty or not. He had motive, means, and opportunity, and now I could put him in the vicinity of the anonymous note at the time when the ink was still wet.

My fingers twitched as I fought the impulse to snatch up the blotting paper and crumple it into a tight ball that I could toss into one of the fireplaces. Which was what anyone sane ought to have done, frankly. Why on earth wouldn't Crispin have taken it with him, if he knew that it could implicate him? It was left in his father's study, yes, and no one but Uncle Harold was likely to see it. The rest of us weren't supposed to go into Uncle Harold's study. Not even Crispin was supposed to be here unless he was specifically invited.

I suppose he must have assumed that Uncle Harold wouldn't give him up even if he did happen to notice that the spots on the blotter matched the verbiage of the anonymous note, and he had been right, hadn't he? Uncle Harold hadn't said a word to anyone, as far as I knew.

Before I could take that thought any further, I heard the sound of a throat clearing behind me, and I swung on my heel, heart knocking against my ribs.

"Oh." The relief was palpable. "Good morning, Tidwell."

"Miss Darling." Tidwell ran a practiced eye over the room. "You shouldn't be here."

No, I shouldn't. I should leave immediately, before anyone other than Tidwell caught me.

I picked up the blotting paper before I walked away from the desk. Tidwell looked as if he'd like to protest, but only until I handed it to him on my way past. "Hold onto this for me, Tidwell."

Tidwell gave both me and the paper a look, but all he said was, "Very well, Miss Darling."

I brushed past him into the hallway, and watched as he shut the door to the study behind us with a pointed *snick*. "The family is gathered in the breakfast room, Miss Darling," he informed me as he turned.

"All of them?"

"His Grace is still in his chambers," Tidwell said, "and Master Crispin has gone—"

Gone? "Gone where?"

"To the constabulary," Tidwell said, and my jaw dropped. Tidwell clarified, "He said he would be back shortly."

Yes, of course he would say that. Telling the butler, "I'm going to give myself up for murder," was surely out of the question. If the village was even where he had gone. He might have made a break for it, and only told Tidwell that he was going to the constabulary to gain a head start.

"Did you see him before he left? Did he seem all right?"

"His lordship seemed perturbed," Tidwell intoned.

Yes, I could well believe it. "Christopher's in the breakfast room, did you say? I must go there."

Tidwell made no move to stop me, so I indicated the blotting paper. "Put that somewhere safe, if you would, Tidwell. The police will want to examine it, I expect."

"Yes, Miss Darling," Tidwell said, with a glance at the paper in his hand. Anything else he may have asked faded into nothingness behind me as I took off down the hallway as quickly as I could without flat out running.

THE BREAKFAST ROOM was indeed full of people when I reached it. Aunt Roz and Uncle Herbert were gone, of course, and had not mysteriously materialized again overnight, but the Marsdens were gathered around one table, snacking on tea and eggs and sauteed mushrooms, while Christopher, Francis, and Constance were sitting at a second table, drinking coffee and picking at bacon and buttered toast.

All three of them brightened when they saw me, and Christopher beckoned.

"There you are. I was beginning to worry."

His eyes landed on my arm, which was better this morning than last night, but which I still favored and tended to keep close to my body.

"Rough night," I told him as I angled out the empty chair between him and Francis and made my way onto it. "I couldn't sleep, so I decided to visit the carriage house, and someone attacked me."

They all turned silent. So did the Marsdens, although they appeared to try to be more circumspect about it.

"Who?" Christopher demanded.

I shrugged, and winced when it jolted my arm. "I have no idea. We didn't precisely have a conversation. I opened the door and turned on my torch, and whoever it was threw a bicycle pump and a blanket at me, and got away."

There was a quickly suppressed snigger from the other table. Laetitia, surely, although Geoffrey has been known to have an inane sense of humor as well, although perhaps not this particular week. Francis's lips twitched. "A bicycle pump and a blanket, you say?"

"The bicycle pump first, to make me drop the torch. Whoever he was, he had good aim. The blanket came a few seconds later, when he knocked me over and ran past me and out the door."

"What's wrong with the arm?" Constance inquired, and I turned to her.

"Thank you for asking, Constance." Unlike some people, who merely seemed to enjoy my suffering. "I don't think it's broken. Just bruised and sore, I think. It's purple and yellow."

Constance winced, and so did Christopher. Not Francis, of course. He's seen much worse.

"Shall I take a look?" he asked.

I glanced around. All the Marsdens were watching, more or less avidly. "Perhaps later. I'm not about to cause a scene by disrobing in the breakfast room."

"Good show," Francis said. "Can you use it?"

"As long as I'm careful." I stretched the arm out and pulled it back in, slowly. "See? Nothing to worry about. If it's not better in a few days, I'll find a doctor and have him look at it."

He nodded. "And you didn't see who it was who maimed you?"

"By the time I had clawed the blanket off my head, the carriage house was empty. And I wasn't about to chase whoever it was up to the house."

"No, certainly not." Christopher shuddered. "I would hope you stayed where it was safe."

I assured him I had done. "The glass on the torch had broken, but it still worked. So I used it to look for oil spills underneath all the motorcars."

"Oh." Comprehension dawned on his face, and on those of everyone else, as well. "Was that what you were doing there?"

"I thought it might at least point to someone other than Aunt Roz and Uncle Herbert," I said. "We know they were in the village, or at least that they motored through it, but we don't know whether anyone else was."

Constance murmured something, and Francis nodded. "And did you see any oil, Pipsqueak?"

"I did," I said, "but I'm not going to tell you whose motorcar it was that was leaking."

He tilted his head to contemplate me. "You do know that I can simply go down there and look for myself, don't you?"

Of course I did. "I'm sure you checked the Crossley after we returned from the Cotswolds the other day. Didn't you?"

Francis allowed as how he had done. "And it was fine. So

not that, then. And probably not the Phantom, as it's practically brand new. Crispin's little speed machine, perhaps? It's had the most wear of the lot."

"I told you," I said. "I'm not saying."

"You'll tell Tom," Christopher asked, "won't you?"

"I don't see why I should do. He said it himself yesterday, that he's not in charge of the investigation. Besides, I'm sure they looked for themselves, don't you think? I wouldn't be telling them anything they don't already know."

Nobody had an answer for that, and I looked around. "Where is Tom, anyway? And everyone else, as well?"

"Uncle Harold isn't down yet," Francis said. "Tommy was here, but Crispin came downstairs and asked to speak to him, and they went off together."

"Tidwell said that Crispin had gone to the village," I said. "He didn't mention Tom, but I suppose Tom might have gone with him, if he didn't come back in here."

Crispin might have wanted the moral support if he was going to give himself up.

"The village?" Christopher repeated doubtfully.

"The constabulary. Or so Tidwell said."

"Why would he go to the constabulary before ten in the morning?" Francis wanted to know, and I watched Christopher turn pale. It wasn't as if we hadn't discussed the possibility of Crispin's guilt at length yesterday, after all.

"Let's not talk about it," I said, and tried to make it sound as if I weren't thinking anything at all. "I'm sure they'll be back soon."

Christopher visibly pushed away any thoughts of speaking he may have had, and nodded. "Let me get you something to eat, Pippa. Eggs? Bacon?"

"Coffee," I said, "if you don't mind. And perhaps some

buttered toast? I'm not feeling well enough for anything else this morning."

My stomach churned anxiously, and I didn't like the idea of what would happen if I tried to put anything but the very basics into it.

"One minute." He pushed his chair back and withdrew to the buffet, where he kept his back to us while he filled a plate and a cup for me. His back was so rigid that I thought he might shatter if anyone tried to touch him.

"Did you speak to St George this morning?" I inquired of Francis, who shook his head.

"He came in here looking like death. His fiancée beckoned him over, and he went and did his duty—"

"The obligatory peck on the cheek?" I nodded. "And then he left, did he?"

"Then he asked if Tommy would come with him, and they went off. I didn't want to ask what it was about, but it was fairly obvious that something was wrong. I assumed they'd gone somewhere for a private chat, but now—" He shrugged.

"Now you tell us that Tidwell said they've gone to the village," Christopher concluded as he put a plate of buttered toast in front of me, along with a steaming cup of coffee.

"That's what he told me," I agreed, and picked up a piece of toast. "Or at least he said that Crispin had done. I don't know about Tom. Thank you, Christopher."

"Don't mention it." He dropped back down on the chair next to me. "I don't like this."

I didn't either. But instead of saying so, I told him, "I'm sure they'll be back soon," before I stuffed my mouth so full that I couldn't blurt out all my concerns and deductions even if I wanted to. This was decidedly not the time or place for them.

The conversation devolved into small talk after that, about the weather and how we might be able to spend the day since we were, presumably, not allowed to leave yet. It was a bit cold and rainy for croquet—which is the Astley go-to whenever we have nothing else to do and when the weather cooperates—but there was always cards in the game room or a rousing game of hide-and-go-seek. When Christopher asked whether we weren't a bit old for that, Francis informed him that that was part of the fun. I ate my toast and let the others talk. And then, because I turned out to be right, there was the sound of a motorcar outside the breakfast room window, and when we looked up, there was the blue streak of the Hispano-Suiza going by, oil leak and all.

"They're back," Francis said, unnecessarily.

I nodded. It must be a good sign, mustn't it, that the H6 was coming back? Unless Crispin had trusted Tom with his precious, of course, while he himself languished in the Little Sutherland jail.

But no, there was more than one figure traversing the drive towards the Hall. More than two even. As they came closer, I recognized Tom's Homburg as well as Constable Daniels's uniform. And surely... yes, that was Crispin's platinum hair that the light reflected off of. He must have forgotten to put on a hat before venturing out again.

"Is that..." Francis squinted through the window. "That's the chap from yesterday, isn't it? The one from Salisbury who came to fetch Alfie?"

The coroner, did he mean? I took my attention off Crispin for a closer look, but by then the chap in question had moved out of sight beyond the conservatory, and the drive was empty.

Tidwell must have seen them coming, because I could hear his footsteps proceed majestically across the foyer to the front door.

"Constable. Detective Sergeant."

There was a pause, ever so slight but noticeable, before—"Your Grace."

My eyes flew to Christopher's. He was staring back at me with the same wild-eyed look I no doubt sported myself. Next to me, Francis muttered something that sounded like an expletive, while, across the morning room, Laetitia had lifted both hands to cover her mouth. Her eyes were shining. It might have been tears, but I doubted it. I would have bet everything I owned that those demure hands were hiding an indecent grin. The Sutherland diamond ring caught the light and reflected it directly into my eyes. I blinked.

Out in the foyer, there was the clearing of a throat, and then Crispin's voice, still froggy, said, "Thank you, Tidwell."

EPILOGUE

"IT WAS UNCLE HAROLD!" I hissed.

It was later that morning. We had left the breakfast room after the denouement, scattering in different directions. Constance and Francis had retired to the latter's bedchamber. Christopher and I had been invited to join them, but it seemed rather odd to be sitting there in a huddle on the bed as if we were children, so after the bare minimum of conversation, of shock and awe and professed confusion, the two of us had excused ourselves and retreated to, of all places, the center of the garden maze. It was one of very few places in or around the Hall where we could be assured of some privacy to discuss the situation without being overheard.

Sutherland Hall was crawling with constables. Uncle Harold's study was under siege, and so was the Duke's Chamber, where Uncle Harold, I presumed, was lying dead in his bed. That would be the only reason why Tidwell would address Crispin with the duke's title, because I could see no earthly reason why Uncle Harold would have abdicated the title while still alive.

"Either that," Christopher nodded, "or Crispin killed him too."

I squinted at him. "Why would he have done, Christopher? He would become duke when Uncle Harold croaked either way, and it didn't look as if he was happy about it happening now."

Christopher had to admit that no, it hadn't looked like that at all. Crispin had been visibly shaken and near tears.

"I didn't think Uncle Harold knew about Crispin," I said, "or I would have suspected him sooner. Everything we speculated about Crispin would apply to Uncle Harold, too, if he knew. Surely he couldn't have known all along?"

Although it would explain Uncle Harold's attitude toward his son if he had known. He'd never been the loving father to Crispin that Uncle Herbert had been to Christopher, Francis, and Robbie—or for that matter to me, once I arrived from Germany. Uncle Harold had always been cold and exacting, someone who would rather raise his fist to his son in anger than embrace him in love.

"Who knows?" Christopher said. "He might have wondered at the time when Crispin was born, if the dates didn't line up. He was able to count backwards as well as anyone. But then Crispin was so very obviously a Sutherland that he probably decided to forget about any suspicions he may have had, if he ever did have any in the first place."

"He would have had no reason to think that his own brother was involved," I agreed. "It wasn't as if your father and Aunt Charlotte carried on an affair. It would have been a one-time thing, I assume. A last Hail Mary before giving up and admitting defeat."

Christopher winced. "So I would guess."

We sat in silence for a moment. It wasn't actively raining at the moment, but the sky was gray and the air wet and cold. I shivered. "What happens now, do you suppose?"

He slanted me a look. "To the title?"

"Among other things, but we can start there."

"I suppose that'll be up to Crispin," Christopher said. "If Father hasn't said anything about it in twenty-four years, he must be happy to let things lie."

"You mean, he doesn't want the title?"

"I would assume that he doesn't. It's a lot of responsibility. The aristocracy is on its way out, Pippa. Keeping up appearances takes too much money and trouble. I don't think Francis wants to be duke any more than Father does, and I certainly don't."

No, of course not.

"Uncle Herbert might just have stayed his hand because his brother was still alive," I suggested. "Now that Uncle Harold is dead—he *is* dead, isn't he?"

"I'm sure he is. Tidwell wouldn't address Crispin as His Grace otherwise."

Yes, Tidwell undoubtedly knew the intricacies better than any of us. "Then your father might feel differently about it now."

Christopher shrugged. "I suppose he and Crispin shall have to duke it out, no pun intended. Although I don't know how they'll be able to prove anything one way or the other. Crispin is an Astley, one only has to look at him to know that, and he's the acknowledged heir. He became Duke of Sutherland when Uncle Harold died. Father could challenge it, I suppose, if he were so inclined, and he was willing to tell the world that he bedded his brother's wife. But I don't know how they'd prove one way or the other whose son he really is."

I didn't, either. "Aunt Charlotte and Uncle Harold

between them committed multiple murders to keep it quiet. Surely that points to it being true."

"It might," Christopher agreed. "Then again, how would anyone know for certain?"

"At any rate we were both wrong about the murderer. It wasn't Crispin at all. It was Uncle Harold."

Christopher nodded. "It must have been. And it makes sense if you think about it. He was there when Hughes left for Bristol. He was here the other night, when we discussed Shreve and Morrison and the Cotswolds. Alfie might have motored them both to Upper Slaughter that night."

"The golden-haired young man the old chap saw," I realized. Not that Alfred had been particularly golden-haired, but he had been a sort of sandy blond.

"Uncle Harold wouldn't have told him why they were going there, so Alfie wouldn't have known that anyone was dead until we came home two days later, and at that point he might have confronted Uncle Harold about it, and Uncle had to kill him."

That was certainly a possibility. "Uncle Harold would have had the time to go to the village after setting Crispin up in the study yesterday morning," I said. "And apart from Laetitia, he was certainly the person here who disliked me the most."

Not to mention that the anonymous note had been blotted with the blotter in the study. If it hadn't been written by Crispin, it could only have been Uncle Harold. No one else would venture into the study and use the desk.

"Until Laetitia and Crispin were properly wedded and bedded," Christopher said, "I suppose he simply couldn't trust that Crispin wouldn't give it all up for you. Framing you for murder must have seemed like a good way of getting rid of you. If not permanently, at least until after the wedding."

The nuptials were coming up in less than a month. Geoffrey had spent more time than that waiting for the Assizes.

"I just didn't realize that he knew about Crispin," I said. "The whole idea was that Aunt Charlotte killed your grandfather and Grimsby to keep it quiet."

"Crispin found out by eavesdropping," Christopher answered. "Who's to say Uncle Harold didn't do the same?"

Well... his dignity, I would have assumed. "You don't suppose your grandfather told him, do you?"

"I don't know if Grandfather knew," Christopher said. "It might have been information that Grimsby kept to himself, the better to blackmail Aunt Charlotte with. The way he tried to blackmail me."

I nodded. He might have done. Grimsby, while he had shared all sorts of less-inflammatory secrets with Duke Henry, had also kept certain things back. Christopher's penchant for ladies' gowns and drag balls was one of those secrets. Aunt Charlotte's night with Uncle Herbert might have been another. It would certainly have been worth paying for. And for Aunt Charlotte, worth killing over, as well.

"But if he did know," Christopher continued, "I wouldn't put it past him to have informed Uncle Harold. He was a bastard."

"That's not a nice thing to say about your grandfather."

"Perhaps not, but he was one. He tried to pressure me into marrying you, don't you remember?"

I certainly did. "What are the chances that Uncle Harold killed his father and Grimsby and framed his wife, do you suppose?" If he had just discovered that she had cheated on him with his brother, it might have seemed like poetic justice. "He wasn't above using Crispin's H6 to go to the village. I'm sure he hoped not to be seen at all, but if he was seen, at least it would be Crispin on the hook and not himself."

And if he had been willing to sacrifice his heir, why not his wife, too?

"I suppose it isn't impossible," Christopher allowed, "and perhaps more likely than not, but I don't think we ought to worry about it. That's all over and done with. Aunt Charlotte confessed. There's nothing to be gained by dredging it up again now. We've got plenty to be going on with without resurrecting all that."

Indeed. "I spoke to him last night, you know."

He glanced at me. "Uncle Harold?"

I shook my head. "Crispin. He showed up at the carriage house a few minutes after the attack. I'm still not certain whether it was him who threw the bicycle pump at me or not."

"Didn't you ask him?"

"Of course I did," I said, "but he wasn't going to admit it, was he?"

Christopher nodded. "What happened?"

"Not much. We had a conversation. He walked me back to my room. I bussed his cheek because I thought it was the last opportunity I might get."

Christopher's brows arched. "And how did he respond to that?"

"I don't know," I said. "I shut the door without looking at him."

"And did he try to get inside?"

I shook my head. "But it did take longer than it should have done for him to walk away."

Christopher's lips twitched. "I'm not surprised. I assume you told him that you suspected him?"

"Not in so many words. But I suppose I might have given him that idea."

Or perhaps the idea I had given him was that his father was guilty. Perhaps he had seen Uncle Harold run away from the carriage house when he came out of the conservatory last night, and recognized him. Just because he had told me that he hadn't seen anyone, didn't mean he hadn't done. Uncle Harold was someone Crispin might want to protect. And perhaps he had gone to confront his father from my door, and that was what had precipitated this morning's events. Crispin clearly hadn't gone to the village to give himself up, so it must have been for Uncle Harold, and if Uncle Harold knew it was coming, he might have taken steps to avoid it.

"It can't have been a natural death," Christopher agreed when I said as much. "There was nothing wrong with him yesterday."

"I think there was quite a lot wrong with him yesterday," I pointed out. "Just as there has been a lot wrong with him for a long time. Although I take your point."

We sat in silence a moment. The mizzle had turned to drizzle, which was rapidly turning into actual rain. The drops hit the sodden grass like small, squashy bullets.

"Would it please you to go back inside?" Christopher inquired politely.

I shook myself like a wet cat. "I suppose we should do. There's nothing useful we can do out here."

"Nothing useful we can do in there, either," Christopher said, "although at least we won't be courting pneumonia."

He got to his feet and extended a hand to me.

"We can be moral support," I said as I let him pull me to my feet.

"I think Laetitia has that well in hand," Christopher answered cynically. "She's not likely to allow you within six feet of Crispin at this point."

Likely not.

"I'm afraid that this has been the death knell to any plan we may have had to force her to relinquish her hold on him. She was dug in deep before, but now that he's actually Duke of Sutherland instead of merely the Viscount St George, it would take something drastic to unlock her claws."

"I can think of two ways," Christopher said as he began walking out of the maze. "Neither is likely to happen."

I fell into step beside him and glanced up at his face. "What are they?" We should consider every possibility. Having to face Laetitia over the Christmas goose for decades to come was a fate too horrible to contemplate.

"Crispin relinquishes the title," Christopher said, "or Father takes it away from him."

"You're right. I don't think either of those is likely to happen. Not unless we could talk one of them into it, but I don't suppose that would be easy to do."

He didn't answer, and I added, "Was that both options in one, or do you have another?"

"That was two versions of the first option, in which Crispin is no longer Duke of Sutherland, and thus of less interest to Laetitia. She might relinquish her claim on him if the dukedom doesn't come with the marriage."

She might. Although it was by no means guaranteed, as she seemed rather attached to his person as well as to the title and money.

"That option seems tenuous at best. What about the other one?"

He looked down at me. "The other option is that you tell him you love him and beg him not to marry Laetitia, and hope that he changes his mind."

"Lie, do you mean?"

"If that's what you want to call it," Christopher said. "His father... excuse me, Uncle Harold isn't around to put pressure on Crispin anymore. He won't be disowned if he breaks the engagement. He's already Duke of Sutherland and can do as he pleases. There'll be a breach of promise suit, of course—"

I nodded. Laetitia wasn't likely to give up without a fight, nor were her parents.

"—and it will undoubtedly be costly, but at the end of it, he would be free, and with his reputation mostly intact."

I snorted. "What reputation is that? He doesn't have one of those to speak of."

"Precisely," Christopher said serenely. "Throwing one fiancée over for another seems rather on brand. And if you make it worth his while, he might agree to do it."

"I'd have to marry him, though."

"I imagine that that would be part of the incentive," Christopher agreed.

"What if I don't want to be Duchess of Sutherland?"

"Then you don't marry the duke," Christopher said. "But if you don't, you'll have to watch him marry Laetitia instead. She'll be sharing his bed and bringing up his children and spending his fortune and ruling Sutherland Hall."

I grimaced. Rock, meet hard place. "I'll think about it."

"Think fast," Christopher advised, as we came out of the maze and headed across the lawn towards the terrasse and the double doors to the drawing room.

As always, this book is written in a mixture of American and British English. If you notice anything weird, it's either because I made a mistake, or because I made a decision to do something I knew was wrong but which I wanted to do anyway. You can let me know if you want, or you can carry on in the knowledge that you caught me. It's up to you.

The expression 'in a pickle' dates back—as so many things do—to Shakespeare, in this case to *The Tempest*, written in 1610-1611. Behold:

SEBASTIAN

He is drunk now. Where had he wine?

ALONSO

And Trinculo is reeling ripe.
Where should they find this grand liquor that hath gilded 'em
To Trinculo. How cam'st thou in this pickle?

TRINCULO

I have been in such a pickle since I saw you last that I fear me will never out of my bones.

There seems to be the suggestion of drunkenness in the Shakespearean usage. Being pickled is another way of saying marinated, sozzled, potted, gassed, ploughed, gilded, blotto, or in a word, drunk. However, Samuel Pepys also used the expression in his diary in an entry dated Wednesday, September 26, 1660: "*At home with the workmen all the afternoon, our house being in a most sad pickle.*" The house definitely wasn't drunk, and the mention of workmen implies that repairs need to be done, so other meanings definitely exist. At any rate, when Pippa says it to Christopher in 1926, it already has a long history of meaning 'in a situation'.

The Slaughters, Upper and Lower, are real places: gorgeous villages in that most picturesque of places, the Cotswolds. There are two Anglican churches in the Slaughters, St Peter's Church in Upper Slaughter and the Parish Church of St Mary in Lower Slaughter. Upper Slaughter also has a tiny Primitive Methodist chapel, built in 1885. It went out of commission in 1954, was converted to a pottery studio at one point, and is currently used as an AirBnB. There had to be a reason why Morrison hadn't settled in Lower Slaughter, and the chapel was it.

Upper Slaughter is one of England's Thankful Villages, a term that didn't come into use until the 1930s, when it was coined by author Arthur Mee. Thankful Villages are small towns where all troops that served in WWI returned safe. There are an estimated 56 Thankful Villages in England and Wales, though none have been found in Scotland or Ireland. On top of that, Upper Slaughter is one of only 14 of them that is Doubly Thankful: it lost no men in WWII, either.

There are eight limestone cottages that form Bagshot Square in Upper Slaughter. They are from the seventeenth century, but were redesigned by renowned architect Sir Edwin Lutyens in 1906, twenty years before this book starts. I don't know whether any of them did or does have a blue door, but I didn't want to designate a particular cottage as a crime scene, since the murder is entirely fictional. But they do exist, and you can AirBnB one if you want to visit the Cotswolds—and who doesn't? It's a particularly lovely part of the world.

A passbook, also called a deposit-book or bankbook, was the way banks kept track of deposits and withdrawals back in the day before computers. I had one growing up, along with a piggybank that held the coins I saved. The bank gave them out —books and banks—as incentive for children to save. When the piggybank was full, we'd take it to the bank, and the teller would open it with a special key—I couldn't get the coins out after I had put them in—and then update my bankbook with the new deposit. The books went away with the advent of computers, although I had one all the way into the 1990s.

The Britishism "to give someone the pip" derives from the poultry disease of the same name, which is more officially known as infectious coryza. *The Oxford English Dictionary* and *Green's Dictionary of Slang* claim that having or getting the pip was used to indicate feeling depressed or out of sorts starting in the 1830s. That's what Christopher claims to feel in the presence of the animal heads in the game room at Sutherland Hall. However, the expression to give someone the pip, meaning to annoy or irritate, has also been in use since 1896, and the game room might make Christopher feel both of those, as well.

The verb 'to soldier' can mean one of three things. One can be a soldier in the army, in which case one soldiers. One can persist steadfastly, usually with a prepositional addition, as in soldier on. And then there's the contranym, which means to laze about, or take it easy. This is what the grooms are doing.

The term hunky-dory dates from the mid-1800s, and is said to come from the Japanese. Japan opened up to foreign trade in the 1850s. Yokohama contains a street called Honchidori, which at the time was lined with bars and brothels: just the sort of place for a bunch of sailors fresh off the boat to flock. The expression means satisfactory, fine, A-OK.

This was a difficult book to write, with a lot of open threads from previous books in the series, specifically *Secrets at Sutherland Hall* and *Blackmail at Beckwith Place*. I hope it all hangs together, but in case anyone has questions:

Aunt Charlotte killed Duke Henry and Grimsby, and phoned Lydia Morrison to tell her to run away because Uncle Harold had figured out the secret they had kept for twenty-four years.

Uncle Harold killed Aunt Charlotte, after she obliged him with a suicide note. He also killed Margaret Hughes, Lydia Morrison, Doctor Meadows, and Alfred the footman. He wrote the anonymous note implicating Pippa. And yes, it was him in the carriage house that night. Crispin did see him run away, and went to confront him, after which he realized the jig was up and decided to take the easy way out.

Crispin killed no one, or at least no one we know about. Nor did Aunt Roz or Uncle Herbert.

ABOUT THE AUTHOR

New York Times and *USA Today* bestselling author Jenna Bennett has written more than fifty books, most of them in the genres of mystery and suspense.

For more information, please visit her website
www.jennabennett.com